NO TURNING BACK

Diandra made an anguished little sound at the back of her throat.

No one had to give him permission; he took what he wanted. He had said so himself. Had he not taken her kiss, and with it the protective covering in which she had shrouded herself for more than a year?

She hadn't expected it; she hadn't wanted it.

She hadn't known she wanted it.

But now she did.

Why, why had she let him paint those sensual verbal pictures . . . why hadn't she acted indignant and offended and just gotten the hell away from him?

Because she hadn't been repulsed, she had been aroused, and she was now paying the price for having opened herself up to all those forbidden thoughts and yearnings . . .

DESIRE ME ONLY

Thea Devine

Zebra Books
Kensington Publishing Corp.

http://www.zebrabooks.com

ZEBRA BOOKS are published by

Kensington Publishing Corp.
850 Third Avenue
New York, NY 10022

First Printing: June, 1997
10 9 8 7 6 5 4 3 2 1

Printed in the United States of America

Prologue

"Damn, damn and damn . . . you would think *that woman* would have the grace and the sense to know she was not wanted and just have thrown herself into the funeral pyre with my father and had done with it!"

"Good God—Justin," his friend Tisbury said with feeling, "how pagan."

"The bastard *married* a pagan," Justin said coldly, still holding his stepmother's letter an arm's length away as he scanned the contents once again.

But the words that had rocked his world still hadn't changed: his immortal father, who had immured himself and his ambitions in the sun-baked *foreign* soil of the last jewel in Britain's crown, had succumbed to the heat or disease or age or all of them and had been buried twelve months past by his second wife, a local of indeterminate age, breeding and lineage who was now determined to come to England and take her place in society and *in his house* as Sir Guthrie's widow and his grieving step-mother.

"She cannot come," he said finally, dropping the thick creamy paper in the trashbasket beside the desk. "I cannot allow it. A creature I've never seen nor met. A replacement for my mother, convenient, and probably fat as pudding and totally unpresentable."

"My dear Justin . . . your father had impeccable taste—"

"My dear Tisbury—have you ever been to Delhi? I swear to you, even the statues begin to look seductive after a while. A man gets sun-logged and desperate in such a sultry climate. And a man like my father, as ambitious as he was, he would look exotic and desirable to the goddess Shiva herself. I tell you, someone had her eye on the main chance, and my mother hardly in her grave. I despise this woman, whoever she is, and I don't want her in my house."

"The Earl of Skene can afford to be generous," Tisbury pointed out gently. "After all, how long could she possibly stay under these circumstances?"

Justin rounded on him. "I see I haven't made myself plain, George. I don't want the drab within a continent of this townhouse or my father's properties."

"*Your* townhouse, *your* properties," Tisbury corrected, still in that moderate tone of voice.

"Damn you, George."

"She cannot be unpresentable, Justin. She was Vicereine for one year before your father's death. She must have manners and surely she knows how to go on in society. I've read all about Lord and Lady Curzon's installation there, and it seems to me there isn't much difference. And how much will she be going out and about if she is in mourning, I ask you?"

"Enough to embarrass me," Justin said tightly. "Enough so that I must bear her company and introduce her to my father's intimates as the woman he chose after my mother.

Whatever she looks like, however she carries herself, whether she has manners or diction or presence or decent clothes . . . a woman of our social strata would *never* foist herself off on her stepson like this—without proper warning or preparation. She is already on her way, a journey that takes upward of four weeks, and with my father not in his grave a year."

"Justin, I beg leave to point out to you that this has nothing to do with your stepmother, and everything to do with your feelings about your father and mother even going out to India in the first place." And that was as plain speaking as George Tisbury was going to get, with Justin in this mood.

"George . . ."

Tisbury didn't miss the warning tone in Justin's voice. "Someone has got to be the voice of reason, man. You know nothing about this woman and you are censuring her beyond anything permissable, even for such a cynic as you. You take no comfort that your father chose her to be his companion."

"He had a companion," Justin said. "And he made a decision. And then—no more companion, no more wife. No . . . more . . . mother—" he stopped abruptly and slanted a look at George to see whether he had detected the infinitesimal waver in his voice, and then he continued, "and this doxy will *not* barge into my life and take things over as if she were my mother."

"I think one can assume she has no intentions of doing that," George said dryly.

"*We* cannot assume anything."

And there was the frosty tone of the *seigneur;* his mind was made up and nothing George could say would sway him.

George sent him a skeptical look.

Justin lifted an eyebrow. "Not to mention that it interferes with my plans to join Alvester in America a month hence."

"Nonsense, you had no such plans."

"Did I not?"

"I'm all ears, Justin."

"A new investment opportunity."

"Indeed? With Alvester? How timely."

"Cattle."

"Ah. Now I gauge the importance of it. And surely joining Alvester in the cow chips takes precedence over receiving your father's widow."

"This is no joke, George."

"No, it isn't."

"Neither incidence is a joke, George. I was—considering—making preparations to travel . . . before this—*matter* came to my attention."

"I see. For cow chips."

"My dear man, for money. Cattle syndicates."

"Just so," George murmured.

"Exactly, given how I've vastly improved the Skene finances. Alvester's making money fist over foot in America running cattle. And he's looking for partners. So instead I must—"

"Indeed—you must . . . Send him a checque, Justin."

Justin sent him a dark look. "Already done."

"So you need not make this journey to admire the scenery—this month."

"I had intended to help round up the cattle," Justin said with feeling.

George almost dropped his sherry. "I would give a fortune to witness *that,*" he murmured.

"I may ask you to," Justin said. "Indeed, who knows what I might ask you to do in the name of friendship?"

"And who knows what I might agree to," George said,

as he bent and picked the letter Justin had discarded from the wastebasket. "Who knows what *you* might agree to, Justin."

Justin stared at him, his bright blue eyes like ice chips. "You win, George. As always. I will do what is *right.*"

Chapter One

London was like a corset—tight, upright, constricting, confining—with no room to move, no room to breathe, and the sky was overcast as if the heavens were about to weep.

She felt like weeping. She could see nothing redeeming in this maw of a city in which she already felt as if she were going to be swallowed up whole.

"Oh! Look—people!"

Her sister, caustic as usual, her eyes bright, her nose pressed to the window and breathing hard as if she were inhaling the sights and scents.

"Indeed—people," she murmured. *Too many people in too much of a hurry and she didn't know how she was going to get used to it.*

"Diandra . . ." Serena's voice was tentative now, almost babylike even though she was only two years younger than Diandra. "It *is* all right, isn't it?"

"Of course," she answered with more certainty than she felt, given she was foisting herself, her sister and a separate carriage full of servants on her husband's son without warning or preparation.

And it was all her own bad manners; she had blamed it on the heat of a hill country summer, and her own restlessness, and a thousand other unquantifiable things, but ostensibly, she had given in to Serena's unceasing demand to be given a season in London, in spite of the fact she was old enough to be considered on the shelf.

But Serena had never considered she had had any advantages; she had complained for a lifetime about living with the heat, scent and caste of a country other than her own. She wanted to go *home*. She begged to go home. And their brother Hugh just wasn't going to pick up and take her.

So Hugh convinced *her*— not that *she* needed much convincing after Guthrie's death—that such a trip would be beneficial to them both.

Now she was here, she thought not. Everything here was too close together. A person's soul could get cramped in such an environment. One needed air and heat and space to expand, to blossom. How could *anything* root under all that cobble and stone?

She felt dislocated and cold, and the only thing that warmed her was the ecstatic expression on Serena's face.

Serena needed this. She and Hugh, they owed it to Serena. Serena had never wanted to return to Bhaumaghar after boarding school.

But Hugh had needed them, for companionship, as hostesses, for family. He had never married. He had cared for their parents until their deaths as he worked his way up the rungs of the Indian Civil Service. And now that he was Governor of Rajam Province, he had to observe rigid codes of conduct and maintain protocol.

He needed his family; he had never expressly said it was their duty, or that he had done his and asked for nothing in return. But he was a single man and he needed them. And they loved him.

And only once did Diandra ever think the unthinkable— that they had had no choice, because they had no other source of support.

She loved Bhaumaghar, and managing Hugh's estate, and hostessing his parties, and moving through the complicated political landscape.

It was Serena who chafed at the restrictions, the weather, the work, the system, the politics. Serena who dreamt up unimaginable mischief among the eligible civilian civil servants. Serena who was bored and constantly in trouble as she flirted with and discarded one man after another.

And Serena who, after Diandra had met and married the highly regarded, exceptionally sought-after widower Guthrie Reynell, suddenly and inexplicably calmed down, made herself indispensible, and began to act in a manner that was faintly alarming.

She ignored her disquiet; Serena was merely going through some mystical phase that she obviously did not understand.

And she didn't have the time to work it out with her.

She was indescribably busy; the three years of her marriage had been intensely sensual, and punctuated by pageantry and protocol. It had been as if she had been waiting all her life to discover carnality and convention. And there had been no time to assess if it were rooted in love or some flaw in her nature.

She hadn't cared; she had wanted it, embraced it, instigated it, had been affected by it to the core of her being.

And now, there was nothing.

She leaned her head back and closed her eyes. *No tears. Too late to cry. Everything was over, and she would not repine.*

This was the real reason she had succumbed to Serena's pleas: Guthrie's death, unexpected, unnerving, disorienting, utterly shattering. A man in his prime, beloved among his people. Dead. Of the heat and the strain on his heart.

And she had buried him, and then she was stunned at the feeling that she wanted desperately to bury herself—in something different, someplace different, someplace *away* from memory and desire.

Except that England wasn't away: England was going to be *her* coffin, and she supposed it would be worth it, to get Serena away from the unnerving influences that she could not even pinpoint.

And there could be nothing more different than these tall buildings, and crammed-together houses, and self-contained parks that loomed up every once in a while.

And the carriages! Coming at them every which way, from streets that radiated off in every direction: cabs and carriages and drays. And shops, the likes of which she could not have conceived, even from her several years at boarding school. Everything she could ever want available in one long line of commercial stores in one trip.

She sat up suddenly as she became aware of Serena's voice breaking into her thoughts; Serena who had been giving her a running commentary all along, and she hadn't heard a single word. "... This is the first place we have to go ..."

Serena sounded excited, invigorated. *Normal.*

"Yes," she murmured, and Serena was off again, pointing out this and that shop of interest, or an itinerant peddler, or a particularly reckless driver.

"It's astonishing," Serena was saying. "You can walk anywhere. Everything is so close. It's paradise ... !"

Or perdition ...

And Justin Reynell might well turn out to be the devil at the gate.

* * *

It began to rain, just lightly, fat drops dissolving like tears on the cobbled street. They drove over the Bridge, past the House of Parliament, the Royal Opera House, Carleton House Terrace, Claridge's ... and she had the overwhelming urge to stop the carriage and register them all at the hotel, and leave Justin Reynell out of it altogether.

But no, it would be worse manners now to back off from allowing him to offer them hospitality. It would reflect badly on him, especially since she was certain he would have already prepared for their arrival. He could, in good manners, do nothing less. And her precipitate letter would be washed over with some Banbury story about his father's wishes—she was sure of it.

It was just that she was getting more and more nervous as the carriage sped toward the residential parks and squares on the outskirts of the city.

Very soon she would be face to face with the bane and pride of his father's existence. And she still didn't know what to think about him after everything Guthrie had told her.

He was opinionated. Arrogant. A genius with money. A born aristocrat, bred to the expectations of his father's title, and all that entailed. A man who lived for pleasure but never enjoyed it.

One of the most eligible men in London who made a sport of evading matchmaking mothers and their spawn. A man who was both purposeful and aimless, profligate and pragmatic, intemperate and tenacious, anomalous combinations that boded nothing but trouble.

And to add to the pot, Guthrie's heir was not much older than she, and that was the most disconcerting and perturbing thing of all.

Yet she had not hesitated to pick up a pen and imperiously announce to him that she was coming without giving him time to consider or refuse.

Perhaps Guthrie's death had been so unsettling, she was really the one who had wanted to get away from Bhaumaghar altogether.

Or perhaps she had unconsciously wanted to leap into the devil's gorge.

But that was not to be thought about now because they had turned onto a broad boulevard, off of which there were tree-lined streets lined with stately white-porticoed brick townhouses, and they were coming ever closer to Cheswick Square.

And then suddenly, they were there; the carriage turned onto a similar boulevard alongside an iron-gated park and again onto a narrow avenue, at the end of which a detached five-story townhouse fronted the street and loomed like a disapproving *grande dame.*

Serena drew in her breath in anticipation. "It's perfect," she breathed.

It's scary . . . Diandra straightened in her seat and reached for her bonnet.

"We'll have to shop for a new wardrobe," Serena said, looking down at her serviceable dress and up again at the house. "Obviously everything I have is inadequate. All the money we spent on tailors . . . Ah—the servants have arrived. Jhasa . . ." she acknowledged as their houseman appeared at the carriage window, "if you would—"

Jhasa bowed and proceeded up the shallow steps to ring the bell. The door opened, and a phalanx of footmen marched out to the carriage, off-loaded their luggage and then disappeared into the house.

Jhasa opened the carriage door and helped them out.

Serena walked past the stamping horses to look at the

park, and took a deep breath of the moist air. "It smells like rain."

Rain. Tears. They would never end, she would drown in them, and she would never know why she cried.

Diandra squared her shoulders and signalled Jhasa and the two remaining servants, Rajit and Gita, who positioned themselves to follow her.

"Mem." Jhasa led the way up the steps.

The butler awaited them at the door.

"Welcome, my lady. I am Millbank. Lord Justin awaits you in the library."

"Thank you, Millbank. My sister, Serena Morant."

"My lady . . ." Millbank bowed and then turned to accompany them.

"My lady—he called me *my lady* . . ." Serena breathed, as she surveyed the opulence of the entry hall. "Oh my, oh Diandra—oh look . . ."

She didn't have to be told. This house was an extension of everything that Guthrie Reynell had been. The Earl of Skene. Wealthy beyond measure. And captivated by the romance of the East. He had left it all to live out his dream. He had ruled a world, lord of all he had surveyed, a king within the royal realm of the Queen.

He had died at the peak of his power and prestige. And he would be revered and remembered forever.

Oh my dear . . . Her heart began pounding as they passed down a long hallway lined with portraits of a dozen bygone ancestors. Reynells all, she saw Guthrie's features in every one of their faces.

She hadn't thought, she hadn't considered . . .

What if Justin—?

But it was too late. They had stopped at a pair of ten-foot painted doors at the end of the hallway, and Millbank was already turning one of the gleaming brass knobs.

"My lady Reynell. Miss Serena Morant. Their man, Jhasa. My lady, enter, please."

She took a deep breath, brushed past Serena who was crowding the door with avid curiosity, and she stepped into the room.

It surprised her; it was high-ceilinged, square, welcoming, warm and comfortable, and utterly unlike everything she knew of him.

And then she focused on him, leaning against a desk near the elaborate marble fireplace, a dissonant *presence* just filling the space and overwhelming it.

Tall. Elegant. Dark. Blazing blue eyes. Clothed in black for mourning, but probably habitually because it suited him far too well. A palpable skepticism about him as he watched her glide into the room, as if he were unsure what to expect, but whatever it was, he wanted no part of it.

His eyes raked over her as she came closer and closer, until she was fairly face to face with him. And his expression never wavered.

It was impassive, unwelcoming, a little shocked, as if he couldn't believe what he saw.

Nor could she; she was so fascinated, she couldn't look away.

"My lady—" he said finally, mockingly.

"Justin," she murmured. *Cut him down before he got the upper hand.* She moved to a chair by the fireplace. "Why don't we sit?"

"My house is your house, madam."

So he had already decided how to address her.

She lifted her chin and met his simmering gaze. "I should hope so," she said tartly. "Serena . . ."

"I'm right here."

"This is Guthrie's son, Justin."

"Yes—"

And what was that *tone* in her sister's voice?

"Serena." Justin, politely.

"So pleased," she sighed, sinking down next to Diandra.

"Look," Diandra said in her most businesslike manner. "I understand I've inconvenienced you terribly . . ."

"That pulls the sheets over it very nicely, madam, but it doesn't nearly cover it."

She stared at him. His irritation was palpable and it was obvious there was nothing she could say to mitigate the circumstances, even if, as his father's second wife, she *ought* to have been welcomed in his house, no matter what.

Perhaps she had depended upon that—too much.

But she knew when to cut her losses.

"Very well." She rose up. "We'll go to a hotel. Come, Serena."

Justin didn't move. "Oh, I think not."

"Really. I had no idea you were thinking at all, Justin. What a nice surprise."

He ignored that. "Your rooms have been prepared. Millbank will show you up. Dinner has been pushed back to seven o'clock. That should give you sufficient time to rest and change. The rest we'll discuss later."

His gaze said *they* would discuss it later—in detail, and without Serena.

She turned to Serena. "You will go ahead and begin changing for dinner."

"But . . ." The protest died on her lips as she read the obdurate look on Diandra's face.

Millbank appeared and Serena reluctantly followed him out muttering to herself, with Jhasa at her heels; Diandra watched them, her color high, her temper escalating as Millbank carefully closed the door behind them.

Justin stared at her pensively.

His father gulled by a woman like that . . .

He could see at a glance exactly what she was: a provincial

parvenue in an educated elegant package. And the sister—discontent and dynamite. Lethal. And his to cope with.

But not for long.

He knew just how to get rid of them.

He turned from the fireplace and poured himself a brandy from the tantalus on his desk, and lifted it to the light. Beautiful liquid. Warm and potent, like her, like the color of her glittering eyes, and her faithless soul.

"So tell me, madam," he said gently, disarmingly, "just how *did* you kill my father?"

She went rigid with disbelief. . . . *everything she knew of him* . . .

She whirled; she didn't think. She reached him in five steps; she watched her arm swing out and strike him, hard, with the full force of her anger and frustration. She saw his goblet fly out of his hand and break against the edge of his desk, and the brandy spatter against the burnished wood and drip down onto the jewel toned carpet.

And in all of that, he never moved a muscle. Never touched his face. Never said a word.

While she—her whole body was heaving, her head was whirling, and she felt as if she had witnessed the disaster instead of participating in it.

And she expected retribution. You did not cross a man like Justin Reynell without consequences. And you didn't back down, from the physical threat of him walking toward you, or from the flaming anger in his ice-blue eyes.

"So what is the truth, madam? Where are the lines? How does one cut down a man in his prime?"

He came closer and closer, his tone level, almost neutral, and all the more dangerous for that, and she kept backing away until she was flat against the closed door.

"What does a man die of, who is healthy and in his right mind, madam? The wishes and will of a penniless nobody?

What plots and schemes did you use to attract him? What aphrodisiacs in your possession? What avarice in your soul?"

She shuddered and he moved tighter against her so that she was totally imprisoned against the door by his arms and the heat of his body.

"Show me, madam. Let me taste a Judas kiss. Let me experience his betrayal."

"Don't touch me."

But it was too late. He swallowed the words in the hot fury of his mouth—for one sizzling moment, he unleashed the thing in her that was the bane and joy of her existance, and all the anger, sorrow and grief of her mourning.

And he knew it. His mouth eased from hers, but he knew he still held the power, and he had tasted it in her.

"How did he die?" The tone of his voice did not change: it remained unemotional, flat, neutral, colored by nothing except his skepticism.

And she thought she wanted to kill him. She raised her hand, and he grabbed it, quicker than a cat.

"How?"

She wrenched her hand away and immediately she shoved him. She did not know where she got the nerve and gut to even touch the high almighty Earl of Skene, but she found it in her fury and her outrage at his high-handed treatment of her.

He wasn't expecting it; he stepped back involuntarily, and then again as she advanced on him the same way he had intimidated her.

"He died of a broken heart, you bastard. He died because of your arrogance and indifference. And *then* he had a heart attack."

And then she turned her back on him and stalked out of the room.

* * *

That set the tone for dinner.

She wasn't surprised, when she and Serena made their way down to the dining room, to find that Justin was nowhere in sight.

Millbank seated them side by side at the oppressively long linen draped table which was ostentatiously laid with gold-rimmed monogrammed plates, cut-glass goblets in three sizes, four branches of silver candlesticks, silver plate and cut-glass accessories, and the family silver with the ornate *R* incised in the shank.

The Earl of Skene making a point, Diandra thought mordantly. *They were there on sufferance pure and simple. He would do what was necessary and nothing more. And perhaps not even that much after this afternoon's debacle.*

She was mortified by her loss of control. And she would not apologize for it. The monster had provoked her plain and simple.

They dined in solitary splendor on leek soup, baked salmon, fresh vegetable salad, potatoes and parsley, and thin glistening slices of strawberry tart.

And when the servants had removed the service and there was nothing but tea and the remnants of tart on the table, she rose up impatiently and began pacing the room furiously to avoid that mutinous look on Serena's face.

But she couldn't avoid her sarcasm.

"Those wall coverings are putrid, Diandra. This place is as bad as Bhaumaghar. What else is there to do here if Guthrie's son won't deign to dine with us."

She whirled to face her sister. "That's outside of enough, Serena. Even when you get what you want, you are dissatisfied. Our first hours here, with no idea what is to come, and it's still not enough. What *is* enough, I wonder?"

"His not joining us is inexusably rude," Serena said defensively.

"Well, your highness, let us give him the benefit of the doubt. Perhaps he had another engagement."

"Oh . . ."

"Yes." She watched Serena's expression visibly smooth out. "So let us be grateful for a hot meal and a hot bath at the end of our journey. And then we will see what tomorrow brings."

Serena rose from the table. "You're right, of course." She folded her hands and closed her eyes for a moment, and then smiled at her sister. "I'll attend to it."

Diandra sank into the nearest chair, not knowing quite why she felt so disquieted. Serena's responses had always been difficult to read. But even in her new-found tranquility, there were these moments of petulant hysteria which were wiped away, just as now, by a quiet moment of . . . *what?*

That was the thing: what *was* this folding of the hands and lowering of the eyes that reversed her mood so neatly and abruptly?

It would be too much to attribute it to either gratitude or prayer; she didn't know what it was, only that it was one of the many small things about Serena that puzzled and worried her.

"My Lady . . ."

And here came Millbank, pausing discreetly at the door, waiting until she lifted her eyes in acknowledgment. "Yes?"

"My Lord would see you in the library."

So much for another engagement. But then, even she had not believed her little fiction. He had probably been holed up there the entire evening, deliberately, just to avoid them; she would not put it past him.

It was almost as if he had not moved an inch since the afternoon. He was leaning against the desk again, watching her as she entered, and there was that same assessing cynical look in his icy eyes.

He dismissed the butler, but did not invite her to take a seat.

The silence lengthened, thickened, congealed.

She knew all about the intimidating nature of silence, and it did not daunt her. But her calm acceptance of it jarred him, and she watched his eyes sharpen with interest.

"We will forget this evening ever happened, madam."

She stiffened. She could still feel the full force of him invading her mouth, and see the dislike glittering in his cold blue gaze. She hadn't even had time to assess what she had felt, what he made her feel.

But one thing was crystal clear: she could never let him get the upper hand or he would devour her.

"I think I will remember it very well, Justin," she said coolly. "Was there anything else?"

He didn't like that either. "You are a piece of work, madam. Do you never take the graceful way out?"

"Why should *I*?" she asked.

He stood up. "We will forget what happened tonight, madam. That is whole of it, whether you like it or not."

She could be every bit as haughty as he. She lifted her chin. "I *don't* like it. Are you quite done?"

"Are you?"

"Not by half," she retorted.

"Let us get down to cases, then." He motioned her to sit, and she sank into a wing chair opposite the desk while he seated himself behind it. "What do you want?"

She made a show of smoothing her skirt just to annoy him. "Nothing more or less than I wrote to you. I want you to sponsor Serena for the coming season."

"Too bad you did not have the good manners to wait for a reply, madam. It cannot be done."

"Of course it can be done. I researched it and planned

for it; it is no accident we have come in March. I wanted
Serena to have the benefit of the preseason, as well as
have time to make acquaintances who will invite her to
private parties. And of course we want her to be presented
at court . . ."

"*Madam . . .*"

"Is there a problem, Justin?"

"*You* are the problem, madam. You are in mourning,
and your sister has nothing to recommend her to London
society—and let me translate *that* in the plainest terms:
she has no money, there is no dowry, and there was no
point to your coming at all."

She stared at him, deliberately showing no reaction.

His lips thinned. "How much do you want, madam?"

"*What?!*" *Monster.* That was as bloodless as a shark.

"How much would it take to remove you from London?"

She was absolutely shocked by his presumptuousness.
She had no words, just a pure violent desire to attack him.

There was a letter opener on the desk. A goblet half
empty. Assorted desk accessories.

"Let me understand you correctly," she said, her voice
deceptively calm though she was shaking with fury. She
marveled that she could keep her composure when there
was marble paperweight so temptingly near. "You are offering me money to leave London?"

"I am offering you the wherewithal to travel with your
sister," he said, offering her the graceful lie.

"In order that you don't have to bother yourself assisting
us," she finished bluntly. "I see. No, Justin. You are not
nearly rich enough to afford that."

She caught the angry flash in his eyes at that; no wealthy
man wanted to be told he hadn't money enough to move
mountains if he so commanded. It gave her the advantage,
just for the moment.

"Believe me, I will do very well without your support.

Let me make myself perfectly clear; with you or without you, Serena *will* have her season. It won't reflect badly on *me* if we are forced to proceed from a rented house in Mayfair. But since you've already had the temerity to accuse me of having something to do with your father's death, have been rude and inhospitable, tried to bribe me, *and* decreed that my sister and myself are ineligible to keep company in your superior set, I must assume you have made your decision, and I will make our plans accordingly."

"Madam . . ." Exasperation in his tone. *Good. Let him stew.*

"We'll be out of your way by tomorrow noon, Justin. No need to discommode yourself at all. Rajit will take care of everything."

She was at the door, and she turned once more to look at him. "Your father would have been so proud."

It was the perfect parting shot; the words hung in the air as she eased the door closed behind her.

She hated him, his smugness, his incivility, his tyranny.

Guthrie's condescending whelp needed to be taught a lesson, but she was too overwrought to even think about that except in the most abstract terms.

That would come. You couldn't be so wealthy, so powerful, so merciless without the gods marking you for a lesson in humility.

It would come. And it would be perfect, and she would revel in it.

Chapter Two

*Abominable, arrogant, top-lofty beast . . . insufferable bastard
. . . who did he think he was . . . ? What did he think she was?*

*This whole idea had been a disaster from start to finish anyway,
and she ought to have known from the way Justin had dissociated
himself from his father that coming to him was the worst thing
she could have done.*

Now it was time to tell Serena.

She rapped once on Serena's door, burst into her room,
and stopped short at the sight of Serena bundled in her
bed, and flanked by candles on the bedstands and window-
sills which emitted an overpowering scent of vanilla.

"Hello—Serena . . . what *is* this?"

"Well . . ." Serena levered herself up against the head-
board. "It was so dank in here, I swear there can't have
been any guests since Victoria's coronation—and hardly
any light, so I thought . . ."

"So you did," Diandra said brusquely, advancing to her
beside and reaching for the bellpull. "Well, it's neither
here nor there. We will be leaving tomorrow."

Rajit appeared at the door and bowed. "Mem?"

"You will please find out the proper agent to lease a house in this godforsaken city, and make sure that we have moved into proper accommodations before tomorrow noon."

"Oh—no, you cannot . . ." Serena cried, pulling at her sleeve.

"It shall be done." Rajit bowed and withdrew, his face impassive.

"It must be done," Diandra said rigidly, easing herself down on the bed.

"No, no—all will go well," Serena said, reaching out her hand. "I've prayed for it. This is just a small setback."

"He's a barbarian. Nothing fine or sensitive about him. He will stoop to anything to humiliate us in order to make us leave. He would even send us away with money in our pockets so long as we agreed not to inconvenience *him*. I will *not* stay in his house another minute longer than I must."

"He will change; he will rethink it and decide for the best," Serena said, trying to placate her.

"Even if he did . . ." Diandra jumped up and began pacing the room. "I have *never* met a man so disdainful, so pompous, so *arrogant* . . . And did I listen when he was described to me? Did I pay heed? Or did I think that manners and morality would carry the day? *I* thought respect for his father would . . . well, how naïve was I?"

"He is too handsome to be such a monster, Diandra. He must be a one who hates surprises."

"Oh, nonsense. He is an indulged, well-fed, pampered, wealthy *swellhead* who thinks he can get away with anything. There is nothing redeeming about him. We will be well rid of him and his high-handedness, I will tell you that."

"I think you're wrong. I think by daylight he will be more amenable."

"Even if he were . . ." Diandra said. "I am adamant we will leave this place. It is cold and unforgiving, like its lord."

"I'll tell you what," Serena said, rummaging under her pillow. "Let us toss my lucky coins and see what comes up."

"Serena . . ."

"Come, what can it hurt?" She slipped out of bed and propelled Diandra over to the fireplace where there was a table set for chess, and two wing chairs opposite.

Diandra sat reluctantly while Serena removed the chess board, set down her leather pouch, and swiped a finger in the ashes.

"There—remember? We make a circle . . ." She moved her finger around the table. "And the two triangles in the shape of a star. And here are my coins . . ." She nestled them on top of the leather pouch and took her seat. "And now, we must focus our energy on the answer to our question. What *is* the question?"

"I have no question," Diandra said.

Serena ignored her dismissive tone. "Then I will formulate the question. Will Lord Justin change his mind and invite us to stay?"

"Serena . . ."

"Shhhhh—keep your mind solely on that question, Diandra, or you'll ruin the whole thing."

Diandra bit her lip and maintained her silence. She hated these childish fortune telling games that Serena liked to play. She put too much credence in them, and carried with her several meaningful objects that she used to foretell the future.

She supposed it was because Serena's life had always been so unsettled—between the death of their parents and their being shuttled from Bhaumaghar to England

and back again. But she had always been uneasy that Serena sometimes put too much faith in superstition.

On the other hand, it was harmless enough—like pulling daisy petals to find your true love. It wouldn't work, it wouldn't influence anything, but it would make Serena feel more in control at the moment when she was planning yet another upheaval.

She leaned forward resignedly as she felt Serena's eyes on her.

"It is for you to ask the question," Serena said after several minutes of intensive silence.

Diandra cleared her throat. "All right. I'll humor you. Will the lordly Justin change his mind and invite us to stay?"

Serena sent her a flickering glance of disapproval, picked up the coins, and then focused her gaze on the star in the center of the crude circle.

"Oracle of the coins, answer if this is in our future," she whispered into the thick vanilla-scented silence, and then she threw the coins into the circle.

The one landed tails up. The other gyrated crazily around the star, clipping the edge of the circle. Serena gasped, visibly clenching her hands to keep herself from touching it.

And then it fell, tails up, just at the rim of the circle, and a good six inches away from the first coin.

"The answer is *yes,*" Serena murmured. She looked up at Diandra. "And the coins never lie."

He had never known a woman like this. He watched her from the shadows as she exited her sister's room and turned toward her own.

She walked with assurance, her posture perfect, her chin held high. She was like a sunflower, all gold and snappy dark center, both pliable and strong, with a will of iron, and an obsidian gaze that revealed nothing, not even under duress.

A man had died, drowning in those eyes. A foolish man who had sought to recapture his youth, and wed himself to a brash beauty who had probably calculated to a farthing just what her take would be if she could ease him into the next world without casting suspicion on herself.

She had made out well too. He knew because, at his father's explicit instructions, he had made the arrangements and signed the papers to transfer enough money to make Diandra Morant an independently wealthy woman.

Pin money to his father, but enough to give the newly married Madam Reynell a false sense of power. He would have thought it was enough for her to maintain a lavish lifestyle in India forever. But it was ever the way when provincials got hold of money: they were forever wanting to buy their way into society and they could never remain where their wealth alone would make them into aristocrats.

Madam Reynell was not stupid.

He watched with interest as she paused and ran her hand across the silky wood of a console table along the hallway wall.

But no, she could know nothing of the antiquity or value of the piece. Or the vase she was touching now.

She probably thought they were pretty things, appropriate to a nobleman's house, as well they were: he had moved them, and many other items, from Skene after his father's death when he had finally begun to come to terms with the fact that *he* was now the powerful Earl of Skene.

How *had* she done it?

He pulled back into the shadows as she turned suddenly as if she sensed someone following her, and then she opened the door and disappeared into her room.

How had she seduced him and convinced him to settle that much money on her?

How had she murdered him and gotten away with it?

It had to be fate that she had placed herself in his hands, and he had reacted emotionally, thoughtlessly, and without considering all the ramifications.

How unwise of him to think she would reveal anything to him.

He cursed himself for a fool; he had had that much time to plan, and he had done nothing but simmered on the inconvenience of having to put up with her and her plebian notion of a season for her lackluster sister.

And then she'd walked in the door and shot everything to hell.

Well, he felt clearheaded and clearsighted now. He had played his hand too soon and too bluntly. It was time to regroup and reorder.

He would take them to Skene, educate the amorphous piece of dynamite, contain her somehow, and proceed from there.

It would cost him nothing. He would have George Tisbury and his stylish Aunt Leonie take care of the details.

For the rest, a season for a little nouveau riche *arriviste* was a small price to pay to avenge his father's death.

She had a will of iron, that was clear. The luggage was piled in the entrance hall at eight o'clock sharp, and she was in the breakfast room taking tea and toast, and reading the morning paper.

"Good morning, Justin," she said coolly, not even bothering to look up. "My man is out and about now, with Millbank's instructions, seeking accommodations for us."

"It *is* fortunate you are packed and ready to leave to early," he said easily, as he poured himself some tea and

then sat down opposite her. "The carriage awaits, and
Skene is a good three hours' drive from here."

"Excuse me?" That caught her attention, and she
looked up, her snappy gaze pinning his with disconcerting
directness. Yesterday might never have been. "Is Skene for
rent, Justin?"

"You must have misunderstood, madam," he said in his
haughtiest tone. "We remove to Skene today to prepare
your sister for the season. My Aunt Leonie will supervise,
and my dear friend Tisbury will join us as well. A month
there with dressmakers to outfit you both properly, and
instruction in every conceivable skill you will need, that *is*
what you wanted, is it not?"

"Why?"

Oh, the woman didn't know tact from a turnip.

He shrugged. "Why not?"

"Trying to buy us off again, Justin? Immuring us in the
country and hope that pastoral pleasures will suffice for a
season?"

"I thought I was being extraordinarily generous, considering my antipathy. But you may proceed as you have
begun, if you wish. Let me warn you, however, a stylish
address is not easily found this time of year. Parliament is
in session and there are two dozen American heiresses *en
scène* preparing for the season; every last house is to let
between Mayfair and Belgrave Square. The hotels may
suffice, *if* there are rooms; the service is excellent, but
there is a steep price to pay for six months' residency. But
they are fairly well filled up by now. So I think your first
plan has the most merit. Throw yourself on my mercy,
madam. I am feeling charitable this morning."

She felt like throwing something at him yet again. *"Charitable,* my lord? *Generous?* You are a stiff-necked, self-centered, high-flown, top lofty, pompous, heartless cock of
the walk, Justin, and those are your *good* points. I will *not*

tolerate your condescension. Or your patronizing attitude."

He felt a wash of heat down his spine. No one had ever dressed him down like that. This woman had gall, besides she was too full of herself. But a title did that to one. Lady Reynell, dowager of Skene. Every bit as arrogant as if she had been born into nobility.

He pulled back on his bitterness. "My house is your house, madam. You have only to say yes."

She stared at him. "I don't believe you. Not after yesterday."

She had the most disconcerting gaze.

"Be that as it may, and I have no idea what you are talking about—you will have what you want."

Burying both humiliating incidents, was he? Time for plain speaking, then.

"Why?"

He hesitated a moment, debating whether to pull out the big gun, just as she had, and then decided he would. "My father would have wanted it."

Her eyes wavered. "Yes, he would," she said slowly. "But I don't trust *you*, Justin. I think you want me where you can contain me and observe me. You haven't changed your mind about your father. You do think there was something questionable about his death. You tried to scare it out of me last night. And when you couldn't buy me, you came to the conclusion it would be better to have me well and truly in your sights."

"And you are coming to the conclusion that no matter what my motivations, your sister stands a better chance of success this season with my name officially behind her. A devil's stand-off, madam."

"I'm not afraid to leap into the abyss."

"As you've proved time and again, madam."

She set down her tea cup slowly and deliberately, and then looked up at him with those disconcerting dark eyes.

"Very well. We will go to Skene. But I serve you warning now—*I'm* not afraid to rattle the devil's bones."

Five carriages, a half dozen servants besides their own, mountains of luggage, the prospect of a three-hour trip, and her sister bursting with excitement . . . it was enough to give anyone a raging headache.

The wonder was *she* felt so calm after that confrontation with Justin. And that was just what it had been: a duel of wills, nothing more or less, and she believed that she had gained the edge because he had made the offer to sponsor the season.

But that didn't mean he wouldn't demand his pound of flesh. He had taken an ounce already.

"I knew it, I knew it, I knew it . . . look—I wore my holy stone all night and prayed for his change of heart. And what happened? We are on our way to Skene!"

"My dear Serena, his change of heart had nothing to do with your coins, your stone or your prayers. He is a selfish beast and he has his own reasons for acquiescing, and that is the end of it."

"No, it is only the beginning. I can't wait. I can't *wait* . . ." Serena breathed fervently as she turned her attention back to the passing scenery.

It was one of those perfect days. They had left the lowering sky in London and the sun shone and the air was fresh with the scent of spring.

Perfect omens for a trip to hell.

Well, she had thought that even as they were making their way to Cheswick Square. And the sensation was more resonant now that she knew Justin Reynell's true feelings and had defined her own.

She could deal with him. She had coped with scullery boys, clerks, colonels, *nawabs*, and maharajahs. What was one overstuffed oversexed aristocrat compared to that?

Three hours . . .

But she had wanted this. For Serena. Nothing for herself except the change, and the penance of girdling herself away from heat and sensuality, away from the swamping carnality that was such an integral part of living *there*.

The shocking thing was, it hadn't died with Guthrie. She was still aroused—by beauty, touch, feelings. It scared her. She had thought that strict tight mourning would repress everything.

Last night's incident proved her wrong.

She had responded to Justin Reynell.

As she felt overwhelmed by the loveliness of the countryside, the clarity of the air, the dazzling warmth of the sun on her face, the painterly perfection of the landscape. She could have been back in the hill country of India; her body quickened with a sense of familiarity as the carriage barrelled along the flat winding roads toward Skene.

One more hour now. *One more hour—to what?*

Serena had already lost interest in the scenery, and was huddled against the squabs, a blank expression on her face.

"Serena . . . ?" She leaned forward and touched Serena's skirt.

"It's like going back to Bhaumaghar, Diandra. Look—there's nothing, no houses, no carriages, no people . . . nothing! What are we going to do? What are we going to do?"

She heard the hysteria threading through her sister's voice. "Serena . . ."

Serena averted her face. "No one told me we weren't going to stay in London. I had no chance to prepare. No chance to . . . "

"Serena . . ."

"It's not fair."

"I see. We're back to being dissatisfied, are we? Very well. We'll turn back and we will try to mount a season without my lord Reynell." She made a move to rap on the driver's hatch, and then paused, hating herself for resorting to a distraction. "Or—perhaps you'd like to consult your cards . . . ?"

Serena's eyes kindled with relief. "Yes, of course—why didn't I think of it? The cards . . . I have them right here . . ." She rummaged in her reticule and withdrew a well-worn deck.

"You shuffle them."

Diandra took them. "Here's the thing: you can only draw one."

"No, no—you know it doesn't work that way."

"Today it will work that way." *Careful here.* Diandra bit her lip as she cut the cards with her left hand. "I'll tell you what. We'll draw nine cards, but you'll only read the last one."

"That's not fair. That won't tell me anything."

"Better than nothing; I want no portents of disaster, Serena. One card, one reading. One meaning only. It should suffice."

". . . I suppose . . ." Serena said reluctantly, responding to the iron tone of her sister's voice. "You deal then."

She pulled her skirt against her thigh to give Diandra room on the seat, and counted as Diandra laid eight cards face down, and the ninth turned over.

"King of hearts."

"Everything good," Serena whispered. "Happiness in the future, love, maybe even marriage."

"That prophecy should cover all contingencies of our entire stay at Skene," Diandra said lightly, as she started to gather up the cards.

"No—no, no—one more card. Just one more . . . *please* . . ."

Superstitious nonsense . . . but Diandra knew she would give in, just as she always did to keep Serena calm and content.

Serena stretched out her hand over the remaining cards and then lifted the first card dealt.

"Oh! Nine hearts. Oh, Diandra. All things good—this is the card of wishes. One wish granted." She closed her eyes and crossed her fingers, her lips moving and her body vibrating with tension.

And then she blinked and smiled. "Now—oh, now I feel much more confident that things are going the way they were meant to. Oh, Diandra, I've told you and told you . . . sometimes you need a little otherworldly help."

"Thank you, I have enough to cope with in this world," Diandra said dryly as she tucked the cards away in her skirt pocket, and hoped Serena did not notice.

"All will be well," Serena murmured, "I'm sure of it now. Do you think we are close yet?"

"Soon, we'll be there soon." *Words to pacify a bored child. Games to distract her* . . .

A rap on the carriage roof, and the footman's face appeared in the hatch above them. "Skene ahead, madam." And then the horn, blaring out ceremoniously to announce their arrival ten minutes ahead as the carriage swerved around a curve and through a stone gate into the park at Skene.

They bowled through an arch of towering trees, and out suddenly, as if emerging from a tunnel, and into a vista of rolling verdant lawns that swept toward the sky, where now and again a copse of flowering bushes or the perfect mirrored surface of a pond broke the landscape.

They saw horses cropping in a far field, dark, sinuous objects against a broad white fence. They saw geese and peacocks and grazing sheep as the track veered up a rise toward a stand of trees, and there, at the top, the carriage slowed, and they caught their first view of Skene.

It was so beautiful, so symmetical, so perfect. She had known that from just the tone of Guthrie's voice whenever he spoke of it. But to see it—its creamy stone exterior, its columned entryway, and shallow stone steps on either side leading to the carriage drive, its curved extensions linking its two wings to the main house—and to see that it was neither formidable nor austere, that it was everything she would have wanted if Guthrie had chosen to return to England—an overpowering sense of loss swamped her, hot tears filmed her eyes, and for one moment, she felt blinded and helpless as the carriage came to a grinding halt by the front steps.

"Madam . . ." Justin's voice, mockingly courteous.

Here already?

She opened her eyes and he was there, leaning into the opened carriage door in such a way that she could not read his eyes.

"What an excellent host," she murmured, holding back the tears by sheer will.

"Welcome to Skene." He held out his hand to Serena first and helped her out and down the step.

He turned to Diandra. "Madam."

She felt her skin prickling. "No welcome for me, Justin?"

"It is hard to read just what the deposed mistress of Skene is thinking."

Fighting words from the arrogant lord. "It is everything your father said it was," she said steadily and held out her hand.

He could do nothing less than take it and help her from

the carriage as footmen scurried from the house to unload their luggage.

"Serena is a child," he said, as he watched her scamper up the staircase to the right, pause on the landing to wave at them, and then continue on to the columned portico.

"Serena has not had an easy time of it," she said, as they followed up the same staircase and met Serena by the immense front door.

"My house is your house," he said, his voice tinged with irony as he thrust open the door and led them into the two story entry hall. "This is the only part that is a bit overpowering."

"How can you say so? Two dozen marble columns and half again as many mysterious doors are not in the least daunting."

"Come—this is simple: the guest wing is through the corridor to your right. The morning room, music room and formal dining room through those doors. The kitchen and family wing to your left, as well as the family drawing room, dining room and library. The saloon is straight ahead, never used but for formal occasions. And here is Tuttle. Tuttle minds us all when we are in residence. He will show you to your rooms, and bring you back for tea after you've freshened up."

Tuttle bowed, and motioned them to follow him. He was a stiffer starchier version of Millbank and Diandra instantly did not like him.

They traversed the curved linking corridor, at the end of which was a beautiful floor to ceiling window that flooded the hall with light. The walls were washed in sunshine yellow, and there was a fireplace at the center, overhung with a luminous landscape.

The bedrooms were just beyond, off of a center hallway, two on each side. They had been allocated the two connecting bedrooms facing the rear of the house, and Serena entered hers and began waltzing around the ornate four-poster bed.

"I do believe Justin means well," she called through the connecting door.

"Do you?" *How can you?* But Serena was naïve in matters like this. She did not see the chafing resentment, or the barely contained *ennui*. Or the fact that he meant to scrutinize them like bugs under a microscope. In this restricted environment, they had to pass muster or he would squash them like flies.

He wanted to do that anyway.

He had wanted to do that last night.

Diandra got up from her bed and began pacing restlessly. She felt not at all like freshening up or resting. Rather, she felt dislocated yet again; there was something about the man that made her feel like committing mayhem.

It was that kiss, and his infuriating attempt to buy her off. And his inexplicable reversal when she had expected him to point out that she could just as easily have taken Serena to the English colony in Calcutta or Bombay where there was a lively social season and just the mix of eligible officers and younger sons that attracted marriage-minded mothers and young women with little prospects.

That was not what she wanted for Serena.

But what to make of him?

We will forget the thing ever happened . . .

"Serena, dear . . ." She paused at the connecting door to find Serena gazing pensively out the window.

She eased herself next to her. "What is it? Serena . . .!"

"Oh!" Serena turned and looked at her, almost as if she were not aware of her presence. "I was just . . . who do you suppose that is? There, on the horizon, to the east, where the clouds are gathering. Do you see?"

She saw.

A figure, gray and ghostly, moving like a wraith against the swelling clouds, and then, in an instant, as they watched, it vanished and there was nothing but the landscape, the roiling clouds and the sense it had never been there at all.

Chapter Three

"So tell me, madam, just what social skills does your sister possess?"

It was the tone of the contemptuous artistocrat; he thought they were savages.

Once again, she felt her hackles rising. Insufferable was not the word for him. He wanted to grind her under his heel. And he wasn't done trying.

Well, she could be every bit as merciless as he. "Exactly what do you mean, Justin?"

He didn't like her bluntless. "Don't be obtuse."

"I'm afraid you must define *social skills*. Do you mean, does she eat with a knife and fork? Can she read and write? You really must be more precise when you ask such a broad question."

Oh, he didn't like being lectured by the likes of her. She was beginning to perceive all his little bullying tricks: the sarcastic question, the cool tone, the haughty look, the thinned lips, the inverted insult.

He did them all to a turn. And there was also the cold

stare that said more clearly than words, I'm surrounded by imbeciles.

She was not amused by his act, and she had all the time in the world to fence with him. Serena was resting, having declined to come to tea after viewing the mysterious vanishing figure, and they were alone together in the library with a pot of tea and frosted enmity between them.

"I'm sorry—you said what?"

"I hadn't said anything, madam."

"Yes, that is very clear. Tell me again what you wish to know."

"Social skills."

"Just what are pertinent *social skills* in *your* world, Justin?"

But he was on to that. "If you don't *know*, madam—"

"Well, we might well have higher standards in Calcutta, Justin. We move among the highest castes and the most ceremonial society. The requirements are very stringent. I think you had best tell me what constitutes social skills in this regressive country."

She watched his face as he digested that. It was obvious he was losing patience with her, and fast. And he wasn't going to give over without a fight.

"I think we will both find out, madam," he said coolly. "And here is Tuttle with tea, and the news no doubt that my aunt and Tisbury have arrived."

"Indeed sir," Tuttle murmured, setting down the tray. "I made leave to bring service for four, excluding the young lady."

"Justin!" A woman's voice, from the threshold of the library, pleasantly fluty with just that hint of annoyance and command.

He rose and went forward to meet her. "Leonie."

She stepped into the room with outstretched hands, and Diandra watched her warily.

She was younger than her deceased sister Pamela, and elegantly dressed in a woolen travelling suit in a shadowed stripe of gray and dark blue, with a draped skirt and pleated hem. Her dark hair was pulled into a double roll at the nape of her neck, which emphasized her flawless skin and dark eyes, and she was covertly looking around Justin's broad shoulders at Diandra.

"And this must be Diandra, may I call you that?"

"Or madam," Diandra said, "whichever you find most comfortable. Justin prefers the latter."

"Does he?" Leonie moved to the couch and seated herself in a drift of perfume and insincerity. "How uncivil, Justin. Oh, and here comes Tisbury who rode admirably to point. Three hours—" she shook her head. "Deadly journey. There's only so much scenery one can admire. Ah, thank you, Tuttle. Tea is just the thing. George, come have a seat beside me after you've paid your respects to the dowager duchess of Skene."

Tisbury was sane, she saw that in an instant. No grudges to bear, and a great fondness, though she couldn't conceive why, for Justin, who was at a cabinet across the room preparing something stronger for himself and his guest.

Tisbury took her hand and bowed. "So pleased."

But she couldn't tell what he was thinking; he seemed amused, rather, but she couldn't take offense because his face was so kind.

He turned to take a goblet from Justin, and Leonie chirruped, "Well, isn't this so very pleasant. How long ago did you say you'd arrived?"

"Not more than two hours," Justin said, seating himself at the tea table, across from Diandra. "We were in the process of discussing the advantages of being raised in India as opposed to England."

"Did you at least have boarding school?" Leonie asked.

Diandra smiled. "We had four years at Rufton Hall. I think you'll find we can read, write and do sums."

Leonie lifted her cup to hide her shock that they had had the advantage of the very best education. "I'm sure you do the school credit," she murmured after she had taken a calming sip of her tea.

"I rather think I did," Diandra said pointedly.

"Yes, of course," Leonie said hastily and turned to Justin. "Just what is wanted, Justin, can you tell me so that I can begin to make arrangements?"

"Dressmakers, dance masters, instructors. Madam and I have been playing word games over social skills. We have no idea in what our guests are accomplished. I expect you to find out."

"I see." Leonie's avid gaze moved from Justin to Diandra. "Of course you're not out of mourning yet, Diandra, so that alleviates one problem."

"I believe I'm still alive," Diandra said tartly.

"Stand up, my dear. Come, come," as Diandra reluctantly got to her feet and presented herself to Leonie's skewering assessment.

She chose not to be kind. "That dress is . . . well, adequate, but certainly not for our purposes. We'll do silk and crepe for you—it has been a year, hasn't it?—since you will be in attendance at functions. Your sister, however, is another matter."

"She's resting," Diandra said brusquely, as she picked up her cup and moved to the window. It faced the rear as well, but to the west, and there was just a sliver of sunlight settling into the horizon through the lowering clouds.

And then she saw it—one moment there, a gray wraith drifting across the horizon like fog, and the next moment gone, as if the earth had swallowed it up.

No, she had imagined it. She was all on edge because

of Serena and this malicious woman. What was the likeli-
hood that she and Serena had really seen anything at all?

She clutched her cup tightly, not half hearing the conversation behind her that centered on which French dressmaker and which dancing master might be available on
such short notice.

"I wish we might have stayed in London," Leonie said
plaintively. "It is impossible to conduct business so far
from Town."

"Nonsense, no one is in Town anyway, Leonie. They're
all out here, waiting to be engaged for the season. George
will help you. He's particularly good with dancing masters.
He knows just what to look for."

"And what will you be doing meantime?" Leonie asked,
and Diandra turned from the window at the coy tone of
her voice.

"I?" Justin said lazily. "I am going to sit back and let
you do all the work while I watch the fun."

He followed her. He wanted to see, he wanted to know.
Too much he wanted to know—about her. He didn't even
understand the impulse.

He watched her on her way back to the guest wing as
she stopped to admire a painting, stroke the lustrous wood
of a piece of furniture, inhale the scent from a bouquet
of flowers that came from Skene's year-round greenhouses.

He watched her at dinner, which was served informally.

Potato soup, fish mousse, veal scallops in wine cream
sauce: she ate slowly and appreciatively, closing her eyes
at the first bite, savoring the taste, the texture, the tang.

She stroked the shank of the cool silver knife, the stem
of the antique wine goblet; and when she stood, as they
were about to remove themselves to the family drawing

room, she touched the satin brocade upholstery of her chair.

She lingered as they crossed the hallway to examine the paintings, to run her fingers over a piece of antique porcelain.

And he watched her as she entered the parlor, her posture ramrod straight, as she moved to take a protective seat close to Serena.

Tuttle had lit the fire and the lamps so that the room was bathed in a soft glow.

Leonie had positioned herself right by the fireplace with George next to her, and Serena and her sister across from them.

Firelight was becoming to Leonie, as well she knew. His mother's baby sister, the unexpected late child who had captivated them all. She was so lovely, so elegant, she had been spoiled by everyone, and now she considered it her due.

She had never married, had flirted with three dozen men, and broke all of their hearts.

And when Pamela had died, they had consoled each other. He knew Leonie wanted more, but he wasn't at all prepared to give it. And he never wanted to have to say the words.

She was tenacious; he knew that too. She was perfectly prepared to wait. And she wasn't in the least happy about this complication, but she also tended to make the best of uncontrollable situations. She would not let the dynamite embarrass him, but it was clear she would look for any opening to disparage Diandra.

And George—looking at him with those soulful eyes, as if it were he putting the sisters through a catechism of their strengths and weaknesses.

Serena was like putty: too naïve and eager to please, no sophistication in spite of her expensive education. But she was malleable, which was in the end easier than dealing with someone like Diandra.

Serena had no problem at all talking about their social life in India, and in fact, he was rather startled at the breadth and scope of it.

"Well, of course, at school, we read classics and did sums—how else could one learn to manage the plantation stores? And embroidery, music, and sketching. And at home, we ride and play lawn tennis. And dance: every month, there are cotillions at the club, you know, and then the bi-annual balls in Calcutta. Not to mention my brother hosts a yearly fancy dress ball. And that is besides the parties, the theatricals, the picnics, the gymkhanas, the contests, the races, teas and discussion groups. And we dine out quite often, and there are always cards after dinner. And good conversation."

"Not in the least primitive," Diandra interpolated dryly. "And don't forget to number cricket, golf, archery and target shooting among our social skills, Serena. And we do ride to hounds as well."

"That's a relief," Leonie said, ignoring Diandra's barbed comment. "Though ladies don't play cricket *here*. In any event, we'll have the dancing master just to make sure. And the dressmaker. Justin can harness up a pony or two so we can judge your seat. Riding costumes, of course. Or do you have one?"

This question was directed at Diandra who felt the full brunt of Leonie's dislike across the room.

"Never mind," Leonie said, before she could answer. "They are probably sadly out of style anyway. New riding habits. Hmm. Tennis. An interesting skill. Marketable, perhaps. Justin, do you play?"

That brought him out of his brooding study of Diandra. "Tolerably."

"Excellent. We must do then. Have someone set up a

court, and the first warm day, we'll have at it. I'm sure Diandra would love to challenge you."

Her dark eyes flashed as they met Justin's.

"I would think Diandra would be up to any challenge," he said blandly, knowing Leonie wouldn't like that assessment at all. He could tell from Diandra's expression she knew exactly what he was about. And Leonie did not. Or wouldn't acknowledge it, in any event. She had no humor at all, Leonie, and she was every bit as self-centered as he.

They were a match in every way.

And all he could do was watch Diandra, abrasive, blunt, elegant, hot-tempered, sharp-tongued Diandra. Soft lips, pliant body; he had felt her give for one telling instant. Soft and hard Diandra, cool eyes, hot mouth: she hadn't forgotten a thing.

And neither had he.

"Speaking of that," George intervened, "why not get up a game of cards?"

"Lovely!" Serena exclaimed.

"Yes, let us test the mettle of our *debutante,*" Leonie said, as she grasped the bellpull. "Tuttle! We want cards. And sherry."

As Tuttle withdrew, she herded them over to a small rectangular table by the sofa where Diandra sat.

Taking charge, as if she lived there. As if she were the mistress.

"Come, Diandra—bring the chairs from the dining room. George, do help her."

She lifted the tabletop and slid it forward so that it formed a square surface and George slipped two chairs under, and Diandra brought one and Justin two others.

They seated themselves and Leonie beamed at them as Tuttle entered with a tray and two fresh decks of cards. "Excellent suggestion, George. You'll pair with Serena, Justin with me. We wouldn't want to overpower Serena the first time, would we? And I know Diandra doesn't mind sitting out."

"Not in the least," Diandra said. "I'm content to watch."

She was content to watch Serena, rather. And Justin. If anyone was aiming to get the upper hand, it was Leonie. She was amazing to behold. And Justin didn't rein her in, either.

Tuttle poured the sherry, and left it on the table, and Leonie cracked open the first deck of cards, handed it to Justin to shuffle, to Serena to cut, and to George for the deal.

Justin, who was to George's left, led with the king of spades and the game was on.

Serena held her own in spite of Leonie's quick, intuitive, and sometimes crushing play. George was there to steady her, his eyes kind and wise. Justin's expression however was totally opaque as he followed Leonie's leads and they took trick after trick.

It didn't look as if he were out to ravage the opposition. He played with logic and a kind of detachment. He knew his cards, and Diandra supposed that extended over every area of his life. His long fingers were quick, his face impassive, his cool blue gaze focused.

Leonie on the other hand wanted the victory. Needed it. To show, to prove, what? That she and Justin could play in tandem on all levels?

Yet Serena was right with them and managed to trump at some least likely moments when she took the lead.

George kept the points and they were not going down by much as they completed the tenth rubber of the fifteen they had agreed upon.

"Perhaps Diandra would like to take Leonie's place," George suggested.

"Not particularly," Diandra said. "Go on and finish the fifteen. That should just about wear everyone out."

Leonie shot her an oblique look, took the cards and began the deal.

And suddenly the table began to rise.

Diandra bolted from her chair as the table wobbled and rose higher, and everything on it slid off and crashed onto the floor.

Leonie shrieked, dropped the cards, and pushed back so hard on her chair she almost toppled over.

Justin and George jacked themselves up simultaneously as Serena heaved upright, screamed and collapsed on the floor.

The table landed with a thump, teetered, and pitched onto one side.

And everyone froze for one fraught moment.

Tuttle came running in.

"My lord . . . I heard . . ."

"Yes." Justin was already kneeling by Serena's side. "I think she fainted. Smelling salts, Tuttle."

"I think I'm going to faint," Leonie said, her voice just a little breathless. "Tuttle—wait! Bring brandy for everyone. What the devil just happened here?"

She and George looked at each other and then at Justin and Diandra who were on the floor, ministering to Serena.

"The table," George said hoarsely. He grasped the edge of it and set it on its legs, and then began a thorough examination of it as Tuttle entered with another decanter, four snifters and the salts.

He opened the bottle for Justin who pushed it under Serena's nose. She came round in an instant.

"Good God, what *is* that awful smell?" She looked up at Diandra. "What happened?"

"You . . . we had a fright," Diandra said because she didn't know quite what to make of it.

"The table is perfectly sound," George said. He got to his feet, grabbed a snifter, poured, and took a long revivifying swallow. "There's nothing. Nothing wrong with that table."

"But we all saw it," Leonie said hoarsely. "It—it lifted . . ."

"We imagined it," Justin said, holding out his hand to Serena.

"No, I know what I saw," Leonie said. She grasped the table. "It went up, just like that . . ." She lifted it from the underside, and then turned it over and set it on the sofa. "There has to be something. Diandra, help me."

"It was all our imagination," Justin said. "The game was tense. Everyone was ready to quit. Although Serena did quite well."

Leonie stared at him. "Nonsense. She was adequate at best; she needs much more tutoring if she is to take her place at the card tables this season. You are being too kind, which isn't like you at all. I don't understand it, and I wish you wouldn't smooth this over. That table lifted off the floor and we all saw it."

"And yet neither you nor George can find anything to account for it. That should surely tell you we are all exhausted and should all retire and forget what we thought we saw."

This evening never happened . . .

Serena sagged against her shoulder. "Did I faint?"

"I think so. I should get you to bed," Diandra murmured, slipping her arm around Serena's waist. "Too much excitement. Everyone, please excuse us."

George stood. Leonie moved so they could pass her. And Justin watched them intently.

She could feel his eyes on her as she shepherded Serena out of the drawing room door; she couldn't get her through the guest wing el to their rooms fast enough.

We will forget this evening ever happened . . .

My lord, manipulating events again, she thought, as Serena sank onto her bed fully clothed.

Or was there something else?

She didn't like the thought that blasted into her mind. No, no, no—Even he would not sink so low.

But in point of fact, he had considered paying her off. What *wouldn't* he do to get what he wanted?

How bored had he been tonight?

She had watched him, especially the way he focused his hooded gaze on Serena periodically as if she were an experiment he was conducting.

If he thought that—and she had every evidence that was exactly what he did think—he wouldn't hesitate a minute to try every trick to make them leave Skene and abandon their plans altogether.

Any *trick* . . .

Forget what you thought you saw . . .

Hadn't he made a devastating kiss disappear?

We will forget this evening ever happened . . .

Not her imagination.

So what else had the table been but a parlor trick, and who better to conjure it than the high and mighty master of Skene?

Chapter Four

They were served breakfast in their rooms the following morning.

"Such luxury!" Serena crowed as she danced into Diandra's bedroom followed by Gita who was pushing a teacart top heavy with fragrant pots of chocolate, tea and coffee, and covered dishes steamy with tantalizing scents.

Diandra was barely awake. "Too noisy, Serena."

"We'll sit by the window. It's all bright and sunny today. And I was too good at the cards last night, I don't care what that witch Leonie says. Hurry *up*, Diandra. Everything is hot and smells delicious!"

Gita began uncovering the dishes as Diandra struggled out of bed and Serena poured herself a cup of tea.

"Give me that." Diandra took the cup from Serena's hands and sipped deeply. "Oh, lord ..." She sank into the chair opposite her sister.

"Wonderful. This all looks wonderful. I'll have the eggs au gratin, the bacon and the spinch souffle. And—" she looked at Serena's eager face, "so will Serena."

Gita served them, and she slowly sipped the revivifying tea, ignoring Serena's telling eyes.

"Diandra . . ."

Diandra groaned. "Do we have to start this early in the morning? Wasn't last night enough?"

"Oh pooh," Serena said. "The table moved . . . so what?"

"You fainted is what."

"Well, it was *floating* . . ."

"Exactly," Diandra said dryly.

"Do you know what that means?" Serena demanded, her eyes wide.

"Someone was playing a trick."

"Di-*andra* . . . I wish you would take these things seriously. You don't *deserve* to know what it means. Let's see what the tea leaves say instead."

Diandra sent her an exasperated look. "I'm not done yet."

"We'll wait."

And she did, her arms folded across her chest, until Diandra resignedly drained the cup. "All right. Take the cup in your left hand and go three times in a circle from left to right. Then give the cup to me."

More games and distractions . . . oh, why not?

Diandra performed the little ritual grudgingly, as she was sure Serena could see, and then carefully handed the cup to her sister.

Serena peered into it and then put it down slowly. "Look—near the trim and handle, an ax shape. That is *not* good, especially with all those curvy lines near it. Nothing is certain. Everything is in the near future. You must be careful. Complications are coming, disturbances—the mushroom, you see? A letter perhaps . . . that's the arrow; money might be coming, signified by those dots alongside. A journey in the distant future . . . see—it's facing the bottom of the cup. But there's nothing here about the floating table."

"I must be careful," Diandra said, a touch of irony in her tone, which Serena missed altogether. Serena knew nothing about irony.

She leaned toward Diandra with the utmost seriousness.

"Well, you must," she whispered. "Maybe we all must. There are spirits in this house, Diandra, and I think one tried to contact us last night."

She didn't try to talk Serena out of her notion. Once it was rooted in her mind, it was as if it were truth. Or Serena wanted it to be truth—Diandra never could quite figure out which, and she didn't have the energy to reason with her.

Besides which, the table had lifted, and whether it was truth or trick, it had been frightening.

"Our problem is that we have been too long confined and we need exercise and fresh air," she said briskly. "I miss that. It has been a month or more since I've ridden or walked. They are barbarians here, I swear. Nothing like that for their women, apparently. *Ladies don't play cricket here . . .* "She mimicked Leonie's snide tone. "They prefer to see them stiff and starched with embroidery hoops in their hands and platitudes on their lips. Well, not me, and I don't care if I am still in mourning. Come, we'll walk the fields and see some of Skene close up."

"Must I?"

"You ought to. It will clear your head and your eyes, and you'll digest all that heavy food so much the better. And think, no afternoon naps."

"This is as bad as the hill country in summer," Serena grumbled.

"But not as hot, so that's a blessing."

"I'd rather go back to bed."

"Then *you* are a barbarian too, sister dear. Fine. Every-one else is staying in, obviously. It's just a sin not to make use of this glorious morning weather."

"And we all know you're a saint, Diandra."

She ignored that. "I'll see you later."

She met no one on her way through the el or in the hallway. The house was eerily still, not even the footfall of a servant disturbing the silence.

She ran down the front steps, feeling full of life, and eager to race across the green velvet of the front lawns. If only she had had a horse, she would have been over the hills already and far afield, searching out the secrets of Skene.

She loved it already, that was the incongruous thing. She would have loved to have made it her home with Guthrie. All that time, he could have come home to this, but he chose India instead. And now she was here, she could not understand how he could have left.

But what was here now? His lord high and mighty of Skene, and his aunt the viper who was intent on both doing his bidding and undermining it.

Was it worth a season for Serena, really? Was it not enough that they were here?

It was enough *she* was here.

She slowed as she reached the crest of the hill where they'd caught their first glimpse of Skene, and she turned to look at the house.

It was bathed in full morning light surrounded by trees and formal gardens, and the undulating landscape beyond; symmetrical, stately, its two els like welcoming arms reach-ing out to her.

This—*this* was not a penance, not for her.

And Justin Reynell knew it, and rather than take direct action, he wanted to scare her away—from Skene, from

London, from any idea she could take her place in the social strata he inhabited.

Clever man.

Not *so* clever.

He might easily read how gullible Serena was, but he still had *her* to contend with, and the acid-tongued Leonie was hardly a buffer between them or the memory of that assaulting kiss.

No, she had taken his measure as well, and there wasn't a childish trick he could perpetrate that would make her return to Calcutta before she was ready.

So let him send on his dancing tables and his mysterious hooded peasants to prowl his property . . .

Even as she thought it, she saw it the next moment, flitting across the cream shaded front steps of Skene; and without taking a breath, she raced off after it as it disappeared into the trees beyond the family wing.

She was too far away, she knew it, and she ran and ran, the pounding of her feet reverberating against the ground, the earth, the clear blue sky—no, the pounding of hooves pursuing her like the devil's own horseman.

Faster she ran, outracing the tentacles of fear that clutched at her heart; she wouldn't look back because he had done it, he had scared her half to death, her bravado was gone, and she was sure she was going to die.

Like an angel, she would fly to heaven; she was lifting off the ground already, held aloft by a mysterious power, floating like a table, tethered to nothing but one strong arm around her waist, and a lathered horse that flew like the wind.

And slowly, slowly it came to a walk, so slowly, until she floated down to the ground as gently as if it were a cloud.

Skene—and heaven . . .

Her heart was pounding wildly as she wheeled to face him.

"You sadist!"

"What the devil were you doing?"

"Chasing ghosts, as you very well know, since you set the thing up."

"Not likely, madam. Manifestations don't interest me in the least, not ghosts, not floating tables . . . which I am not at all sure *you* did not perpetrate."

"What?!" Oh, he had guts and gall, she had to give him that, shifting the whole thing back on her. But what a tactic, and whose word carried weight, after all? The *seigneur* could get away with murder, if it came to that.

"The table," he said conversationally as he began to lead his mount toward the house; she had no choice but to follow, "the table was an excellent stunt. Admirable. You must tell me sometime how you effected it—when, of course, you are ready to admit you were responsible."

Oh, she just had to take the wind out of this blowhard's sails.

"How fascinating you should deduce that, my lord," she said silkily, "when the thought had occurred to me what an excellent device you employed to try to shock my sister and myself out of proceeding any further with our plans."

He didn't like that. His jaw tightened, and there was the faintest darkening of his cheekbones.

"I don't do children's games, madam. If I weren't amenable to your being here, you wouldn't be here."

"Or if I weren't determined, my lord."

He stopped dead. "You truly think that carries any weight?"

"I truly do, Justin. I am used to managing things and having my way. My sister might be susceptible to trickery and superstitious nonsense, but I am not, and you might as well know it now, and tell your loyal tenant, whoever it might be, that the timely appearances of a ghostly figure will *not* frighten me."

He gave her a considering glance, his eyes cool and blue as the sky above. "I have no idea what you are talking about."

"Of course you don't, Justin. Just tell your accomplice I have seen through his chicanery, and the game is ended."

"There is no game, except that which you have instigated, madam, and it is foolish beyond words to think that parlor tricks would influence me in any way."

"Which is why it is all the more likely it is you who are pulling the strings to discard what you have already decided was an unnecessary burden. I knew it when you changed your mind, Justin. No man turns an about-face so quickly. Your bribe didn't work, so you thought to get us out of London to get rid of us altogether, just as I surmised . . ."

"*Enough* . . ."

He was furious, she could see that; no one stood up to the *seigneur*, it was obvious, and he looked about ready to throw her in the dungeon.

She wondered idly if Skene even had dungeons as she calmly watched the telltale muscle in his jaw as he fought to regain some control.

There was a secret here: if she made *him* angry and she remained collected, the balance of power shifted into *her* hands.

She rather liked that.

"I'm bored to death with this talk, madam. Do what you think you must, and when I get tired of the nonsense, I will toss you out."

"Oh, there's fair warning. Judge, jury and executioner. It is a very satisfying plan, Justin. Who could doubt you?"

"Indeed," he said haughtily.

"Well, we shall see," she said and again had the satisfaction of seeing his cheekbones wash with angry color again. "It isn't all up to you, you know."

"I beg to differ, madam. And I live to see the day you capitulate."

"And I of course live to see the moment your schemes are exposed."

"Then we are at point, madam. And I am too weary of this stupid conversation to make the next parry." He hoisted himself up onto his restive mount. "You might try going at it with George for a while. They are all in the family dining room waiting for you. The dressmakers arrive in an hour."

"And you depart, and who knows what next we might see ruffling the drawing room curtains. Convenient, Justin if another table has a mind to go floating around the room."

He stared down at her coldly. "Convenient you will have credulous witnesses, madam. But there has never been the like at Skene before you arrived, and that speaks for itself."

"Indeed, Justin. Until *we* arrived. The wonder of it . . ."

"Do you *never* shut up?" he said harshly, cutting ruthlessly into her vitriolic response.

She considered the question for a long, teeth-grinding moment. "No, I don't think I do, Justin. May I go on?"

"No, but I'm going to." He smacked his mount and it reared up dangerously close to her. "You won't win this one, madam."

She didn't back down; she wondered if he expected that she would.

"But who is to say I will lose?" she asked sweetly.

He made a disgusted sound, the *seigneur* again, tall and imperious in the saddle, just waiting for the moment he could blast out of her presence.

"*I* do, madam."

She said nothing, but he hated the smug expression on her face that spoke more clearly than words. Quite obviously, she did know when to hold her tongue. And she knew to do it when he least expected it.

But her dark steady gaze had veered away from his and the expression on her face had changed.

"Justin . . . !" she whispered urgently, and he twisted around to follow her pointing finger.

He saw—he thought he saw a movement in the trees . . . and then out again, gray as smoke, and as insubstantial, floating in the topiary . . . and then gone—

He grasped her arm and pulled her up in front of him before she even comprehended what he was doing.

"Hold on!" He nudged the mount and they took off, racing down the carriage track toward the house and moments later into the trees, and then pulling up in the gardens behind the family wing.

There was nothing there, just the blazing light of the sun, the gorgeous sky, the brilliant garden color, and an apparition that had disappeared into thin air.

There were patterns laid out over the dining room table and bolts of material propped up on every sofa and chair in the drawing room.

Black silk, watered silk, grosgrain silk, velvet and crepe, brocade satin, tricotine, cashmere, French sateen, mohair, challis, nun's veiling . . . she touched them all as if she could imprint the colors and textures on her skin.

Serena was already swathed in two cuts of silk and lace goods, and she was rubbing her face against the softness of the material.

"The color, for madamoiselle . . . *non* . . . tan does not do well for her. Green, perhaps—try this . . ." The speaker was a small spare woman who radiated impatience and energy. She was dressed in black, and she had a thin sharp face and gray hair that was braided up and out of her way around her small neat head.

Leonie held up the green silk next to Serena's face.

"Yes. Better. Take away the tan. Now . . ." Her incongruously delicate fingers began tucking and draping the green silk around Serena's languid form.

"Ah, here is Diandra," Leonie said, as she noticed her at the threshold. "And Justin. My dear, this is a party for ladies only."

"And yet there is George, lounging in the drawing room, tea to hand and ready to render an opinion at the instant."

"Oh, well—that's George. What are you doing here anyway? I thought you went riding."

He chose not to answer her. "That color will do well on Serena."

Leonie cast a critical look at Serena. "Perhaps. Perhaps a shade darker. Nothing too bold for Serena. Don't you love her skin? So clear, with that subtle color. And those eyes. Diandra's are so dark, and Serena's so light, more of a gray-green, don't you think? Yes, that green will do; it pulls out the color in her eyes."

She motioned to Diandra. "Louise will be dressing Serena. And Helaine will tend to you. She waits in the dining room. You have only to select the styles and trim you want."

Well, that was easy enough. Serena was enjoying the attention enormously, and that *was* part of what she had wanted her to experience in England. But she didn't like feeling as if she were a piece of wallpaper about to be hung up to dry.

Leonie was just as overbearing as Justin and adept in all little tricks. The dismissive hand. The critical look. The disparaging remark.

They had no manners, none of them. All they had was money. And boredom. And she and Serena were a respite from the boredom. The moment's diversion for these jaded aristocrats.

So what was the gray spectre that kept disappearing?

Justin had seen a movement in the trees, a wisp of morning fog . . . and thin air when they emerged in the garden.

A trick? A distraction from his high-handedness? He trusted her not, not even to return to the house to proceed with the fittings.

He was going to watch her every moment and expose the hoax.

"You are too excellent, madam," he had said coldly, as he eased her off the horse. "You almost had me believing . . . until I saw *nothing* with my own eyes . . ."

"How adroitly you planned it," she interrupted furiously. "What does your accomplice have—some kind of telescope by which he knows when you are afoot and when he is to appear? Oh, I congratulate you, sir. If I didn't know better, indeed, I would have left today on the evidence of the table alone."

And now he was watching her as if he expected her to conjure something up from under the dining room table where she was looking at pattern drawings and samples of trim.

It was enough to make her edgy where before she had felt calm and in control. But it would not do to let Justin see her uncertainty. She must ignore him and concentrate on the matter at hand.

Nevertheless, there was not much she could accomplish except to choose the style of dresses she wanted, and in which material and trim they would be made up.

Helaine, her seamstress, was as tall and spare as Louise was short; and she was no nonsense. She knew the way the thing must be done. Everything by the book. Anything in lavender deferred until summer. Lace she might have, subtle and elegant, for evening wear; ribbon and velvet

trim, buttons and pleats, cord and braiding, yes. Crepe
and silk for lightness. Patterns, brocades could not be considered. Ruching and bows were too frivolous. Jet beads
were too fast. No puffs, panniers, or contrasting material.

But there was shadow-striped silk, and lustrous crepe
with passamenterie coiling all over the selvage; strips of
velvet for the collars and cuffs. Sleek braid to accent a
vested basque, and the hem of a draped skirt.

It was possible, just possible, to maintain some semblance
of style in mourning. She made her choices, and Helaine
took her measurements. They chose the fabrics and trims,
and by the end of it, she was exhausted.

She had had no idea that even black must be mated
with the tone of her skin or that there were so many subtle
shadings, and so many ways to fit a dress.

Leonie sent them to their rooms to rest. They were
having guests after dinner for dessert and cards, and she
was sending Louise to Serena with one of her own dresses
to be made over for the occasion.

"She thinks we are as provincial as can be," Serena
muttered as she allowed Gita to unhook her dress and
loosen her stays. "As if being fashionable were only possible
in England and nowhere else. I think I don't like her."

But her eyes lit up when Louise entered her room with
the dress.

"Ohhhh . . . it's beautiful—look, Diandra . . ." She held
it up, a confection of bronze silk trimmed with a pleated
bodice and vertical lace insets in the skirt. "Maybe she did
mean well . . . oh, may I try it on?"

Diandra sank onto her bed and watched the flurry of
motion as Louise and Gita removed her sister's morning
outfit and helped her slip on Leonie's dress.

It was big on Serena's slender frame, and Louise immediately began pinning and tucking the bodice to make the
necessary adjustments.

"A stitch here, a tack there improves the fit and all can easily be removed later for Miss Leonie," Louise murmured, her mouth full of pins, and her needle flashing. "Oh, but the color does well for you, madamoiselle. A little rouge to emphasize the cheeks. A pretty fan in hand. Madamoiselle's figure is to be envied. *Voilà*—it is done."

"This is so elegant," Serena breathed, as she viewed herself in her mirror. "Who must these guests be?"

"Is there anything I can do for *madam*—?" Louise asked.

Diandra shook her head, and Louise and Gita removed the bronze dress and Louise took it away with her to secure the alterations.

Serena climbed back into bed and nestled under the covers. "I could grow used to this."

"Yes, I can see that. A nap is in order before the strenuous task of bathing and dressing for the evening. And of course Gita will see to your other wants. I, on the other hand, want to go for a ride, so . . . I think I will change and find the groom."

"You know, I just don't understand you, Diandra. Why not spend the afternoon resting? What else is there to do?"

Diandra closed the connecting door behind her gently without bothering to reply; Serena didn't expect it anyway, and her voice was drowsy with the anticipated pleasure of drifting off for the rest of the afternoon.

She on the other hand felt restless and fractious. The whole incident this morning with his high and mighty lord of Skene . . . and the spectre—gray fog that only she and Serena could see? For one moment, he had seemed to believe her—and then it all came down to dissembling and distraction.

The thing had been there, yet when they got to the garden, there was nothing; and he, if he could not see it, that was the end of it. So easy for him. But wasn't that the way of men, to leave one with no room to maneuver whatsoever?

Well, she could be as obdurate as he. His incivility was enough to prove to her that he was the *provocateur*. She was not going to decamp and she was going to go for a ride.

Leonie stopped her as she strode through the connecting hallway.

"My dear, is *that* your riding habit?"

She bristled. "It is serviceable enough, Leonie."

Leonie made a sound that might have been *pffft*. "Come—Helaine is still here. We must get you fitted today for a new habit." She turned her head as George sauntered out into the hallway. "Don't you agree, George? Look, the elbows are worn, and the skirt is . . . well, disreputable is hardly the word for it."

George smiled at her. "Truly proof she must be an excellent rider. This is a well used costume."

"Indeed," Diandra said frostily, allowing Leonie to pull her back into the dinning room. Helaine was there, cutting patterns on the dining room table. A few words in French; a clap of the hands, and George disappeared, Gita came running, and before she knew it, the offensive habit had been removed so that Helaine could deconstruct it, and Gita had been sent for a walking dress to replace it.

Too much, too much—she was preternaturally silent as Gita dressed her and Helaine gathered up her scissors, patterns and materials and left.

"Are we finished?"

"Oh, quite," Leonie said. "Why don't you join me in the drawing room, my dear; we'll have some tea and a chat."

Tuttle had already set out the tea things—the steaming pot, the tiny sandwiches, the miniature pastries.

"Lovely," Leonie said, motioning Diandra to take a chair opposite her. "Shall I pour?"

Diandra took the cup and sipped. This way, at least, she had the advantage of Leonie, who, having issued the invitation, was required to maintain the conversation.

"Tell me, Diandra. How did my sister die?"

It was the last question Diandra had thought to hear, and she scalded her tongue as she drank too deeply in her dismay. And after all, what could she tell Leonie? She had been on the sidelines then, watching Guthrie move through the social circles of Calcutta from a very great distance.

"She just . . . disappeared," she said carefully, setting down her cup. "It was determined that she had committed suicide, that she had drowned, but her body was never found."

"Yes . . ." Leonie murmured. "One day there, one day gone."

"All her clothes, and a note, were found by the river-bank. It was during monsoon. She might not have jumped. She might just been swept away, except for the careful placement of the clothing and the note."

"But the body was never found."

"No."

"And how long after did you meet Guthrie?"

The question was slick, neat, offhanded, and lethal as a knife.

"I had met him previously," she said. "And renewed my acquaintance more than a year after Pamela's death."

"I see."

Did she? The tension in her was palpable. "And you married when?"

"The year after," Diandra said through stiff lips.

"When he already knew he would be Viceroy."

Jury, judge, executioner: Leonie was asking the questions that

Justin had already answered in his own mind. Without asking her. Without caring what the answers might be. Oh, they were all the same, she and he, spoiled, childish, inhospitable . . .

Or—feeling threatened?

She leaned forward as if to get up and Leonie's hand shot out and stayed her.

"Why *did* he marry you?"

Even she did not know that; Guthrie loved her, she loved him—that was the right answer, and Leonie had no right to know anything else.

"He loved me," Diandra said, "and I loved him."

"And then *he* died. How fortuitous."

She felt the shock all the way down to her toes. This was war—and a battle of equals, even if Leonie did not think so. Leonie must be put in her place—and quickly. There had been enough of her little digs and taunts that she had been willing to overlook for Serena's sake.

But this—this was offensive in the extreme.

"How insulting. The gloves are off, I perceive, and we will not be civil or even mannerly? I can do that, *Aunt* Leonie. Do test me. *I* have been a Vicereine, and believe me, your little intrigues are nothing compared to the politics in Indian upper circles. You are *not* dealing with some ignorant *parvenue,* dear Aunt. I hope you will take that into consideration in the time we must spend here. And I hope that is all you will have the bad manners to ask me."

Leonie rose to her feet, and stared down at her contemptuously. "And I hope that is all you have the bad manners to ever say to me. There's gratitude. I take you and your rag-tag sister and try to make something presentable of you, and you resent my request for information about my dear only sister? *That* is beyond bad manners, my dear. That is obscene and cruel. Perhaps *you* have something to learn . . . if you even *can* be educated at this late date. Nothing I have tried to do for you yet has made an impression. But that is ever the way with colonials. They believe their provincial society moves in exactly the same way as England. And they take a steep steep fall when they cannot measure up. Do excuse me. I cannot bear to be in the same room with you."

Leonie flounced out of the room, and Diandra sat back in her chair, her hands shaking, her face flushed. Oh, but that woman was not going to get the best of her. Never. She had not begun to feel the wrath of the Vicereine who could be every bit as arrogant as any born and bred aristocrat.

Leonie would never speak to her that way again. And when they returned to London, she was going to rent a house and remove herself from that woman's poisonous presence, and become the toast of the social season besides.

Chapter Five

And then—three hours later, when she and Serena came down for dinner, they were welcomed into the formal parlor, where Lord and Lady Hoxton-Shope were already seated, as if *they* were the guests of honor, and Diandra had the distinct feeling she had fallen down a rabbit hole.

Lady Hoxton-Shope was as portly as her husband was fine-boned and slender, and they were of indeterminate age and married years, who, apparently, adored dining out *and* playing cards, especially at Skene, where, to their great regret, Justin was hardly ever in residence.

They were delighted to meet *her*, and charmed by Serena's modest blushes, and amenable to being herded around by Leonie who was acting the part of an overactive border collie, licking, lapping and nudging everyone where she wanted them to go.

Their hostile conversation might never have taken place, and Diandra was content to leave it like that.

Bored aristocrats rewrote history to suit themselves obviously. And you didn't air dirty laundry, dirty secrets or dirty words.

They dined on split pea soup, stewed tomatoes, stuffed and grilled mushrooms and baked Dover sole, followed by dessert in the family drawing room: seed cake, lemon cookies, tea and coffee, brandy and cards.

The conversation centered on local topics and mutual friends, and every once in a while, Lady Hoxton-Shope kindly directed a question to Serena about their lives in India, or requested a detail of some imperial incident from *her.*

Leonie and George kept everything moving nicely, and Justin pinned her with his icy blue gaze like a butterfly in a box and hardly said a word until Tuttle was summoned to bring in the table and fresh decks of cards and decanters of sherry, and then, "I'm not of a mind to play tonight. Let our guests have the pleasure—George and Serena will pair and Leonie will supervise all. Meantime, I will conduct my lady Diandra on a tour of the house."

He looked at Leonie as he was speaking, daring her to raise an objection, but how could she, in her guise of the perfect hostess? And Serena could care less about the house.

"You have seen all of the formal rooms . . ." he was saying as they strolled from the drawing room, and as they emerged into the reception hall, he dropped all pretense of cordiality, "and now I will have you where I can see *you.* How dare you abuse Leonie that way?"

The question hit her with the speed of a gunshot.

So this is how it is to be. Every insult, every transgression has been laid at my door and still it is not enough . . . I must pacify Leonie as well. Well, this I will not do, not even for Serena.

"I believe that is none of your business, Justin. Now what will you show me?"

"The door, if I had my way."

Her anger boiled over. "Then you shall. I will be perfectly content to return to London tomorrow and see to
my own situation. You've done enough, as much as your
father would have expected. I don't need you, Justin. Surely
a Vicereine who is widow of an Earl would be welcome
anywhere—unlike your Aunt Leonie, who has nothing to
recommend her but excessive rudeness and bad manners
and her futile desire that you notice her. But *that* is none
of my business, and the difference between us is that I
know it. The only thing I wish to pursue now is packing
my bags and getting out of here."

She turned away from him then, but he was blocking
the entrance to the guest wing, and she did not wish to
go within a dozen yards of him, so she stalked down the
hallway toward the saloon.

She could hear the animated play from behind the drawing room doors and she was aware that he was following
her and that once she entered the saloon, there was
nowhere else for her to go.

*Calm, calm, and retain the power . . . they were all snakes,
ready to strike the moment they saw a weakness. And she had kept
her weaknesses hidden—she had thought . . .*

She pushed open the doors to the saloon. It was furnished luxuriously, with every chair, table and molding
washed in gold and lit by two softly glowing sconces on
the wall. There were two doors, one leading to the library,
from which there was no egress except into the drawing
room; the other . . . she moved toward it quickly, turned
the knob, and stepped into darkness of a dungeon.

He paused at the top of the steps, waiting until he could
barely see the flickering light of her candle, and then he
began his descent.

He could see the light moving steadily down the short

corridor toward the *voudrais*. She would have passed the
wine cellars and the cold storage cellars, which were all
neatly closeted behind wooden doors and stone arches;
probably she would have opened at least one.

And now she must have come to the *voudrais* with its
ornate arched doors and luxurious satin curtain beyond.

He didn't think it was locked; there had never been a
reason to lock what was an open secret among men, and
the relic of an era of twenty years before.

He heard the doors creak as she opened them. She
would then part the curtains and step out onto a stone
parapet that overlooked the opulently furnished *salle
d'entrée*. There were stairs on either side, and if she were
curious enough, and he was certain she was, she would be
down those steps and past the first room already.

Or maybe not. As he parted the curtains, he saw her
below him, holding out her candle and circling the room
to get a better look at the brocade sofas and thick tufted
chairs that were now pushed back against the walls.

Slowly, she paced toward the back of the room and the
next thick satin curtain that divided the possibilities from
the choices.

She whipped the curtain open and stepped down into
the next tier, the lushly carpeted and exquisitely furnished
bagnio, and further on to the next curtain and the next
tier, the *boudoir*, and finally past two massive golden doors
into the exclusivity of the *seraglio*, and the echoes of its
secret perversions.

She sensed him following her. Her posture was taut, her
shoulders tense; she understood the sense of what she was
seeing, but he could not tell what she was thinking as she
turned slowly and started back toward him.

He waited for her at the step at the entrance to the
bagnio.

"What is this place?"

Nothing in her voice. So cool, she was, as if she couldn't identify the musky scent that still, after all this time, permeated the rooms.

"This is the *voudrais,* madam. The place of fulfilling every illicit fantasy. The place where all restraints and constraints are left at the door and you are free to do what you will. *Fais ce que tu voudrais.* It is engraved over the door. Do what you will. Anything." His voice flattened. "Everything. Nothing is forbidden."

Her eyes widened, and she turned slowly back to look at the *bagnio.*

"In the *salle d'entrée,* they gathered and then chose a partner for the night. In the *bagnio,* they removed their clothes and began the evening's foreplay. On the couches, on the floors, in groups, or singly if they wanted to sample a wide variety of tastes."

He grasped her arm and propelled her forward. "And when copulation was imminent, they moved to the *boudoir.* Goddesses moved among them, naked and insatiable, willing to spread their legs for whomever wished to penetrate them."

And down the step into the *seraglio.* She was trembling; finally, a weakness, a chink in her bravado. She was disgusted. Thoroughly repulsed and repelled. And he reveled in it.

"And those who wished to indulge in their perverse desires choose the privacy of the *seraglio.* A country house weekend was an indulgence of the senses in every possible way."

He pulled aside a curtain to reveal a cubicle in which there was just a backless, armless overstuffed sofa centered on a thick carpet.

"In the dark, oblivious to anything but their own desire, they did whatever they wanted; everything was provided.

Nothing was profane. And since it was one big family of neighbors and nobles, nobody told. And everybody knew."

She closed her eyes and swallowed. "Your father?"

"Probably." He didn't care to elaborate, and perhaps he didn't want to think about it at all. But the *voudrais* itself dated from the turn of the century, so at least two generations of Earls of Skene had availed themselves of illicit pleasures in this bordello of oblivion.

"Picture it, madam," he went on mercilessly, "picture them entering the *salle d'entrée*. The excitement. The heart-pounding anticipation at the thought of a fresh naked body to try out. The women would lift their skirts, expose their nipples, tempt and entice the men to choose them. They would offer kisses and caresses, and whisper of obscene delights. They would revel in the men freely fondling them anywhere they wanted. They would start to strip off their clothes in their excitement. They would take the men one and two into the corners and on the sofas, and begin their primal seduction. A taste of their charms. One at their breasts, one with his hand rooting between their legs; and she with each hand feeling her lover where he wanted it most.

"Picture it, madam—"

She made a strangled sound.

"—and that was the *salle d'entrée*. Once the choices were made, and their excitement was at a peak, they fell into the *bagnio* and began the full seduction. They removed their clothes and they spent themselves over and over in whatever licentious ways they could imagine or invent.

"Later, they removed to the *boudoir* to avail themselves of the ladies who sought further pleasure by copulating with every available man in any position she could devise.

"They would keep count, madam; it was a competition to see how many men they could fuck. That was all they wanted, a man on his knees between their legs.

"And for those to whom this was unpalatable, there was the *seraglio*. Here were explored other pleasures of the flesh and the fetish. Man to man; woman to woman; virgins and voluptuaries, this is where they came, to cells as hermitic as a monk's where they could render their perversions in the sanctity of silence.

"Skene's dirty secret, madam."

She didn't say a word. She turned away from him and began walking back toward the *boudoir*.

He had shocked her, he had done exactly what he had wanted to do—scandalize her beyond redemption.

He wanted to shake her, and he did not know why.

She was already through the *bagnio* and heading toward the parapet.

He followed her slowly, watching her wavering candle as she mounted the steps.

He wanted to mount her in the seraglio . . .

His step faltered, she saw it, noted it, never changed her expression, never moved, not even when they heard the first of a series of short, echoing raps.

He froze.

Rap, rap.

Ghostly, reverberating eerily through the cavernous rooms of the *voudrais*.

Rap, rap, rap.

He raced to the steps, grabbed her candle and her hand and pulled her down the corridor to the basement stairs.

Rap, rap, rap, rap.

Up the stairs and through the saloon, the library and into the drawing room where they were all immobile around the card table.

Rap, rap.

They all heard it, echoing like thunder through the house.

Rap, rap, rap—staccato, impatient almost.

Serena had the presence of mind to stand up and call out, "Is someone there?"

Rap.

"Is it—" she looked around her and George nodded that she should continue on. "Is it a spirit?"

Rap.

"Once means yes?"

Rap.

Leonie was white; the Hoxton-Shopes looked terrified. Diandra had sunk into a chair and was watching Serena warily; and Justin's icy gaze, which ranged between the two of them, was skeptical altogether.

But there was no denying the sound. It was hollow and resonant and eerie at the same time. It came from everywhere and nowhere; it filled the drawing room and the library and the hallway, and reverberated in their souls.

And Serena, tall and brave, standing up to a entity she could not see.

"Are you a spirit?"

Rap.

Every flame flickered.

"Do you come from this place?"

Rap.

"Are you long dead?"

Rap, rap.

"No." Serena looked around at them, wide-eyed, and then gripped the edge of the card table to steady her trembling hands. "Who are you?"

Rap, rap, rap, rap, rap, rap, rap . . . steady, angry sounds. Serena gasped in fear.

The table rose up, scaring her almost insensible as it bounced furiously up and down under her hands. She pulled away from it violently and it crashed to the floor. She backed away from it slowly, her whole body shaking.

"Who are you?" Serena's voice, unnaturally shrill.

Rap, rap, rap, rap, rap, rap—

"Can you spell?" She still had some presence of mind while the rest of them were rooted in their seats.

Rap.

"Tell us who you are."

She spelled out the letters as the entity rapped: ". . . m . . . n . . . o . . . p . . ." The rapping stopped.

"P . . ."

Rap.

"A . . ."

The rapping continued: ". . . j . . . k . . . l . . . m . . ." and paused.

"M . . . Pam—Pamela?"

Rap.

"Yes," Serena whispered.

And just as she confirmed it, Leonie screamed and the lights went out.

Nobody went to bed.

"This is ridiculous," Justin said. "Leonie, get up and stop this nonsense."

"Excuse me," Leonie moaned from the sofa where she was lying with a cold compress. "You didn't hear those sounds or see that table?"

"It was a trick," Justin said succinctly. "I don't know how or why, but it was a parlor trick. And it was *not* my mother."

"Oh, how can you say so? It sounded just like her."

"Leonie . . ." He was out of patience with them all. Even George, the most sensible and level-headed George, had been utterly gulled. And he couldn't tell in the least what Diandra thought.

"She followed them," Leonie whispered. "She came back to tell us. Even Diandra said, no one knows what happened to her. She was presumed drowned but they never found the body. Isn't that right, Diandra? *Isn't it?*"

"You know better than I what happened, Leonie. I barely knew them at the time. That is what was reported."

"She was waiting," Leonie said. "Waiting for the moment she could come back and tell us. She came with them." She pointed at Serena and Diandra. "And now she's ready to communicate. We need . . . we need—we need a *séance*. Or a medium. Or—a ouija board. Justin . . ."

"Oh good God, go to bed, Leonie. There are no ghosts or spirits . . ."

"But you heard it, we all heard it."

"*Never* until those two came here."

"Well then it's true, Pamela came with them. It makes all the sense in the world, and we shall get to the truth of it tomorrow. I will arrange for someone to come who can bring us Pamela's message." She sat up then, and she looked at Diandra. "Then we'll know the truth about everything."

It sounded like a threat. Diandra made a movement and then checked it. Serena's eyes were still glazed with fear. The table still lay overturned on the floor, and the Hoxton-Shopes looked as if they couldn't wait to excuse themselves so that they could spread the titillating details instantly among their friends.

They hadn't engaged to stay over, but Leonie wouldn't hear of them leaving at that late hour.

She was curiously and suddenly calm, now that she had decided on a course of action. She rang for the servants to make up the extra bedroom in the guest wing, and to provide all the necessities, and she escorted them there herself, with Serena in tow, and Diandra following behind.

She closed Serena's door behind her in relief. "That was absolutely chilling."

"Where were you?"

She could not repress a shudder. *Of longing? Of dormant desires that he had aroused by his mere words? And how could she be thinking about that on the heels of the evening's turmoil?*

But she could, she was . . . and she wanted—what?

"Dear Justin was showing me the more interesting parts of the house," she murmured, turning her flushed face away from Serena's sharp eyes and busying herself with pulling down the bedcovers. "We could hear the rapping sound everywhere."

"I told you. I *told* you there were spirits here."

"You are quite prescient then. Shall I call Gita?"

"Please. I'm so tired. I was scared out of my wits."

"And now?"

"I think Leonie is right. Pamela followed us. She can't mean us any harm. She's *family*, after all. There is something she needs resolved, Diandra and she was waiting for the right time to accomplish it. So I'm not afraid any more."

Neither am I . . .

She tugged the bellpull and a moment or two later, Gita tapped at the door. "Come to me when you are finished tending to Serena."

Gita bowed, and she brushed past her and through the connecting door to her room, and threw herself on the bed.

Tricks and flummery.

Do what you will.

All fear . . .

All pleasure—

All mixed up—apparitions, entities and life beyond the grave—

She couldn't think, she couldn't allow herself to feel. She would let Gita undress her and pamper her and then she would go to sleep.

It had to be a trick—it had to be . . .

All tied up with the voudrais—*Justin trying to shock her and scare her away, every trick in the book because she would not be deterred from her course.*

She had promised her brother Hugh, and she had promised Serena, and she would follow through. Serena was blooming.

And Serena had had the guts to challenge the "entity" . . .

"Mem?" Gita, softly, at the door.

"Come."

Gita was like the fog, wafting in with gentle touches, soothing presence, and familiar scent . . . handing her the lotions with which she rubbed her body every night, and her freshly ironed cambric nightgown with the lace trim edging the collar, lapels and wristbands.

After Gita brushed her hair and plaited it into a loose braid, she slipped into a wrapper of figured black sateen that tied neatly in front, and dismissed her servant.

No entities rapping now. No flickering candles.

She paced the room impatiently and then opened the connecting door a crack. Serena lay curled in slumber and there wasn't sound anywhere.

She closed the door gently and opened her hallway door.

Dead matte middle of the night silence.

Do what you will . . .

They did, they came in the dead of night when no one could see them and everyone else was intent on the same voluptuous gratification.

No ghosts or rapping then; only the rocketing sound of permissive sex with anyone and everyone, and the moans of slaked desire and aroused need.

She made an anguished little sound at the back of her throat.

Do what you will . . .

No one had to give them permission; they took what they wanted. He had said so himself. Had he not taken her kiss, and with it the protective covering in which she had shrouded herself for more than a year?

She hadn't expected it; she hadn't wanted it.

She hadn't known she wanted it.

But now she did.

The thought made her shudder.

She did.

Do what you will . . .

In the silence, where no one could find her, where morality and scruples were inconsequential, she could surrender to the illusion of lust without conscience or consequences.

Why, why had she let him paint those sensual verbal pictures . . . why hadn't she acted indignant and offended and just gotten the hell away from him?

Because she hadn't been repulsed, she had been aroused, and she was now paying the price of having opened herself up to all those forbidden thoughts and yearnings.

She itched to touch the creamy upholstery of the sofas, to sink her bare feet into the rough texture of the carpet, to lie naked on the velvet sofa in the cells of the *seraglio* where a lover would come and take her and she would only know him by his touch and the feel of him possessing her.

This, this was what he unleashed with his Judas kiss and his gospel of carnality.

This, this, this—her skin ached to be touched . . . oh, but no—she had foresworn that when her husband died. She had adhered to the discipline, she had closed herself down, made herself immune from all those feelings, all those needs.

Rap, rap, rap—and now Pamela was here to remind her of what she had taken from her. She could almost believe Pamela had come to claim what was rightfully hers.

Do what you will . . .

Perhaps she had lived a hedonistic life by Guthrie's side in the years before he emigrated to India. Perhaps hers was the secret, and they had disturbed her rest in a place of undiluted pleasure.

Her body was hot with longing.

She lit a candle, slipped out the door and closed it gently behind her.

No raps. No ghosts. Not a sound but her thrumming pulse and errant heartbeat.

Down the corridor of the el to the reception hall. Through the saloon and into the library.

A moment's hesitation at the door before she pushed it open. A black hole loomed before her, and she stepped cautiously into the void.

Down the steps, no ghosts pursuing her—down to the corridor, shining the candlelight on the ornate double doors of the *voudrais.*

She paused before them and lifted the light to illuminate the words engraved in the stone lintel above: *Fais ce que tu voudrais . . .*

Permission begged and granted.

She pushed open the doors and paused on the parapet.

Darkness all around her, except for her light. And silence, a thick voluptuous silence. And ghosts—*her* ghosts.

She entered the *bagnio* and removed her wrapper, and then went on into the *boudoir.*

She could just see a rim of dim light under the golden doors to the *seraglio.*

He was waiting; she had known he would be waiting.

Her ghosts . . .

She removed her slippers and stepped down into the rich carpet of the *seraglio,* and closed the doors behind her.

He was waiting for *her.* She set her candlestick down and walked slowly down the aisle of cells, each one shrouded by a luxurious satin curtain, each one its own private pleasure palace.

Her body tingled in anticipation. *Everyone knew. Nobody told.*

The devil's bargain, the price of lust and longing.

And tonight she was willing to pay.

She paused at the endmost cell, and pulled back the curtain.

He was standing behind the sofa, dressed in black, his arms folded, his face concealed, and the shadow of the rampant male part of him jutting in the shadow.

She felt a spurt of drenching excitement flow through her vitals. *This—oh, this—just the feel of that part of him first; let him be master, and then I will master him.*

"What do you want?"

"Do what you will," she whispered, climbing onto the couch and surrendering her body to his hands.

She felt him grasp her hips and turn her over so that she was face down on the velvet sofa. She felt his hands lifting her gown over her hips and then his warm fingers exploring her buttocks, her crease and her wet flowering fold.

She arched her back to give all of herself to him. She felt him stroking her, between her buttocks, between her legs, she felt him delve quickly into her wet and out again, in and out, in and out, with one finger, with two, with three, with four—she gasped as he penetrated her and enveloped his fingers in her hot wet sheath; she moved against him, in and out, in and out.

His relentless fingers rode her and still he did not take her. In and out . . . she was naked and open and willing, her body hot to surrender to his potent maleness, and still, he did not take her . . . in and out, in and out—she writhed and begged with every movement of her body, and still, he did not take her.

She climbed onto her knees to entice him, and still, he did not take her. His fingers only rubbed and thrust and felt her nakedness as she moaned and made sizzling guttural sounds at the back of her throat, and wriggled and undulated beneath his knowing fingers and still, still, still—

She was so wet, so hot, filled to bursting by his expert fondling, she wanted to explode all over his thrusting fingers—but she wanted his ramrod manhood inside her, that and nothing less.

She watched it elongate in the shadows; watched it move with every thrust of his fingers, with every grinding motion of his hips. Watched how it wanted her, how it couldn't wait to possess her.

She wanted to suck the creamy life out of it so it would never bury itself in any other woman but her.

She wanted him to ram it deep inside her, hot and hot and tight, and leave it there forever . . .

Her ghosts . . .

She wanted . . . the pure carnal pleasure of him, him, any him, this him—her ghosts . . . her pleasure—

He mounted her; with one slick thrust he entered her as he held her buttocks and stood above her and drove himself into her.

"Ah-h-h-h-h-h-h . . ." *Yes, yes, yes, yes, yes . . . too long, so long*—her moan of agonized pleasure reverberated all through the *voudrais* but she was oblivious to everything but the feeling of him pounding against her. Hard, hot, tight, hard, hot, tight . . . he had a will and a penis of iron; he could move mountains, he could move her—she felt herself climbing to the peak like the rush and roar of a waterfall, and then tumbling, tumbling, and cracking onto the rocks below, sharp, crystalline, clear, and then breaking suddenly, and caught in the backwash of his release as it spumed into her and eddied away into nothingness.

Women lived for this . . .

He eased himself from her, and away into the shadows. She understood the rest. She did not look at him as she levered herself into a sitting position and then off the couch and through the curtain. She picked up her candlestick, retrieved her wrapper and then returned, on silent cat feet, to the sanctity of her room.

The thing never happened.

They all knew and nobody told.

Screaming, streaming pleasure, contained where no one could examine it and only the participants were witnesses.

She had broken her vow of chastity, and bowed to the ultimate commandment of Do what you will.

She wondered if she would be damned forever.

Chapter Six

The dancing master came the following afternoon.

Diandra thought it was perfectly in keeping with Leonie's intent to keep up appearances that she and M. Lespin were drinking coffee in the drawing room when she and Serena came downstairs at noon.

The guests had only just left, having slept in, because of the previous evening's excitement, and after partaking of an extensive midmorning breakfast; Justin and George had gone out with them, to accompany them as far as the turnpike.

But of course no one had notified her or Serena and so they still had to have breakfast before the lessons, for which Justin was paying an hourly fee which Leonie was not loath to point out, could commence.

"I beg your pardon," Diandra said coolly, as she poured her tea and helped herself to some toast, "I was under the impression the event of the day was to be a—medium or a psychic to entertain us."

"To *entertain* us? No, she will attempt to make contact

for us, Diandra. But then, you seem to make a point of misunderstanding. I'm certain I made it plain that we are to have intensive instruction these two weeks while the dressmakers are working on your wardrobe. I will of course accompany Monsieur on the pianoforte and thus save Justin the expense of paying someone to come play."

"Of course," Diandra murmured. "Or it may be that Pamela could accompany us. Did she play?"

"We were both well trained in the musical arts," Leonie snapped, "and I don't appreciate your making light of last night's contact. It was very meaningful."

"It was very eerie, and we don't know that it was Pamela."

"You mean, you don't want it to be Pamela," Leonie said. "You have every reason to not want to hear any message she might have for us, don't you, Diandra?"

"Do I?" *But she was already haunted by ghosts.* She sipped her tea with every evidence of indifference to Leonie's barbs. "I'm shocked you should say so. What can you mean?"

Now she had forced Leonie to choose because of her blunt question. She would either have to voice whatever poisonous thing she had on her mind, or she would say nothing, and she didn't like either position, by the look on her face.

She chose to hedge. "But you were as shocked as anybody last night, Diandra."

"Indeed I was." She saw no reason to deny it.

"But perhaps not for the same reason?"

Clever Leonie, circling around and coiling like a snake for the strike. But she wasn't going to let Leonie squeeze the life out of her or Serena. "Perhaps you'd care to elaborate?" she asked again.

"You know just what I mean," Leonie said impatiently. "And it's neither here nor there right now," she added as Justin and George appeared in the doorway. "It is time to move the furniture, bring in the pianoforte, and the lessons to begin."

She rose gracefully and held her hands out to Justin. "George can play. M. Lespin can test Serena, and Justin and I will demonstrate correct form."

"I am grateful I ever took lessons," George said dryly, as three footmen entered and began shifting the furniture, and three more began rolling back the carpet, and two others rolled in the pianoforte from its alcove behind a sliding panel on the far wall.

George seated himself at the instrument and tried a few experimental notes. "Excellent sound." He began a lighthearted waltz, and Leonie prodded Justin into the center of the room and left him no choice but to swing her into the dance.

Diandra couldn't look at them, wouldn't look at him. She hadn't thought about what she would do or say or anything. She had stayed in bed and pushed the memory of the pleasure, into the dark dungeon of her soul.

Everybody knew. Nobody told.

Somehow he had known; somehow he had divined her shame and her secret, and he had granted absolution.

Do what you will.

And so she had done. And now it was as if it had never happened, and the knowledge was her cross alone to bear.

"Come," M. Lespin said to Serena. "Let us dance."

There was nothing Serena loved to do more than waltz, and she went eagerly into M. Lespin's arms and they began the dance.

"Excellent, excellent," M. Lespin cried as they swayed and turned effortlessly around the room.

Leonie frowned and missed a step as Serena and Lespin circled around her and out into the center of the room. Justin instantly caught her up and they finished the sequence, but before she realized it or she could protest, he relinquished her hand and swept Diandra up into the waltz.

"Justin . . . !" Leonie's voice was a discordant wail above the music.

He waved her off. There was no protest on Diandra's part either; her eyes were closed and she was following him with an elegant almost boneless movement of her body.

She loved the music and to dance, and she especially loved the feeling of his arm around her waist, and the strong certain way he steered her through the steps and sway of the dance.

Danger here—his swooping her up was so unexpected, she could only capitulate—

Just like last night . . .

But she wouldn't think of that.

This evening never happened . . .

Do what you will . . .

But there was Leonie, morally outraged that she would even *think* of dancing this soon in her mourning. Her lot was to grieve and wait, preferably hidden behind some decorative screen where no one could see her. Leonie wished she were invisible, especially to Justin.

George diplomatically ended the dance after the next twelve bars, and M. Lespin clapped his hands appreciatively.

"Really, Diandra. And Justin, you should know better."

"I know better," he said, his cool gaze on Diandra's flushed face.

In the dark, permissive, persuasive, all there, all hers, sensing, knowing . . . better—

Diandra turned away first. *Unbearable. Inconceivable. How could she have thought she could face her fall from grace by the light of day?*

She moved to one of the sofas, out of the way, as Justin

took over from George at the pianoforte and M. Lespin and Serena went on to the polka, the schottische, a quadrille and a contra dance.

George was very adept at the figures, but Leonie was not pleased that Justin had abandoned her, and much as she tried to hide it, it was obvious she had not expected that Serena was that competent on the dance floor.

"Well, I'm delighted; you could have saved your money, Justin," she said finally and insincerely, when they were all exhausted from their exertions. "And Diandra, you did the proper thing. A widow must withdraw and set herself apart, and make it known that she grieves continually, even as she does what must be done for her younger sister."

"I'm grateful I meet your standard of correct behavior," Diandra murmured.

"We will break for lunch," Leonie said, pretending not to have heard her. "And perhaps Justin might consider throwing a small party before we return to London, where we can test Serena's skills."

"But what if Pamela shows up?" Diandra asked. She couldn't help it. Leonie's sanctimonious pronouncements were beginning to rub her the wrong way.

"We examined the table," George said, "and all the underground rooms, and we found nothing. There is either a clever hoaxster at work, or this is the real thing."

"We'll find out this evening," Leonie said. "There is a woman in town who is said to have psychic abilities, and I have engaged her, after having told her the whole of last night's incident, to try to make contact with Pamela."

She looked around at their bemused faces. "Well, we have to get to the bottom of this, don't we? What if it is Pamela? What if she has a message for me—or for you, Justin? Or what if she can't rest because she needs to tell us what happened to her—" she lowered her voice, "and who is to blame?'' Don't we want to know, Justin? Don't we?''

He could still feel her supple body beneath his hands, still feel the essence of her enveloping him, and the scent of her sex enticing him—and he didn't want to know anything else.

It was unexpected, all consuming, and it was done. It would never happen again.

We will forget this evening ever happened.

He watched her. She was excellent at pretending she was innocent. What a show she had put on last night. He could almost believe she had enticed him beyond all reason. Circe, cloaked in mourning, spinning and weaving plots and plans, and—into the bargain—ensnaring the too gullible Leonie into believing her sister, his mother, had a life beyond the grave.

And somehow it was all intertwined: all the seemingly supernatural manifestations and her powerful surrender to the seduction of the *voudrais*. No one was immune to its illicit temptations. Not a widow, not a lord, not father, not a man.

Not even a woman who was intent on preserving all she had gained at any cost.

He slammed his hand down on his desk.

It was enough; he understood suddenly and completely what it was all about. It was the one thing he hadn't been able to reconcile—why she would go to all the trouble of trying to bamboozle him with apparitions and trickery— but now it was abundantly clear.

It was what every magician used to preserve the illusion, and Diandra Morant Reynell, Dowager of Skene, had become a master at it.

Distraction.

Keep the eye moving—a floating table, an invisible ghost, an entity that "talked"—never allow a moment where a question could be asked, an explanation be rendered.

She had kept them all upended over the moving table and the so-called spirit while pretending the deepest skepticism that either existed.

Magical.

Who could look into those unfathomable dark eyes and believe otherwise of her?

Even he had been caught; he had marked her with his scent, and now, he was ready to commence the just cause of avenging his father's death on her.

So it would be.

He would play it through—but for no more than another week or two—to see where she was leading him. Now that he understood, he could play a vastly different game, and he could easily put himself at one remove from her.

And because of that, without conscience, he could just as easily take her, at her desire, all over again.

Finally, she had been able to sneak away from Leonie, away from the stultifying atmosphere of the house, to the familiar barn-smell and noise of the stables.

"A nice afternoon for a ride, my lady." George was right behind her, almost as if he had followed her. And deliberately too.

She stopped and waited for him to catch up with her.

"Some fresh air is wanted," she said. "I'm used to outdoor pursuits and I'm feeling very closed in."

"Indeed. Here, let me choose a mount for you. I'm well acquainted with the stables. Been Justin's friend since childhood, you know."

She hadn't, but she watched with interest as he chose a

pretty little mare with a hint of the devil in her eye for her and gave her to the groom to saddle up.

"Can you handle her?"

"Absolutely, and anything else," she said stringently, as she checked the cinch and saddle and then allowed the groom to help her on.

"Now, now, my lady." He was up and beside her in an instant. "Let me show you Skene."

Of course, he had a purpose. He had been too quiet, too accommodating, too kind. And Justin's childhood friend too. Justin's instrument, more likely.

They rode in silence across the rolling fields beyond the house. Though it was late afternoon, the air was warm and perfumed, and a brisk breeze had risen.

This was the weather she loved. She could have been riding in the hill country. This felt like home.

Would Skene forever affect her like this? Or was it some residual effect from hearing Guthrie speak of it with such love and longing? There was something about it still, even with the enmity of Leonie, the entities and apparitions, and the open skepticism of Justin.

Even after her wanton surrender to Lethe, the goddess of oblivion. Would she ever forget? Would he?

Do what you will . . .

She had; she had run from Leonie and her viper's tongue and she wondered how long she would be able to put up with it, or *him*, for that matter.

"Let's talk, my lady."

George was beside her as she contemplated the house from a half mile away. It looked like a doll's house, something she could take apart and put together at her wish and whim. Controllable, when every else seemed very out of control.

"Must we?"

"You *are* frank. Admirable trait. Even Justin must appreciate that you do not dissemble."

"I think not, my lord. I think Justin does not like to put himself out for anything."

"Very true, that. But you must understand—his mother gone, his father remarried, and then suddenly the Earl was gone too, and all a thousand miles beyond anything he could do about it. And that *after* His Lordship had decided to emigrate to India and left Justin behind."

She knew that part. "He was in school."

"He was a boy. The only son. His Lordship was not thinking of anything beyond the possibility of being appointed. He wanted to become part of the fabric of life there, to know the people, the politics, the way of things. It was an exotic adventure to him."

"And Pamela hated it."

"He told you that?"

"It was possible to infer it from all he didn't say," Diandra said carefully.

"She missed the boy, of course. They should have taken him with them. He felt abandoned, left behind, unwanted. And he never wanted to be in that position again. He wanted control, my lady, of everything around him. His life. His money. His need to know, at every next moment, what was around the corner. Your letter jarred him. He still mourns. And resents the fact that His Lordship chose to remarry and stay on in India."

"A very profitable stay, however," Diandra pointed out.

"One of her Her Majesty's best," George agreed instantly. "But the toll on Justin was very great, very hard. He has a genius for money, but I expect you know that."

"Yes, I understand his skillful handling has multiplied Skene's resources many times over."

"And he doesn't believe in what he can't see with his eyes or hold in his hands, my lady."

"Who does?" she asked lightly.

"I was hoping you would gain a better understanding."

"I understand everything," she said. "We foisted our-selves upon him, and he was resistant, to say the least; then grudgingly amenable; and now downright hostile since he believes for some inexplicable reason that I am somehow responsible for the mysterious happenings here. Imperti-nent females he will endure, but ghosts and floating tables and noisy entities—never. Who can blame him?"

"Indeed," George murmured. "And look, it is almost time for tea. Shall we head back?"

She couldn't say no, that she would much rather ride until sundown. She stoked her mare into a gallop and raced along the back fields with George close behind her.

The wind in her face, the hot sun, the blur of green, brown and blue—for ten glorious minutes, she was in heaven. She did not want to rein in and slow down but a quarter mile from the house, she pulled up again to wait for George.

He was out of breath by the time he caught up with her. "You are amazing, my lady. Justin would forgive the devil for that seat."

"Justin *is* the devil," she muttered, as she nudged her horse into a walk.

"A hasty judgment, at best," George said, and she sent him a sharp look.

Or was *that* the message?

She couldn't decide.

They went on in silence, slowly, companionably, without conversation, and with the outbuildings coming closer and closer.

"If you would dismount, I'll take in your mount," George said.

"Too kind." She reined in, and slipped to the ground, and he followed suit.

"Excellent ride, my lady. I hope we might do it again."

She had all the niceties at her fingertips. "I would enjoy that—" she began and stopped dead. *"George . . ."*

She could just see *it* over George's shoulder, gray fog in human form, wafting away into the trees.

He wheeled around at the urgency in her voice and then turned back to her, puzzled. "What? What do you think you saw, my lady? It must have been your imagination. There was nothing there."

The woman's name was Agatha, and she was a spiritualist from the closest village who was known to communicate with entities through the medium of a divining board. Hers was elaborately scrolled and incised and it lay on the card table in the drawing room, and Leonie and Serena were staring at the small velvet pouch that lay on top of it.

Agatha had come to tea, and she was in the process of enclosing them in a protective circle when Diandra and George burst into the room, which was shrouded in darkness and lit by a dozen strategically placed candles.

"Shhhh . . ." Serena and Leonie turned simultaneously to warn them, and Agatha motioned them into the protection of the circle, and made another pass around the room murmuring incantations.

"We are all feeling quite safe," Justin said from his position on the sofa, "and quite confident you can begin now."

"Hush!" She was a dumpling of a woman, dressed in black head to toe, with neatly bound gray hair tucked under a proper cap. She continued on until she deemed the spell was in place, and only then did she pull a chair up to the table and place herself at the alphabet end of the divining board.

"All is in readiness," she pronounced as she seated herself. She reached for the pouch and reverently withdrew the planchette. "We can begin. Who will be the respondent?"

Leonie turned to Justin. "Justin?"

"Leonie?" he answered in kind.

She hesitated, her hand at her throat, almost as if she felt some kind of pressure not to move from her place beside Agatha. "I—let it be Serena. Serena was brave last night, and my sister's spirit responded. Serena?"

Serena looked at Diandra, who shrugged, and then she took her place opposite Agatha. "What must I do?"

"Clear your mind and heart, my girl, and fill your consciousness with reverence for the privilege of being able to communicate with a soul from the world beyond. Put your fingertips on the planchette, and I will put mine opposite. And now we make the convocation."

She closed her eyes and rocked back and forth. "We beseech the spirit, the entity, the soul who has made its presence felt, to hear our pleas and our questions and honor us with communication through the medium of this blessed board. Is the spirit present?"

There was a moment's hesitation and then the planchette moved, seemingly of its own volition, from one letter to the next as Serena spelled out the message.

"Y . . . e . . . s . . . Yes. But I didn't move it . . . I didn't—"

Agatha's eyes popped open. "What is it you wish to know?"

Serena swallowed hard and looked at Leonie. Leonie nodded and Serena asked, "Is this . . . is this Pamela?"

The planchette moved again. "Y . . . e . . . s . . . Yes."

"I told you, I *told* you." This from Leonie, her voice hoarse, her hand clutched at her heart. "Will she—will she answer questions?"

A pause. "Yes."

No one moved. The silence thickened. It was almost as if they could feel Pamela's presence in the room.

Agatha's voice broke into the stillness. "What do you wish to know?"

"Where has she been?"

The planchette moved. "Waiting."

"For what?" Serena whispered.

"To be heard."

Agatha took over then. "We hear you now. Tell us what you wish us to know."

"Regret."

"For what?"

"All."

"You are missed."

"Son."

Agatha looked at Justin, whose eyes were like ice.

"He has mourned."

"Loved."

"He hears you. Tell us what you wish us to know."

"Drowned."

"So it was reported. Tell us what you wish us to know."

"Vengeance."

"For what?"

"Returned."

"What do you avenge?"

"Life."

"On whom?"

"Murderer."

There was an awful dead silence after that, and then Leonie shrieked, "I knew it, I knew—"

"Shhhhh—" Agatha, agitated. "Shhhh—is that what you are trying to tell us—that you were murdered?"

"Vengeance."

"Oh my God—" Serena then, her hands trembling on the planchette. "Tell us—tell us who—"

"Don't—" Agatha in a furious whisper, and then out loud, addressing the board. "Tell us what you want us to know."

"Murderer."

"Tell—" and then she broke off as the planchette went into a frenzied swirl around the board, seeking letter after letter, and neither her fingers or Serena's could seem to control it.

"Oh my lord, my lord, my lord, my beautiful dead sister," Leonie moaned with tears streaming down her face.

And then, as quickly as it had begun scrolling around the board, the planchette suddenly stopped, almost as if it had found what it wanted.

And it was pointing directly and most decisively to the letter *D*.

"I knew it, I knew it, I knew it—" Leonie jumped to her feet and reached across to grab Diandra.

Immediately Serena released the planchette to come to Diandra's aid, George grabbed Leonie from behind, and Justin knocked the board and planchette off the table.

"The connection is broken," Agatha intoned. "The spirit will speak no more."

"The spirit has spoken too much," George said, pinning the struggling Leonie. "Are you out of your mind, Leonie? This is witch's tricks. Conjuring. No basis in reality."

"No, no—she was here; I felt her spirit, she *was* trying to communicate."

"Oh truly—that someone whose name begins with the letter *D* murdered her? Nonsense. That's the stuff of fiction. Calm yourself, for heaven's sake. You are making a scene."

She stopped struggling, too calm suddenly. "Of

course—you're absolutely right, George. I'm embarrassing myself. The *séance* was shocking."

"Anyone can manipulate the planchette whose fingers control it. Do be sensible, Leonie."

"We must obtain one," Leonie murmured, but George didn't hear her. He was picking up Agatha's board and planchette as Agatha rocked back and forth, muttering, "Desecration. Blasphemy. Lost souls. Provocateurs . . ."

She looked up at George as he handed her the board and her pouches. "Never call on me again. The protective spell is broken. Do what you will, but you will never find the answers here."

Diandra felt a chill. *Do what you will . . .*

"We will obtain our own board," Leonie said again, her voice louder.

"As you will," Agatha said. "Evil lurks and finds its way through the protective circle. I will not accept your gold," she waved off George as he attempted to give her a crown. "I accept nothing from the godless." She tucked the planchette pouch inside the larger pouch that contained the board, and then she stood. "I will find my own way home."

And in the blink of an eye, she was gone, and George could not catch her even though he raced to the front door faster than she ever could have walked.

"We're well rid of her," Leonie said. "The problem with these mediums is they will not tell what is real, what is truth. They remain neutral and let the thing speak for itself, never interpreting, never giving advice. And so what are we left with? My poor dead sister wandering in the afterlife, seeking vengeance on a murderer," and she turned to look at Diandra, "whose initials begin with the letter *D*."

* * *

"Well, madam, congratulations. An excellent bag of tricks. I am now to believe a medium's divining board has accused you of murder. Or maybe your cleverness lies in the fact you are sure no one would believe it ... and like all magicians, you took the risk. Or was it too just a distraction?"

"I do not know what you mean; I'm as shocked as anyone," Diandra said furiously.

"You are too good. Even I don't know what to make of it. George—" to George who had just entered the library after making sure Leonie got to bed with laudanum and a compress, "—tell us your impressions. What did you think of the redoubtable Agatha?"

"Scared the daylights out of me," George said, pouring a tot of brandy and joining Justin by the fireplace.

"Well, it seems we must get at the truth now," Justin said, "and madam must tell us the whole of how my father died."

It must have been close on midnight by then. After Agatha so mysteriously departed, Leonie had called for tea, and they spent two hours reconstructing what everyone had seen and felt and heard and what it could have meant.

Diandra felt like the condemned man waiting to consume his final dinner.

And that was served informally an hour later.

They hadn't crucified her—yet.

So the question remained, what to tell Justin with his cold skeptical eyes, and George, whose expression was gently encouraging.

She didn't want to tell him anything. Why relive the horrible moment? She had come downstairs after a sleepless night and, assuming that Guthrie had fallen asleep in his office yet again, had gone to awaken him.

She shook her head. "There is nothing you do not know, Justin. He died at his desk of a heart attack."

"Four years after Pamela disappeared, and was presumed drowned."

"I did not know him then. I only know what I read in the papers and what local gossip recounted. He and my brother became acquainted thereafter when he came to Bhaumaghar to hunt tigers. And I met him then. I did not know your mother at all. And that is all that needs to be said."

She was hiding something—he knew it. Distraction, diversion, dissembling . . . she was so good at it. And wasn't it curious that all those words began with the letter *D?*

"Indeed." George, objective and rational. "I think this whole *séance* has put us all on edge. I believe what Diandra says. And so should you, Justin. Best advice. And now, I'm going to bed."

"Gentle George," Justin murmured as he exited the room. "Wants everyone at peace, and everything moving smoothly and calmly. Doesn't have the capacity to deal with spirits and ghosts."

"And you do?" Diandra asked, not a little contentiously.

"Flummery, madam. I just wish I knew how you did it. You beguiled my very susceptible father, seduced poor gullible George, hoodwinked your own sister, and you've utterly mystified me."

"Oh, I think not," she retorted. "No, Justin Reynell knows what, where, why and how every moment. You do nothing without a hidden agenda, Justin. Don't think I'm not aware of it. I've thought all along you're the trickster. You have the wherewithal *and* the will to do it. And what a coup if you could conjure up a murderer to explain the death of your father. That is something you cannot get a grip on. And I've played right into your hands, more's the pity, believing that in his name you might summon up some charity and hospitality for myself and Serena. And *still*, you are skeptical and accusing by turns, and trying very hard to convince yourself of my culpability when my only crime was to love your father.''

There was a thick silence after that. She stood up resolutely and walked to the door.

"Did you?"

She almost didn't hear the question.

And she didn't hesitate. "I loved him."

"And last night?"

Oh God, this on top of accusations and apparitions.

"I loved that too," she whispered, and closed the door firmly behind her.

It was all tied up. He knew it. And he had reminded her for a purpose. And she knew it too.

He sat in the library with his brandy and waited.

The clock struck midnight. One. One-thirty. Two.

He sat motionless, waiting.

Do what you will . . .

Pure unalloyed masculine fantasy played out in the dark dungeon of the soul; he knew it, she knew it. Believe in absolution. Wallow in sin.

A man's credo.

What did my lady Diandra believe in?

He had watched her so carefully, the way she inhaled the scent of a flower, or touched a luxurious fabric, or savored the taste of food. A creature of the senses, honed in a country of heat, color, caste, custom so different from his own.

Unfathomable. Unknowable. And yet, in her eyes, a certain knowledge, a perceivable hunger. And all around her, an air of suppression, and carefully controlled impulses.

Not last night. What had it been about last night?

A body. A need. A cataclysmic moment of possession. And then she was gone, silently as a nun.

He listened to the silence, certain that soon, he would hear her soft footfall in the hallway. And certain as sin that he would follow.

No one was immune to the lure of the *voudrais*. Not a cloistered widow. Not a worldly lord.

She resisted it as hard as she could. With every fiber of her being. Once was enough, to alleviate pain, to conquer desire. The penance was self-denial, and she was so familiar with that.

She lay in her bed, still as a nun, her mind ranging over the evening's events.

Distractions.

He had said it.

Illusions.

Maybe everything in this house was an illusion. Even Justin. Even the *voudrais*.

Do what you will . . . where in life could a person be exempted from the consequence of his actions?

If he were tempted to take action . . .

If *she* . . .

Nights were the hardest. She could get through the days, but at night, alone, she could only remember and yearn for what was no longer possible.

But not now. She had breached memory and longing; she had reduced the equation to from obliteration to absolution.

Her body propelled her; it was as if she were watching herself rise from the bed, shrug into her wrapper and then slowly make her way through the dim candle-lit corridors to the destiny of her other self.

She watched herself walk down the long underground hallway to the *voudrais,* and without a qualm, push open the doors.

Embrace desire, all who enter here . . .

Where would he be waiting this time? Closer, sooner, hot shuddering excitement swamping every other emotion. The forbidden, anything she wanted, she had only to ask . . . her knees went weak at the thought of it.

Through the *salle d'entrée* and into the *bagnio,* quickly, quickly, her breath catching, her heart pounding. Here, now, where . . . ?

There, reclining on a sofa almost as he knew what she wanted of him this time.

She knelt before him, no words needed.

Let me worship you . . . her hands told him, her knowing well-taught hands seeking him where she had never thought to touch a man ever again.

He responded instantly as she rooted between his legs, stroking him, cuddling him, fondling him, loving the feel of him elongating between her fingers and the surge of his hips as he urged her sensual exploration.

Oh, but this was not nearly enough, to have him so hot and hard and *there* and not be able to feel the naked essence of him.

He knew instantly what she wanted, and while he was divesting himself of his clothes, she slipped the wrapper from her shoulders and let it pool around her naked body.

And then—oh, and then . . . her hands enclosed him reverently, and she rubbed his firm ridged tip against her lips, softly, softly, then flicking her tongue against it wet and light, soft as she closed her lips over the tip, softer still as she sucked him gently, softly into her hot wet mouth—the tip, very most tip of the the most elemental part of him.

Just that, just that—how she had missed that, holding that primal maleness and licking and tugging it, and sliding her hands all over that hot hard shaft.

It was so luscious, so responsive. She held him, she teased

him, she munched him, she played him like a flute, swooping her tongue up and down the underside of him, and then all over him, a trail of wet from the root to the tip of him, and then back again to take his firm scrotal sac into her mouth and roll it around against her tongue.

What it was to be a man; she felt his strength and virility in the very center of her being. She wanted to capture it there and keep it there forever. She wanted . . .

She rubbed him against her hard pointed nipples. She cushioned him between her breasts and enclosed him in her mouth and rested, soft, soft, letting him feel her naked breasts, the heat of her mouth, her passion, her need.

He reached for her, wild with wanting her, and she would not relinquish him. She pulled him more tightly into her mouth and he moaned, his hips rocketing up to ease her way.

She held him there for a long voluptuous moment, her one hand snaking under his body to cup him and keep him.

It was too much; even she knew that from experience. He was deep within her mouth and he wanted to move, to seek, to possess, and she wouldn't let him go. She moved with him, anticipating every frenzied motion, her mouth encompassing him, sucking him, pulling, prodding, and adoring him.

He bucked, he twisted, he pushed at her violently as she brought him closer and closer to the peak. She knew, she knew: he didn't want that, he wanted *her*, her body, her heat and her flesh, and all she wanted was to possess the carnal essence of him in this searingly erotic way.

She felt him climbing, capitulating as his body's voracious need claimed him. In that one sweet moment, he was utterly and completely in her hands, captive of her mouth and her hot heaving lust for the elemental maleness of him.

She rimmed his thickness with her teeth, with her tongue, with the long erotic sucking motion of her mouth as he began the drive to climax. That was all she wanted, all she needed; her mouth, his gorgeous luscious shaft deep, hard, hot against her tongue, prisoner of her rapacious need to possess it.

She heaved with his body, not letting him escape her voracious sucking; he would never get away, never. He rolled, he pushed, he jammed himself up into her, but she stayed with him, pulling and sucking and loving his rush to completion.

She couldn't get enough, nor could he; the eruption was hard and tight and explosive, and she stayed with it, every last pumping moment of it, every thrust and throb and jolt until she had drained him dry. And she kept him with her until his body stopped shuddering, his hands entwined limply in her hair, and he slept.

It was enough. It was so good; it was too good. It was hers. She had given nothing of herself, her body, her need. She had taken, and it was good.

Slowly, silently, she eased herself away from him, and as silently as a nun, she left him.

Chapter Seven

She woke with the taste of him in her mouth and the scent of him on her hands. And the news that Agatha, the medium, had been found dead on the road to Skene.

"But it was teatime, after all," Leonie was saying when she came downstairs to join them in parlor. "It wasn't dead of night. And she was the one who decided she was going to see herself back to the village. What is the fuss?"

"The thing is," George said patiently, "we were the last to see her, *I* found her, and that is her board and planchette on the table."

"But—she must have left them. I found them here this morning." Leonie touched the velvet pouch. "So odd . . ." her voice trailed off. "Some reckless driver must have knocked her off the road. What other explanation could there be?"

"Nevertheless, the constable wishes to come and question us," George said.

Leonie picked up the pouch. "We won't tell him about finding the board here." She looked around at them,

Serena, George, Diandra. *"Nobody* will say a word about this . . ."

But that was difficult, too. Everyone knew about Agatha and her board and her spells, and Constable Streatfield went straight to the heart of the question.

"Had Agatha been weaving spells and summoning spirits with her board?"

Leonie looked at Justin who had accompanied Streatfield, and took the lead easily. "Well, yes, she had. We had her in for an evening's diversion, Constable."

"I see. Did she have any success?"

"It could be said she did. The board certainly was responsive, but whether it was real or of her own devising, who can tell?"

"Perhaps someone didn't like the message of the board," Streatfield said. "If you would care to tell me what it was, that is."

Leonie flashed a look at Justin. "The spirit said it was my sister Pamela, and her message . . . her message was that she was—she was there, that she was watching over us, and that . . . that she sent her love to Justin."

"And that was all?" Streatfield was plainly skeptical. "Agatha's spirits are never so benign."

"It has been a while since my lord has been at Skene. Perhaps that's why. She has been waiting to deliver her message of love from beyond."

"Now really," Streatfield murmured. He looked around that them. "You all were present at this *séance?* You can corroborate what the lady Leonie says?"

One by one they nodded, Serena, George, and Diandra, who had been covertly watching Justin, after a moment's wrestling with her conscience. Justin, who had no conscience whatsoever.

"And then what happened?"

"The session was over. And she left."

"Found no money on her."

"Then someone took it," Leonie said.

"No marks."

"Very odd," Leonie said.

"Board was gone."

"It was a beautiful object," Leonie said. "Perhaps it was taken too."

"What time did she leave?"

Leonie appealed to George this time. "Five-thirty, I should think," George said. "Declined to be driven."

"Really? Odd, that. Never known Agatha not to take up an offer to ride in a nob's carriage. So. This is what we know: Agatha came to you at three-thirty, having been invited for teatime to have a *séance* with her board. In the course of that, you allege she contacted the deceased sister of my lady Leonie, Lady Pamela Reynell that was, who forwarded her love to Lord Justin and her assurances that she was watching over . . . you? him? Skene?"

"Just watching over *us,*" Leonie said.

"Then when the *séance* was finished, she left, on foot, and was found early the next morning on the turnpike by Lord Tisbury. Her board was missing and her purse. And that is all we know."

"Exactly," Leonie agreed.

"And you'd never met her before."

"Never."

Streatfield looked at each of them in turn and they nodded agreement, except Justin.

"I'd heard of her," he said finally. "It is not the kind of parlor game we normally indulge in at Skene."

"Indeed not," Streatfield murmured. "Why, I wonder, this time?"

The trick, the trap—how would Leonie explain it away?

She smiled faintly. "Well, we are here with Justin's sister-in-law who has come from India to sample the delights of a season. We brought her in to entertain Serena, who has a little talent in reading cards and tea leaves . . .''

Diandra shivered; was she making it up, or did she know that about Serena? Whichever it was, the explanation seemed to satisfy Streatfield.

"So, you are Lady Pamela's sister," Streatfield said, as he continued making notes. "And Lord Tisbury is the friend of the Earl. Miss Serena is his sister-in-law. And Lady Diandra is . . . ?"

More traps, more tricks.

Diandra looked at Justin. His expression was inscrutable.

In the dark, they were the sum of their body parts and their mindless hedonistic immersion in pleasure. In the light of day, no benedictions applied.

Do what you will.

It was Leonie who defined the thing fully, almost as if all the interrelationships hadn't struck her before. "Lady Diandra is the second wife of Justin's father—my sister-in-law—and Justin's . . . stepmother."

Streatfield finally left, his little book bulging with notes.

"That will be the talk of the village," Leonie murmured. "What a disaster. How that poor woman could have been killed in broad daylight, I will *never* understand."

"Pamela killed her."

Everyone looked at Serena in shock.

"What?"

"Pamela . . ." Serena began and then sensed that she was treading on thin ice. "Well—the woman is dead and her board is sitting on our table—isn't that a message . . . from Pamela? Remember? Leonie said yesterday, we should get a board? I mean, you can't just go into a store and buy one . . ."

"Serena," Diandra said warningly. Really, the thing was getting out of hand.

"Well, did you ever tell them about the ghost we saw?" Serena demanded defensively.

Leonie swung toward Diandra. "Ghost?"

"Fog," Diandra said promptly.

"A gray ghost," Serena said staunchly, "floating over the back fields."

"You thought you saw it—once," Diandra said, "and it's neither here nor there. There are no ghosts." She regretted saying the words the moment they came out of her mouth, because she just knew Justin was going to disagree.

"And you've seen it, how many times, madam?"

"Fog," she said succinctly.

"Indeed," he agreed tightly. "And smoke and mirrors. And you will all kindly keep your delusions to yourselves from now on. We have another couple of weeks here before we return to London, and we do not need Streatfield chasing us down at Cheswick Square. I am going there today, to make some arrangements." Which was something he had decided not twenty minutes before. This thing was going to follow them. He could feel it in his bones.

"I will be back tomorrow for dinner. And I count on George to keep you all in line. Leonie—you will *not* use the divining board."

"But Justin . . ."

"Serena—not another word about Pamela."

"No sir." Her tone was too meek.

His icy eyes settled on Diandra. "Madam—"

Her voice was even frostier. "Justin."

Nothing more needed to be said.

He rang for Tuttle, his bag was brought, and he left them standing in a rigid tableau of compliance.

And the minute he was out the door, Leonie locked it and brought out the board.

"We *have* to know."

"God, Leonie . . ." George sounded disgusted.

"Oh please. Would you go to the window and make sure he got off? He's riding down, right?"

"Leonie, this is not the way—"

"George . . ."

"I'll keep watch." Serena darted to the window as Leonie lit the candles that had not been removed from the previous evening's *séance,* and drew the curtains on the other window.

"Diandra . . ."

"Don't do this, Leonie."

"Ridiculous." Leonie removed the board from its hiding place under the sofa. "You just don't want to know what Pamela has to say. You're scared. I'm not scared. There is a message here for us."

She set the board on the table and waited until Serena drew the curtains to signify that Justin had gone.

"We need the blessing," Serena said. "And the circle of protection."

"Nonsense, we have the board; we don't need anything else."

"No," Serena said, "we need it." She began circling the area just around the couch, the table and the board with her arms outstretched.

"We beseech the oracle to bless our board and this circle of protection. We pray that the spirit, the entity, the soul will hear our pleas and communicate with us through the medium of the blessed board, and consent to answer our questions."

She sent a deep speaking look to Diandra, and then she

seated herself facing Leonie whose fingers rested lightly on the planchette, and placed her fingers opposite.

"Is the spirit here?" she asked, and her voice was hoarse and shaking slightly.

A long long pause.

"It won't work," Diandra said.

"It will."

"Not because you want it to. Serena . . . !"

"No. There can be no discord in the room or the spirit will not manifest itself. Either clear your mind and accept it, or go away."

She swallowed a further protest. George was looking horribly uncomfortable, and rooted to the spot.

Curiosity obviously was going to win out over good sense, as much for her as for him.

Serena waited. The silence lengthened. The sense of things eerie and unexplained permeated the room. The feeling of expectation increased until the very moment that Serena asked again, "Is the spirit present?"

Diandra held her breath. No one moved.

And then the planchette began spelling out an answer. "Y . . . e . . . s . . ."

Serena licked her lips. "Is it . . . Pamela?"

"Y . . . e . . . s . . ."

Leonie blinked, as if she could not believe it.

Serena said, "The old woman is dead."

The planchette moved.

"Meddling."

"Should I . . . ?" Serena whispered, looking at Leonie.

The planchette moved again.

"Power."

"Who has the power?" Leonie asked.

"You."

"What do you want to tell us?"

"Murderer."

"The old woman was murdered?"

"Protect."

"Where are you?"

"Here."

"What do you want to tell us?"

"Murderer."

"Who? Who is the murderer?"

Immediately the planchette launched into a frenzy of movement all around the board until it stopped on the letter *L*.

Leonie gasped and relinquished the planchette. Serena grabbed her hand and placed her fingers back.

"Who is the murderer?" she asked, her voice firm and her eyes fixed on Leonie's white face.

The planchette did not move.

"What do you want to tell us?" she asked again.

Nothing happened.

"You *must* tell us. What do you want to tell us?"

There was a long long pause and then the planchette spelled out: "Necessary."

Serena shook her head. "What does that mean? Is she talking about herself or the old lady?"

"Ask her," Leonie whispered.

"Tell us—what was necessary?"

The planchette did not move.

"What do you want to tell us?"

"Murderer . . . murderer . . ." Serena read, and then the planchette began scrolling wildly and uncontrollably all around the board.

And then Leonie screamed as it shot off the table and the whole thing tipped to the floor.

"You don't meddle around in these things," George said disgustedly after he and Diandra shared a pared-down dinner of chicken in red wine sauce, potato pie and glazed carrots. There had been strawberry mousse and vanilla ice cream for dessert, and they were now ensconced in the library with tea and brandy, and the firelight going; Leonie and Serena had chosen to have a tray in their rooms.

"Oh, Serena has been doing tea leaves and amulets for years," Diandra said, waving it away. "It's harmless."

"That old woman was harmless. Why did she have to die?"

"Why does anyone?"

"Gave me a turn, finding her, and her board missing, and nothing to say how she died. Streatfield will not let it go. The villagers are a superstitious lot, and they believed in her powers."

"So does Leonie, apparently."

"I'm going to remove that board from this house and leave it where someone will find it," George said resolutely.

"I think that's a good idea."

"Tonight."

"Did you see where she put it?"

"Actually . . . no—"

"It *was* under the couch."

They looked at each other and simultaneously rose and headed to the drawing room.

George got down on his hands and knees and felt under the sofa. "Damn. It's not there."

"What if she has it with her?" Diandra whispered. "I wasn't watching her."

"Neither was I," George admitted. "Well, let's just do a thorough search of the room."

They did that, going through every drawer, behind every curtain, under the carpet, the chairs, in the pianoforte alcove, all to no avail. They went on to the dining room and poked into every corner and drawer and storage space.

"She must have it with her," Diandra said resignedly.

"She took it upstairs, and there is no way we can force her to give it to us. And I think you're right: it would be better if it could be found somewhere very far away from here."

"We haven't searched the library yet," George said, brushing off his trousers from yet another hands-and-knees exploration under the sideboard and cupboard spaces in the dining room. "That's a fine place to hide anything, what with all the bookshelves, chairs and the desk."

Diandra caught his elbow. "This is just trickery, right? I mean, it was Leonie and Serena pushing the planchette around. The board can't really—"

He looked at her consideringly. "I wish to hell I knew," he said, as he preceded her into the library. "It scared the be—"

He broke off and went dead still. She pushed her way past him into the room. And just stopped in her tracks.

The board and planchette were right there on Justin's desk with the velvet pouches folded neatly beside them.

The house was dead silent.

It was almost as if it were Justin whose presence gave it any kind of life. Leonie had not emerged from her room in the family wing, and she knew for a fact that Serena was asleep.

How could she sleep so soundly after the death of that old woman and their violation of the board?

But that was now taken care of; George had packed it up and taken it away hours ago, and what he had done with it she did not care to know; only that he was going to make sure that someone would find it at first light of day.

The house was quiet, too quiet. If there were restless spirits, they were not abroad this night. Or else the board had scared them away.

And she didn't care to speculate how the board had turned up on Justin's desk, even though George was of the opinion that Tuttle had found it and brought it in since he knew they were there.

She liked that explanation. It was sensible. It made sense. And it divested the board of any supernatural powers. It was simple. The moment they went into the drawing room, Tuttle had brought the thing to the library.

And now, George was somewhere on the turnpike looking for a likely place to leave it where someone would find it. And know what it was. And turn it over to Streatfield so that he would never come back to question them again.

Done.

The house was so still. The kind of stillness that was a prelude to salacious thoughts, illicit yearnings. The kind of heightened silence in which a lover sought surcease.

That kind of quiet, when you knew that pleasure was a promise away, and you slipped down the staircase and into its arms as willingly as any courtesan.

The kind of enveloping voluptuous silence that only amplified your voluptuous cravings because there was nothing to stop you thinking of what you had done, what you wanted to do, what you were going to do . . .

Nothing to stop her.

Everything was possible in the dark. Things that were never even conceivable in her brother's house in Bhaumaghar where she kept a tight rein on her emotions, her desires, her lust.

And yet, here, in the dark, it had taken only a word, an image, a spurt of memory, and a rising need, and her body was no longer her own. She had known that already. Someone else had conquered it, tutored it, pleasured it . . .

Abandoned it.

She shook off that thought.

Do what you will . . .

There was nothing to stop her.

Silent as fog, she drifted down the steps and down to the netherworld of indulgences. In the *bagnio,* she slipped off her wrapper, and naked, her senses thrumming with excitement, she entered the *boudoir.*

The air was sultry, heavy, suffused with the scent of sex and surrender.

She lolled on the sofa, inhaling the essence of *him,* hot with the memory of possessing him with her mouth and her hands.

She wanted nothing more than to have him at her mercy again. The need pulsated in her as real as breathing. She craved the joining of hard to soft, heat to wet, and the saiety of completion.

And she knew the way to surcease; she had been taught that as well. And in desperation, she might . . . she just might—

She wanted . . . and she knew she should not have succumbed to the lure of the *voudrais;* she had known that this could be the only outcome—that she would give in to her lustful nature no matter what the consequences.

A year was too long to suppress the wanton in her. She had proved that with one night, one carnal joining; and then a feast, because she could not keep away.

Even tonight, she needed to the benediction of the *voudrais* to even allow herself to *feel.*

Do what you will . . .

It might have come some other time, some other place. But better that she had surrendered to it here, in this dark welcoming place, where she could slip off her clothes and her constraints and give herself over wholly to the pleasure she craved.

"Did you think I could stay away?"

Did she imagine the whisper in the dark because she wanted to hear it so badly?

She opened her eyes slowly as his large hot hand grasped her thigh and moved slowly down to her ankle, and then determinedly parted her legs, and removed her hand.

He was naked, long and strong, and thick and hard, and ready to mount her and ride her to oblivion.

She shifted her body, spread her legs, and canted her body toward him, in a blatant invitation.

He hovered above her, his shaft prodding her velvet fold, slipping in and slipping out, slipping in and back out, in and out, just at the point of letting her feel his heat and hardness and his power.

She undulated her hips to entice him. He responded by inserting just the tip of him, the luscious ridged tip that she had sucked and nursed to creamy ecstasy, just that, into the heat of her feminine fold.

She held him there, squeezing him, wriggling against him, taunting him with the hot promise of her body.

He waited. He watched her as she tried to tempt his full probing possession of her. She wanted it; her body ached for it, and still, he held himslf just *there*.

He wanted her to beg for it. He wanted to be the only one who could give it to her, like that, and like that, and like that, as he rammed himself into her inch by long hot hard inch. The only one who could make her body ripple and squirm and thrash with such abandon.

The only one who could make her heave and buck against him in ecstasy. The only one who could answer her naked siren's call.

He thrust into her hard and slow, hard and slow, and she opened herself to him as she undulated with him, hard and slow, hard and slow. And deep. And wide. And hard and slow, like that—and like that, as he hovered above her, connected to her only by the most virile male part of him; like that, deep and hard, resting within her, letting her cradle him in her tight textured heat, her body spiralling down against his to encompass every last inch of him until he was buried to his very root.

They rocked together violently, hip to hip, joined tightly, erotically in a carnal dance of war.

She wanted to tempt him beyond all reason. He wanted her to lose her soul.

He couldn't keep from moving. She needed his virile thrusts. Her squirming body demanded them. Her shimmying hips enticed him.

Her body arched to receive him, seeking his relentless primitive power. No man was immune to the siren's call to possess her. It was what she begged for, what she could not live without: the rock hard feel of a man inside her and the driving explosive culmination of his desire.

He was coming that close to it; his thrusts were savage, hard, elemental. Her body tightened, lifted, and took him and took him and took him; she moaned in rhythm with the floodgate of feeling as he swept her with him into a wrenching drenching release that left her drained, sated, done.

He eased himself onto her, and she bore the weight of him joyously, feeling him joined to every pore of her body.

She slept.

And sometime in the night, she awakened with a start to find herself naked and alone on a sofa of the *voudrais*. There was a candle lit someplace in the distance, and her satiated body was draped with her wrapper. But he was gone, his presence and his possession as evanescent as a dream, and the only proof of their vigorous coupling, the deliciously musky scent of his sex.

Chapter Eight

Imagined it, imagined it, imagined everything. The simple explanation, just like Tuttle's finding the board and leaving it in the library.

The simple explanation; she had had a deliciously erotic dream and sleepwalked to the voudrais, and slept in too late already.

Serena had come to awaken her. The dressmakers were due back today for the first fittings. She didn't want to miss that.

She rather thought she did. It was going to be difficult watching Serena with a trunkload of lovely dresses while she was still relegated to wearing black.

Helaine was waiting for her in the library; Serena was already closeted with Louise in the saloon, and Leonie was supervising all.

"Into the library with you. No time for breakfast now, Diandra. You should have come when Serena called. The ladies have but two hours to spare."

And in that short period of time, they intended to pin, tuck, trim and mold each dress individually to their bodies.

Diandra had had no idea how elegant a black dress could be, until she tried on the first of Helaine's samples.

It fit her like a glove. Its high collar accentuated her neck, her jaw, her cheekbones. The skirt was slashed with figured silk panels and swept gracefully to the floor from beneath a draped overskirt of the same material.

Nothing fussy for her. Every dress was clean lined and devoid of excess trim to show off her figure to advantage. There was the silk crepe with the faceted button trim, the silk with ribbons and lace overlay for evening, the sturdy twill with tucks and pleats for afternoon. Every piece was meticulously fit to her body, tacked, sewn and then removed for the final finish.

In between, she took some tea and toast and a great deal of unanticipated pleasure in watching Serena parade in her frothy fashion dresses: silks, stripes, foulards, challis, a walking suit, a tennis dress in white linen lawn, a riding habit of black twill, light spring dresses in spring colors, a ball gown of ivory laid over with lace and golden ribbons. Could any girl be happier?

Serena waltzed around the entry hall with her pretend partner, and when George entered from the drawing room, she caught him up in her dance and swirled him all around the room.

"I can't wait to get to London," she crowed as George finally begged off and Leonie looked just a little disgusted at the display.

"There will be time enough for that," she said dampingly as she helped Louise and Helaine gather up the dresses and pack them for transport back to the village. "Anyway, it's a beautiful day. I think we should spend it outside."

"You, Leonie?" George looked amused and skeptical.

"I had Tuttle set up a net in the lower field. I thought Diandra and Serena might enjoy some tennis. It's perfectly all right—in private," she added, as Diandra was about to comment. "It *has* been more than a year. And I would like to see Serena's form."

"Leonie doesn't play," George interpolated wryly. "She merely *judges.*"

"Somebody must," Leonie said. "Come along, everyone. We want the best light and the warmest time of day. High tea when we return."

As if cucumber sandwiches and tarts were a decent bribe, Diandra thought grudgingly. A game would have been wonderful without Leonie's *superior* presence.

Nevertheless, she would not let Leonie spoil things. It was a warm and cloudless day, George—if no one else—was excellent company, and Serena had a sunny smile on her face as she chose a racquet and swung it experimentally.

It was a scene out of the pictorials in *Queen Magazine.* The country house weekend. No ghosts. No messages from beyond the grave. No furtive coupling in a place of deceit.

Just the beautiful girl, the eligible admirer, her proper chaperone and a family friend. Charles Dana Gibson could not have sketched it better.

George was checking the tension in the net. Leonie had seated herself in the referee's position and Serena was loping around to the opposite side of the net as she picked her choice of racquets.

"Are you ready?"

Serena nodded.

The court was not unlike theirs at home with the net centered over a patch of springy grass outlined by an unevenly drawn chalk foul line. She struck the first ball over the net, and it felt good to be in motion and in control.

They did a practice volley, and then got to down to the game in earnest, with Leonie calling the fouls, and George watching with great amusement as Diandra took the first set, 6-3, 6-2.

"You're tired now," Serena called out to her.

"You think, my girl. I've just gotten my first wind."

"You're out of practice," Serena taunted. "I was just setting you up anyway." She struck the ball and Diandra came in to meet it.

She didn't have much of an underhand stroke, but she managed to tap it over the net; Serena couldn't get it in time, and looked disgusted as George called the score at love-fifteen.

"I've got your measure now," Serena said, popping the ball toward her again. Serena was serious, Serena meant to take her out by any trick possible.

It would be so easy to pull up and let her take the point.

She would never have thought to do it, and Serena knew it. It had been the same at home; that deadly competition in the most unlikely things. But here there was an audience, and a need to win at all costs.

Perhaps it was good for Leonie to see Serena as an implacable player with a style and talent all her own. Not so malleable. Not so disreputable or contemptible. Serena needed that, and what were her puny principles by contrast? They wouldn't make Serena feel better.

She adjusted her position, pushed aside her better instincts, and let Serena take the second set.

Tuttle brought lemonade and they took a quick break before the next set. And then Diandra took the first game of the third set, and Serena got grim. A battle to the death, Diandra thought, but she could not figure out quite why.

She had never raced around the court so much in her life. Serena was determined, and she was equally unyielding, and between the two of them, they kept the ball in a rally for five minutes at a time before one of them scored a point.

"Getting too old for this," Serena jeered as she took another point that put her at advantage.

"Deuce back to you, my girl," as she returned service with a neat placement to Serena's opposite side where she couldn't get to it.

She stepped behind the service line and lifted her racquet.

But Diandra's eyes were not focused on the ball. She was looking beyond Serena to the field behind her.

Serena sent her puzzled look, but then she saw that Leonie was gazing in the same direction, her face dead white, and she slowly turned in time to see a wisp of gray disappear into the blue sky, and to hear Leonie's strangled cry before she slumped to the ground.

"I didn't see it, whatever it was," George said for the hundredth time as he applied a cold compress to Leonie's forehead.

"It was *not* an *it,*" Leonie moaned. "Oh my God—it was Pamela. I *know* it was Pamela. She had a gray cloak exactly like that, I remember it well. And I saw her. I *saw* her. She's here, just as she said . . ."

"My dear Leonie, you're making connections and constructions where there is nothing. Pamela is dead."

"Pamela . . . is with us in spirit. Have we not talked to her? And now I have seen her. That was your ghost, wasn't it, Diandra? That's what you've been seeing since you arrived here? How could you have known? I wish you had known, we could have made contact sooner . . ."

"Leonie you are getting out of hand here. What did we see, after all? A wisp of gray floating across the back field. It was gone in a minute, and I'd swear on my oath it was a patch of fog."

"And I know it was my sister . . ." Leonie said, sitting

up. "We have to do something about it. We have to find her. Contact her again . . ."

She broke off as Tuttle appeared at the door. "Beg pardon, my lady. Constable Streatfield is here."

"Oh—oh . . . Diandra, would you—?"

She went to meet him but he was already over the threshold. Leonie immediately sank back on the couch and gave George her compress to rinse out again.

"I'm sorry to see you out of sorts, my lady," Streatfield said.

"Tennis," George said. "Too much sun and now she has the headache. What can we do for you, Constable?"

"I thought you'd be interested to hear that we have recovered Agatha's divining board."

"Really?" Leonie bolted upright and then sagged back against the sofa cushions again as George leaned over to apply the compress.

"We missed it in our first pass of the surrounding woods. A neighbor, a farmer, found it. Knew just what it was too. But that is the way of it, ma'am. Evidence in unlikely places. And perhaps the murderer as well."

"Exactly," Leonie said who refused to be scared by the implicit threat. "Now what was it you wished to ask us . . . ?"

"I just came to tell you about the board, my lady."

"I see."

"And the wooden pointer. In velvet bags, neat and tidy. Like someone had hidden them, intending to come back and get them. Of course, the damp stained them . . . the bags, I mean—"

"How very singular. Well, if that is all, Constable . . . ?"

"For now. Maybe I'll have some more questions later, my lady."

Leonie eased herself to a sitting position. "But we might very well be leaving for London in a day or so, Constable.

In fact, I believe that was the very plan. So what happens in that event?''

He looked puzzled for a moment. "Have His Lordship come see me, my lady. I'm sure we can work it out."

She watched him with an eagle eye as he withdrew from the room and then she leaned back against the pillows. "My head. My head feels like it is going to split open. George—some tea, please. I don't suppose *you* know how the board wound up outside of this house?"

But George pretended not to hear her as he poured her tea and she decided her head was aching too awfully to pursue the subject for the moment, and she went on to more important matters.

"Serena, you play an excellent game. Diandra—you are too aggressive by half. I think I'm just as glad you won't be playing in town. But you did see the ghost, didn't you? Diandra?"

She didn't want to admit it or to give credence to Leonie's theory it was Pamela. "I saw something," she said reluctantly.

"You two should be ashamed of yourselves," George said roundly. "There was *nothing* there. It's a trick of the light or the air. Or something. Neither Justin or I have ever seen such a thing, and I for one am sick of the whole subject."

"There was something there." This from Serena. "I saw it, I did."

"Mass hysteria," George muttered. "For which the universal panacea is . . . tea." As Tuttle entered the drawing room with the tea cart, piled high with the promised sandwiches, cakes and tarts.

"Well, look, Justin will return tonight," George went on, ignoring his recalcitrant audience, and focusing on Tuttle's arranging the service and setting out the teacups. "Your dresses should be ready tomorrow. I don't think it would be too difficult to remove to Cheswick Square by dinner time."

"I'm not leaving Pamela," Leonie said.

"I'm sure she will come with us," Serena said comfortingly and then turned to Diandra. "Perhaps you'd like to give your opinion?"

"I would be just as happy to return to London so we may begin to address the reason why we came in the first place."

Serena waved a dismissive hand. "Oh, that."

"Yes, that."

"Have some tea, Diandra. There isn't much we can do about it now, except tell Justin and let him decide."

Tea sounded good, too good. And she was exhausted. On top of Leonie's headache and the pressure of Streatfield's visit.

She needed a quick dose of rationality. Skene was a fictional world populated by eccentrics and supernatural entities. Neither were real, *she* didn't feel real. Her behavior wasn't real, it was time out of mind in a place that had no function in actuality.

When they got back to London, she would wake up from the dream.

The only problem was, she didn't want to.

They assembled for a sketchy dinner later on.

"The house is too quiet," Leonie complained. "And I still don't understand how the constable got hold of Agatha's board. I was sure I had it. And now we can't talk to Pamela."

"Pamela will let us know if she wants to talk to us," George said with some irony, which was utterly lost on Leonie.

"Do you think?" she murmured hopefully.

"Leonie . . ."

"Well, didn't she first contact us by rapping?"

"It takes too long."

"*George* . . ."

"I can tell fortunes by reading cards," Serena said.

"Can you?" Leonie said, diverted. "How droll. I would love to hear my fortune."

She summoned Tuttle to bring in a fresh deck and they assembled in the drawing room.

Serena shuffled the cards, gave them to Leonie to cut, and then laid out a cross. "I see money—love and happiness, perhaps marriage. Only, beware, happiness comes at price. Look—the ace of spades. The most negative card in the deck. Preceded by two other spades, foretelling of sickness and bad luck. But don't make changes, that won't affect anything. Someone is your enemy."

"What a terrible fortune. Take it away—at once!" Leonie swiped her hand over the table and sent the cards into a jumble. "Read for your sister."

Serena looked at Diandra. "Or maybe the coins?"

"The cards will do," Diandra murmured. She hated them both, and Leonie was obviously displeased, so what had been meant as a parlor game had turned into something vastly more serious.

And anyway, she already knew there was danger.

Serena shuffled the cards and laid out the cross, shuddering slightly as the ace of spades turned up yet again.

"Love, happiness, perhaps marriage; there is money is involved, and there is the card of death and bad luck. Jealousy. A man you know could be a friend or an enemy; you would be wise to let a woman guide you."

"Odd they are so similar," Leonie said.

"It works that way sometimes." Serena folded the cards into the deck.

"Perhaps Pamela is at work, trying to tell us something."

"Leonie—" Diandra this time. "It's a parlor game."

"Nonsense. And besides, you have a vested interest in trying to deter me from contacting Pamela. What if her message has to do with you?"

Well, it had—in a way. But the planchette had also pointed accusingly to the letter *L*, which Leonie chose to ignore.

"We only have your word for it that you didn't know Pamela. I think she's trying to tell us something different."

The gloves were off. Leonie's patina of civility had worn thin. And there was no other way to combat her other than by direct attack.

"I hope she tells you *something,*" Diandra said. "She was very emphatic about the letter *L* the previous contact. Whatever can she have meant by that?"

"We won't ever know, will we?" Leonie said sharply, sending a simmering look at George. "Because that bumbling fool Streatfield got hold of the board somehow. We'll just have to compensate when we get to London. We have to find out the truth. It is very obvious to me that Pamela has come to help us discover the truth."

"Whose truth?" Diandra asked softly.

"Why, her truth, of course," Leonie said. "The truth about how she died. And maybe the truth about why her husband went and married *you.*"

She'd had just about enough of Leonie and ghosts and Skene altogether. Her accusations were as clear as a bell: Diandra had wanted Guthrie Reynell, and she had gotten him.

She wished it had been like that. She couldn't hardly remember just how it had been. Guthrie in mourning for the missing Pamela, and seeking to divert himself with some hunting. Hugh, her brother, having been introduced to him at one or another of the clubs that were an integral part of the colonial social scene. And then Guthrie turning up in Bhaumaghar one hot sultry hunting season.

And staying on, enjoying the countryside, the company, the pampering by Serena and Hugh's servants.

Oh, yes—Serena had had one monstrous crush on Guthrie. And he had been so gentle with her, so sweet. He wasn't that old, either. And he was just waiting to step and become interim ruler of the country. The moment Gladstone took control in England, his place in history was ensured.

And meantime, he hunted tigers, mourned his wife while investigators searched for her body, and in the process, fell in love with *her*.

She hadn't been aware, not at first. He was Hugh's good and generous guest, who seemed to come out to Bhaumaghar almost every other month. He had business in the province. Or he was meeting with the maharajah of *some place*. Or he had heard of particularly good hunting in a nearby suburb.

Whatever the reason, Guthrie Reynell was a frequent and welcome guest, and she couldn't have helped getting to know him and admire him when he sought her company so often.

Serena hadn't liked it, of course; but she was young, too young, and she considered herself just a friend who was available to another friend when he came to visit. And when he would consider remarrying, after the mystery of his wife's death was solved, he would choose a woman on his own social strata.

She knew that. Serena did not. Or would not consider it.

When she thought about it, it seemed to her that it was then that Serena had begun investing her hopes in superstitions and omens. Almost as if amulets and rituals would make a difference in how Guthrie regarded her.

So unrealistic. She had been so young, and all the mumbo-jumbo had seemed so harmless. Especially because Diandra had been so sure that Guthrie did not want either of them.

And she had told Serena so when Serena's hocus-pocus seemed to be getting out of hand.

"Are you planning to sneak a love potion in his brandy *pawnee?*" she had asked once derisively, and it seemed to her that after that Serena had become secretive and resentful.

The end of it was not pretty. Guthrie proposed to *her*, and Serena had taken to her bed, and refused to stand up as her maid of honor, and the whole thing was an awful mess.

She hadn't wanted to marry Guthrie. She was not high born enough, she didn't know if she loved him, she was too young, she wasn't nearly up to the task of becoming Vicereine, and she could *not* wound Serena like that.

Hugh had convinced her. It was her life. Serena would get over it. Guthrie loved her, and if he thought she could take her place among the elite and by his side, who was she to gainsay him?

It had sounded so logical at the time. And she had been forever grateful to Hugh for his steady good sense. She *had* loved Guthrie, as her life, her gentle teacher, her lover, her king.

He was like a god to her. And he had come down from his throne to initiate her into the rites and pleasures of men and women together, and to teach her the way of being a lord's chosen wife.

She had been malleable, of that she was aware. But she also had a will and mind of her own. She had had the best education, at Hugh's insistence, and she had walked the thin tenuous line of his governance of the province and had done so successfully and with uncommon grace.

Serena, her charge, had been another matter altogether, but once her marriage to Guthrie was a fact, Serena had done a *volte-face* that had made her dizzy with its rapidity and totality.

She hadn't given up her dependency on tricks and magic, but she was back to her old self, and helpful and good company besides.

Guthrie's unexpected death had devastated them all.

She didn't like thinking about it.

But this business with Pamela and messages from beyond the grave was unnerving her. Leonie believed too strongly; she had to get Serena away from Skene and away from Leonie. Leonie wanted to find spirits and life and blame where none existed.

And Serena was too suggestible.

There were explanations for all the manifestations: she was sure of it.

But there was no justification whatsoever for her surrender to the *voudrais*.

This would be their last night at Skene. Tomorrow she would send Jhasa ahead to find suitable accommodations, just as she had threatened a week before. A hotel would do; money was no object.

She wandered around the drawing room, touching objects. The house was so quiet, everyone was asleep. And yet she was pulsatingly awake and not at all afraid of spirits inhabiting the dark.

It was curious to her that she was drawn to this subterranean night life. In India, her life had centered around the light: the morning, so cool and infusing her with a throbbing energy to do, to accomplish; she would ride in the morning, supervise the house staff, and meet with Hugh daily to discuss his schedule and any entertaining he planned to do.

And then in the afternoon, her reward—letting the energy flow into rest and relaxation in preparation for the early evening when the social events of the day would begin, and she, Hugh and Serena would walk to the club for dinner, for tennis, for conversation, for business, for music, for cards.

She wasn't used to being this idle. Or this upended. Prior to coming to England, her life flowed in a graceful, useful path and no one knew her secrets.

And now . . .

She paused by the door that opened to the *voudrais*.

Now she knew his secrets too.

She pushed open the door to the *voudrais*.

He ought to dismantle it. He ought to tear it apart and take a wife and forget there had ever been such a thing to tempt mortal women.

So why did she feel she belonged here, even tonight?

She lit the candlestick, and for the last time, she went down the steps and into the *salle d'entrée*.

The doors were always open, like a lover's arms.

The erotic scent enveloped her like expensive perfume.

Was this where her god had honed his skill? Oh, if she had ever known about this—no, she hadn't been ready to know about this. She had been a frightened fawn in the hands of a man who knew just how to train her, with all the rebuffs and rewards that would make her into his perfect odalisque.

So wasn't it fitting that she had succumbed to the lure of voudrais?

And that its motto was a blessing and an atonement?

She was in the *boudoir* now, her senses overwhelmed with longing. *It wasn't enough—it was never enough . . .*

That was the one thing Guthrie had taught her, and the one part of her that she had to most strenuously suppress.

Never enough.

Pleasure was such an evanescent thing. Memory and desire went hand in hand—and she had not yet learned how to separate the one from the other.

She only knew how to obliterate her yearnings and nullify her feelings.

But not here. Not here.

Do what you will . . .

For three unconscionable nights, she had. Wasn't that enough to last the rest of her life?

Except she couldn't imagine life beyond the *boudoir* door at that moment. Everything seemed centered in this one place: dormant desires, hedonistic philosophy, libertarian free thinking, a total contradiction of how chastely she had lived and what a wanton she was in reality.

She felt at home here.

The thought was startling. She had experienced the freedom and the liberation of the *voudrais*. Even now, the sultry air wrapped around her like a second skin, and she wanted only to be naked for her phantom lover.

When would he come tonight? If she were waiting . . . *if* she were waiting . . . in the *seraglio* this time, in private, behind the curtain, stretched out languorously on the sofa . . . yes—

She placed the candle on the small table in the corner of the cell and slipped out of her wrapper.

This was the room of the first encounter; she felt an especial fondness for this place. She lay face down on the sofa, rubbing her body into the satin tufts that felt so slick and cool.

So easy just to drift off into a delicious erotic dream . . .

Feeling two large hot hands grasping her hips and pulling her onto her knees. Feeling a hot naked body covering her, pushing his thick pulsating shaft between her legs so that she rested on its iron length as she braced herself on her hands.

And then, oh then, his hands cupping her swinging breasts, feeling the weight of them, the sensuous curves, the tight hard nipples. He wanted her nipples. His fingers stroked them, played with them, thumbed them, fondled them and squeezed them.

Her body reacted, squirming against his hips, against the jut of his penis between her legs. She loved all of it, the fingering caress of her nipples, the swamping unimaginable pleasure, the thrust of him between her legs, her buttocks writhing against his hips.

He covered her breasts, and slowly lifted her upright against his chest.

Oh, this was better, so much better. He still had her nipples, but she had *him,* all of him she could straddle between her legs. And she had her hands, and she could touch him and rub him and squeeze him in concert with his luscious seduction of her nipples.

They were so hard, so tight, so bulbous under the expert caress of his fingers. And he couldn't get enough of them. He held them between his thumb and forefinger, stroking, rubbing, squeezing, feeling them, feeling her explosive response.

And she held him, her fingers constricting convulsively around his massive erection with every caress of her pleasure points.

She couldn't get enough. She arched against him, and ground her hips downward against his jutting male root.

He responded by pulling lightly at her engorged nipples, once, twice, and then just squeezing them ever so gently, and then holding them, holding them.

She could just feel his fingers there, holding, holding; her hands played all over his towering manhood, grabbing him each time her body twinged as he played with her. All that power, all that force focused in her hand.

All that pleasure streaming from two lush points of her body—all that silver cascading through her veins—molten silver, hot, shimmering, fusing into one hard explosive crack of thunder that smote her like a mallet. And she cracked—into a thousand jagged pieces of blinding silver as her body went out of control, spasming wildly against him, her hands squeezing and pumping in tandem with her gyrations.

He came thirty seconds after, spewing his cream all over her hands. She wasn't even aware; she rubbed his essence into her skin and then she sagged limply against him.

Gently, he pushed her down onto the sofa and he covered her with his warm, throbbing body.

A gorgeous erotic dream . . . she thought it as she drifted to sleep wrapped head to foot in a heavy blanketing warmth.

Hours passed.

Or maybe minutes.

But the sound was unmistakable, echoing through the *voudrais,* and throughout the house.

Rap! Rap! Rap!

She bolted off of the sofa. She was alone in the *voudrais.* She reached for her wrapper which had been draped over her and slipped into it, feeling naked and vulnerable suddenly, and too too alone.

She grabbed the candle and slowly eased her way out of the cell, out of the *seraglio* and to the parapet steps.

Rap! Rap! Rap!

She heard footsteps pounding above her, and Leonie's voice in the distance.

They were eerie, those raps, after these several days of having heard nothing except the messages of the board.

She flew up the steps and doused the candle as she entered the library. They were all in the reception hall.

She darted into the drawing room, and exited into the hallway from there.

Rap! Rap! Rap!

They all heard it: George who had just emerged from the family wing el, Serena, still yawning and looking faintly scared, Justin, following behind George and buttoning his shirt, and Leonie, emerging from the family dining room, with the divining board and planchette in her trembling hands.

Chapter Nine

They returned to London the following afternoon.

Leonie refused to give up the board and planchette, she had wanted to have a *sèance* then and there, and wound up hiding it among her clothes so that if Justin wanted it, he would have to unpack every trunk she had brought.

She and George travelled in the one carriage, Serena and Diandra in the other, the servants in a third, and the trunks and tenderly wrapped dresses that had been delivered that morning, in the fourth.

Justin rode, stopping off briefly to speak to the constable, as Streatfield had requested, and leaving their direction in London, with the assurances that everyone in the house party could and would be available anytime he desired.

And then it was three long arduous hours through the winding countryside to the outskirts of London.

He had never wanted so badly to return. Things were going too fast and getting too far out of hand.

This whole business with the manifestations . . . and last night—they had searched the house yet again, the footmen, Tuttle, the Indian servants, himself, George. Nothing was overlooked, not a space, not a drawer, not even the *voudrais*.

They found nothing.

But Leonie had found the divining board and the planchette. In the family dining room. Right on the table, with the velvet pouches folded neatly beside.

And Streatfield had never said a word about it.

Too many mysteries, both private and personal, and all of it precipitated with the arrival of Diandra and Serena. And Skene was obviously not the place to pursue the answers; there were too many distractions there.

The carriages barreled down the avenue alongside the park, turned into Cheswick Square and drew to a shuddering halt. Millbank was at the door almost the moment they stopped, and a phalanx of footmen marched out to his command and efficiently began removing the luggage from carriage three.

"Yes-s-s," Serena whispered as they entered the house.

"Don't get too comfortable," Diandra warned. "I'm looking for suitable accommodations."

"Whatever for?"

"For my comfort," Diandra said tartly.

"Your luggage has been brought to your rooms, ma'am." Millbank, polite, removed, effective.

"Thank you, Millbank." She mounted the steps, with Serena lagging behind her.

"I don't want to leave here."

Diandra ignored that. "I'll have Gita draw you a bath."

"I don't want a bath. I want . . ."

"Why don't you change, at least? We'll have tea and then we'll talk."

Only she didn't want to talk. She felt charged with energy. She had slept the whole way, in spite of Serena's attempts to engage her in conversation—speculation, really, about the rappings and the divining board, and who had killed Agatha, and her certainty that Pamela would follow them to Cheswick Square—and she was ready to attack and search the whole of London for a place for them to stay.

"Tea and talk . . ." Serena murmured. "Talk and tea— it seems like that's all we ever do. Now we're in London, we have lots more choices. Why don't we go *out* for tea?"

"Can we settle in first?"

"I thought you said we were leaving . . ."

"Serena . . ."

"I'll tell you what: I'll read the cards, and they will tell us exactly what to do."

"If you must," she said grudgingly, because she did not want to go downstairs and face Justin. Or her fantasies.

Surely she hadn't imagined that bone-crackling pleasure . . .

But that was over now; whatever it had been, it was done. She had entered a kind of heaven and had been cast out again. Forbidden fruit. A woman should never taste forbidden fruit.

She cut the deck of cards with her left hand, as Serena reminded her, and then began unpacking their new clothes as Serena laid out the cards.

"Oh dear. Bad luck intersects everything else. Look— someone may take advantage of you. There's money coming, the future looks good, except there's a possibility of some kind of accident. Not serious. And there are good signs surrounding that card: money, romance, good health, friends. But beware of a stranger. And don't make any changes in spite of the forecast of trouble. *Don't make any changes,* Diandra."

"Serena . . ."

"It says right here."

"I'll think about it. We'll see what Justin has to say. He must be tired to death of apparitions and spirits."

"You don't understand, Diandra. Pamela will be heard. That's why Leonie has the board. Pamela has come with us. Don't you feel her presence? Don't you want to know?"

She didn't want to know. She felt curiously removed from her intentions suddenly. Nothing seemed important. Everything had been reduced to the lay of a deck of cards and the shattering memories of the *voudrais*.

She could stay or go; it would make no difference. She was irrelevant to the will and whim of invisible spirits. Serena and Leonie were the real sisters under the skin. The thought was bizarre—like everything else that had happened since they arrived in England.

It was strange to think as well that London now represented freedom to her. And that even though Cheswick Square was situated in a private enclave, she could still look out the window and see the movement and motion of the city beyond its park gates.

It was all very odd. As if she had been transformed somehow. Or she really had fallen down a rabbit hole.

Leonie was to stay on at Cheswick Square and coordinate the social activities. It was an amusing idea, to visualize Leonie with a tray of calling cards in one hand and the divining board in the other, calling upon a spirit to approve the suitability of an engagement.

"Well, the gossips have been at work. There's already a mention in the paper, and a note that we will be at home starting this week. Justin has taken a hand to launch you properly," Leonie said to Serena when they came down to tea.

"Let me see!"

Diandra peered over her shoulder as Serena read the brief paragraph: *The Earl of Skene is hosting his sister-in-law, Miss Serena Morant, and her sister, Lady Diandra Reynell, his stepmother. After a week in the country, Miss Morant will be receiving at Cheswick Square under the auspices of Lady Leonie Hull.*

"Succinct, with all the relevant details."

"Sufficient at any rate," Leonie said. "It will do. Cards will come and then we will decide where and with whom Serena will be seen socially. Oh, and you too, Diandra. You will be invited as a matter of course. There may be some invitations you will want to decline. But I'm here to instruct you on these matters."

"And I bow to your superior wisdom," Diandra said, seating herself at the tea table with the paper which she had plucked from Serena's hands.

"Lovely to have an immediate mention in the social column, don't you think?" Serena said.

"Very opportune," Diandra murmured, but she wondered just how Justin had gotten that done over and above whatever else he'd accomplished in Town—and simultaneously back at Skene.

But she wasn't going to think about that. The only question was why, given his skepticism and disinclination previously to act on Serena's behalf.

"You do know what Justin is letting himself in for," Leonie said.

"Well, no—"

"Every marriage-minded mother who has an eligible son will be knocking on that door in hopes of bagging two for the price of one. He will have to appear at any number of odious parties and dinners on Serena's behalf, since he is her host, and he will have to be civil to people he would normally never speak to even in passing. It is a great sacrifice."

"How tiring it is to be a god," Diandra murmured.

"Or his helpmate," Leonie said.

Leonie, warning her in the most round about way, that

what she had inferred from the first was indeed true: Leonie wanted Justin, and now that they were in London, she meant to stake out her territory.

Why would she fear his father's widow?

"I will help as much as possible," she said.

"You are a sweet and biddable girl, Serena," Leonie said, ignoring her offer. "Men like that. And there is just a little bit of the exotic about you. You have conversation, you have the requisite skills. You should do very well going around and about and getting a taste of the season. We won't expect to be asked everywhere, but Justin's name is enough to secure the very best invitations."

Serena sighed in delight. "This is more than I ever expected."

"Your modesty is becoming," Leonie said. "Diandra, however, should try to look a little more tragic."

"Not seriously. It's been a year, Leonie. I don't particularly want to be buried as well."

"Too soon. No frivolity at all for you."

If only Leonie knew . . . "But who was that well acquainted with Guthrie here?"

Leonie sent her an exasperated look. "Me. My family. Any number of parliamentarians. Those who sponsored him to India. I promise, there will be no dearth of those who remember him, and would be put off by seeing his widow as some kind of gadabout. And they all knew Pamela."

The name dropped like a stone and there was a sudden silence.

"So there will be comparisons and resentment," Diandra said bluntly.

"There may be. You must act above reproach. It would help if you weren't so young and beautiful. Maybe if we swathe your head in black . . . to hide that hair. Well, we have to work with what we have . . ." Leonie said resignedly, "and around whatever invitations arrive."

"So kind," Diandra retorted. "I think I've lost my appetite."

"Perfect. Stop eating dinner. We want a gaunt effect, I think. Yes, skipping a meal should do that very nicely. Very clever of you, Diandra."

She bit her lip. Leonie had no sense of humor, so this wasn't a joke. She meant every word.

"I'll see what I can do," she said acidly, but even that was lost on Leonie.

The doorbell rang insistently. Leonie looked up and smiled smugly. She rose to go to the dining room door where she would wait for Millbank to deliver the first of the expected calling cards.

But he had no salver in his hand and there was a puzzled expression on his face. "I'm sorry, my lady. I don't understand it. There were no cards. There was nobody there."

"A delivery boy playing tricks," Justin said later, dismissing it. "Unless madam engineered it somehow?"

"Madam hasn't been out the door the whole day," Diandra said stringently. He had summoned her to the library early in the evening, and she was just waiting for some snide remark. "Or out of Serena's or Leonie's sight. Or were you hoping, Justin?"

"Nothing has been explained to my satisfaction," he said roughly. "You are still here on sufferance because now so many people are aware of your presence in Town. And that was before the formal announcement in the paper. I still don't like it, but I'm stuck with it, and so you will disabuse yourself of any notions of leaving Cheswick Square for other quarters."

"Oh my, Serena has been busy. I'm thrilled to know you

are suffering *and* despite that, we must strive to maintain your reputation . . ."

"Which reputation is that, madam?" he asked dangerously.

"For—cordiality and benevolence, of course. Among your peers. You certainly would not want to be seen as an ogre. How fortunate we have come to know the *real* you."

"Have you?"

The question sat between them for one long fraught moment and anything she had thought to say stuck in her throat.

"I daresay I . . . could," she murmured, meeting his crystalline gaze boldly. But she could read nothing there.

Nobody told.

Neither would he. And whatever she knew about him was a secret safely locked in the underworld of the voudrais.

She had taken her pleasure with the freedom of a man, and what did a man do but discharge his seed and then walk away?

Hadn't he?

The Queen of Hearts was not invited to this tea party.

"This ghostly nonsense has to stop."

"As if I had a part in it . . ."

"I believe that was the theory."

"Then explain the divining board turning up in Leonie's hands when we had heard explicitly that a neighboring farmer had found it and turned it over to your Constable Streatfield."

"I can't."

"Tell me how I could have done that."

"You could have found a similar one."

"They are not sold in tourist shops, Justin."

He got up up from behind his desk and began pacing around the room. "I can't explain it. Or the rapping. That could have been the wind."

"Or it could have been our collective imagination. I

believe you tendered that theory when a table floated of its own volition.''

"I don't know how you did that, madam, but that I know you did."

"Tell me why."

"Distraction, madam. You are an expert at it." Their eyes met and held; she checked her fury that he would even allude to the nights in the *voudrais* like that. "There are still questions about my father's death. You've answered nothing, you've thrown yourself on my mercy—"

"You have none," she muttered.

"And I will not let you get off scot free."

"You haven't, have you?"

"You will meet the price of this boon for your sister. Believe me, you will."

"And I promise *you*, Justin, it will cost you. And I will make sure you pay." She got up and went to the door. Enough was enough with him. "And I will make very sure the price steep."

At war again.

And too steep for whom? She felt like she was the one about to fall off the mountain.

What was it about Guthrie's death?

Justin's rage was just under the surface, and she was so convenient as a whipping boy. She was the interloper, the child-bride, the usurper of his mother's throne. From a ten-year-old, all of that would have been understandable. From a grown man, it was unconscionable.

And she would not excuse it. Ever.

They were all going out this night. All but her. That was the other thing he had to tell her. A musicale, a last-minute invitation, and not something his father's widow would attend. They would be gone several hours, no more.

Oh, she hated this, she hated this. Guthrie would have hated it too. He wouldn't have wanted her walled away like this.

Still, it was the first of the opportunities she had sought for Serena. Why wasn't that enough? Why?

This house didn't seem quite so eerie and still. The bustling of the servants was more evident as they prepared the rooms for slumber, and maids emptied ash bins and dusted around the rooms that had been in use.

Like elves, deep in the night they were, unobtrusively providing everything before it was demanded.

Justin's library was extensive. There was reading matter here for a century at least. More philosophy and current affairs than anything, but also the odd novel here and there that she took down and leafed through.

But she didn't want to read. She wanted to laugh and listen and dance in brightly lit places with elegant people.

That would happen. She would make sure of it.

She dismissed Millbank, who was hovering over her like a worried hen.

She wandered through the house, admiring the furnishings and appointments. She spent some time with the ancestral portraits. She read the paper front to back, sitting in Justin's chair.

She heard the music in her heart as she explored every nook and cranny of the house, playing hide and seek with the servants as they made their evening rounds.

So it seemed perfectly natural she would find the secret door in the basement, and that her curiosity would provoke her to open it.

But she didn't expect to find an opulently furnished cell, the town equivalent of the master's *voudrais*.

* * *

Now it was clear, the attractions of Town at the onset of the season. There was riding in the morning in Green Park, either on horseback or in a carriage—which was Leonie's choice for herself and Diandra. Afterwards, they changed in preparation for shopping or having lunch. And changed again for visiting, after which they would prepare for dinner.

Within several days, Serena had a basket of calling cards, had returned a half-dozen visits, and had received invitations to one reception, the theater, a ball and two private parties.

Cheswick House bustled with all the preparations. A half-dozen new dresses were not nearly enough. Two more dressmakers were called to stitch up a gown for the ball and a dozen more afternoon and evening dresses.

Serena was hopping with excitement. Her name was in the paper every other day. She was deemed charming, delightful, refined, striking. Diandra was *the tragic young widow,* graceful, restrained, *grief-stricken and game.*

"The wonder is, with all the Americans, that you've gotten all this notice," Leonie said. "It really is in deference to Justin, you know."

"It hasn't hurt you either," Diandra said, as they prepared for an evening out.

"It is true; I am generally not so much on display," Leonie admitted. "It is nice to have that attention. But it never lasts long. A new exotic bird will fly into the coop and divert the roosters before too long."

They were going to the opera, a safe enough activity for the weeping widow. Diandra was dressed in black silk, cut close to her body and covered over with lace which matched the draped underskirt.

She felt excited, elegant, eager to get out.

"That hair . . ." Leonie murmured. "We must do something about that hair. A hat perhaps?"

"I only wear them in the sun."

"A—mantilla, perhaps? Ummm . . . A length of lace, just to . . . cover—it would match the dress as well." With Leonie, the action followed the thought. Which meant she had it ready beforehand, and she draped it over Diandra's hair before Diandra could protest. "That will do."

Anything to keep the peace. Serena was wearing autumn gold, with long gloves, dangling earrings and a headdress to match. Leonie was in blue.

George was their escort; Justin was nowhere in sight.

But she didn't care. She loved the music, the crowds, the after theater crush.

Suddenly, everything seemed exactly the way she had hoped when she had first planned to bring Serena to England. Everything was perfect.

They didn't linger long over refreshments; the crowds were overwhelming. The evening out was enough.

Even George said so, and George disliked opera intensely.

But even he was susceptible to the magic of the music and the mystery of the night.

As his carriage turned into Cheswick Square, he was the one who saw it first: the ghostly gray figure floating in a cloud of mist.

Leonie screamed, "Pamela!" and started to open the carriage door. George grabbed her one side, Diandra on the other, as she fought to break free of them and run after the figure. "Pamela!"

It didn't hear her; it drifted across the road and into the park, and it was gone in the next instant, illusive as air.

"We will summon Pamela."

Leonie was adamant, and she sat at the dining room

table with the divining board in front of her, and she held onto it tightly with both hands.

"Pamela is here. You all saw her. Don't deny it."

"Leonie . . ." George began, trying to be the voice of reason.

"I won't listen. We will summon Pamela."

"That's Agatha's board, my dear. You don't want to use Agatha's board. Surely that's bad luck."

"Nonsense. Serena—the circle of protection, and I don't care if Justin comes in and breaks it."

Serena looked at her blankly, then she blinked and smiled and said, "I think we should summon her too."

"Do the circle."

Diandra felt a chill go down her spine. Something wasn't right here. There had been no manifestations in this house since they had returned. Why now, why tonight? Why Serena's eagerness to aid and abet Leonie?

No one believed in ghosts, in the voice from beyond the grave. But this had gone beyond a mere parlor trick. She didn't know what it was, except that at this moment, she felt very nervous.

Serena walked around the room, her arms outstretched. "We beseech the oracle to bless our board and this circle of protection. We pray that the spirit, the entity, the soul, will hear our pleas and consent to communicate with us through the medium of the blessed board."

She seated herself opposite Leonie and placed her fingers firmly on the planchette.

Leonie drew in a deep breath. "Is the spirit present?"

Diandra made an involuntary move, and George grasped her arm and shook his head. The thing was in motion now; she could do nothing to stop it.

A long long pause before the planchette started moving. "Y . . . e . . . s. Yes."

"Is it Pamela?"

No answer.

Leonie shot a puzzled look at George, and tried again. "Is it Pamela?"

The planchette did not move.

She tried another tack. "What do you wish to tell us."

Slowly, the planchette began to move.

"Waiting."

"Waiting for what?"

"Time."

"What else do you wish to tell us?"

"Love."

"Is this Pamela?"

"Watching."

"Why won't she confirm for us?" Leonie asked plaintively.

There was a movement behind George. Justin had entered the room.

The planchette moved furiously.

"Love."

"Is this Pamela?"

"No."

Everyone held his breath. Leonie gave tremulous voice to the question. "Who?"

"Watching."

"Who?"

Not a movement. Not a sound. Long long seconds passed. No one dared move.

Not Pamela.

"Who?" Leonie asked again, her voice hoarse.

Moments more passed.

And then slowly and painstakingly, the planchette spelled out the shocking name:

"Guthrie."

Everyone froze.

Nobody spoke. Leonie's hands were shaking on the planchette. She looked up at Justin, and shook her head as he took a step forward.

"Is the spirit there?" Her voice was a bare whisper.

The planchette did not move.

"Who are you?"

No movement.

"Are you Guthrie?"

No answer.

The silence thickened as the planchette remained motionless.

"Is the spirit there?" Leonie asked in a strained voice.

Nothing.

Nobody moved. The silence was deadly, awful, threatening.

And then: "Goddamn all of you," and Justin stepped into the circle, swiped his arm across the table, and knocked the board and planchette out of Leonie's hands, and they stared in horror as the board cracked in two when it hit the floor.

Chapter Ten

He was in such a rage, she thought he would kill them all.

"How *did* you do it, Diandra? *How? How?*"

He wanted to shake her. He wanted to lash out at someone. The abomination of it—taking his father's name in vain, making it into sleight of hand, a party trick.

Leonie couldn't move. She stared at the broken board, made a move to pick it up, and then stopped. "How could *you?*" she whispered brokenly. "Now how will we contact Pamela?"

"There *was* no contact with Pamela."

"God, you are cruel," Leonie cried.

"And what is this? Tell me what this is? A devil's game? You don't care who you blaspheme, do you, Leonie? Do you?"

"I'm going to bed," Leonie said, her voice laced with hurt and anger. "You can't *make* someone believe. Pamela is here, whether you believe it or not. Are you coming, Serena?"

Serena flashed a glance at Diandra and followed Leonie out.

And then it was just Diandra and George, and Justin standing at the head of the table, his hands knotted around a chair.

"This will stop, right here, right now, this minute. Millbank will burn the board. And if there is another manifestation of any kind in this house, I will ship you back to Calcutta and announce to the world what I've done. Do you understand me? Do you, Diandra?"

What a threat; as if she cared what anyone in London thought. But Serena . . . oh, Serena—

"I swear to you—"

"George . . ."

George blew out a breath. "I don't understand it, Justin. I don't."

"This was not part of our bargain."

"No."

"I could have been a thousand miles away from here by now but for duty—doing *what is right.*"

"Granted, Justin."

"I can't reconcile what happened here tonight."

"Nobody can."

"And I've had enough of trumpery and deceit."

"I know. Go to bed, Justin."

"I want to wring someone's neck." He looked directly at Diandra and she cringed. "I could kill Leonie for pursuing this."

"Go to bed, Justin."

"Damn them all . . ."

"Justin . . ." There was a distinct warning in George's tone.

Justin looked at him closely and then nodded. "This isn't the end of it though."

"We know."

They watched him withdraw from the room.

There was a long potent silence.

"It wasn't fair," George said finally.

"I don't care what he thinks, I didn't do it," Diandra said.

"He doesn't believe that. And I don't know *what* I believe. So you'd best go to bed too, Diandra. There's nothing you can do here."

They rose together, and he took her arm to escort her out the door.

There was a faint thumping sound behind them.

"What was that?" He whirled suddenly, almost knocking her off her feet. "Oh, dear God—Diandra . . . look!"

She wheeled around.

The board was back on the table, fused together whole, the planchette on top of it, and the velvet pouches folded neatly beside.

The board was gone by morning.

"Well," Leonie said huffily. "Millbank has done his job, and we'll just have to find our own board. Meantime, we have a ball to attend. Diandra—the black satin for you. Serena—the ivory dress that Louise made for you. For this, we call in a hairdresser and all the maids. This is the opening event of the season."

It took a full day to prepare for it. The morning ride first, for exercise to stir the body; breakfast in bed after. A long leisurely bath. A day of lounging around in one's robe, making sure one's dress was ironed and properly laid out. And then, the hairdresser came into their rooms and worked on their hair one by one.

Leonie first, her dark hair drawn up and rolled and tucked and pinned, with several stray strands caressing her neck and cheeks.

Serena next—the vision of innocence, her hair wound around in the style of a Greek goddess and festooned with pearls.

Diandra last, her gilt hair parted in the middle and drawn up in a loose knot on top of her head.

The dresses came next, and after everything was tucked, tacked and smoothed out, it was six o'clock and time to leave for the ball.

"You'll be behind the screen, of course," Leonie said. "No dancing. Your appearance is a mere formality; you are Serena's chaperone, after all. You may engage in conversation. You may not encourage any gentlemen. You are permitted to accept condolences. I daresay someone will want to reminisce; it is up to you whether you have the stamina to listen. I really think that dress is too fast; it doesn't look like mourning at all. Do you have your lace mantllla? Are we ready?"

She was like a general, gearing her soldiers for battle.

But she knew what a crush it would be even as early as when they would arrive at Lord and Lady Langham's townhouse,

Diandra had never seen so many diamonds, tiaras and beaded gowns as they pressed their way up the steps and into the reception hall.

And Leonie knew everyone, and made brief introductions as they moved along the reception line.

George joined them, his expression dead serious, but at what point Diandra couldn't say, because she had been too busy looking at everyone and everything. He just turned up suddenly at her elbow.

They entered a two-story ballroom that was awash in light from overhanging gas chandeliers. Above them, in an alcove, an orchestra played. Below them, two steps down into the ballroom, couples were waltzing. And there were chairs set out all around the entry tier, and there were knots of people sitting and talking, and moving from group to group.

Further to the right of where they stood, close by the windows, there was a small lace folding screen, behind which Diandra could just make out a half dozen ladies sitting and talking.

Her *purdah,* obviously. But what did it matter—Leonie was introducing Serena to everyone and even as she stood poised on the steps, she was being solicited to dance, and her card was filling fast.

Or perhaps there was some method in Leonie's madness: they had come reasonably early, well before the heiress contingent, when young beautiful women were at a premium, as even she could tell from looking around the ballroom. An excellent strategy on Leonie's part.

For that she was perfectly willing to be consigned to the *cemetery.*

"Oh, and who is this?" one matron demanded as Leonie escorted her behind the screen.

"This is the my lady Diandra Reynell, the window of the Earl of Skene. Perhaps you've read she's in Town, from Calcutta, with her sister, Miss Serena Morant? Diandra, this is Lady Theresa Pettigill."

Lady Theresa eyed her through her quizzing glass. "I see. Well, have a seat, my dear. I daresay we can be as entertaining as any coxcomb on the dance floor."

And they were, those elderly ladies. Not for them the niceties of societal mores. They were wicked gossipy old ladies and they talked more about Justin than she'd ever thought possible.

Of course, they were garnering information too. One of them had known Guthrie, and they'd all known Lady Pamela Hull.

"Tragedy, that," Lady Theresa told her. "Never could figure out why he was so avid to go. Pamela didn't have any say in it, that was the worst thing. He was going, and he was going to leave the boy, and she could stay or come as she wanted. She couldn't let him go alone now, could she? But then—the boy—he had to stay. They put 'im in boarding school and then sent 'im up to Christchurch. Genius with money, Justin is. Crazy with grief when Pamela was reported dead. Shock when it came through about his father. He couldn't go, either. Didn't want to. Didn't know what was the point about going to India after the fact. Can't imagine how he received *you*."

That was blunt. And to the point. She had never ever thought about how Justin had gotten the news or how he grieved. Had never thought about anything but her own desire to get Serena to London.

No wonder he'd gone top over tail when his father's name was spelled out on the board.

"He was very gracious," she said carefully. "I had written to him several months earlier. He engaged Lady Leonie to supervise my sister's debut, and it's all been very— cordial."

"He's a mannered man," Lady Theresa said, tapping her arm with her fan. "But he's simmering inside. Trust me. No man likes to have what he loves taken from him like that. Taken twice too: once by the service and the second by fate. How difficult is that for a boy?"

"He's not a boy now."

"Ah, but he grieves like one," Lady Theresa said.

Another stunning insight, almost physical in its intensity.

"And look, he's here, he's dancing." This was Lady Margaret Bagnot. "Well now, I haven't seen him in several years. He's standing up with his sister-in-law. Wasn't she a one, coming so late to her parents? Round and about Justin's age, she is. Never married, not that she wasn't asked. They do look well together."

Diandra peeked out from behind the screen. And there

he was, waltzing with Leonie, whose transgressions apparently were shelved in her closet back at Cheswick Square. It was like nothing had happened last night. He was smiling, animated, social, trading off partners, and then dancing in sucession with one and another of the young elegant women who started to crowd around Leonie.

He even danced with Serena.

"He needs to get married." Lady Theresa, nodding sagely.

Lady Theresa's comment shocked her. And her succeeding thought: *not* to Leonie.

"Oh, he needs to start thinking about an heir," Lady Theresa said. "And doesn't he look grand with Grace Partram?"

Grand, Diandra thought irritatedly. Just . . . grand. Any one of those beautiful women would have made him a suitable wife, but he hadn't yet chosen one. And it wasn't for the lack of *their* trying.

They were all beautiful—and grand. And hungry for his title. While he—he craved retribution, and only then would he banish all his ghosts, past, present, real and imagined, and finally lay the dead to rest.

In the end, he came for her, and long before the ball was over. It was well after the arrival of the heiresses, which caused an enormous stir. And even though Serena was relegated to the sidelines, she wanted to stay on, and Leonie and George were willing.

He, however, had had enough. Had she?

She was enjoying the company no end, she assured him, but yes, she was ready to return home.

He paid his respects to her companions, remembering something personal about each of them, as he took their hands in turn.

"Bring your stepmother back to us," Lady Theresa said. "She's excellent company."

He sent her a simmering look. "We do know that, ma'am. And we will, I promise we will."

They came out into the brisk night air, and his mood turned grim, almost as if he had removed a mask.

There were carriages already lined up two by two in front of the townhouse. He would have walked if he had been alone, but he found the Skene carriage easily enough, and they rode back to Cheswick Square in a suffocating silence.

Millbank opened the door. "Brandy in the library, sir."

"Much needed, thank you." He handed over his cape. "Madam?"

She didn't like the look on his face. "Must I?"

"In fact, you must," he said, and she didn't think she wanted to argue with him.

She preceded him into the library and took the chair opposite his desk where she had engaged him the first time

The first time . . . when he was desperate to get rid of her and not above bribing her, attacking her, insulting her, accusing her of chicanery and deceit, and having had a hand in his father's death.

And then all of that mitigated by the visit to Skene and the sumptuous netherlife of the voudrais—*which had nothing at all to do with him or his world.*

She would do well to remember that.

He poured his brandy, took a sip and began prowling the room.

"Just tell me how and why you are doing this, madam, and we'll consider the episode closed."

She stiffened. "I thought you closed it very effectively last night."

"The board is missing."

She caught her breath.

"I can only assume you took it because you are the only one who saw what happened."

"I didn't see anything. It was on the table, in one piece, twenty minutes after you threw it on the floor."

"Exactly. So we come to the point, madam. The board is missing when I distinctly said I wanted Millbank to dispose of it. I don't believe in spirits and ghosts and divining boards bringing messages from the beyond the grave. There can be only one answer, the one I deduced all along—it is your game, your distraction, and I am ending it now. You sail from Dover in one week."

She felt the shock from the top of her head to her toes, and she said the first thing that came into her head. "I don't think so, Justin."

"You will not make a scene over this, and you cannot embarrass anyone but yourself if you persist in remaining where it is clear you are not wanted."

Oh, but he had wanted her . . .

. . . grieving like a child . . .

Only after Guthrie's name had been spelled out on the board—

"I tell you again, this is none of my doing, Justin."

"I don't believe you." He eased behind his desk, pulled out the top drawer and withdrew two envelopes which he placed on top of the desk.

The letters lay there, innocent, primed, explosive. And he sat there and let her wonder about them, and about what they had to do with her.

And then he picked up one of them and handed to her.

Second shock: Guthrie's handwriting on the envelope.

"Read it."

His voice, his eyes were ice.

She opened it slowly and removed the single sheet inside.

My dear Son,

    I am writing to impart the most awful news a father could ever deliver to a son: your mother is missing and believed to have died in a suicide attempt.
    Her clothing and a note were found beside the river which was swollen from the rain. The authorities believe she was swept away, and that she jumped of her own volition.
    Every attempt has been made to find the body, with no success thus far.
    Yet I still hope, while I mourn for my beautiful Pamela and for your bereavement as well, my son. I'm at a loss to see how to proceed from here.
    I will write when there is further news.

                                     Skene

"There *was* no further news, was there?" she asked in a flat voice as she refolded the letter and gave it back to him.

"There was this, two years later." He handed her the second letter.

My dear Son,

    I write to ask you for your blessing and good wishes. By the time you receive this, I will be married. She is Miss Diandra Morant, the sister of the Honorable Hugh Morant, the governor of Rajam Province who has been my great good friend these several years past.
    I feel your pain for the ongoing loss of your mother; I assure you that everything conceivable was done to try to recover her body, and when none of the efforts prevailed,

she was officially declared deceased six months after the accident.

I hardly dared hope to find companionship ever again, let alone a consuming love, but I have, dear boy. Diandra is my flower, my angel, my innocent, my love, and she comes to me at a time when I take the greatest step in my life and my career, and by God's grace, I do so with her by my side.

I cherish the memory of your mother, dear boy; I will always love her. No one could ever replace her. She has a place in my heart no one will ever touch. But I pray that you will wish me well in my new endeavor and with the new companion of my life, and I hope there is some solace in your knowing that I am content.

Skene

N.B. I have detailed the arrangements I wish to implement for my Diandra, now and in the event of my death. I trust you will carry out my wishes.

She could hardly bear to read the words. *My flower, my angel, my innocent* . . . such a callous thing to write to a son a mere year after his mother's demise. Or had he been so deliriously in love? Had she?

"How did you do it?" he murmured. "Made him forget honor and family and succession and everything he had held dear."

"No, he gave it all up when he went to India," she said slowly. "I didn't seduce him, Justin. India did."

"I could almost believe you. I can see why he did. The *arrangements* tell all. *Now and in the event of my death* . . . I know just how you manipulated that. He was lonely and besotted and you were young and willing. His *flower* . . . You could have stayed in India forever on that money; you could have lived like a queen. No one would have had a question in the world about his death. Why would you leave yourself open to that?''

He was right, of course. She would have been perfectly content to stay in Bhaumaghar. "I needed to get away; Serena *wanted* to get away. Hugh encouraged us. It was as simple as that. I never thought . . ."

"And so we were invaded by ghosts."

"You cannot believe that."

"You don't want to know what I believe. It isn't pretty. And it isn't nearly as simple as you paint it."

"Why don't you color it in for me, Justin? Complete the picture. Let me see with your clarity of vision."

He stared at her for a long moment, debating. She could feel it: she could feel the impact already, and he hadn't said a word.

"You are an adventuress, madam. A tart, a whore, a manipulator who caught a vulnerable man in a moment when he was lonely and needed solace. And you reeled him in beautifully. I wonder he didn't see through you. You are every bit as strong-willed as Pamela ever was, and he called you *his innocent*. How deluded could he have been? It has been a pleasure matching wits with you, but now you have taken it one step too far, and you have to bear the consequences. I will no longer honor you as his widow.

"And I promise you, I can bankrupt you. You may have the money, but I hold the investments, and that on my honor, madam. And while I have been very fortunate on the Exchange, there have been some years that I have taken great losses. One can never predict the ups and downs of the Exchange, Diandra. I trust you understand me."

"Perfectly," she bit out. There was no talking to the man. Not at all. She was to take her money and Serena and return to India and play lady aristocrat there. She had never been so humiliated in her life.

. . . grieving like a child . . . ha! This was not even a man, this was a monster, determined to wield power and destroy innocents.

And this on top of every other insult. She was breathless with rage, shaking in her impotence, mortified by her surrender.

And she hadn't done anything at all. Guthrie had done this, and Hugh, by his insistence that she come.

She had an odd chilling thought as she rose stiffly from her chair and made her way to the door.

Everything led back to Guthrie.

She had no idea what it meant, she didn't want to think about it, and she was already planning the remove from Cheswick Square.

So she didn't see it until she had almost breached the top of the stairs, and she nearly tripped over it because she didn't expect it to be there.

But there it was, right in front of her on the landing: the divining board, the planchette and the neatly folded pouches.

Gita would not touch them, and so Diandra gingerly picked them up, after debating whether she ought to just leave them there, and brought them to her room and laid them on a table.

Under light, they looked like gorgeous items of silky burnished wood that was pleasing to the touch, with the letters incised in scrolling print on the board, and the planchette fashioned in a small rounded triangle on a tripod of brass.

She pushed it with her fingertip and it slid easily across the board to touch the letter *S*.

Surely not purposefully?

She didn't believe in it anyway. And if she were smart, she would plant it in Leonie's room and let Justin's wrath rain all over her.

Or, she could just . . . try it—

She placed her fingers on the planchette and waited.

She noted that her hands were trembling, and her arms, and that there was a peculiar resonating shimmer in the planchette, and in her body.

She noted that everything went very very still, and that the only thing she was aware of was her fingers pressing against the slickly finished surface of the planchette.

She felt as if everything were in shadow and the whole of her energy was concentrated on the board.

As if there were a bright light and she was at the center of it.

As if everything were illuminated and perfectly clear.

And then the planchette moved, spelling out four succinct letters which she read out loud: "S . . . t . . . a . . . y —stay . . ." and then she involuntarily lifted her fingers from the planchette, almost as if they had been forced away.

Had she felt something?. Or had she imagined it?

This evening never happened.

Everybody knew. Nobody told.

Ghosts and Guthrie, somehow interrelated, but all in her imagination because madam was invited in no uncertain terms to leave. And now she had been given an unnerving message to stay.

She heard Serena come in sometime toward one o'clock, and she only wanted to sit and recapitulate the small triumphs of the evening.

It was Lord this and Honorable that who had spoken

for her in dance after dance, and the kindest of ladies, and many compliments on her dress, and Leonie was perfectly wonderful, and why had Hugh immured them in Bhaumaghar when they could have been living this delightful way in London?

How to tell her they were being given their *congé?* Better now than first thing in the morning.

"I'm afraid all plans have changed, Serena."

"Oh? How is that?"

"Well—we *are* leaving, as I have wanted to, but not by my desire. Justin has had his fill of ghosts and tricks and he lays it all at my door and will not have us in the house another week. We sail for Calcutta Monday next."

She watched Serena's face melt down from utter happiness to complete dismay. "I don't believe you. And I won't go. This can't be true, Diandra. You must have angered him somehow and you have to go apologize this instant. We are not leaving."

"It's true, and we are."

"I'm not. I'm *not.* This calls for the direst methods, the strongest charms. Where are my bags? my coins, my holy stone? We were getting along so well, he and I. He danced with me, Diandra, and he was so charming."

"They do know how to put on a good face."

"He's not a liar."

"They can do what they want. He was very specific and very precise about the means by which he intended to coerce me."

"He can't do that. No matter what he said, he can't. What can he do? He wouldn't dare do anything."

"Money," she said simply, and it only intensified the threat. She had learned so well how to live with it, and she never wanted to be without it again.

"But—but . . . Guthrie—"

"He holds the investments that pay into my funds."

Serena sank onto her bed as if her knees had given way. "He can't do this . . . no, I won't let him do this . . ."

"Serena . . . we'll just pack and go to a hotel. I won't stay here past tomorrow morning. And he won't make a scene at a hotel."

"Well, I'm going to help. We'll make a circle of protection, and he won't be able to cast us out. I need a candle. Gita! A lighted candle. And my holy stone—" She looked up into Diandra's wary eyes. "Oh, don't be stupid, Diandra. This can only help. Didn't we change his mind the first time?"

She hadn't thought *they* had. "I don't like this, Serena."

"You don't know anything. I'm going to do it anyway." She reached out as Gita handed her the candle, and paced her way around the four corners of the room, murmuring to herself.

Then she walked in a circle around the entire room, speaking so that Diandra could hear her words: "Oracle of the night, I beseech you, grant us protection from whomever would harm us, and keep us safe in your holy light."

She blew out the candle and sat down. "There. It's done. And tomorrow he will change his mind."

But she could not sleep. The combination of Serena chanting spells and her own eerie possession of the board was enough to unsettle anyone.

She tossed and turned and finally awakened so early in the morning, no one was about. Easier that way. She could begin packing and planning, and have it half done by the time Serena got up.

This trip had been a horrible exercise in futility and humiliation. And it hadn't diminished Serena's dependence on superstitious nonsense one bit.

Her mind worked furiously as she laid clothes and accessories out on the bed.

She would reimburse Justin for the expenses he had laid

out in their behalf. She would give the maids a little extra for their help. She would be especially grateful to Leonie for her willingness to take them on.

A hundred details occurred to her as the sun rose and she had everything arranged to her satisfaction.

What to do about the board, however, was a searing and troubling question.

She summoned Jhasa at eight-thirty. "This time, we are truly in need of place to stay. Can it be done by noon?"

"As you wish, mem," he murmured as he bowed and withdrew.

He was treasure—unobtrusive and intuitive, and he would not fail her.

She and Rajit brought in the trunks. "Is Miss Serena awake?"

"I will ascertain, mem."

Her people were loyal, and she counted on that. Gita began laying the clothes into the trunks and alleviated that chore.

Now she had only to decide what to do about the board.
. . . *stay* . . .

The message was a clear as if it had been spoken.

And simultaneously, there was a sharp knock on her door. She opened it to find one of the footmen with a tray of tea and scones, followed by Leonie who was greatly agitated.

She stopped short as she saw the trunks. "Put the tray on that table, thank you. Diandra, what's this?"

So Justin hadn't told her. "The short version? Justin wants us to leave and so we shall. This morning."

Leonie ran her fingers through her already touseled hair. "But you can't do that, Diandra. Something awful has happened." Her voice broke and she stopped for a moment to regain her composure. "Something horrible.

Grace Partram was found dead this morning, in the park, and the inspector says nobody is to leave the house."

"See?" Serena said from the connecting doorway to their rooms. "I told you. He changed his mind. We don't have to go."

[faded text from previous page visible at top]

Chapter Eleven

Fate . . . in the vaporous hands of spirits that worked in mysterious ways . . .

Lovely Grace Partram, swirling away with Justin at a dance, beautiful and grand and dead now—

It was inconceivable.

Serena looked so smug. "You really must have faith, Diandra."

Diandra ignored her. "Tell me the whole."

Leonie clasped her shaking hands together. "She was found this morning, in the bushes, strangled. No one knows how; she lives in Mayfair. She left the ball well after we did and wasn't seen since. The inspector, Stiles, I think his name is, has been to all the surrounding houses, but as you might guess, no one attended the ball except us, and so we are the focal point of his questioning right now. He will want to see you and Serena, and he was adamant that no one was to leave this house until he said so."

"We'll be down directly then." She was amazed at her calm, and furious at Serena's complacency. "Serena . . ."

Her sharp tone made an impression.

"Yes, of course," Serena murmured. "Of course, we'll answer any questions."

She sounded so subdued, but Diandra knew better. The moment the door closed, Serena pulled her into a wild waltz around the room. "I told you, I told you, I told you. The charm worked. The circle protected us. You'll see, Diandra. Everything will work out just the way we want it to."

Nothing, however, was more real than Inspector Stiles. He awaited them in the library, quiet, unobtrusive, the kind of man you wouldn't look at twice on the street. But tenacious as a bulldog; it was in his eyes. He was seated at Justin's desk, leafing through a small notebook, and he looked up as they entered and waved them to two chairs that had been placed in front of the desk.

"Good morning, ladies. Lady Diandra?" He looked at her first, made a note, and then acknowledged Serena. "So . . . this is what we know. Miss Grace Partram was seen last night at the Langham ball. This morning she was found dead in Cheswick Square park, and so we are questioning everyone who attended the ball, and of course, particular attention attaches to those living in or around Cheswick Square. Now, Lady Diandra, had you ever met Miss Partram?"

"No." Was that too simple an answer? She tried to gauge how much to explain, and then jumped right in at his encouraging expression. "As you may know, we have only just arrived from Calcutta so we really haven't had time to make the acquaintance of anyone in town. I believe the invitation to the ball was tendered on the Earl's behalf as a kindness."

"You hadn't met her?"

"She was pointed out to me by Lady Theresa Pettigill when she was waltzing with the Earl. I have never met her."

"Miss Serena?"

"I believe—I do believe that Lady Leonie Hull, my sponsor, introduced us. But it was such a crush, and there were so many gentlemen asking for dances and I don't think I could honestly say whether I met her or not."

"I see." He made a note. And he made Diandra exceedingly nervous. "But you can say, Lady Diandra, that because Lady Pettigill called your attention to her, that you were made aware of who she was?"

"Yes."

"And if someone had asked you to—oh, deliver a message to Miss Grace Partram, you could have identified her and done so?"

Nothing to hide. "I believe so."

Another note. He looked at Serena. "Miss Serena?"

Serena looked startled. "What?"

"Could you have identified Miss Partram if someone had asked you to point her out?"

Serena hesitated a moment. "I—no, I don't think so. There were so many people, Inspector," she added with a helpless little wave of her hand.

"Of course there were," he agreed instantly. "Nevertheless, that's very helpful. Now, I assume I may contact you here in case there are any more questions?"

No hesitation there. "Oh, absolutely, Inspector," Serena said confidently. "We'll be here."

"But what else could he ask?" Leonie said after he had left. "We've all known Grace forever, she was sweet as a flower, and I can't imagine who would ever want to harm her."

"So you got a reprieve, madam," Justin said tightly, later, in private. "How clever. Of course, it isn't too much to

assume you might commit mayhem in the name of further-
ing your plans.''

"Oh, I see. Since you think I had a hand in your father's
death, you deduced that by extension, for some outrageous
reason, I went after that poor girl? Are you crazy, Justin?
Or just desperate?''

Even he didn't know. She was outraged; but she was
always on the offensive with him. He had deliberately put
her there. But it didn't diminish the pull-tug he felt. He
wanted to shake her, throttle her, throw her on the floor,
and take her ten times over.

She was never more desirable than when she was retaliat-
ing against some of his more shocking allegations, and on
any given day, he couldn't have defined what he believed
about her and what he didn't.

"Perhaps tonight is the night for a *séance*, madam. Perhaps *that poor girl* could tell us. If, of course, you would
hand over the divining board.''

"You are crazy. I don't have it.'' *Small, small lie.*

"Don't you . . . ?''

"I won't play word games with you, Justin. Or try to
convince you. We are here for the duration of the investiga-
tion into Grace Partram's death, and you'll just have to
come to terms with that.''

"Exactly,'' he murmured. "Terms. I like the idea of
terms.''

She felt like throwing something. "You are in no position
to bargain, Justin. There is nothing you have that I cannot
obtain for myself.''

She could have bitten her tongue once the words were
out of her mouth. The look on his face was positively
diabolical.

"Really, madam?'' His voice was silky smooth, his eyes
like blue fire. She knew exactly what he was thinking and
what he meant. "I could think of half dozen things *I* could

do for you that . . . well, suffice it to say, we could come to some kind of accommodation. While it is true that Stiles would prefer to have us all in one coop, as it were, you are perfectly free to leave. I obviously can't force you to return to India when he requires your presence in London.

"But who is to say what ridiculous rumors would be bruited about if you were to leave Cheswick Square in the wake of that poor girl's death? Some kind of nonsense about spirits and *séances* . . . ? No, I think we do have something on which to bargain, and I think, Diandra, you already know the terms."

"Hardly blackmail, Justin."

"Call it an excuse then."

"Very pragmatic. Very male. You've called me a whore and now you wish to make me one."

"And you've taken your pleasure like one. All you need do is continue on."

"How nice for you."

"And you," he shot back; he knew exactly what he was doing and why—he wanted her, and he wanted her with the fury that other men must have desired her. He wanted to devour her and contain her.

He wanted to *know* the whole of how she made men so wild for her that they lost every vestige of sanity. He wanted—

"It was all in your imagination, Justin," she said finally. "We will forget you even mentioned the matter."

"Oh, I don't think so," he said, and she knew he was right: it was there, on the table, compounded of knowledge and desire. She could close the door on him, but she could not shut out everything that had happened, or the murder of poor Grace Partram.

Grace Partram, looking just grand . . .

. . . he needs to be thinking about an heir . . .

. . . and she needed to stop thinking about—that—

His proposition was making her crazy. She was going to stay as far away from him as possible.

And she had too many things to do anyway: she needed to cancel yet another suite of rooms that Jhasa had engaged for them. And she and Serena needed to ready themselves for an evening out, a private dinner, which Justin would not attend, and where she was sure the whole of the conversation would center around *poor Grace Partram.*

"I think the inspector would do well to call in a medium," Leonie said as they drove to the Carstairs townhouse which was a short distance away from Cheswick Square in Belgravia. "He said it himself, there are no clues, no motives, no one who wished her ill. How else can he pursue the murderer then? He truly needs some otherworldly help. I wonder if Pamela . . ."

"Dear Lord," Diandra interrupted exasperatedly. "Pamela is dead. The girl is dead. No one is going to speak to us from beyond the grave."

"You have too little trust," Leonie said. "And you don't believe anything we've experienced. But Serena does. She and I both have think a message will be revealed to us."

"For heaven's sake . . . how? *Do* the Carstairs have a divining board?"

"Oh, do you know, I never thought to ask them . . ."

They were all crazy. She was going crazy.

And the Carstairs home was too evocative of things that reminded her of Bhaumaghar. Colonel Carstairs had served in India, it turned out, and had brought back many souvenirs and artifacts, pictures and furniture, and all of it decorated his townhouse.

The scent of sandalwood permeated the air and she felt, instantly, all the emotions, longings and pangs of memories that she had sought to escape by bringing Serena to London.

Nor could she take any pleasure in Serena's inclusion

in this social evening; it reminded her too much of other evenings in the sultry heat of a hill country summer.

For Serena's sake, she suppressed her desire to leave the house the instant she walked in, but all through the opening minuet of introductions and assessments, all she wanted to do was bolt.

It turned out to be a pleasant enough dinner; the Carstairses had invited several other friends, including two eligible Honorables for Leonie and Serena. But all the conversation centered around the murder, and any likely suspect, of which there were terribly few, and Leonie talked far too much about spirits and contacting the dead.

Before they even set up for cards, Diandra pleaded a headache and begged to be excused. They hardly even noticed when she left, and she was driven back to Cheswick Square in the Carstairses' carriage.

Millbank let her into the house and she fled up to her room and threw herself on the bed without even undressing.

A moment alone, without ghosts, manifestations or indictments . . . she closed her eyes and drew in a deep breath. Silence in the house. A bone-deep pulsating silence.

A contemplative quiet that soothed her. The kind of quiet she had immersed herself in after she had come to terms with Guthrie's death.

Had she loved him?

. . . My angel, my love, my flower . . .

All those feelings, buried in such a shallow grave—not interred with him . . .

How could he have left her like that, with every need and longing dangling after her like apron strings; surely he hadn't wanted someone else to catch them? To catch her?

His creation, his creature of the senses . . . his innocent who wanted nothing more than to please him . . .

She had learned that well . . . what she hadn't comprehended was how to submerge all those voluptuous feelings when the source, the mentor, the creator was gone.

Nor had she appreciated that there were traps around every corner—a beautiful flower, a lovely painting, a sultry day, a scent—anything had the power to arouse that glistening passion that would subvert her life yet again.

Even a man.

The worst man.

A vile man with a vile proposition.

He hadn't even needed to say it. It was between them, no matter how hard she tried to suppress it.

And did she care when her blood pumped so heatedly through her veins?

But she knew the answer to that. When the blood was hot, all that mattered was a body and a moment.

And this had become the night she wanted to seek the moment.

He had been the one who had instigated it, with the subtle message of the voudrais. *She could have another life, it said. And it would be completely separate and apart from everything else.*

Just like a man.

Or a woman of the evening . . .

She inhaled deeply. No scent of sandalwood here, yet it permeated her soul. And a dinner with the Carstairs that caressed the memory of dinners at home: touches of cumin, coriander, tumeric and saffron laced through stuffed fish, pilaf, cauliflower and beans, and a spinach salad.

Tastes that sat on the tongue like spirits conjuring up echoes of the past.

She would not give in to it.

Or she would . . .

Who would know, after all? Everyone was out, Leonie would not be leaving the Carstairses' until well after midnight, if not later, by the look of things when she had departed.

Her need was like a river, roaring in her ears, in her mind, rushing to drench her molten core.

What man has taught me . . .

Slowly she undressed, savoring the moment. It was the moment when her breath caught short, and her imagination went wild. When she slipped out of her dress, her petticoat, her corset and her padding; the moment she released all constraints and her body became soft and moist, and pliable, and willing.

Only then did she feel the sweet spot of recognition when need and excitement converged and obliterated every logical objection, every common-sense consideration.

She closed her bedroom door softly behind her and, by the light of a candle, she made her way down to the basement.

The netherworld, the place apart, the land of pleasure peaks— and the valleys of guilt. But that she left outside the door.

It was arranged exactly as it had been at Skene. The ornate double doors leading to a lush velvet curtain, through which she emerged into a cell very similar to that in the *voudrais*.

The walls were draped in velvet. The floor was covered with a dense oriental rug. There was one small mahogany dresser in one corner, and a lamp on that. And in the center, an armless sofa, tufted in a rich creamy brocade.

. . . do what you will . . .

She set the candlestick down next to the unlit lamp, and she removed her wrapper and lay down naked on the sofa.

It was warm in the cell. She felt a sense of heightened anticipation, as if she knew something would happen, that psychically she had called to him, and in spite of her denials this afternoon, he would answer.

No, not he—someone . . . who could join with her, couple with her, explode with her . . .

All she wanted, all that mattered—

She never heard him enter, didn't see him at all. Her eyes were closed and at the moment she became aware of someone, she felt a cool cloth pressed against her eyes.

"You knew I would come . . ." His voice was barely above a breath.

"I knew—"

"Don't move—"

She couldn't. Her body felt heavy, languid, almost drugged. He hadn't touched her, but it felt as if he had. Or the texture of his voice had, like warm thick honey spread all over her.

And then something else touched her, and she couldn't grasp quite what, because it flicked all over her, like light hot drops spattering her body, soft, arousing, a touch here, a swipe there . . . it took her breath away; it made her skin ache, longing for the next erotic contact.

She was not to move. She was not to know.

His hand, hot and firm, stayed her when she stirred.

"Be still."

"I can't."

"You will."

And he waited; that was the worst part, when he knew that she wanted it, badly.

She felt it suddenly dancing for an instant on her ankle. A moment later, on her mouth like a feathery kiss. A long pause, and then it brushed between her breasts. A dot against her wrist and her pulses jumped. A tap behind her knee. A swirl over her nipples. A tap on her hipbone. A light breath of sensation behind her ear and down her jaw. An immediate jump to her toes. And a long lingering pull up to her thighs and between her legs, followed by a long throbbing pause.

Her body tingled. She reached out her hand and felt it

graze her palm. An instant later, it nestled again between her legs and she pushed against it.

But it was as ephemeral as air. There was nothing there but her escalating need.

It touched the base of her throat, and then swirled down to her belly in an intricate sensual pattern.

She shivered and it was gone and nothing touched her for a long long while except the sense of his heat and control.

She was not going to beg.

She lay still, so still, the touches still resonating deep inside her. Now she didn't want to know what was the source of such sublime pleasure. She wanted to feel it; her body ached to experience it. She could still feel its erotic track burning her damp skin.

She was certain he knew it, the way he knew everything else about her. She moved her hips subtly, impatiently. She couldn't wait, she wanted it, she needed it.

At his mercy.

No, at the mercy of the point of pleasure, which was exactly where she wanted to be.

She felt the touch again, just at her feminine fold.

Yes . . . she had been waiting for this—the touch, the place, the moment of fulfillment . . .

She braced herself to receive it, but there was no penetration and she made a low keening sound at the back her throat.

She felt it come between her legs again, pushing them apart this time so that she was exposed to this most luxurious sensation. Something was brushing her between her legs in long luscious strokes, and she undulated wildly, trying to find its hard thrusting center.

But there was only the titillating sensation of something swirling around her thighs and between her legs, teasing her, taunting her, and daring her to capture its elusiveness.

And just as suddenly, there was nothing, just the dark and the spangling sensations against her skin, and the craving for more.

It was so quiet, a deep-seated, hungering stillness while she waited for what would come next.

And there would be something next; she felt it, she was certain of it. Every nerve ending in her body screamed for it.

Slowly, insidiously, he was there, the hot carnal caress of his tongue seeking her, enveloping her, insinuating himself into her. Deeper into her, moving, pressing, exploring her.

Like that, and like that—she spread her legs wider, she laced her hands through his hair, she bore down on him, and she rode the pointed thrusting invasion of his tongue.

All in the dark, all, her fantasies swirling in the dark like thundering horses; like the thunder of blood coursing through her veins so that she knew she was gloriously alive—

Like that, in the dark, with touches and kisses, and deep stroking movements of his tongue, he seduced her all over again, in the dark.

There was nothing else, just the point of his tongue against the pleasure point of her, coaxing her, pushing her, taking her, just that, just that, just that—she tried to hold back, she tried not to fall, and then she felt the telltale twinge of the first molten spasm that sent her spiralling over the edge.

Down she fell into a slide of incandescent light, white-hot, glittering on her skin, crackling all over her body in sizzling convulsions from her head to her toes.

He held her and he felt every torrid undulation of her climax. And when she was done, he pulled her legs over the side of the sofa so that he could fit between them, and he knelt and rubbed himself against her bush and belly until in one mighty spurt, he ejaculated all over her.

In the darkness still, she tried to hold him there, to contain his root and his seed. She loved the feel of it on her heated body, and the stickiness of it as she rubbed into her skin.

It made such a difference in the dark. In the dark, everything was possible; no thought required.

Only he was not in the dark, and after many long moments, neither was she. She felt something touch her skin, and then the certain sense that he was gone.

She lifted the cloth from her eyes, and levered herself up on one elbow. She was alone in the room, and draped across her belly was the answer to all questions, and his chosen instrument of torture: the corded tassel from the belt of her wrapper.

"The dear inspector still hasn't a clue as to why poor Grace was murdered," Leonie said the next morning. "And now everyone's scared there's a killer on the loose."

"There is," Diandra said dryly.

"But that's ridiculous. That means everyone will stay home and the season will just disintegrate. I for one won't have it. We have too much to do. We had great fun at the Carstairses' last night. Too bad you were indisposed. I trust you are better this morning and up for our usual ride."

Up wasn't quite the word she would have used. *Up* was what had transpired last night in the *voudrais*. But men, and the women who serviced them, never spoke about that. "Of course. Serena will be down in a moment."

"She's showing to good advantage. That should please you."

"It does, except that my purpose was not particularly to have anyone offer for her."

"It's hers," Leonie said trenchantly. "And why not? If she had money behind her, she would do just as well as any other girl, barring the heiresses. They are something else again. However, Honorables don't pursue them, but they do go after girls like Serena. I don't suppose you've considered settling some money on her?"

That was a fast jab; she felt her head spin and she had to think a moment before she answered. "We hadn't talked about, the possibility of her meeting and marrying someone here. But yes, of course, I would—"

"Good. And I trust you've got a will besides."

That was none of Leonie's business. "Yes," she said succinctly.

"Excellent. But I expect that was one of the conditions of your original settlement. Guthrie was nothing if not very thorough. When he married Pamela, he—well, that's very much in the past, of course. Everything probably reverted to Justin anyway. The only important thing was if you were willing to provide for Serena, and you are, so that is the end of that."

They took their morning carriage ride, following Serena who cantered alongside in her usual fashion.

There didn't seem to be any fewer people out in the park that morning. Serena veered off once or twice to speak with an acquaintance and then came trotting back to join them with a juicy tidbit about someone they knew.

Here and there were knots of people in conversation; others waved and called a greeting. Some were racing along the park trails, just barely avoiding an accident.

It was a party in the park every morning. No ghosts, no murderers, no fear. Everyone came for a hour or so to see and be seen, and then back home for breakfast.

It was a very nice morning ritual, and Diandra only longed to be able to ride beside Serena, but Leonie had put her foot down about that.

"And did the Carstairses have a divining board?" she asked idly as they watched Serena take off again to greet another acquaintance.

"No," Leonie said, "but they know a medium . . ."

"For heaven's sake—"

"I thought you were serious," Leonie snapped.

"I can't believe you are."

"There's a woman who is known to be able to contact those on the other side and to bring messages to their bereaved. I think . . . I think we should have her come in—"

"Leonie, don't do it."

"I'm sorry. I think Pamela still has something to tell us, and I don't care what you or Justin think. I am going to ask Madam Petrovna to come to us, and then, for once and for all, we'll see."

She was serious. And Madam Petrovna was positively rabid on the subject of life beyond the grave.

"The spirits are out there," she said in her thick Russian accent as she paced around the candlelit parlor, marking her space like a cat. "They are all around you, watching you, keeping you from harm."

She stopped suddenly in front of Diandra. "Yes, you. He says, yes, do what you will."

Diandra stepped back involuntarily. She couldn't mean that; it wasn't possible Madam understood that what she was saying had some meaning for *her*. Still, the woman's eyes were sharp and knowing, luminous and black in her wrinkled face, and she nodded as if to emphasize the message and then she turned to Serena.

"He says—don't."

Serena blinked as that flat black gaze bored into hers. "I don't know what you're talking about."

"He knows," Madam Petrovna said and turned away. She accosted Leonie next. "He says . . . he won't."

"What? What are you talking about?"

"The spirit, he's over your shoulder and he tells me to say, he won't."

"Who won't? You're talking in riddles. I thought you were casting a circle."

"Oh, but before I close out the spirits, I must speak for them."

"You've spoken, and we're waiting, so go about your business so we can begin the *séance.*"

Was Leonie as unnerved as she? Diandra couldn't tell if the message meant anything to her at all.

"You must heed the message, my lady."

"If I knew what it meant, I would," Leonie said waspishly. "Come now, are you ready? Oh, I forgot, George is supposed to take part in this. No, *insisted,* and that we hold it at teatime, just like we did with Agatha."

"Ah, Agatha, yes . . . she is here . . ." Madam Petrovna murmured. "Yes . . . she says, evil lurks . . ." She looked around at the three of them. "She says . . . the circle is broken."

"You haven't done the circle. We're waiting for George."

Madam seated herself at the table. "As you wish."

The doorbell rang and the sound reverberated all over the house.

A moment later Millbank appeared. "There was no one at the door, madam."

"Nonsense, George was there."

"There was no one there," Millbank repeated, his face impassive.

"This is a bad idea," Diandra said. *He says . . . do what you will . . .* She couldn't shake the words.

"And anyway, here comes George," Leonie announced. "Where were you?"

"Came through the carriage house, why?"

"Never mind. Madam Petrovna is here and we are ready to begin, per *your* instructions, George, though why I'm listening to you, I cannot understand. Madam, this is George Tisbury."

"Yes," Madam said, as if she knew. "We are ready to start." She rose up again and walked first to the four corners of the room, murmuring to herself, making a circular motion of her arms as if she were drawing in the spirits and energy that hovered around her; and then to the center where she stood, her head bowed for a moment, as if she were gathering her powers for the service of those who had called her.

"We may begin. Please sit in a circle around the table and join hands."

They did as she requested, and she joined them and linked her hands to Diandra on the one side, and Serena on the other.

She bowed her head and they were enveloped in a preternatural silence. No one moved. The air thickened. Something oppressive seemed to enter the room. The candles flickered and then went out.

Leonie gasped as they were enveloped in darkness.

"Is the spirit with us?" Madam asked softly.

There was a tension in the room, and a tautness about her, as if she were trying keep herself centered between the hovering energy and her connection with those around the table.

She lost the battle; her body slumped, her head fell forward, and she answered in a voice totally unlike her own.

"I am here."

The room turned cold. Seemingly no one had the wit to speak; Serena finally continued the questions in a trembling voice. "Who is here?"

"She who seeks justice."

"Justice for what?"

"Untimely death."

"Who are you?"

"One who watches and waits."

"Are you Pamela?"

"I am she who will be heard."

"We are listening; what do you wish to tell us?"

"Love is fleeting."

"Are you Pamela?"

"I am she who believed."

"What do you wish to tell us?"

"Evil lurks." The voice was fading.

"Tell us more," Serena said urgently.

Silence. Utter bone-dead silence.

And then suddenly, across the room, a glowing light moved along the floor. Slowly the light came toward them, taking shape slowly until it seemed to form the figure of a woman.

"Who are you?" Serena whispered, her voice shaking.

"The one to whom evil was done." The voice was papery, dry, barely a whisper; the thing hovered, as if it were waiting.

"What do you want us to know?"

"Evil is innocence. Innocence is evil."

The figure moved and then stopped, almost as if something invisible barred its way; it wafted toward them again, and stopped with a gesture of frustration. And then it lifted an arm and pointed. "She destroyed my life—that one . . ."

Who? Who? They could barely see each other in the dark. The figure held them mesmerized. It seemed to just float and threaten, and yet it couldn't move toward the table.

"Murderer—murderer!" the voice shrieked. "They will know the truth, they will know—justice . . . will . . . beee

. . . dooonnneee . . .'' The voice faded and the glowing body suddenly seemed to melt away before their eyes.

Nobody moved; nobody spoke. The silence was deafening.

The thing was gone. One lone candle flickered to life, casting long black shadows across the room.

Madam came to, lifting her head, the blank expression on her face easing into one of recognition. "It is over?''

No one answered, and then Leonie said in a voice that trembled just a little, "What was *that*?

"I gave what is given me by the spirits,'' Madam said.

"What was that thing?''

Madam looked startled. "What, what thing?

"There was something, something surrounded by a white light and it spoke to us.'' It sounded crazy; it sounded as if they had all imagined it. A thing came amongst them, delivered an ambiguous message, and disappeared.

"No, no, no. I saw nothing,'' Madam said agitatedly, looking around at them. "I can't answer for what you saw. I conjured nothing.''

"It delivered a message.''

Now Madam looked frightened. "Tell me what.''

"Love is fleeting. Evil is innocence. It accused one of us of murder.''

"No, no—no such thing happened; I would have been aware.''

"You spoke first and then the thing came . . .''

"No, I am not aware. It was not of my doing. This is not to be taken lightly. Spirits do not appear on a whim. There is something urgent here, something you need to attend to.''

"Yes, only *I* must deduce what it is and who was accused,'' Leonie retorted. "I did not summon you here to be told that.''

"You summoned me here to be the instrument of the

spirit, and so I was, my lady. Even I cannot define by which channel the spirit may seek to enlighten you. I did what you asked. You have your message. My job is done."

But she looked pale and uncertain and would say nothing more. "I did what you asked," she repeated as Leonie disgustedly escorted her out.

"They are all like that," George said stringently, but even he seemed a little wary. "There is always something melodramatic. And then everything else is six of one, half dozen of the other. They never give you a straight answer. And they leave you to interpret everything which they couch in the vaguest terms possible. When will Leonie catch onto it?"

"Fine—you explain what happened in there."

"Now Diandra, of course it was some trick. And Justin will kill us if he hears about it."

"It scared me."

"A very effective trick. We'll give the room a good going over and we'll figure it out."

"And she delivered messages from the spirits before the *séance*—"* Diandra began, and then thought the better of it.

. . . he says . . . do what you will . . .

"Amazing how they do that," George murmured. "As if it had any meaning at all." And then he looked at her closely. "Or did it?"

"I don't know," she said after a moment, deliberately lying. *But how could Madam have known that? How?*

And the spirit, how could she have done that?

They searched all over the parlor, she and George, and they found nothing to indicate any chicanery.

"She's good at her job," George said. "Didn't Leonie say she came highly recommended?"

"I don't recommend anyone being accused of murder by an apparition."

"She must have had an accomplice."

"But she looked as chilled as we felt."

"It was a trick," George said pragmatically, his voice gaining strength because things had returned nicely to normal.

And then the doorbell rang again.

A footman came to the threshold of the parlor.

"No one at the door, my lady."

She looked at George and he looked at her.

"What is going on here?" she whispered.

"Someone is playing tricks, and we're just never going to know who," George said. It was the only explanation, really. Nothing ever happened for no reason.

I want to know . . . but the only thing she really wanted to know was who was being accused of murder, and why someone was resorting to tricks and illusions to do it.

And murder.

The following morning, the papers reported that the well-known medium and psychic, Madam Petrovna, was found in her apartments by a friend, apparently dead of a heart attack.

Chapter Twelve

Justin was furious. "Do you mean, Leonie, that I can't leave the house for half a day without your calling in every spiritualist in the whole of London?"

"Just Madam, she came highly recommended."

"And conjured up something that scared the devil out of you. What the hell went on here yesterday?" He wheeled around toward Serena. "Serena."

Serena seemed to shrink back for a moment at his wrath, and then she answered bravely, "Oh, but she was so good, Justin; she had messages for us—I mean before that . . . awful apparition—there was nothing untoward . . ."

"Except Leonie's ridiculous idea that Pamela lives beyond the grave, which was fed by this stupid *séance.*"

"We didn't know it was Pamela," Leonie said defensively. "It never identified itself."

"No, it just made a wild accusation of murder. Madam?"

"I have nothing to add," she said. All his sanctimonious anger—too self-righteous. And after all, where had he been yesterday afternoon? She felt a chill snake down her spine.

Who better to play the role of trickster than the one who bore the most antipathy? Hadn't she believed that at Skene—that he would stop at nothing to get them back to India and out of his life?

But murder? That was too much. He might hate her for usurping Pamela's place in his father's life; he might be burdened with an unbearable guilt for not having gone to India with them; he might be mourning them still and hating her, but she couldn't believe he was capable of murder.

And for what? Some inexplicable occurrences that seemed rooted in something supernatural?

He could not be that vindictive.

But—she didn't know.

No, she knew . . .

Leonie knew too, exactly what she was going to say to Stiles, and it was a repeat of the story that she had told Streatham. They had brought in Madam at the recommendation of the Carstairses as a parlor trick, something to entertain Serena who had a slight interest in spiritualism. None of them had been prepared for what she conjured up. She had left the house around six o'clock, and they had had no contact with her since.

"Is that so?" Stiles asked each of them in turn. "For the girl?"

Yes, yes and yes, even Diandra, who thought, against her better judgment, that it was wiser for all of them not to explain too much.

"I see," Stiles said, making a note in his little book. "You understand you all were the last to see her alive."

The silence tightened.

"Yesterday was the first time you'd ever met Madam Petrovna?"

Leonie answered for all of them. "Yes."

"She was contacted by you, Lady Hull?"

"Yes."

"The Earl did not take part in the *séance*?"

Justin answered. "No."

"It lasted about an hour or an hour and a half?"

Leonie again. "Yes."

"And ran the usual course—Madam had you join hands, she summoned the spirit, seemed to go into a trance, and then the spirit *spoke* through her in a different voice?"

"Yes."

"And then during that time an apparition appeared that seemed to be a glowing light in the shape of a figure."

Leonie swallowed; it sounded improbable and impossible. "Yes."

"And it spoke to you."

"Yes."

"And pointed to one of you, accusing that person of murder."

"Yes."

"And then disappeared?"

"Yes."

"And Madam claimed no knowledge of this apparition."

"She said she didn't conjure it."

"But that could have been part of her act," Justin interpolated, his exasperation simmering just under the polite tone of his voice.

"Indeed, my lord, but none of madam's clients that I have interviewed have reported such a thing. It seems out the range of her usual—*act*—shall we say?"

"You may say," Justin said tightly.

"And then, after disclaiming the apparition, you escorted Madam out the door, had the footman call her a cab, and you never saw her again."

"Yes," Leonie said, her eyes on Stiles as he made yet another note, and then looked up at them.

"I appreciate your cooperation, my lord. I think that will be all for today."

For today—ominous words, as if he were going to pursue them as well as Madam's alleged ghosts and apparitions.

"An unfortunate accident," Leonie said dismissively as the door closed behind Stiles. "She must have had a heart attack; what other explanation is there?"

"Ghosts," Justin said sarcastically.

"I think you should not make fun," Leonie said seriously. "Something is obviously going on here. And at Skene. And we've had doorbells ringing and no one at the door. Which I didn't tell Stiles because . . . well, why? He thinks we're eccentric enough as it is."

"There is a logical explanation," Justin said, his icy gaze veering toward Diandra, "and I promise you, before long, I will find out what it is."

That threat didn't scare her at all. Especially when they were away from Cheswick Square and she could think clearly.

Except the death of Madam had fogged everything up again.

They had an evening engagement, but she took Serena on an outing to the British Imperial Museum anyway. Not that Serena was interested in antiquities, but she thought the jewelry at least should hold her attention for an hour.

And that it did; they exclaimed over the intricate workmanship and beautiful stones. Serena made sketches, while Diandra contemplated fragments of temple walls. They sat on stone benches and luxuriated in the silence, which seemed to open a path to confidences.

"Justin is very handsome," Serena said idly after a while.

The statement jolted her. "Very forbidding, you mean."

"And eligible . . . ?"

"But you knew that."

Serena smiled. "The ladies talk, a lot. They all want him. They're envious that we are even in the same house with him. They're all curious about him. I don't tell them anything; why should I?"

"Indeed."

"Anybody could have him, if she could fix his interest."

"Theoretically," Diandra said uneasily. She did not like where this conversation was going. "Who has asked for your help?"

"No one. Well, perhaps . . . someone," Serena murmured coyly. "It doesn't matter. I'm the one who has the advantage. And Leonie. And . . ." she slanted a look at Diandra, *"you."*

Diandra shivered. "This is all nonsense, Serena. Yes, I do believe Leonie has some affection for Justin, but it is obvious he has never looked her as other than a relative. And a rather exasperating one at that. And you're not helping with all your superstitions and magic and all."

"The spirits will speak," Serena said.

Diandra blew out an impatient breath. "Or someone is speaking *for* them, and if you continue on this way, suspicion will attach to you."

"What about the board?"

"What about it? The board is gone."

"Guthrie spoke to us . . ."

"No, I refuse to believe that. You or Leonie manipulated that board."

"I didn't, I swear I didn't."

"I don't want to talk about it."

"You wouldn't," Serena said. "I don't care. I want to stay here forever, Diandra. When everything is over, I don't want to go back to Bhaumaghar."

Another breath-stopping statement. Diandra took a moment to think of a reasonable answer. But she wasn't feeling reasonable at all, especially because it was obvious that this was the point of Serena's consenting to come out with her.

She felt a spurt of anger and impatience. "Just how do you think *that* will work, my dear? Leonie isn't going to issue you an invitation any time soon and Justin can't wait to get rid of you."

"Why, it's perfectly obvious. I'll get someone to offer for me."

Why was she not surprised? Because Leonie had paved the way, talking about settlements and wills?

Still, Serena's certainty was unsettling when she had no inkling that there was anyone at all interested in her.

"Do you have someone in mind?"

"Maybe I do, maybe I don't," Serena said coyly. "Would you hate that?"

"Have you met someone?"

"Maybe . . ."

"Serena—"

"Don't be stupid, Diandra. It's too soon to tell anything. I'm putting all my resources toward it. And I expect nothing less than success."

Diandra felt a chill. *Charms and omens and magic—of course . . . she should have known. What else would Serena depend on?*

"I hate it when you put your trust in superstitions," she said sharply.

"Well—I don't care. You don't have to do anything. I'm making my own destiny. And if it works—all you have to do is go back to India."

She hated it. She was furious with Serena for her smug surety that all would work out as she wanted and all on the basis of *her* whims and desires and some chants and charms.

And all she had to do was go back to Bhaumaghar . . .

As she dressed for their engagement that night, she was shaking with anger that Serena thought it was that easy, and that much in her control when everything was utterly out of control.

And the woman who stared back at her in the mirror— that was not she; where was the face of placid serenity she had cultivated? Where was the demure widow who wanted nothing more than to sacrifice herself so no one would discover her secrets?

She was not the woman in the mirror. That woman, dressed in a close-fitting black silk evening dress, she was someone else altogether, and her face showed it. There was passion in her eyes, and exasperation, and high color in her cheeks; and an awareness that she had tried so hard to suppress.

. . . do what you will . . .

Serena was doing just that. Had she ever thought she had any control over Serena? Bringing her to England had not been the answer to the problem of Serena. And now there was a new overlay, besides all the paranormal nonsense; there was to be the spectacle of Serena in pursuit of a mysterious suitor.

Why hadn't she noticed?

She thought back as she twisted and pinned her hair, and she couldn't remember a single man in whom Serena had evinced an interest. Of course, they had barely been out and about: the ball, several dinners and card parties. The musicale. And tonight, the theater, at the invitation of Lady Pettigill who had taken a fancy to *her*.

And dinner out, afterwards.

The *preseason*. There was too much activity already for someone used to the more leisurely pursuits of a station club. Everything was too different. But Serena fit right in.

Serena slid right in like a chameleon just waiting for the moment.

And in fact, she loved it all—the gaiety, the music, the chaos of the social events, the maneuvering and manipulating to garner the most favorable bachelor's name on a dance card or as a partner for dinner.

And somewhere in there, Serena had fixed the attention of an eligible man.

And hadn't told her dearest sister.

What was going on?

But it was all of a piece with everything else. They had pushed aside the deaths of Madam Petrovna and Grace Partram, and it was go about your business as usual.

She couldn't do it. The disturbing *séance* weighed on her. The messages, the glowing figure, the accusation.

Who and who and what?

And she was still in possession of that bedeviled board.

. . . Stay . . .

It was as if someone had breathed the word in her ear. She whipped around, and there was no one there, and yet the command had been clear, precise, and uttered in a papery whisper that close . . . that close to her.

She started shaking all over again.

There was a knock at the door and she jumped, and opened the door with a trembling hand. It was only Gita, with her mantilla and her reticule, coming to tell her they were all waiting for her downstairs.

She closed the door behind her as she stepped into the hallway. And she stopped.

Was there the faint scent of something wafting in the air?

She brushed it off; she was not susceptible, she wasn't. It was just the air was so sweet, so fragrant . . .

And then a moment later, the scent was gone.

She paused at the head of the stairs. Gita was in her

room; the others were in the hallway. She could hear them, Leonie particularly, ordering everyone around. She could hear Serena's high clear voice, and George's deep rumble, all of which sounded strangely reassuring.

Nothing unusual. Just a whisper and a scent. Madam's message from beyond. A mysterious gray figure. Floating tables. Mysterious rappings. A hidden divining board that had spelled out Guthrie's name. An apparition that glowed. Serena's childish reliance on magic and charms. And two deaths.

No—three. Three deaths. Three people dead, poor Agatha included. They had forgotten all about Agatha.

Nothing to be afraid of.

At all.

She mentally shook herself. She had to stop this.

The scent of lilac permeated the air again, suddenly, as if someone were blowing it like a soap bubble. It was just there, matte, cloyingly sweet—she whirled around, but no one was there down the hallway toward her room.

She turned the other way, toward Justin's room. And she grabbed onto the banister tightly.

She could barely see it, but just ahead of her was what looked like a thick patch of fog just hovering at the end of the hallway. Slowly, as she watched, it took shape into a gray mass that could have been a gray hooded cloak, and then just as suddenly as it had appeared, it vanished, and there was nothing except the dim light of the hallway sconces, and the receding scent of lilac.

Nothing, nothing, nothing—nothing to be afraid of . . . I'll just—I'll just . . . follow it—

She made herself move; she made herself step back onto the landing and walk slowly down the hallway toward Justin's bedroom.

The lilac scent lingered here, and she had the most

desperate urge to just turn around and race down the stairs to the comfort of light and companionship.

She inched her way along the wall instead, her fingers groping for anything that was solid and of this earth. A hall table. A doorknob. Her heart pounded wildly as she got closer and closer to Justin's door.

What had she expected to find? There was nothing, just the fading scent and an unusual coolness in the air.

Or, she had imagined it altogether, because she was becoming too susceptible to all the nonsense.

Because she felt guilty? Or because she was indulging herself at the same time she was supposed to be chaperoning Serena?

She didn't know anymore. Everything was too mixed up, and overlaid by all the mysterious phenomena.

There had to be an explanation. But as she stood helplessly in the hallway, with just a whiff of lilac surrounding her, she wasn't sure there weren't ghosts or that she wasn't a figment of someone's imagination.

. . . *Go* . . .

She started violently.

It was—it was a whisper in her ear, as tangible as the hall table she was clinging to.

There was no one, and nothing, in the hallway. Not a servant in sight. Flickering gaslight sending eerie shadows ahead of her and behind. Portraits of ancestors watching.

And a ghostly whisper in her ear, as precise as a knife. Go . . .

It could have been any of them. Anything, anyone—or just a horrible awful trick designed to scare only *her*.

She turned and raced for the staircase, leaving her mantilla in a drift of black lace behind her.

He had had enough. It was time finally to expose the hoax and give her no option whether to stay or go. Two deaths were more than enough, and it wasn't something he wanted that obnoxious Stiles investigating in his house one minute longer than was necessary.

But somehow the two were linked, and he intended, finally, to discover how.

There was no question in his mind: Diandra was the key. Diandra had reason, motive, wherewithal, imagination and presence of mind to conjure spectres, not the least of which was her culpability in his father's death. It made the utmost sense to him.

He needed only to find one little suggestion, one small piece of apparatus.

He watched from the dining room window as the carriage pulled away from the curb. She was gone now and it was time; he had politely refused the invitation to the theater for the sole purpose of taking on this task.

He dismissed the servants, went upstairs, and eased his way into Diandra's bedroom.

It was as neat as if no one were occupying it, but he knew that her dresses were neatly hung in the armoire, and that her things would be meticulously placed in the drawers.

He had no qualms about tearing the place apart.

The bed first . . .

The bed—but there were never beds in the voudrais *. . . what would it be like to have her in a bed, covering her, containing her whole body solely by the potent thrust of his? . . .*

Jesus . . .

He was not going to think about her that way . . .

He ripped off the bedspread, the cover, the sheets, the pillows and the mattress.

Nothing. Nothing. Nothing.

Into the closet next, pulling out dress after dress, searching each for secret pockets and secret devices.

Still nothing.

Into the dresser drawers. Here now, all kinds of things, personal things. Diandra things, scented in violet and rose. Underthings. Corsets. Padding. Petticoats. Powders, perfumes, jewelry, nightgowns edged in lace, silky stockings, lacy garters, incongruous in his large hands.

On her long legs wrapped around him . . .

Damn her—

Diandra things, all feminine and fine, spilling all over the roughness of his hands and enticing him—and nothing, nothing, nothing among the boning and stiffeners that even remotely resembled a gadget for a ghost.

She had been more clever than he thought. And she had neatly diverted him with the help of his most distractable part.

But that was *there* and this was *here,* and the two had nothing to do with each other.

And he wasn't nearly done with her. Not yet. Not here.

Not ever . . .

It was gone.

By the time she had gathered her wits, told them to go on without her because she had a headache, and got upstairs, the lace mantilla was gone.

It wasn't in her room—Gita denied seeing it altogether, and it wasn't in Serena's room, or downstairs, or in the closet, or anywhere she could think of that a servant might have mislaid it in those ten minutes that she was not too gracefully bowing out of going to the theater with them.

It was one small thing. One small *earthly* thing.

There was no more scent of lilac in the upstairs hall.

She walked cautiously down the hallway toward the spot where she had seen the apparition.

Just by Justin's door. Just there . . .

She knelt on the floor and touched the carpet. There was nothing on the carpet.

There was nothing along the walls except the tables and paintings hanging above, and two doors, one of which was Justin's room.

But . . . the other—?

She touched the knob and recoiled. The thing was cold as ice.

She reached out and grasped it and turned it.

The door was not locked. She pushed it open, and immediately the matte scent of lilac surrounded her.

She shivered, a chill coursing down her spine.

But it was a bedroom just like any other—comfortable, beautifully furnished with a tester bed, a washstand, an armoire, an overstuffed chair by the fireplace, a chest of drawers on the far wall, and beautiful dark green brocade draperies puddling onto the riotously flowered carpet.

Nothing to suggest a ghost.

Except the scent.

Her hands were like ice as she lit a candlestick from the mantel and moved into the room.

Whose room?

The ghost's room . . .

No, no, no—too fanciful by half . . .

But it was cold in the room, and the scent of lilac permeated the air.

On the dresser there was a silver tray with brushes, mirrors, combs, and a silver jar.

She put down the candle and opened the jar.

Lilac-scented powder, overwhelming in its saturating smell, wafting into the air—fragrance of ghost . . . she covered it quickly, screwed the top tight, and replaced it on the tray.

And then she noticed the initials on the silver-backed

hand mirror; ornate entwined letters, easily decipherable. She picked it up to have a closer look: *P . . . R . . .*

Pamela.

She dropped the mirror involuntarily, just as she heard a scratching noise in the armoire.

Mice, surely, but her heart was pounding so hard. Her chest felt so constricted, and the room was so cold . . .

She picked up the candlestick and moved toward the armoire. It was a huge piece of furniture, almost ceiling height, burled walnut with rounded edges and a cornice, and a beveled mirror panel in the door.

She saw her own reflection in a halo of eerie shadows as she approached the armoire; she saw her hand shaking, her face pale with fear.

She had only to pull open the door. The armoire would be empty. Pamela's clothes would be long gone. It would all be her imagination.

She reached for the little glass knob, she swallowed hard, and then she yanked open the door.

There was nothing in the armoire—except a long gray hooded cloak—

She felt faint, she almost dropped the candle, and then she was scared out of her wits by a violent voice behind her.

. . . "What the hell are you doing here?"

His voice—how? Was it even he? She couldn't even be sure of that; she turned slowly, slowly, slowly—and he was there, on the threshold, holding a branch of candles, looking beyond her into the armoire, seeing what she had seen . . .

Able to corroborate what she had seen—

"What the goddamned hell . . . ?" His blazing eyes pinned her as she tried to move toward him. "How did you do this, how did you set this up? Where did you get that cloak?"

Now he came toward her threateningly—and she started to back away, not sure then if the threat was the ghost or him.

—and there was a sound—the faintest sliver of a sound . . . and they both halted in their tracks and whipped around toward the armoire, lifting their candles to illuminate the interior—

Only to find—the cloak had vanished; the interior was empty, the gray cloak was gone.

Chapter Thirteen

"How did you do it, Diandra? How?" He was kneeling beside the armoire and examining the interior, his branch of candles on the floor beside him. "Amazing. Utterly gone."

She couldn't say a word; she was frozen, just a block of ice with a candle in her hand, the scent of lilac in her consciousness, and a witness who thought she could conjure ghosts.

It was unbelievable. The whole of it. Just inconceivable. And he didn't help when he got to his feet and held the light up her.

"You look ghastly."

She felt like a spectre herself, like she was standing outside herself and watching it all as if it were a play.

"I saw . . . I saw the gray ghost."

"Did you?" Plainly, he didn't believe her. "How convenient."

"You saw the cloak."

"An illusion, obviously. It's not there. Although how you worked the mirrors, I'll never know."

And that was that. She was the trickster and nothing would convince him otherwise.

"Was lilac *her* scent?"

He knew who she meant; his face hardened and his voice was terse when he answered. "Yes."

And so there it was: Pamela was haunting them, and this room—*her room*—was her place of rest.

It didn't reassure her to know that.

"Was this her room?"

His answer shocked her. "No."

"Then what—" She broke off. Another mystery: something of Pamela's in this room, just enough for someone to make the desired inference.

Someone—or *her?*

There was nothing in the armoire; the scent had almost dissipated and the air had warmed up considerably, probably from the violence of his emotion.

What was going on here?

"It's time to cut to the chase, Diandra." He loomed over her with his branch of candles, and she immediately took a step backward. "It's time for the truth."

"You've said that now for the past month, but you're only interested in your truth, Justin."

"Oh no, I know my truth, my lady. It's your truth we need to hear now."

She made the mistake of looking into those icy eyes.

"All those pretty lies you and Leonie told the good inspector. Not to mention Constable Streatham. Do you know, they still don't know how Agatha died. Very supernatural, the villagers are thinking. It's really hard to credit a sudden heart attack that explains everything so conveniently and convincingly."

"I have said all I am going to say."

"It's damned next to nothing."

"Because there *is* nothing."

"I don't believe it."

"We are now going around in circles, Justin. This is none of my doing. I'm so tired of telling you."

"Yet you stayed home on the pretense of a headache— and suddenly the ghost turns up in the guest bedroom. Really?"

She turned on her heel and walked out of the room. There was no talking to him, not at all.

He was after her in an instant, grasping her arm, pulling her away from her bedroom door, and thrusting her toward the stairs.

"Let's talk some more about this sudden headache, Diandra."

"I have one now," she muttered.

"Brandy is just the thing then."

He ruthlessly propelled her down the steps, and toward the library.

"Millbank . . . !" His shout echoed all over the house.

The butler came running. "My lord?"

"The Napoleon brandy for madam, Millbank." He pushed open the library doors. "Perfect for your lying tongue, madam." His eyes caressed her thinned lips. "And your lying eyes."

He nudged her into the room, and so she saw it before he did, the divining board on his desk with her lace mantilla draped over it, and the two velvet pouches beside.

"How perfect." He stood contemplating it, a snifter of brandy in his one hand and the lace mantilla in the other. "You must have an accomplice, madam. There's no other explanation."

"Only the one I'm tired of giving. I have no idea how this thing got here." Her voice sounded shaky; she was just a little shocked. She had thought the board was so well hidden no one could ever find it.

"But how opportune that it did. And you did an excellent job of repair, Diandra. I congratulate you."

No use even trying to convince him she had done nothing, or to even describe just what had happened that night.

"I wonder if we shouldn't ask a couple of questions of our own."

She didn't have to wonder. She didn't want to touch the thing. It was really too much, the board on top of the apparition and the vanishing cloak. And the death of Petrovna. Mustn't forget that. Three deaths. Three.

And a divining board that had unburied itself and turned up on Justin's desk.

She felt just faint enough to take a sip of brandy. Excellent brandy. Strong enough to scare away ghosts and see through illusions.

Enough!

"Perhaps if we ask the board," Justin was saying, "we might get a straight answer." He set aside his snifter and sat down opposite her and stared at the board.

"I'm not doing this," she said.

"No, of course you won't. You're afraid. Or you're involved."

"I'm so tired . . ."

"Yes, I know. Tired of denying it. Tired of pretending. Tired of me, of London, of Leonie, your sister . . . tired, tired, tired. Put your fingers on the planchette, Diandra."

"Go to hell."

"Devil's board, my lady. Do it."

She felt the chill all the way to her toes. She could almost believe spirits were watching. So comforting to know *something* was always there.

She wasn't afraid. Not now. The brandy had burned her tongue, and his words had seared her soul. Millbank had lit the fire, and the room was warm, intimate, made for secrets or revelations.

She placed her fingers on the planchette and sent him a challenging glance.

He placed his opposite.

The planchettte vibrated and moved.

And then stopped.

"Excellent, Diandra."

She ignored him. She didn't believe it; she didn't want to pursue it, but his skepticism left her no choice. "Who is with us?"

No answer.

His hand was heavy on the wood, deliberately heavy, she thought, and holding it back because he was so certain that she was the motive power.

"Is there a spirit with us?"

No answer. But he was pushing down hard on the planchette so that there was no vibration, no float to it.

She gritted her teeth once again. "What do you wish to tell us?"

A long moment, a tremor, a sharp little movement to the left—and then it jerked and began spelling out the message.

"Do what you will . . ."

She looked up at him, her eyes wide.

"Clever, Diandra."

He didn't believe it. *She* didn't believe it. "Ask it something."

He held her gaze for a long moment. "I will. I will ask the spirit, Who killed my father."

She felt the shock all over her body. Just that. The one defining thing he needed to know. That she was the one. That there was a reason, an explanation, a meaning to his father's death.

The planchette did not move.

"So much for that," he said disgustedly.

"You thought I'd confess?"

He removed his hands from the planchette. "I expected it to lie, just like you."

"Justin—"

"Well, you tell me. You tell me how and why and what so that it makes some kind of sense. Why don't you try that, my lady, instead of your tricks and trumpery?"

"I told you. I came down one morning and found him dead at his desk."

"What a bald statement that is. What an epitaph. Just like that—no illness, no complaints, just good night dear and gone the next day?"

"Exactly like that."

"I don't believe you."

She took her fingers off the planchette. "You believe something," she said boldly, holding his eyes.

He didn't look away, and she saw, for one explosive moment, the war going on within him, and it had nothing to do with the past, and everything to do with *her*.

The planchette began to move. Neither of their hands were on it, and they watched in horror as it just floated across the board, spelling out letters.

"B . . ." she read, her voice shaking. "E . . . L . . . I . . . E . . . V . . . E. Believe." She looked up at him. "Oh my God—"

Even he looked a little pale; but he wouldn't back down. "Excellent trick, Diandra." He leaned forward and lifted the board, and the planchette fell to the floor. "There has to be some mechanism under here by which you control the movement."

"Yes, by my strength of will," she retorted.

"I'd believe that over and above the thing moved by itself."

"It moved itself."

And even she could see, there was nothing about the board. It was flat underneath and there was no place to attach a wire, a string, or even a magnet.

"I *will* burn this thing." He picked up the planchette and examined it, and then placed it back on the board.

Immediately it began to move, scrolling wildly around the board, almost as if it were furious at what he had said.

He grabbed it—and dropped it instantly, and looked with shock at the red mark on the palm of his hand, while it swung back and forth crazily across the board like something inhuman.

And then suddenly it stopped.

The air thickened. There was the faint scent of lilac, a wisp of fragrance around them. Something swirling around them. Something hovering over them.

Evil lurking.

She felt it with every pore of her body. Something was with them, inexplicable, unknowable, unnerving. She felt paralyzed; she felt suffocated.

And he was immobilized, and still holding his hand palm upward, almost in supplication.

The board vibrated; the planchette began to move, to spell out a word.

She leaned forward and something shoved her back.

He read the word. "Murderer." His eyes skewed toward her and she made a movement to rise from her chair.

She couldn't. Something held her back. Forcibly. She felt almost catatonic with fear, but she forced herself to ask, "Who is with us?"

The planchette whirled around the board.

"Is it Pamela?"

It stopped and began spelling out letters again.

"Killed him."

"Who—who killed him?"

"Wanted him."

"Who? Who?"

"Liar."

"Who killed him?"

"Morant."

Oh, my God—what?? And Justin's face—on the testimony of a divining board gone haywire? Now he believed?

She felt frantic suddenly. "Which Morant?"

"She who—"

"Which Morant?"

"That one."

"Give us a name."

"No name."

"Tell us *who.*"

"Poison."

"Tell us—" The note was in her voice, pure panic, and Justin knew it.

"Do what you will . . ."

"Tell us!"

The planchette swirled around one more time and suddenly tilted off of the board. In the space of a instant, everything receded: the scent, the heaviness, the pervasive feeling of evil, and they were left staring at each other.

He picked up the planchette. Nothing happened this time. He turned it over in his hand and examined the underside yet again, and it was the same as before: there was nothing there that would have propelled that object without the use of human hands. There was nothing underneath the board, nothing, nothing, nothing to explain the phenomena they had witnessed.

"Millbank!"

Millbank came running.

"Make sure the footman burns this—tonight."

"Oh, my lord." Millbank sounded appalled as he gingerly picked the thing up.

"Just do it."

He withdrew from the room, and as he exited, the tension eased; she felt less petrified, less threatened. What *was* it about that board? Especially that she was thinking about it as if what had happened were the norm?

Nothing was normal, and this was just totally out of body and scarier than anything that had happened already.

She didn't even know what to say: the thing had all but accused her of murder, had verified everything Justin had thought of her. She wondered why he wasn't calling in Scotland Yard. She wondered why he just sat there looking at her.

"I didn't do this," she whispered finally.

"I'm going to have the footmen tear apart this room, my lady. I'm going to find out just how, just why. I've been away enough so you've had free run of the house—and of this room. I don't believe in entities and messages from beyond the grave. And I know you've spent at least one evening in here—supposedly reading. That is only sane explanation."

"I accuse myself of murder?"

"But you didn't—it didn't, let us say for the sake of discussion. It gave no name, it said only *she who* and *that one*. It's a very clever trick to divert attention from you, Diandra. Most diverting."

"How did I make it burn your hand?"

"Something electrical. I know we'll find it when the room is dismantled."

"And what about the cloak—and the scent?"

"You imagined it all, my lady. I saw nothing."

"You saw it. I know you saw it."

"In retrospect, I'm not at all sure."

"You bastard."

"No one has seen the ghost but you—"

"And George," she interpolated. "And Serena, once."

"George is too suggestible. A dear fellow, but ever willing to give anyone the benefit of the doubt."

"Even you," she spat.

"Or you."

"And you are just so calm about what happened this evening . . ."

"I know you engineered it somehow. And I'm going to find out how."

"Dear God . . . what if—what if I didn't?"

"There can be no other explanation."

"And you weren't scared out of your wits?"

"No, I was merely admiring your resourcefulness."

"Nonsense. You were terrified."

"And you are an excellent actress, madam. And with that, I think this performance is finished."

And now he wanted her to go. She was absolutely terrified to go, but she forced herself to rise from the chair and walk to the door.

To open it.

The hallway was illuminated by wall sconces that cast long shadows into dimly lit corners.

She would have to cross over the shadows and mount the steps. Go back down the landing where she had seen the apparition.

She took a very deep breath and stepped into the hallway.

Evil lurking—

She felt it as if it were tangible; it felt like she was walking through a congealing thickness, like pudding. It felt cold, dank, sour.

She held out her shaking hands and touched . . . nothing. But almost immediately the sensation dissipated. Just evaporated into thin air.

She stood dead still, her nerve endings jangling like a pair of cymbals. She wasn't afraid. None of this was real.

She chanted the words over and over as she girded herself to continue to her room.

Serena would be home soon. Leonie's grudging voice would be issuing orders. George would stay the night, reassuring and sane.

None of it was real. Something was making it all happen, and Justin was right, he would find out what and who—and then he would probably send them packing.

But she was ready, even if Serena was not.

. . . oh, Serena . . . with her little triumphs and her charms and her naked desire to have the life of a princess . . .

She couldn't imagine why she had ever let Hugh talk her into bringing Serena here.

She pushed one foot in front of the other and thought about the fact that if she and Serena hadn't come, there would have been no ghosts, no deaths, no messages . . . no *voudrais* . . .

Especially—no *voudrais*—and all those feelings and needs would have remained tightly corseted within her, and she would have returned to Calcutta as whole as she had come.

But now—she felt splintered a half dozen ways. She wanted what was best for Serena. But for the first time in a long time, she wanted something for herself. And that was *not* supposed to have happened.

At the staircase now. Easy. She mounted the first step, and the next, and the next . . .

Right to the top where Millbank had left a lamp on a table just by the landing. Bless Millbank.

And finally into her room where more lights were burning, and Gita was waiting—along with the board and planchette on the bed and the pouches folded neatly beside.

* * *

She almost fainted. She didn't scream. She was actually very calm. There was a sense of inevitability about it. Justin thought she was guilty, and by God, the board was going to turn up in the most incriminating fashion.

She allowed Gita to help her out of her dress and into her nightclothes, all the while she stared at the board and didn't try to move it.

Maybe she couldn't move it . . .

"Gita—"

"Mem?"

"Did someone give you the board?"

"Oh no, mem; it was here when I come to turn down the bed. It cannot be moved."

Oh Lord no . . .

"What do you mean?"

"Oh, I tried to place it on the table, but . . . it will not be moved."

I need a circle of protection—

No! I need to not be thinking like this . . . I will not let this scare me—

God, Serena . . .

She felt Gita's nimble fingers working at her corset. Any moment, she would be free of restraints. She would move the board. And she would get some sleep.

She raised her arms and Gita slid her freshly laundered nightgown over her head, and then bent to remove her undergarments and stockings. Her slippers were already at her feet, and she slipped into them.

There was a pot of chocolate on the table near the bed. The covers were turned down invitingly, and all that remained was to move the board.

"Oh mem," Gita protested as she moved to the bed and put her hands on the board. "Oh mem . . ."

She sounded afraid for her, as if something awful would happen if she lifted the board.

And yet she felt no fear as she stepped up to the bed and grasped the edges of it as Gita mumbled something that sounded like a prayer.

She moved it easily; she didn't know what to expect, but there was no resistance at all—there was only a paper-thin whisper in her ear as she set it on the table next to the chocolate pot, and then a hammering pounding at the door.

He blasted in like a gunshot.

"You took the board. Goddammit, you took the board. I could throttle you. Who is she? Get her out of here—" But he didn't have to say it twice; Gita scuttled away just as he spied the board on the table. "What the hell—so you didn't have time to hide it . . . that piece of hell—I'm taking it and I'll burn it with my own hands."

He reached for the board to lift it—and the resistance almost toppled him backward.

She just stood there, gaping. He couldn't move it. Couldn't get it off of the table. He was ready to throw the table and the board right through the window. He toppled it upside down, sending the chocolate pot rolling and spattering hot liquid every which way, looking to see how she had attached the board to the table.

He found nothing. "I'll burn them both."

"Justin, no—that beautiful table . . ."

"Watch me, madam."

He went to lift the table—and it wouldn't move.

"Justin . . ."

"What the hell is going on here?"

The table wouldn't budge.

"How did you do this?"

"I didn't . . ."

"Goddamn it to hell—" He couldn't move it an inch, and he was in such a fury. "Damn you, damn you, damn you—"

She felt the tears streaming down her face. "I swear . . ."

"Liar." The message of the board; she felt as if she could never escape it. *Liar. Murderer. She who—*

She who—what?

She felt his hands on her shoulders, pushing her back, back, back against the door. She felt the hard wall behind her, she felt his wrath, his helplessness that something uncontrollable had invaded his house, and he needed to contain it, he needed it to be her.

It *was* her; everything in her life was out of control, and the only constant was him. His derision, his disbelief, his mistrust, his . . . mouth—ah, this she hadn't expected, not this.

Not this hard, demanding, devouring loss of self.

This was not a thing apart, separate from themselves and all that had happened. This was something different, explosive, dominating—he needed that from her, and perhaps, just perhaps, she needed to give it to him.

His hands were ruthless; he took her body just as mercilessly as he took her mouth. His hands were everywhere, seeking, probing, feeling . . . and she didn't care, she just didn't care.

Her emotions were too high, and he was too rock solid, angry and *there*. She wanted to climb onto him and into him. He wanted to imprint himself on her, on her mouth and her body, he wanted that hard thrusting possession of the thing he couldn't have; he wanted it.

She was easy, so easy; he tore off the nightgown with one hard yank, and nudged his knee between her legs.

And there it was, the center of her being, riding that rock-hard thigh while he took—it was the only word for it—took her breasts, her mouth, her sighs.

She was an animal, living in the moment, caged by his arms, his mouth, his leg, waiting for *her* moment like a predator stalking its prey.

She straddled his leg, rubbing herself against him, arching herself against him like a sinuous cat.

Everything, he could have everything. Here there was no time for play. She reached down between his legs and cupped him in both hands. She held him just there, feeling the weight of him, the hardness, the tensile contraction of his muscles as he felt her confident probing between his legs.

Oh, this she knew—that lush sweet spot just behind his taut sacs that begged for a knowing finger to stroke it. And the light nipping pinch of the sacs themselves, just enough to make him squirm. And then the tight constricting grasp of his penis, all hers, contained in her hand.

That—just that . . . just thumbing the ridge back and forth, over and over, and then a quick slide of her hand down the pulsating shaft. Over and over, up and down, while he ravaged her mouth, and fondled her nipples, and every part of her that he could reach.

And this was the thing; she wanted him right there, right then, against the wall, high, hard, tight, spreading her legs, pummeling her body, she wanted him.

She pushed away his leg, she tore at his trousers, and when she had freed his most vital part, she hooked her leg around his hip to entice him.

He needed no invitation. There was no gentle probing, no easing his way into her. With one mighty thrust, he rammed himself into her. And she was ready, she was wet, she was poised for that ineffable moment of penetration and the instantaneous stormy connection of their bodies.

This, this, this—she loved, she wanted the ferocious violence of his possession. He took her against the wall, against the wind, against his will, even.

But she wanted it. It took nothing at all to stimulate that aching suppressed need in her. That was the scariest thing: it was right at the surface, all the sensuality, all the carnal appetite for everything she had ever experienced before.

And he wanted to devour that; her body and soul, he wanted. He wanted to be the first and the last, and he would never be. And the ghost with whom he competed was the most impossible rival.

He poured his frustration into her; she met every thrust, every savage assault on her mouth. She pushed him with her insatiable body and urgent response. Nothing was forbidden here. There could never be enough of this swamping and tumultuous sensation that pulled her into its undertow.

She felt it coming then—and the almost frantic need to escape it, because she knew, she knew . . . it would obliterate her completely just as it had before.

And then there was no help . . . everything swirled away from her and coalesced into that one potent point of pleasure—and just cracked her body in two.

She was gone. Gone, her body racked with jolting spasms that were echoed in his own convulsive thrusts. Upward and upward and upward—there was no end to it, no end to him and his volatile possession of her.

He wanted to drain her, to pump every last fathomless sensation from her spangling body. Every last . . .

She let him. She let him.

She let him.

And when the last tumultuous feeling eddied away into a skeining little curl in the nether regions of her body, she felt his hands at her buttocks, felt him lift her, and, still joined with her, he carried her to the bed.

There, he eased himself away from her and let her look her fill of him, still powerful in his lust to possess her again, as he slowly divested himself of his clothes.

She loved that; that was the best, to be able to feast her eyes on the jutting tactile whole of him and only the distance of several inches between the essence of him and her eager hands, her questing mouth.

She was soaked with his ejaculate and she reveled in it. Just watching him, aroused her all over again: the economical movement of his body as he stripped, the smooth curve of his buttocks, the long length of his legs, the thatch of hair on his broad chest that slithered down toward to the hard luscious root of him.

She knew it so well already. Better than herself. And she only wanted to feel the slick slide of him embedding himself in her, filling her, penetrating that yearning hot part of her.

She loved lying there naked for him. She wanted to push him past sanity, past anything else but wanting to couple with her.

She saw it in his eyes, those icy eyes, blazing now with carnal need; he was almost there, almost there.

She lifted herself up on one elbow. She reached between her legs and swiped some of his heavy cream onto her finger, and then, holding his eyes, she gently rubbed it against her taut pointed nipple, and then inserted her finger into her mouth.

Oh yes, that did it, that—she made a hissing sound of pure female satisfaction as he roughly pushed her onto her back, climbed over her, covered her and mounted her without words, without preliminaries, with nothing but the lust in his soul.

She groaned she wrapped herself around him like a ribbon, and gave him her mouth, her body, her hot wet core. She quickened as he crammed himself into her; she loved the first penetration, she loved the strength of it, the thickness of it, the length of it thrusting to find the depth of the textured heat of her.

She loved it just there, deeply embedded, holding tight, all hers, every last potent inch of it. There was nothing more delicious, more luxurious, more supremely female than to be naked beneath a man and to have his body wholly and completely between your legs and at your command.

She couldn't help moving; she wanted him deeper still. She writhed against his hardness, his heat, enticing, sinuous little movements designed, as she well knew, to make him lose control.

She spread her legs widely and ground downward, wanting to feel his very root, wanting to feel his hair grazing her aching skin.

And his kisses—rough, overpowering, dominating, seeking something in their fury. She didn't care; her mouth was his, she surrendered everything to him.

But his body was hers and she wanted to wring everything from him.

It was a slow excruciating mating dance. There was nothing he could do to her resilient body that she didn't want or didn't invite with her swinging undulating hips and the husky love sounds she made at the back of her throat.

And he couldn't get enough of her. He wanted to imprint her body on his, he wanted to thrust himself into her forever.

He felt violent about it, volatile with emotions that he had thought were buried. There was too much to this that had nothing to do with her—or him, and he didn't care. It scared him that he didn't care, and that every scruple he had was focused solely in the long strong thrusts of his body into hers.

That was what he wanted: the moment, the blast of

voluptuous pleasure, the desire to do it again and again and again.

But only with *her*.

The gods were laughing, and he—he was primed and tempting fate.

His body vibrated like a violin. He could not have imagined such a sex partner. He couldn't have predicted *her*.

Her body was sleek, resonant, giving. Her mouth was as voracious as his, and she met every thrust of his tongue with rapacious and inventive enjoyment. Her hands were all over him, feeling him, stroking him, kneading his taut muscles, and riding the tense press of his buttocks as he pounded against her. And in his mind, the image of her naked and sucking the last bead of his cream with such intense pleasure.

A man could get entangled in a woman like that. A man could explore her sex forever. A man could never want to let go . . .

He wanted her this way forever, naked and open for him, awash in his cream, and moaning in his arms.

Every throaty sound she made reverberated deep within him.

What man wouldn't succumb? Even he, tight and skeptical as he was; even he. She was real and there and fearless in her desire for him.

And he felt every nuance of her response. She was close, that close, to release. Her body rippled under him with a wanton urgency. She was coming, coming, coming; he braced himself on one arm and used his free hand to hold down her hips. He wanted to feel it, feel her, every movement, every shimmy, every subtlety of her culmination.

He was in control, and she was coming—he couldn't wait, he couldn't—he felt himself seize up and stiffen, and fighting it every inch of the way, he fell over the edge into a violent consuming surrender to her.

On and on it went, a spume of pure molten pleasure he poured into her endlessly, endlessly, he could have ridden her forever, spewing himself into her, taking her body, letting her ride until the bone-crackling moment she gave herself to him.

The mystery of her was that she could control when. Her dazzling dark gaze sent him a knowing message: she had broken him this time, and she would take all the time in the world to come. And he was still so hard and hot for her, he could have gone on for hours.

But there was an urgency in her. She loved her power and her wanton nature. But she loved gratification even more. A woman who loved her nakedness and her sex and the pleasure coiling all through her shimmering body.

From him. From his strength, his heat, his penis, yes. He wouldn't let himself think about anything else—just that body, those guttural sounds, that slick wet resilient heat that enfolded him so perfectly—just that, as she wrapped herself around him and gave herself up to undiluted ravishing pleasure that shook her body from head to toe.

And then silence. Delicious bone-weary silence. He didn't move; she let him stay, reveling in the hard thrust of him still inside her and the feel of his bare skin against hers.

The fragrance of sex permeated the room.

. . . this . . . she had lived for this once upon a time . . . but that was before . . . and she wasn't going to think about that as she cradled him, all of him, in her arms and between her legs.

The lights flickered and went out.

Footsteps sounded; Leonie's voice, Serena's in response. Somewhere in the distance, a door opened and closed. They ignored everything; he remained long, strong and rigid within her. She thought she slept, but perhaps she didn't. Perhaps she dreamt this perfect union, a thing apart from everything else.

Perhaps not.

It felt so real.

Sometime deep in the night, he whispered in her ear, *I want you, I'm so hard for you . . .*

And she whispered back, *I feel it, I want it, give it to me . . .*

This time it was quiet torture, everything centered on him, his heat, his lust, his prowess; she wanted only to be the receptacle of his passion.

He gave her her desire; he rode her to point, until his body was lathered over with sweat. In the dark, she focused on the point, on his pumping thrusts, on the keen edge of pleasure that spiralled all over her.

She loved it in the dark; everything was magnified in the dark. Everything was magic, perfect, and he was so very there. And she had nothing to do but feel his raging desire for her. He was out of control with it; she had seduced him well. He only wanted to conquer her. And this time, she wanted to surrender.

She braced her heels against his legs, and she reached down under him and grasped those luscious taut sacs that were so wondrous and free. Grasped them firmly in her hand and worked them with her fingers, and then slid her fingers still further between his legs to that delicious spot directly behind them, and began rubbing and stroking that.

Oh, just that . . . perfect—his body shuddered violently; she had him wholly and fully in her hand just like that, and he was squirming to get away from her knowing fingers.

Just like that—she grasped him again tightly, and she felt the very moment of his capitulation as his body stiffened again and unleashed the potent fury of his release.

He was all hers just then, but she had no time to revel

in it; her body betrayed her. Her stunning sizzling culmination took her utterly by surprise, taking her over completely, and inundating her in a backwash of sensation so intense she almost fainted.

And still he was hard; and still he stayed.

But when she awakened in the morning, he was gone. And so were the table and the board.

Chapter Fourteen

And so there it was: she had succumbed in her own private *voudrais* and to the high emotion of the moment.

And now her sins were divided between *here* and *there*, and kept in secret behind closed doors.

It was early, and Serena was still asleep, her clothes scattered every which where in her room, evidence of how tired she had been, how late they'd come home, and obviously of what a good time she'd had.

There was no sign of the board or the table, and after her struggle with it the previous night, she found its disappearance a little eerie.

But perhaps *he* had been able to remove it. Or Gita had. Or one of the servants. No matter. It was a minor mystery compared to what else had happened last night.

Even she couldn't credit it. By light of day, the whole thing seemed out of kilter and like a plot of a gothic novel.

The hallway, so dark and forbidding by night, was flooded with sun from the third floor landing window, and it was hard to conjure up the spectre of the night before, floating so amorphously at the other end.

She even felt brave enough to enter the guest bedroom. It was a different room by day. It was a corner room, and there was light everywhere. No scent of lilac. Nothing in the armoire. No sign of the divining board or the table. The bed neatly made and awaiting the next occupant.

And so down to breakfast in the dining room. Leonie was already there, and leafing through the *Daily Tatler*. "I was so hoping we would get a mention," she said, "oh, but there's nothing here—as usual. You would think they were deliberately avoiding us. You should have come to the play last night. Lady Theresa was a little unhappy that you'd declined to come. On the other hand, that left room for Serena to exert her somewhat limited charms, which—in that company—seemed more considerable than they are."

"Just as long as she didn't prattle about ghosts and the like," Diandra murmured, helping herself to baked eggs, fried tomatoes, asparagus, biscuits and tea.

"George wishes to get up a shooting party at Skene, and I think that would be ideal. That way, we can control the guest list and exclude those noxious heiresses who have enough places to go anyway. We'll arrange it for next week—whoever is at loose ends, that will be fine, and Serena can get a taste of a weekend house party. I'll set everything in motion today. Meantime, tonight—let me see . . ."

She took out a notebook which was neatly annotated with a calendar and a list of engagements. "Oh yes, the Esterhams' dinner. You're invited, and you will come. They have three younger sons, all perfect for Serena. The usual livings: church, army, banking. But—viable nevertheless. I think they'll all be there. And then the daughter—she's

Serena's age. They ought to hit it off. And that would ease the way for her later on. Don't renege on this one."

"I wouldn't think of it," Diandra said.

"Justin will come too. Yes. I think that will do. The figured silk for you. Oh, and Serena . . . hmmm—something a little more dramatic—I'll have to think . . ."

And off she went, marshalling the troops and planning maneuvers.

It actually proved to be quite a congenial party. The three Honorables, Harry, Albert and Joseph, were personable and out to make an impression, having been apprised beforehand just who the sister of Miss Serena Morant was. And to that considerable weight was added the presence of the present Earl of Skene, his sister-in-law and Serena's sponsor, Lady Leonie Hull, and his friend, Lord George Tisbury, Viscount Penbarrow.

The daughter, Christabel, was a lively slender redhead with blue eyes and fair fair skin that looked almost translucent in the light. She performed on the pianoforte before dinner, and got up games afterward for those who were not serious about cards.

Her brothers hung around Serena in the most enchanting way, and, watching them vie for her attention, Diandra felt appallingly middle-aged.

And insanely envious of the way Christabel handled her brothers—and Justin.

Ah, Justin. She had watched him the whole time, across the dinner table, and conversing with his hostess and host, with Leonie, with mutual friends, and then with Christabel, turning the pages of her music, and escorting her to dinner, the perfect guest.

But Christabel Esterham was of *his* world, and not that netherworld of rumpled sheets and spewing passion. What did the genteel Christabel know of relinquishing control and drowning in a tidal wave of sexual hedonism?

And what did Diandra Morant know about being a lady?

Consciously, she removed herself from that realm. It would have been so easy to fall into a fit of envy. But this was not her purpose. That was being well served by this invitation and the interest of the Esterham sons in Serena. And by Justin's small attentions to her during the course of the evening.

All very proper. Just what she had wanted. What she had envisioned when Hugh had proposed the trip.

When George set up at the pianoforte, and the dancing began, she was relegated once again to the perimeter of the group, with Lady Esterham and her mother-in-law for company.

This wasn't too comfortable either. Lady Esterham was intent on playing matchmaker for Christabel, and her object was *not* a Viscount.

"Well, Justin has been paying her marked attention tonight," Lady Esterham commented to Diandra as the group commenced a reel. "It isn't as if he hasn't noticed her prior to this. His attentions, if anything, have been tepid. But tonight—"

Oh yes, tonight. As opposed to last night, and the voluptuous gratification of his possession. Christabel Esterham would never know the like of it. And she just couldn't keep the thought out of her mind.

It was the guilt. It was the indulgence, in a place and at a time when she had least expected it. She *had* to keep herself removed from it. She had to treat it just as a man would: something apart from his everyday life.

That was what she had wanted: the freedom to yield without the price of her emotions. And she thought she had covered that very well.

". . . he's old enough now; he's sampled enough women," Lady Esterham was saying, rather baldly, Diandra thought. "He needs an heir, but everyone's been saying that for a year or more. He's sensible to it. But he's not always so charming. I do worry for Christabel. He would be something to keep in hand."

Diandra didn't let herself dwell on that statement for one minute. "Indeed, he has been most accommodating to me and my sister."

Lady Esterham ran her eye over Diandra's form fitting gown. "Yes, he's done very well by you. It's the talk of the social set how he took you in, given what happened to his parents. I don't think Justin tends toward forgiveness. And you are very beautiful, even if Leonie has wrapped you in black from head to toe. But there can be nothing untoward there. Leonie is the one in love with him. But there's no interest in that quarter; and besides George Tisbury is in love with her."

Diandra pressed her lips together, staggered by this tid-bit of information. How had she not noticed?

"But he's always around where she is," Lady Esterham pointed out, and indeed, there he was, waltzing with Leo-nie while the Honorable Harry took a turn at the music. But Leonie only had eyes for Justin who was dancing with Christabel and—wonders—making her laugh.

A moment later, he swung Serena out onto the floor and finished the dance with her while Leonie sulked on the sidelines, and George attempted to mollify her.

"A lost cause," Lady Esterham murmured. "She has wanted Justin forever, and she thought eventually . . . but after Guthrie remarried—well, Justin was in such a rage, he went out of circulation for a year. All on account of *you*, my dear. How do you like having such power?"

"It's rather daunting," Diandra said. "I cannot credit that."

"It's true. He holed up at Skene and no one saw him for months at a time. Except George, of course. And Leonie, sometimes. But he didn't ask for her comfort. Your arrival was a blessing. At least she can be around him on the pretext of helping your sister. But I hope you are not aiming too high for her, my dear. It won't wash at all."

That was blunt. And a warning.

"You have younger sons to marry off," she pointed out gently, pointedly.

"And what do you have?" Lady Esterham asked with malicious curiosity.

Diandra smiled as she rose to her feet; it really was necessary to tower above these noxious snobs. "Money," she said succinctly. "Pots and pots of money."

That put her in a whole different light; she saw Lady Esterham whispering the whole rest of the evening to her mother-in-law, to Harry and Albert who promptly set about getting to know Serena better.

It was a sexual quadrille, without the heat and tearing need, and fueled by the coin of the realm, even for Justin. Especially for Justin.

He seemed quite taken with Christabel.

And Leonie was unreasonably upset. As if everyone didn't know her dirty little secret.

Perhaps she thought they didn't. But at least there was no mention of the supernatural events at Cheswick Square. There was enough else to occupy her, and Serena had been warned not talk of her penchant for charms and chants and spells.

So the evening passed, and Diandra spent a good deal of it observing George. Kindly goodhearted George in love with the self-serving wasp-tongued Leonie. The perception overset everything, and she felt a bristling anger that Leonie had never loved anyone but herself.

But that was George's problem, and obviously he had been steadfast and loyal without scaring her away. Leonie depended upon him. She used him abominably, and he came back for more.

Nothing like Justin, but as loyal to him as anyone. She began to see as she watched them, and it was much more entertaining than feeding her niggling envy.

She wasn't going to succumb to that. Rather, she wanted to examine rationally what she was feeling, why she couldn't just put it out of mind, out of sight the way he could, and take her pleasure at her convenience.

Well, she had. But she hadn't expected the residual effect; it made her ever more aware of the traps she could walk into.

And Lady Esterham, with her piercing gaze, watching her, now she knew that the dowager widow spoke the coin of the realm. It didn't matter who her antecedents were, after all, or that she had supplanted Pamela in Guthrie Reynell's affections.

. . . Nobody told . . .

She imagined them all down in the *voudrais,* their faces contorted with lust. Yes, that was the way to bring them all down to size, including Lady Esterham. Including Justin.

She blew out a deep breath. This was the way of disaster. She had made the decision, no one else. And if she had thought the constraints of London society would keep her baser nature at bay, she had been appallingly off the mark.

Serena danced over to where she was sitting. "This is more the thing, isn't it, Diandra? Those Esterham brothers—so immature. But so good-looking . . . and then Christabel—do you think Justin's being so nice to her for a reason?"

"Just good manners," she said, temporizing. She most emphatically did not want to speculate about Justin's motives.

"Well, he's been very nice to *me,*" Serena added. "Christabel may know how to play parlor games, but she has no conversation whatsoever. It does make me thankful for our years in Bhaumaghar. At least *I* know how to talk to people."

"I'll assume you're not talking about the phenomena at the house . . ."

Serena sent her an exasperated look. "Not to these people. They are too too proper. Haven't you heard all the talk of bloodlines? Especially Justin's? They are desperate for him to marry. Far more so than he is himself."

"How interesting," she said carefully.

"I think they memorize everyone's pedigree, and the one thing you can have better than that is money."

"That I figured out," Diandra said, and gave Serena a little push back to the younger company.

She had to forcibly make herself stay where she was. She hated dark corners and being a widow and not being able to participate in the games and the dancing. She *hated* it. Someone should have told her; she resented the fact no one had told her. And she would certainly advise Serena against fixing the interest of an older man. It was too bloody confining.

On the other hand, Serena had intimated there was someone *she* was interested in.

But no one in this crowd. She would have noticed, she was sure she would have been aware.

"So—you grew up in India," Lady Esterham said, easing herself back down beside Diandra.

"Indeed," she said politely. "My parents died when we were young. We lived with my brother who is the governor of Rajam Province."

"I see." Lady Esterham didn't know quite what to ask next.

"And of course there was the time in Calcutta when I was Vicereine."

Oh, yes—that got her attention.

"Marvelous," Lady Esterham murmured. "We read all about it. But of course, when Guthrie died . . ."

"Exactly. Who could have known? I was in despair."

"And yet so—providential . . . ?"

"I'm not quite sure I understand you, Lady Esterham."

"My dear—no children, you so young, he so wealthy . . . and now, here you are."

"Yes, I felt a season here would greatly enhance my skills as my brother's political hostess," Diandra said evenly while she contemplated committing mayhem on the woman. *The condescending witch . . .*

"Everyone who is anyone has come to Bhaumaghar, as you may know, Lady Esterham. The hunting is extraordinary; my brother's hospitality is legendary. I do hope you will come when you are passing through—India, that is."

"I'm sure my husband is well aware," Lady Esterham murmured.

"I did so enjoy my year as Vicereine," Diandra went on. The woman deserved it—every little nick and twist of the knife. "Let me tell you about it. It is almost like being queen of the country. There is ongoing ceremony and ritual. You live in a palace, with servants to attend to every command. You entertain every manner of ruler from countries all over the world. You have your charities, and a litany of very special duties that devolve on the Vicereine. An enormous wardrobe—there are state occasions several times a week, you know. It was the most wonderful year of my life . . ."

"I'm sure . . ." Lady Esterham said.

"And of course, as Hugh's hostess, I entertain quite royally all throughout the year. I believe later on this year, we are expecting the President of the United States, as a matter of fact. But forgive me, I must be boring you to tears."

"So very interesting," Lady Esterham choked. "The President."

"Oh yes. And Gladstone as well, you know. He was horribly upset when Guthrie died. Well, it just changed things all around for him, and he went and appointed . . . no, no—I don't need to bore you with current events now, do I? Although he did ask me whether . . . I must stop this, really. This London sojourn is really to give Serena a taste of Town life. She does seem to be enjoying herself."

Lady Esterham looked totally nonplussed, and Diandra wondered if she hadn't troweled it on too thick. But she didn't care at that point. Leonie was was right there beside her suddenly, and she wondered how much she had heard.

But then it was obvious she had come to signal the end of the evening for them, and thank goodness for that.

"Ah, I see we are about to take our leave. Lady Esterham, lovely evening. It's been a pleasure."

"Indeed. We will see you again, I'm sure."

She had the common courtesies down at least. It was only when you stepped into her parlor that she entangled you in the sticky web of social snobbery.

But it was over; another evening done. She had dodged Lady Esterham's poison darts quite efficiently, and given her something to chew on besides.

It was all she could hope to accomplish. And Serena never had to know.

She had decided she was a creature of the night. Night was so easy; darkness cloaked every vice and shrouded every sin. The night was another world, another place, utterly removed from the demands of mundane day-to-day living.

In the dark, all fantasies were possible, one could give life to one's clandestine self, and no one would ever tell.

And in the dark, all secrets were sacred, cloaked in the benediction of silence and collusion.

She lay awake, deep into the night, her body betraying her yet again. She could count on nothing. She wanted everything. And she was past the point of regret.

Her body was stiff with wanting, almost as if it had a memory apart from her own. She felt the ache to be touched, to be kissed, to lie stretched out against a hot hard male body that would . . .

Oh, but she didn't want to think about that. That path was futile. She was not as entitled as a man to seek her pleasure. She was only empowered to know how she could.

It was so horrendously unfair. That, and the emotions that went hand in hand with it. Stifling her envy this whole evening. Watching Justin and George leave for their club. Knowing they could buy anyone on the street for an evening's pleasure. And walk away.

She wasn't strong enough. She thought she could do it. She had thought . . .

But all the powers of Eve, what use were they in the end? She was left squirming in bed, and nothing more to be had.

Had she loved Guthrie? She was still wrestling with that, and her guilt.

He had been *her* lover, her tutor, her guide. He had opened the book, showed her the pages, taught her the worth of her body, worshipped it, and made her feel as glorious as a goddess.

She had been *his* goddess. But no one should have to make love on a pedestal, and now she didn't know what she was except a woman in heat who knew exactly how to satisfy her lust . . . with no one to accommodate her.

That had been his legacy. And her determination never to unleash that carnal, uncontrollable part of herself.

Well, that was all gone to smoke now, irretrievable, irrev-ocable, irredeemable.

And with Justin Reynell.

It was enough to make a saint cry. And yet she didn't want it any less.

And she wanted it with him.

Her cross to bear. Her sins of the flesh.

She should be wearing a hair shirt. She should be sleep-ing in her corsets to remind her that the body was weak and she was more powerless than most.

Ah, but she could never have envisioned *this*. Him. Them.

She ought never to have come to England.

And she didn't know how she could ever leave.

He came to her anyway, after a night of carousing and flirting with insipid misses who would spread their legs for a farthing and not think twice about it. And that was after the deadly evening at the Esterhams, and his deliberate attention to the milk-faced Christabel, and the utterly per-nicious Serena.

He had been too generous to her already, but that was all of a piece. He knew what they were saying about him, he wanted to play with them, and he wanted the languishing pleasure of a responsive woman to whom no declarations must be made.

He watched her covertly the whole evening: the cool haughty expression on her face when first she arrived; the fire in her eye as Harriet Esterham began her assault, her deft check on Serena at all times, her perfect posture, and how, in every light, the opaque black of gown made her seem more sensuous, and even more unobtainable.

But he knew better. He knew that body naked and rock-ing with indescribable pleasure. He knew those breasts and the strength of those hips, the taste of that mouth and tongue, and the hot slick satin between her legs.

But the last thing he wanted was to be enslaved by that body. The last thing he needed was to be dependent on her caresses, on the expert tug of her mouth. He didn't want to know her, he only wanted to have her.

And so, after a futile night seeking the like, he came to her in their dark netherworld where nothing had to be said or admitted.

They could live for this: the heated touch of his hand on her silky skin; her instant luxurious response, her body stretching opulently and seeking his caress.

All he wanted to do, just feel that voluptuous reponse, just slide his hands all over her, lifting her gauzy gown to get at her thighs, her buttocks, the small of her back that curved so sensually into the flare of her hips.

She was made for such pleasure, she couldn't wait for it as she shifted herself and spread her legs so that he could tantalize the wet heat between.

And then he turned her boneless body so he could caress her breasts. Such breasts—so firm and weighty with those hard pointed nipples that drove him to distraction.

He wanted to drive himself between her breasts and spew himself all over those nipples. He was so engorged by the thought, he almost came. But a man needed to cultivate restraint, even under such provocative conditions.

He undressed himself with precision as she watched and he watched her naked body writhe and arch to entice him back to her bed.

Nothing could have kept him away. He climbed onto her, straddling her yearning body and he began his deliberate seduction of her nipples. All he wanted, just those hard succulent pleasure points in his mouth, first one, then the other, back and forth, back and forth, until she was ready to scream for mercy, and he was on the verge of eruption.

And then, he shifted himself so that he was positioned between her breasts and she immediately pushed them up and around his towering erection so that he was pillowed between them, just where he wanted to be.

Her eyes were bright and knowing. Her hands cupped her breasts so her nipples were erect and in his line of vision. And she licked her lips in anticipation as he began to move.

Long strokes between her breasts, long, almost to her mouth, he wanted to make it to her mouth; he pushed himself hard between her breasts so that the very tip of him just touched her lips, once, twice, the third time she caught him, taking that sensitive tip right between her lips and squeezing.

And again, to a long lush lick of her tongue. And again, to a sucking aching kiss and she held onto him and held on just with the suction of her mouth and her hot flicking tongue, devouring him, eating just the luscious tip of him, all hot wet sucking licks and tugs while she cradled him between her billowing taut-tipped breasts.

He kept going back for more. Each stroke took longer and longer as her expert mouth worked the tip of his penis toward ecstasy.

And she loved doing it. She loved him between her breasts, his rigid manhood craving her mouth, and her succulent kisses.

And he adored the the lush soughing sounds she made at the back of her throat as if *she* couldn't get enough. It became a game: would he thrust deeply enough for her to catch him? And if he didn't, would he miss her juicy sucking? And could he ever get enough before he exploded . . . he felt like he could go on and on forever between her breasts and her hot eager mouth.

In his mind, one more thrust, one more, one more again, between her lips and into paradise, and one more still . . . he pulled back for still another lusty plunge into the heaven of her mouth, and his potent sex erupted with the force of a volcano—wet and wild and pumping everywhere, all over her nipples, her breasts, her mouth, her face, her hair covering her, bathing her in the hot cream of his desire.

He couldn't move, couldn't, couldn't couldn't. Didn't want to. Could have died and gone to heaven right then.

But she immediately began rubbing his ejaculate into the skin of her breasts, her face, her body, as if she loved it and craved it; into her taut nipples, as she looked at him with those dark unfathomable eyes, as if she had known all along his forbidden fantasy.

He had never known anyone who loved it like that.

Her body arched as she continued to caress the residue of his desire into her body; there was so much, it was drying so fast, she wanted it so much . . . she rubbed it on her legs, between her thighs, on her hands, back around her breasts and her nipples again, all the while watching him, watching his ramrod manhood respond to the caressing strokes of her fingers rubbing the essence of him into her own body.

"I'll be wearing it tomorrow," she whispered, brushing her lips with her sticky fingers. "I'll be clothed in your cream." She licked the tip of one finger, and he wanted to cram himself into her mouth and spew all over her again.

He wanted to give her half what she had given him.

He was rabid to taste her; she was primed and ready for him, he could feel it as he explored between her legs, and she opened wider and invited him in.

A moment later, he made her goddess and he was her abject slave. There was something about such deep carnal kisses, and that he could control pleasure with just his tongue.

She went off like a shotgun the moment he touched her, hot shuddering spasms one after the other after the other as he delved deeper and deeper into the velvet of her sex.

He wouldn't let go; he spread her legs wider and wider, going as deep as he could into the mystery of her, pulling her with sucking kisses similar to her own, making her bear down on him harder and harder, until, until . . . she cried out for mercy.

Too much was too much; he was as raw and satiated as she; he eased himself away from her and collapsed beside her, fatigued and gratified to the bone.

It was like a fabulous dream. She was sure she had dreamt it, because she was not allowed to merge the netherworld of dark erotic passion with the mundane morning rituals of having breakfast, riding in the park, and then changing for an afternoon of making calls.

They left cards at the Esterhams', and went on to visit with several of Leonie's friends.

A boring lot. Easy to think of other things and still carry on a conversation. But she didn't like the talk of Justin and how he had been seen out and about and what a nice refreshing change *that* was, to have such a worthy *parti* among them.

If only they knew . . . if only they had tasted his passion . . . and were brazen enough to wear his cream . . .

They knew to a shilling his annual income. It was absolutely appalling. And they discussed with circumlocuitous candor the prospects of each and every eligible heiress, including the Americans who were cutting a wide swath through London society.

Leonie was used to it, of course, and knew just how to do social chat and steer the subject away from both Justin and herself. If anyone had an inkling where her interests lay, Diandra saw no sign of it.

There was no talk of spectres and *séances,* though they did discuss the the resolution of the case of Madam Petrovna, whose death was accounted a heart attack for want of any evidence to the contrary, and the fact that there had been no progress finding who had killed the unfortunate Miss Partram.

They all lived for the gossip of the moment and to be the one first with the most current *on-dit.* And Leonie was considered to be one of the very best sources because of Justin's position and his reentry into the social scene.

She lapped it up, all the while keeping her distance. She knew just how to do it too, telling some deliciously shocking tidbit while actually she revealed nothing of consequence, and she timed perfectly when they had to leave.

"Never tell them anything. They're a bunch of leeches, and they're always sucking blood," she said trenchantly. "Never satisfied. Always looking to tear down someone a little higher than they. But they are amusing on a boring afternoon. And they'll tittle-tattle about you, Diandra, for a little while, and then go on to the next case."

But she wasn't so sure there would be a next case when Justin met them at the door with a copy of that day's *Tatler* in hand. And he was furious with her yet again.

All considerations out the window. The erotic life of my lord begins and ends at the bedroom door . . . do what you will—as long as nothing else intrudes.

"Madam is about to become a nine days' wonder—what the hell did you say to Harriet Esterham?" He thrust the paper into her hands. It was open already to the appropriate page, and the paragraph was dripping in innuendo.

We are fortunate indeed to have among us the former Vicereine and widow of the Lord Guthrie Reynell, first Earl of

*Skene, who is visiting family in London, along with her
sister, Miss Serena Morant, for whom she has hopes of
contracting (or perhaps purchasing?) a suitable alliance.
They have been seen at various social functions in town,
among them dinner last night at the home of Lord and
Lady Esterham, and guests, who were regaled with the details
of Lady Reynell's year in India as consort to the Viceroy,
his lordship, the now deceased Earl, in which my lady likened
herself to a queen. A deposed sovereign now, we say, with
no royal dominion whatsoever, and no right to claim one.*

It was horrible. She put the paper down slowly. Retribution was certainly swift among the nobility. A hard lesson
to learn, especially at Justin's expense.

He was staring at her as if she were a stranger, his eyes
icy hard, his mouth a thin line of contempt.

"Fortuitous indeed that Leonie has gotten out the invitations to the shooting party, or we'd all be dead ducks this
week in Town. You are all going out to Skene by morning,
and we will hope this idiocy will die down by Saturday. As
it is, this will be fodder for the cows to chew on for the
next couple of days, and *I* will have to defend it."

"Indeed," Leonie chimed in. "And not only that, this
will put a damper on any interest in your sister you had
hoped to cultivate. You made the family—and Guthrie—
look like fools into the bargain. But then—what can one
expect? Not everyone has a Justin who can distract the
gossips. And he will do so—for family honor and for his
father. *Not* for you, Diandra, and you'd do well to remember that. Of course, we will pack and leave for Skene today,
Justin. You are right about that. But at a leisurely pace.
And we can let them know this was a planned event and
we are not decamping in the face of that scurrilous paragraph."

"Exactly. I will join you on Saturday . . . and I'm serving

notice now, madam: there had better not be any ghosts, spectres or manifestations. You've done quite enough."

"I will monitor her behavior," Leonie said. "It's quite obvious she cannot be left to her own devices in company. It was really bad of you to point up your advantages, Diandra. It's a point of courtesy never to do so in company like that."

She felt a wave of heat course all through her body. This was too much, even for Leonie. And it was not so bad as the paragraph made out. And she didn't care anyway.

Not true: she wanted nothing to interfere with the coming months of Serena's time in London.

Who besides Lady Esterham could have even related the essence of the conversation to the gossip mongers? She had said nothing that was so off the mark that someone would want to stoop to smearing her publicly.

It had been a private conversation—or so she had thought. She had been naïve. The artistocracy was always ready for diversion; it was true in Calcutta as well as London, and she should have taken that into account.

Now Justin despised her and they all must suffer, most of all Serena.

Worse, they would never know who tattled, and she hated that most of all.

"You really ought to go begin packing," Leonie said.

"Of course, you're right. I suppose apologies are superfluous at this point," she said to Justin.

"You're lucky it's midweek, madam. They would dine out on it for a fortnight otherwise," he said tightly.

She mounted the steps without a comment, Serena following docilely behind her.

Who, who, who?

And then she turned, just as Leonie cornered Justin on some pretext. She could see them reflected in a hallway mirror, as she was sure Leonie could, and she knew exactly how Leonie must have liked how they looked together, him so tall and she so petite and fragile.

And then Leonie looked up at her, and there was no mistaking the hard, self-satisfied, malevolent look in her eyes or who had leaked that conversation to the *Tatler*.

. . . *wearing his cream* . . .

He was so consumed with his awareness of that, and of his bulging erection, he could hardly work up enough anger over the paragraph in the *Tatler*.

. . . *wearing his cream* . . . smeared all over with the evidence of his lust for her—what man wouldn't take her thirty times over to bathe her in the essence and scent of his sex.

God, he wanted her . . . and Leonie was in his way as usual—he could barely hear what she was saying, he didn't give a damn what she was saying . . . his eyes, his consciousness followed Diandra up the stairs and out of his sight.

Into the privacy of her room where she would strip off her clothes and await the pleasures of the night.

No, he wouldn't succumb to her tonight. He wouldn't. He wanted surcease without thought, without price. He could spend himself on anyone, and he just might. There was enough diversion in town to satisfy the appetites of a pasha.

Would she be waiting?

How many men would kill to be devoured by that hot mouth, how many?

He knew just what he wanted to do, next time. He wanted to soak her in his seed and bathe her himself. The fantasy reared to life instantly and he had to forcibly restrain himself from going after her, stripping off her clothes, and visiting his hot straining head on her naked body.

Leonie was in the way. She was always in the way.

They were going to a private party somewhere . . . Millbank would know . . . they were going together, with Serena, but Diandra would have to stay home; unavoidable social obligation, he *must* attend, as much to protect Serena as the defend the gossip. Everything must remain as normal as possible before they left for Skene.

He understood, he understood, he understood—would she never *move*? He felt like lifting her like a piece of furniture and setting her someplace else. He agreed to everything, but he didn't know what and he didn't care.

She was wearing his cream . . . had begged for it. Had hungered for it. Had luxuriated in it. Had caressed her nipples with it . . .

God, he couldn't wait to have her again . . .

It was a long, long night, compounded of fantasy and reality. He was just as nice as he could be to Christabel Esterham; he accepted Lady Esterham's apologies for the outrageous behavior of some unknown guest of hers who had made the details of a private conversation public.

He sat between Leonie and George for dinner, and bent over backwards to charm Serena. He deflected the barbs about his royal stepmother with light-hearted wit and disguised his anger.

And all he could think about was Diandra, wearing his cream.

He couldn't wait to get back to her. He was hard for her, bulging for her, hot for her.

And to have to wait only increased his lust to spend himself on her.

And there was still the ride home with Leonie and Serena, and the pulsating minutes ticking by as they got themselves upstairs and finally to their rooms. Long, fractured moments that went on forever as he envisioned Diandra naked in her bed, wearing only his cream, and swamped with the desire to devour him again.

The waiting was excruciating. The creaks and groans of

the house; the movements of the servants, like elves behind the scene. Sconces lit. Firescreens carefully placed. Doors locked. No rapping. No spectres. Just quiet, quiet, quiet as the house, the servants, settled down for the night.

And still he waited, deep into the netherwold of the night when all things were permissable and nothing was forbidden.

And only then did he make his way upstairs, divesting himself of his clothes as he went, and releasing his hot jutting erection into the night.

He was naked as he eased his way into her room. She was waiting for him, he felt her come pulsatingly to life as she sensed his presence.

No words were needed. He climbed onto the bed and into her mouth and almost shot his seed right there.

But no, she had a want and a need all her own, and she knew just how to give him the power. She held him tightly as she positioned herself beneath him so that he was angled just over her taut pointed nipples.

And then she began to pump him gently, gently, gently. And slowly but surely, he began to ejaculate, slow, slow, slow as he watched her direct his essence onto her nipples, just her nipples; the cream of him thick on her hard hot nipples, coating them with his sex and his scent, only there and no place else.

Her body writhed as his essence thickened around each nipple; she strained against the feel of it coating each sensitive pointed tip. And she held him like a vise, her mouth wildly kissing the hot ridged tip of him, and licking the last luscious pearly dew just from his head.

"I want you to think of me wearing your cream on my nipples," she breathed against his rock-hard member as she kept caressing it and licking it.

God, he loved it. He loved it. He wanted to fondle her drenched nipples. He wanted to come all over again.

"I love the feel of your cream on my nipples," she whispered. "It's so thick—like you . . ."

He was going to come. He just was going to come, from her provocative words and her expert hands; he didn't know how he was going to contain himself long enough if she kept on this way.

No man should have to suffer like this, wanting everything, having to choose one thing . . . something . . . in—or out—or all around . . .

No logic to this; he was not in control. And he wanted her almost out of his mind—nothing but complete immersion would do.

He pushed her back onto the bed, mounted her, and rode them both to ecstatic oblivion.

He left her before daylight, and watched without expression the next day as the luggage was loaded in the carriages, and with the servants, she, Serena and Leonie set off to Skene.

Like nothing had happened, except it was all burned in his brain.

He actually thought he could do without her, that he had spent himself so entirely on her, that he wouldn't miss it, wouldn't want it, couldn't care less if he had it.

But he went so crazy without being able to see her or touch her, he wound up going to Skene two days earlier than he had planned.

And he brought with him the horrific news that Christabel Esterham had been found dead in Green Park.

Chapter Fifteen

Christabel had been found the next morning after they had returned to Skene. Justin had elected not to stay for the funeral. George would come at the weekend, but it looked as if there would not be much more company.

Everyone was in shock: Christabel and Grace Partram dead, and for no discernible reason that anyone could tell. Stiles would want to question anyone who had seen Christabel at any social function in the weeks prior to her death, but they didn't have to make a special trip back to London for that. At the two parties they had been at there were enough witnesses to even eliminate his need to speak with them immediately.

It cast a pall on everything. Serena went into a fit of moping that they had left all the fun of London for the funereal atmosphere of Skene where there was absolutely *nothing* to do. And the house party might be cancelled as well. Justin had no idea if anyone would feel like coming out after the funeral, but he had held the invitation open.

Leonie was horrified, but in the depths of her eyes,

Diandra could see her frustration that her own indiscretions had been pushed aside for juicier stuff.

She was shocked. Beautiful Christabel with her flaming hair, lively manner and pale, pale skin. Christabel for whom Lady Esterham had begun entertaining high hopes just on the basis of Justin's attentions to her that awful night.

Poor poor Christabel.

But Justin didn't look overset by the tragedy; merely irritated that he had to pretend grief for someone who had been at best a passing acquaintance to whom he had chosen, for one insignificant moment, to be kind.

But he had seen the danger of that, perhaps too late. Everyone had seen Lady Esterham clinging to him in tears and with incoherent references to his growing attachment to Christabel and how now it was all to dust.

He couldn't imagine Christabel at all, and he thought it was kinder to let Lady Esterham keep her dreams; he didn't have to act on them, or disappoint her, now. He knew exactly what the story would be: *Skene was on the verge, the very point of offering for my darling Christabel when the tragedy happened. Imagine—Justin Reynell, my prospective son-in-law . . .*

Fodder for her friends, but mainly the gossip mill. And then she would curse the fates or God or whatever she believed in, and she would throw herself into finding suitable wives for her sons.

He didn't feel in the least callous dismissing her like that. Nor did he feel like revealing he would never have offered for Christabel, who was pale as a milkmaid in comparison to Diandra.

Diandra haunted his dreams. He had never had anyone like Diandra; she was the woman he had always wanted—and the one he should never have had.

But no such considerations were on his mind as he

stalked the halls of Skene looking for her the morning he returned.

Leonie, however, wanted to hear details.

"There were no details," he told her impatiently as he snapped his crop against his thigh. "Someone from the Yard came calling to tell us, having gotten our names from Lady Esterham's guest list. I could tell him nothing, and here I am."

"George will know," Leonie said fretfully. "And why would Stiles want to talk to us yet again? What had we to do with Christabel Esterham?"

"Not much," Justin said succinctly. "And now, could you kindly tell me where Diandra has gotten off to?"

"Why?" Leonie demanded suspiciously.

"For the very reason I told you. No more ghosts. No more manifestations."

"Nonsense, Pamela's here whether *you* wish to acknowledge it or not."

"Leonie . . ."

"Believe what you want, Justin. She was my sister, and I think she has come to find her murderer."

Sometimes she wondered about Serena. They had gone for a ride, after Serena had evinced some teary sympathy for Christabel's fate, and almost immediately they were out of sight of the house, Serena wanted to climb down from her mount, and cast a circle of protection.

"What? Honestly, Serena—this has really gone far enough."

"Oh no no no—You know I read the cards the first night we came, and you remember the ace of spades turned up right in the center of the cross. I still shiver when I think of it. Honestly, Diandra, what if Pamela has followed us back here? What if she means to harm us? What if *she* killed those poor girls?"

"I thought we were finished with all that spirit business."

"You can't assume anything, Diandra. Just because they haven't made themselves known doesn't mean they aren't lurking and waiting for the right moment. And after all the signs we've been shown, and you're still skeptical?"

"What signs were those, darling Serena? Two dead mediums?"

Serena began pacing off four corners. "There's a reason why Leonie decided for us to come back here, and it had nothing to do with a shooting party. She was guided to use that as an excuse. And now we're here, we want to exclude any harmful spirits or any who mean to do us harm."

"Serena, I am really beginning to doubt your sanity."

"This is the place it all started, Diandra. There's a reason why we've been led to come back. You don't have to do anything. You're in the circle of protection." And she began to chant. "Oracle of the circle, grant us the sacred protection born in the unbroken ring of our trust. There. Safe, now."

"Serena . . ." She was more uncomfortable with the ritual than she realized, but surely that had more to do with all the unnerving events of the past month than Serena's amateurish forays into magic.

And then too, the nights; the otherworldly nights where she was a creature of the senses, nothing more, nothing less, counting the moments until her dark invader returned.

It was all too mixed up in her mind, and she couldn't get quite clear what one had to do with the other and what any of it had to do with Guthrie. Or was it that he had created both of them and that somewhere in time it had been ordained that it was inevitable they would find each other?

But that was just as amorphous as Serena's spells; life didn't work that way. And she was pragmatic enough to know this idyll would burn itself out like a flare very soon.

Until then—oh, until then . . . she had used every carnal art at her command shamelessly. Wantonly. And was overjoyed that they would return to Skene with its erotic underworld.

Another week and then the full brunt of the season's events would begin. And a year and half since Guthrie's untimely death.

And here was Serena pacing out lines and murmuring chants. There was something so very wrong about that; it was too far away from what she had planned for Serena when they had first embarked on this trip.

She was supposed to have gotten over that. She was not supposed to be summoning ghosts and oracles. She was to have laid aside her charms and her fortune-telling cards, and gotten wholly involved in all the social occasions.

Well . . . she had done that, but her dependence on superstition lingered in the background, and here it came full bore at a time when Diandra least wanted to deal with it.

"I really think that's enough, Serena."

"It will do, for now."

They mounted their horses and turned toward the house.

"I really must cast a circle in our rooms as well," Serena mused. "You never can tell."

"I beg to differ with you. There's been nothing for the past two weeks: no rapping, no apparitions, no messages. Whoever is playing these tricks has finally desisted."

"You are too gullible, Diandra. It's not over."

"It had to have been Justin," she went on stubbornly.

"No—you've told him what he wanted to know. It's not Justin."

"Then who?" Let her answer that, Diandra thought. Let her give a name to her certainties those things existed.

Serena drew in a sharp hissing breath. *"Look—"*

She looked—toward the house, and she saw it, the drift of gray just rounding a corner and disappearing into nothingness . . . she couldn't believe she was seeing it, not here, not anywhere—and she took off after it as if her life depended on it.

And she came right up against a stone wall—and Justin too.

"Where is it?" She knew her voice was sharp and peremptory and gave nothing over as to how much she had wanted him to be there; and now she could not comprehend why he had chosen to resurrect the gray ghost back at Skene.

"Where is what?" Diandra, the huntress, flying at him like a whirlwind. It took him precious moments to even grasp what she was saying and by then she lit into him full bore.

"Where did it go, Justin? Where are you hiding it? And why are you doing this? Why now?" She wanted to attack him. She wanted to wrest him to the ground and stomp on him. She wanted him groveling at her feet.

She was furious and she had the odd thought that it had very little to do with the unexpected appearance of the apparition.

Perhaps it was the unexpected appearance of *him* . . .

"Wait a minute, what *are* you talking about?" Her emotion, her anger was making his mount restive, and he had to work to control him just as Serena barrelled into stable yard to add another commotion.

"Do you see it? Did you? The gray ghost?" She was off her horse in a minute and racing around the side of the house.

"Damn her . . . !" Diandra dismounted like a circus performer and dashed after her sister, and he had no choice but to follow.

"Where is it?" She whirled as he cantered toward her. "Why are you doing this?"

"I? Not I. *You,* madam."

"Oh, don't start that again, damn you. It's your house, it's *your* ghost."

"And it passed here not five minutes ago," Serena chimed in. "But there's nothing here now. It's just gone."

"If it ever existed," Justin said. "You two could be in collusion."

"Dear God . . ." Diandra muttered.

"No," Serena said. "It's Pamela. I *told* you, Diandra. She's not done with us . . ."

"I will not listen to this," Diandra said. "The thing was right . . . there—" She pointed. "And it just floated around this side of the house and disappeared. In broad daylight. Who but one of your minions could perform such a feat, Justin?"

"Someone in league with you, madam."

"Maybe the two of you are in league with each other," she said disgustedly.

And didn't the expression on Serena's face change as she considered the idea?

Anything was a possible, she thought irritatedly, grabbing her horse's reins. Better to get away from both of them than fall into their trap.

His trap.

Which trap? Did it matter?

She would wear mud and thatch for him before he would ever trap her *there* again.

But as she walked her mount back to the stables, she wondered just how long that resolve could last.

He watched her, watched her, watched her, first in the stables as she cooled down her horse, brushed him, touched him, murmured to him, and fed him, and he marveled at how easily she could compartmentalize her life.

Just like a man.

He didn't like that. Not when he had been having wet dreams about her.

Nothing in her manner indicated that voluptuous night world they shared had any meaning to her. She was as pragmatic as a courtesan, going about her daily business, dressed to the collarbone as the widow she was, prim, proper, poignant, purposeful . . . infuriating.

He didn't want to know if she ever thought about . . . *him;* God, he hated the situation, just hated it. A rival of the memory of the person he loved—and hated—in equal measure. It was almost too much—except in the dark of the night when nothing mattered except the swamping sensational surrender to the senses.

He followed her into the house, curious now, as she veered toward the saloon and library rather than heading down the guest wing el.

He understood immediately: she was going to find a ghost. She was as tired of the game as he, only she still thought he was activating it.

. . . *his house, his ghost* . . .

Sometimes he thought the only ghost in his life was his father . . . but he refused to go there; all the time, he refused to think about what his father's ambition and defection had meant to him.

It was just not possible to dwell on it without letting feelings surface that were better buried. Easier to bury himself in Dian-dra . . .

And he didn't want think about that either, either who she was or what she had meant to anyone connected to him.

He kept well behind her as she slipped behind the door that led to the *voudrais;* he saw the flicker of candlelight and when it disappeared, he followed carefully behind her.

But she didn't intend to enter to *voudrais;* rather, she was looking for another outlet, one he knew didn't exist, and he watched from afar as she groped along the wall, seeking any aperture, any opening.

She would have to come back to the *voudrais.* He waited until he saw her elongated shadow move toward the stairs to duck behind the doors.

A moment later, a glimmer of light shone under the door, and then she pushed them slowly open.

She didn't see him at first. She lifted her light to illuminate the *salle d'entrée,* looking at it with new eyes.

And then she sensed another presence, and wheeled just as he closed the doors behind him.

"Following me, Justin?" Her tone was cool and calm, belying the instant heat she felt flaring up between them. This she didn't need, not now. Not him closing the doors behind her and effectively closing them off from the real world. Leaving her the choice as well, by not locking them.

"No ghosts here, Diandra."

"Oh, I think there are a couple," she murmured. She felt instantly and strangely dissociated from herself. She was acutely aware of him and the rising tension between them and fact they were alone in the place that reeked of hedonistic sexual indulgence.

And she knew he had come after her here deliberately.

And she didn't know whether she hadn't wanted him to.

"You're not going to find ghosts in the catacombs of Skene," he said.

"And you should know," she countered.

"Or you should," he retorted. "It's your ghost. And your show."

"Touché, Justin. But the fact remains, it's your house and something *was* out there."

"On your word and your sister's? I don't think so."

"Well, we are at *pointe* then, are we not?"

"We could be," he murmured, knowing just the sensual images he was deliberately evoking.

He moved closer, and she edged away. But there was no use protesting; she was already slipping away into the seduction of the *voudrais*.

He locked the double doors. "Perhaps you're seeking this ghost," he murmured, reaching out to touch her face, and leaving a hot little trail of sensation down the side of her cheek.

There was something in the air, there had to be. She shivered at his touch, her body instantly felt languid and moist, her clothing felt superfluous, and everything inside her quickened, . . . waiting, hoping, yearning.

She hadn't come here for this, and he was doing nothing more than looking at her with a raw hunger in his eyes that was utterly enslaving.

Who had the power after all?

His desire was as fierce as hers. More so. She had made it so, deliberately, even calculatedly.

You take your pleasure like a man . . .

Oh, but her response was pure woman—

And she felt in her heart there wasn't much time.

"You remember the *voudrais*," he was saying in a low seductive tone. "In the *salle d'entrée*, you view the menu for the evening. I would ask you, madam, to make a choice even before we proceed to the pleasures of the *boudoir*."

"A choice now? But there is so much delicious flesh to choose from."

"Come with me then."

She knew if she moved, she would commit herself to a choice. But now that he had closeted them off from the rest of the world, it was a choice she wanted to make.

The game was on, and she willingly took his arm, handed him the candlestick, and let him escort her down the steps, through the *salle d'entrée* to the *boudoir*.

"Perhaps here, madam?"

"So difficult," she murmured.

"Would madam like to sample someone?"

Did he know, or was he inventing this game? He seemed to know it very well. Did she care?

"I would kiss *you*," she said after a moment's consideration.

And his kiss was leisurely, luxurious, masterful, arousing little darts of pleasure that attacked her vitals and left her feeling weak and wanting more. It was a long slow slide into a shimmering sensual indulgence, his kiss.

A voluptuous prelude. A sexual feast in itself

He kept kissing her as they slowly inched their way toward the *bagnio*.

"You are invited to remove your clothes, madam," he whispered against her lips.

"But I haven't made my choice," she protested breathlessly.

"Surely you have."

She looked at him consideringly. "I think you'll do."

"I hope I may service madam adequately," he replied in kind. "Shall I strip you?"

"By all means, do."

He set down the candle and went to stand behind her. An easy task this, because she was still in her riding habit and not encumbered by pads and buckram

He reached around to her jacket buttons first, slowly undoing them and letting his hands slide down over her breasts to her waist, and then slowly helping her shrug out of the jacket. The blouse came next, practical cotton, but it felt as sensual as anything as he worked it away from her body and let it fall to the floor. The skirt, the petticoat, the corset cover, God he hated all that excess material that kept him from being able to touch her luscious bare skin. The boots, the stockings—almost naked now, and shivering in anticipation, the corset laces ripped apart and unwound from her body and just tossed to the floor.

And then she was his, her nakedness in his hands, and against his questing mouth, and he was so hard for her he thought he would split open right there.

He couldn't stop caressing her. He wanted to feel every inch of her, and even that wasn't enough. He wanted five hands so that he could contain all of her in his hands.

"Tell me what you are wearing," he whispered as he gently squeezed her hard pointed nipples between his fingers, remembering her as she was the last time she was naked and in his hands.

"Oh, but I'm in want of bathing again," she murmured. "There's a particularly luscious cream I use . . ."

He growled ferociously; God, he wanted her . . . he lifted her and carried her into the *seraglio,* and into a cell where he laid her on the sofa on her belly.

"You shall have all that you want, madam." He couldn't get out of his clothes fast enough.

She wriggled her bottom. "You know how I love that treatment."

He straddled her legs and grasped her hips. Where to begin? He was like a rock; he wanted to slide himself into her hot willing writhing flesh, and he wanted to rub himself against the soft cushion of her bottom until he spewed every ounce of his seed all over her body.

He positioned himself against her buttocks, and there was no question—this was his fantasy, this—the slow subtle pumping of his hips against her ripe bottom, he was so hot, so hot, he wanted to shoot himself everywhere.

And she, she was wriggling and bouncing up against him, enticing him to heave himself all over her.

He wanted it to last; he wanted to give himself a long strong ride on her buttocks, he wanted to pump away forever—and the minute he thought it, he tensed and his body betrayed him, and he came in a long hot enervating gush of pure pleasure.

He bathed her in it, all over her buttocks and her lower back. All that luscious cream, just as he had fantasized, and as he got his senses back, he began stroking it into her skin, and pushing her thighs apart to rub it between her legs.

Yes . . . she loved that, she loved it—lush against her skin, made by her and his lust for her, she absolutely loved that, as his large hands massaged the evidence of that lust into her body and the most feminine part of her.

She couldn't see anything; she still lay on her belly, and all she could feel was his hands and the wet of his ejaculate, and the lush movements of his hands as he spread her legs and rubbed her there.

And kept rubbing her, and inserted his fingers, one, two, three, and began seeking her pleasure point, and seeking her mouth, and then finding that wholly naked part of her that belonged solely to him.

Her body rocketed out of control under his expert hand. He knew just where and what and how much pressure; his kisses were intoxicating, she lost herself in his mouth, in his hands, she was utterly gone, marked by him forever, and wearing his cream.

They lay in a rich, thick silence; he covered her, and he felt the sticky residue of himself against his skin.

She was drained and still, and it was as if they were the only people in the world, and nothing existed outside the cell.

He cupped her breast; her nipple was taut, alive, as he stroked it and she reacted.

"I want to wear it on my nipples again," she murmured lazily, reaching under his body and grasping his rigid erection.

"You can wear it everywhere, madam."

"Yes, you are very ready to service me again."

"Is madam ready?"

"I'm always ready," she whispered, and he eased himself away from her, turned her to face him, and maneuvered her so that she was at the edge of the sofa.

This was a wonder to her: he knelt at the edge off the sofa and lifted her legs against his chest, and her body as much as it took for him to be able to penetrate her.

She could see everything: the long hard thrust of him entering her, and then the piston movement of his body as he took her. Rhythmic, rhythmic, his body was like a musical instrument, driving her body to a resonant response at the clear coupling connection between them.

Servicing her in the absolute sense of the word—and it was the most voluptuous moment she had ever experienced; he owned her by virtue of that one long strong muscle that possessed her so commandingly. She was a slave to it, and to him. She wanted it just like that, and him, just like that. She could do nothing else but lie there and take it, and that was the only thing in the world she wanted to do.

Her climax came slowly, achingly, curling its way through her shimmering body, and then bursting explosively into her very core in successive, shattering detonations of pleasure.

He held himself tight, tight, tight—he fought his gratification, and fought it until the last shuddering wave passed through her body; and then he drove into her once and out again, and unleashed himself once more on the luscious planes of her writhing body, and collapsed beside her, spent.

How fast could a man heat up again?

Instantly.

He had no idea how much time had passed. And he didn't care.

And then he heard footsteps above the *voudrais,* and Leonie's voice calling. The real world intruding. He could have stayed there forever.

He could take her one more time. He could do that, just gently easing himself into her, just gently because she was so warm and soft and hot and wet for him still.

He could do that, and then once, twice, three times—and very very gently discharge himself into her welcoming fold.

Just that, just that, as she slept—or maybe she was aware: there was a faint shuddering response of her body—dear God, how was he going to leave her when he wanted so much more?

His clothes next—he left the candle—then he was gone as silently as a ghost.

"George has come with the worst news," Leonie said when he finally joined them in the family parlor.

"And what is that?" he asked distractedly.

"There won't be company this weekend; they've all gone to mourning Christabel Esterham. And I'm royally put out about it."

"Nonsense."

"Well—what will we do this weekend? Skene is deadly in April—except for the hunting."

"Then we'll hunt," he said decisively. "I would make book that Serena and her sister both have done, and you won't, and George probably won't mind doing, and so—we'll make due."

"So kind," George murmured.

"In the name of friendship," Justin retorted.

"How I do regret losing my perspective that one heady moment."

"And you can keep Leonie company," Justin added, and George looked at him sharply. But there was nothing in his manner to suggest he meant anything more than he had said.

"Where is she, anyway?" Leonie demanded.

"Who?"

"My lady Diandra of course. We know where the insipid lamb is: in her room getting ready for dinner. But Diandra seems to have disappeared."

"I expect you wish I had," Diandra said from the doorway, "but I am here, and—" her gaze rested on Justin for a fleeting second, "ravenously hungry."

"Dinner is in an hour so you are early in that respect. The rest of us must change."

"I'll never change," Diandra whispered, pitching her voice so that only Justin could hear her.

"Oh, very well, we'll do cards and parlor tricks tonight," Leonie said grudgingly. "Perhaps Serena can play something for us, Diandra?"

"Very likely."

"Then that's settled. In an hour then. Everyone—time to change."

She herded them out, nipping at their heels like a border collie, and Diandra sank onto one of the couches in relief.

She had made a quick change; she felt as if half of her padding was shifting or falling, but she took care of that in a moment after the others left.

She said yes to sherry when Tuttle inquired, and he lit the fireplace and left her alone with her thoughts.

Except she didn't know what were her thoughts; she had gone chasing a ghost and wound up in a dream. Which was the reality?

No, there was no reality here. This was a life totally apart from anything she'd ever known, and the supernatural overlay made it that much more alarming.

Not to mention the sex.

And the murders.

God, yes—the murders. They ought not forget the murders.

Or the manifestations.

Where had the gray ghost disappeared to?

She was beginning to feel very spooky, and she jumped when Tuttle appeared before her suddenly with her glass of sherry on a tray.

She took a delicate sip, and the heat curled down her throat and warmed her.

She should go back to India.

The thought blasted out of nowhere. And it was so right, so comforting. They had gotten enough of a taste of an English season. There wouldn't be too much more: just the same invitations to the same dinners, parties and balls, and later, the regattas and Ascot and polo and tennis and back to the country. No presentation at court for Serena, she hadn't had the forethought to arrange it, and now the American heiresses were too much in the way.

So what would they be missing? Besides the possibility of someone fixing his interest on Serena, of course. But Diandra had yet to see any one of the young men she had met even close to coming to the point.

They didn't even need to go back to Bhaumaghar. She could set up in Bombay or Calcutta where there was an English colony and a rich social life, surely enough to occupy Serena in the foreseeable future.

And they could just get away from these supercilious aristocrats, and Serena would just stop giving credence to all that supernatural nonsense.

It sounded like a plan to her. Justin wouldn't be sorry at all to see her leave, and she wanted to go long before she began falling in love with him, and while she could still take her pleasure *like a man*.

And the unanswered questions would remain unanswered. Sometimes things happened for no rhyme or reason. Sometimes there were signs and omens that were just unexplainable.

And sometimes people died.

Two spiritualists and two young women. People? An odd lot, actually. Two spiritualists, both of whom had come to them at Leonie's behest. And two young women. Two young women.

Odd, odd, odd—that, and the séances, that glowing vanishing figure, the messages, the accusations of murder, the doorbell ringing and no one there. And the gray ghost. The cloak in the closet. The rappings. The divining board which had utterly disappeared. The voice whispering in her ear. Serena casting circles of protection and reading coins and cards. And the floating table.

Leonie's unshakable belief that it was Pamela's spirit engaging them: Oh God, how was that possible? How was that possible? And why could it not have been Guthrie? Why did it have to be murder and accusations and inexplicable manifestations?

Let it be Guthrie then. Let him come back and explain everything; it all came back to him anyway . . .

Dear God, she had tears in her eyes. She set aside the sherry. She missed Bhaumaghar, and Hugh, and her tight comfortable world at the plantation. She wanted no more upheavals, no more surrender to her baser instincts.

She wanted safety and peace and more than anything a predictable end to the story.

George gave them all the gossip at dinner. Everyone was prostrate over Christabel's death. Stiles was at a dead end. Everyone had seen her at that party or this; there was no one strange lurking. She had always been in the company of her brothers or friends, and she had gone straight home.

The story was the same as that of Grace Partram: they were as loved as flowers and no one had any motive to want to kill either of them.

"Lady Harriet is just overset. Took to her bed, came out for the funeral and back again. Parties cancelled all over the place. Dinners, not, however: one must have somewhere to go to gossip. And theater must go on, of course, and I suppose there's justification to attend. So we're just as well off here as back in Town."

"Hardly," Leonie said.

"Truly. Absolute pall over the place. You'd get sick of them rehashing the details. That's all they talk about. The heiresses don't qualify; they're keeping things going single-handedly, along the nobs who are shopping for brides. So that's the end of it, and it will all wash out in two weeks' time."

"I'm sick of it already," Leonie said.

"But those poor girls," Serena murmured.

"More for their brothers," Leonie said. "Would anyone care for more bread?" She was determined to be a malcontent. There was a malicious look in her eyes as she passed the bread plate to Diandra. "You're very fortunate, my dear. A murder doesn't always push the latest *faux pas* out of public consciousness."

"Lucky for me," Diandra said.

"One has to know how to get on. One can't just plop oneself down in the middle and expect the protection of your husband's name and Justin's title."

"Indeed, and I'm so grateful for even that."

"You ought to be. Justin has been generous to a fault, and hospitable kind-hearted and gracious . . ."

"And I am his father's widow," Diandra interrupted coolly. "What is your point, Leonie? We are not some strangers he has taken in off the street."

"Well, it's as good as if you were. What did he know about you? How does he know you are who you say you are?"

"Oh, I think he believes *that* much at least, Leonie. Must we go on with this exercise?"

"All right: I'll be blunt. Forgive me, Justin—George. I think you should go home."

It was so exactly what she had just been thinking, that Diandra squared her shoulders, looked Leonie straight in the eye, and said, "No." And she was shocked to find that she meant it.

Leonie shrugged. "Truly, there is nothing more for you here, Diandra, and not too much more you can do for Serena. If no one has shown interest by now, she probably won't have a suitor. So what is the point?"

Diandra looked at Serena, whose face was faintly flushed. "The point is, we are staying. And the rest is none of your business."

Oh, Leonie didn't like that, not at all. It was as if the two of them were alone on the playing field, and Leonie was determined to win at any cost because she knew she was losing whatever small hold she had on Justin.

Justin was the prize.

And Diandra knew she had already won it. And she could not afford to be magnanimous in victory; no one else knew. She and Justin, a brief glancing of their gazes across the table. He knew. He wanted. Her. She had made sure of it.

And she would have to live with the consequences.

"Pamela wants you gone."

That came out of nowhere and all of them sat up in shock.

"Leonie—" That was Justin's warning voice. "Don't."

"The gray ghost is back, isn't it? Weren't you chasing it all afternoon? Don't tell me—I know. Pamela is back and she wants you gone."

"I'll let her tell me," Diandra said.

"And she will. And if that's what it will take, fine."

Justin looked helplessly at George. George shrugged and then said, "Perhaps some music will soothe our savage souls. Serena plays. Won't you, Serena?"

She bit her lip. "Certainly." She didn't want to, not now. Diandra could see that she was on the edge of tears from having been talked about as if she weren't there, and in such a vicious way.

They adjourned to the drawing room. Tuttle lit the gas, the sconces and the fire, and directed three footmen to bring out the pianoforte.

Serena seated herself at it; George arranged a branch of candles beside the music, and she began to play.

She liked to play; it was a place where her melodramatic instincts were not misplaced, and she could be as flashy as she liked.

And she was, to Leonie's distaste, which was reflected in her expression.

George sat with her afterward, and they played a genteel duet, and then George took over with a Mozart piano concerto that soothed Leonie's sore and heaving breast.

After that, they took coffee and dessert and Leonie looked around said, "Who wants to play cards?"

"How about if I read the cards?" Serena suggested. "You know I do have some talent there. Perhaps Leonie would like to learn her future?"

Leonie froze. And then she said through stiff lips: "Of course. Tuttle—bring out the table. We'll take brandy in here. More coffee? Anyone? All right then—here's the table. By the fire, please. And the chairs. Justin . . . ?" There was something in his eyes, and a warning note in her tone. "This isn't something to fool around with."

"It's a party trick, Leonie."

"Not since Diandra came to this house."

He was shocked to hear her words eerily echo his own thoughts. But why was she so leery when it was she who adamantly believed Pamela's spirit was haunting them?

"I'm sure Serena will be kind," he murmured, taking his place opposite George.

Serena was already seated and cracking open a new deck of cards. Leonie poured another cup of coffee for herself and settled in on the couch as Serena shuffled and handed the deck to her to cut.

"Left hand, please."

Leonie halved the deck and Serena completed the cut and picked it up, pausing to look deeply for one long meaningful moment into Leonie's eyes.

Then she laid out the cards, her expression carefully blank.

"How interesting, Leonie. These cards are not good. They show misfortune and bad luck—and even with the possibility of serious love and an advantageous marriage, you have the three worst luck cards negating everything— right there: the ace, ten and nine of spades. I see nothing that will even moderate that to some degree."

"How convenient," Leonie said. "Nothing good, everything bad."

"Sometimes it happens," Serena said. "There are success, prosperity and good luck cards here, but the placement of the others seriously affects them. Now, there *is* an indication of an important message—perhaps that will alleviate some of the bad news."

"I'm so relieved," Leonie muttered.

Serena looked around as she expertly shuffled the deck. "Anyone else? Diandra!"

"Fine."

Serena handed her the cards; she halved the deck, Serena capped it, and began to lay out the cross.

"Well," she murmured. "A better aspect here. I see danger and temporary misfortune. Maybe a quarrel or a disagreement will send you on the road to adventure, perhaps with the hope of obtaining some money, or seeking a fortune—but you see, there is the nine heart, the wish card, and that's allayed with the cross cards, all of which are favorable: they predict a prosperous future, true love, wealth, success and marriage which might be postponed, but will come to pass. Goodness, Diandra."

"Adventure and marriage, my, my," Diandra said. "Neither of which interests me in the least." She slanted a look at Justin. "I wonder what your cards predict for my lord?"

"Oh yes, let's find out." Again Serena shuffled the cards, handed them to Justin to halve, capped them and began to lay out the cross, her hand wavering a moment as she placed the last card. "How very odd. Very fortuitous cards, Justin. You too are slated for adventure: three cards indicate some kind travel or journey. Nine heart turns up for you too—every indication is for good luck, success and fulfillment. And marriage—not soon—but here: queen heart and queen club indicate you will meet the woman of your dreams and you will marry her. Only two negative influences: the seven heart—you might keep a wary eye, not everything is all positive. And there is something, shown by the queen spade, that you must beware of. It could be a person or a situation. Or both. But the cards don't specify."

"So kind," Justin murmured.

"How delightful," Leonie said, now actively annoyed that her cards had been the most negative thus far. "Why don't we read Serena's cards?"

Serena blinked. "My cards?"

"Why not? Let Justin shuffle and Diandra will lay out the cross. You can read them. We all have taken note of the most meaningful cards, so we won't let you hedge."

Serena looked around at all of them. "Certainly. Justin?" She handed over the cards and Justin shuffled. She cut them, he capped them, and he handed the deck to Diandra.

She slowly placed the cards, angling them toward Serena whose face showed nothing as the first card turned up the ace of spades.

Card of misfortune and death. Everyone knew it. They all waited for Serena to speak.

She placed her hands on either side of the cross. "It's not a good fortune," she said finally. "Besides the first indication of misfortune that everybody knows, there is also a suggestion of some kind of dispute, which might lead to a separation—" She looked up and met Diandra's sympathetic gaze. "The queen diamond indicates a woman who interferes: that could be anyone, even me. Any success, the two heart, will be counteracted by the negative cards or indecision or poor planning on my part. And the six heart denotes an unfortunate weakness in me . . ."

She broke off as the lights flickered and went out. They were engulfed in darkness and firelight—and then suddenly the table began to lift, pulling Serena with it.

They all sat dumbstruck as the table swung back and forth crazily for the space of a minute, and then it crashed to the floor, and Serena slumped down beside the sofa, the cards scattered like snow all around her.

And before they could even move, they heard the rapping.

Rap, rap, rap.

"Damnation." Justin, on his feet and at the door. "Tuttle! Jhasa!! Rajit!!"

The servants came running.

"Get the lights. Get some water and smelling salts. Brandy for everyone! Someone search the house. I want to know exactly where that sound is coming from. *NOW!!!*"

The raps echoed through the house.

Rap, rap, rap.

Diandra was on the floor beside Serena who was struggling to sit up.

"What happened? Oh! I remember—the table . . ."

"Yes, the table," Diandra said briskly. "Are you all right?"

"I think so."

"All right—up on the couch then." She helped Serena up. "Here's a tot of brandy—" She took the snifter from the footman who had rushed in with a tray. "Go on . . ."

"It was so weird," Serena murmured as she sipped the pungent liquid. "It was an awful fortune."

"Not worse than Leonie's."

Simultaneously, they turned toward Leonie who was standing by the fireplace. The lights had not come back on, except for the candles which the footman had lit, and she looked rather aggressive standing there, almost as if she were going to challenge the spirit.

But the spirit was strangely silent.

They could hear the servants running every which where, their footsteps pounding above them and below, and they could hear the shouts as each area was searched and cleared.

It took a half hour, during which Justin and George were actively involved in the search and came back periodically to report.

"It is a most elusive ghost," George said at one point.

"You won't find her," Leonie said. "She's waiting until all this foolishness is done, and then she will come to give us her message."

"Leonie—" George said warningly; as patient as he was, he had had enough of her nonsense.

"It's Pamela. I know it's my sister."

"Oh God—" He left the room in disgust, but he and Justin were back in fifteen minutes.

"There's nothing, damn it—just nothing—"

Rap, rap, rap . . .

"Goddammit—!" Justin again. *"Tuttle!"*

"No!" Leonie was insinuating herself between Justin and the door. "Let it speak."

"For God's sake, Leonie—"

"Let it speak!"

She was so serious, more than serious—it was as if her life depended on it.

He nodded at Tuttle, who understood exactly what he had to do, and he turned to Leonie. "Ask your questions."

She lifted her head to the ceiling—or heaven, Diandra couldn't decide which. "Is the spirit still with us?"

Rap, rap, rap.

"Will you answer our questions?"

Rap, rap, rap.

"One for yes, two for no?"

Rap.

"Are you Pamela?"

Rap.

"Do you want to give us a message?"

"Yes."

"Are you seeking something?"

"No."

"Someone?"

"Yes."

"Is it someone connected with your death?"

"Yes."

"Is it the person responsible for your death?"

"Now wait a minute—" Diandra protested.

"Yes."

"Is that person with us?"

No answer.

"Can you name that person?"

"Yes."

"Will you?"

No answer.

There was a long silence.

"Pamela?" Leonie's voice was uncertain now. "Are you there?"

Silence.

"There is some reason she won't speak," Leonie said. "Some negative influence somewhere. Or she doesn't want the person to know that she knows the true story. That would give the guilty party a chance to make alternative plans, wouldn't it?" She looked at Serena who stared back at her with wide eyes. "How smart she is. I think she won't be back tonight."

Tuttle entered the room. "There's nothing, my lord."

"And yet we heard it, we all heard it. How can that be? What about the attics?"

"Yes, my lord."

"And summon the servants. Everyone will be escorted to bed. I will root out this demon tonight, I swear it."

George took hold of Leonie's arm. "Come."

"You don't believe it."

"I don't have to believe it, Leonie. It just *is*. So come . . ."

Gita edged into the drawing room. "Mem?"

Diandra turned. "Take Serena to our rooms. I'll be along in a minute."

"Di-andra!" Serena protested.

"Really. I won't be but a minute, I promise."

Gita led her away and it was just she and Justin, staring at each other across the room.

"And then there's the table," she said. They had utterly forgotten about the table in the wake of the rapping and Leonie's histrionics.

"I'll goddamned take it apart," Justin growled. "There has got to be an explanation." He grabbed it and took it into the butler's pantry which was adjacent to the drawing room.

And then she was alone in the room, warmed by the flickering firelight, and everything seemed obvious and normal, except for the cards scattered at her feet.

She got down on the floor to gather them up, although she knew one of the servants would get to them eventually. At least she could take some kind of action while the footmen went ghost hunting and Justin axed apart a table.

She swiped her hand under the skirt of the sofa, feeling for some missing cards.

But she touched something else. Something unusual. Something that ought not to have been there.

She drew it out slowly, her heart pounding wildly.

It was a tube with a swiveling cavity at one end of it, and a mechanism at the opposite end that, when she depressed it, pushed out an extension rod.

Oh my God—

She stared at the thing, utterly confounded. And then she felt under the sofa again and pulled out a second one. Two of them. Under the sofa. Exactly where Serena fell.

She licked her lips as she hooked her elbow into the

cavity and depressed the mechanism. The rod popped out, extending almost a foot beyond her fingertips. If she held her hand flat, she could slip it under any flat surface. A book. A rug . . . A table . . . and—*lift* it . . .

Dear God—a magician's rod, hidden under a sleeve to conjure an illusion—like a floating table . . . like—oh my God, oh my God . . .

And therefore only one conclusion: Serena was the trickster, using sleight-of-hand to bamboozle them, and playing them all for fools.

Chapter Sixteen

Serena!

Serena?

She couldn't move, she just couldn't. *Serena . . .*

How? Why?

A noise behind her . . . or was it by the door—she couldn't let anyone see—she had to hide, had to protect . . . no one could know she had found these incriminating rods . . .

She shoved them back under the sofa, and began gathering up the cards with shaking hands.

Serena . . .

"Diandra . . . !" Justin's voice, harsh and irritated. "What the hell are you doing?"

She levered herself up onto the couch. Her legs were wobbly, and she felt lightheaded. *Serena . . .* "I just . . . the cards—" She was holding onto them like a lifeline.

"The servants will get them in the morning."

"And the table?" Oh, at least she had the presence of

mind to ask about that. *They had all been so distracted by the rapping, they had ignored the table.*

They shouldn't have ignored the table.

But if Serena had levitated the the table, then maybe . . . maybe—oh, no no no, she didn't want to, she couldn't let herself even speculate about it.

There had to be some other explanation, there had to be.

But they had been saying that all along . . . all along—

"Nothing. I took it apart inch by inch. There was nothing."

She had expected that. *Now.*

Dear God—

And under the sofa, inches from her feet, one explanation. One place to point an accusing finger.

How could she deal with that?

What explanation could there be?

Serena . . .

It was incomprehensible.

"Get some rest, Diandra. We're not going to find anything out tonight."

But we did—I have . . . I have to get those rods out of here . . .

"You're right. You've done everything you possibly could. None of it makes any sense." What else could she say? She was talking too much anyway. She should just go to her room, and later, much much later, she could sneak back out to the drawing room and retrieve the incriminating apparatus.

At least he wasn't accusing her of being the perpetrator. "Come, madam."

She set the cards on the sofa, and let him help her to her feet.

She felt as if he could read everything in her face, and see deep beneath the sofa where the magician's rods burned like a beacon, beckoning him to an ineffable discovery of deception.

Her heart was pounding so violently, she was sure he could hear.

Because now, in her effort to protect Serena, she had made herself a partner to it.

Serena was sound asleep.

She closed the connecting door to their rooms and sank onto her bed.

A nightmare. And Serena slept the sleep of innocence while she jumped to outrageous conclusions.

It was the whole tenor of the night; it was enough to spook anyone. And the apparatus—it could be Leonie's as well. Leonie *was* going off the deep end about Pamela.

And Leonie *believed.*

Yes, Leonie of all of them had faith—

She leaned back against the pillows and tried to reconstruct the last twenty minutes of the evening in her mind.

Serena's cards, overwhelmed with misfortune—negative influences, indecision, weaknesses . . . and then the lights went out and up went the table—with Serena hanging onto it.

Serena . . .

She closed her eyes, envisioning it. Not in the air for more than a minute and then down it came—and Serena, in a faint, just by the sofa.

Serena . . .

And then the rapping—

But it had quieted when Justin sent the servants running . . .

And it had been there again suddenly, with Leonie defending it. Answering her questions. And refusing to name names.

It made no sense. None.

And the magician's apparatus under the sofa.

Leonie had been nowhere near the sofa.

Serena . . . all of it back to Serena again.

But why?

Why, why, why?

She couldn't rest knowing that apparatus was under the sofa where anyone could find it. Even now, the servants could be—

No. *She* would take care of it . . .

She was edging her way through the guest wing el before she even completed the thought in her mind.

. . . now . . .

Through the reception hall and into the drawing room which was cast in shadows by the banked fire in the fireplace.

Down on her knees, scrambling by the sofa, shoving her hands under, wary of the noises and the cold and the shadows. And the spectres of her past.

To find—there was nothing under the sofa, not a card, not a ball of dust. The extension rods were gone.

She lay in bed, shaking. *The things were gone.* She couldn't believe that either.

Or had she dreamt them?

No. Gone. Which meant what? A servant had found them? Someone had taken them?

Someone meaning—Serena?

Her hands were clammy.

What was going on here? Serena was still in bed. She had made sure. And breathing deeply and naturally, deep asleep.

But—there had been that half hour or so as she had waited for the house to bed down when Serena could have crept into the drawing room and removed the rods.

But then anyone could have done . . .

Where was her loyalty to Serena?

Anyone could fake being asleep . . .

She didn't like where any of her thoughts were leading her. The simplest thing was to wake up Serena and *ask* her.

Oh truly—and what did she think Serena would say? Oh yes, I conspired to trick everyone?

Serena, who believed in charms and omens and the placement of the cards? Who cast circles of protection and spoke to spirits?

God, it made no sense, no sense.

When had that all started? She wished she could remember. Long before they came to England. Long before Guthrie's death even. Maybe before she had married him?

Serena's outrageous behavior had changed: she had calmed down but she had become more overtly dependent on talismans and superstition.

Then? But why?

And it had been something that had bothered her, but also something she could put off dealing with. How many times had she sloughed it off by thinking what harm could it do?

And here was the end result: Serena's implication in all the supernatural nonsense.

But—the evidence was gone . . . Serena was no more entangled in it than she—on the surface.

Only she had seen the extension rods.

She—and whoever had taken them.

There was a connection here . . . why couldn't she see it?

She tossed and turned for hours, listening for some sign that Serena was awake and that she could somehow approach her.

The deep night sounds of the house were subtle and eerie. Creaking noises. The footstep of a servant making the rounds through the guest wing. The wind. The clock in the el chiming, like a ghost keeping count of all the lost hours. A hissing sound.

She drifted off to sleep.

And her dreams were a nightmare, all of it surrounding the death of Guthrie, her finding of him, the endless questioning, the endless procedures, the endless phantasmagoria of his funeral preparation, all of it, all of it, as clear as glass—she could even smell the smoke and feel the heat blisteringly close to her skin, and she thought, *it all comes back to Guthrie—*

And she woke up suddenly, frighteningly, paralyzed to find her bed in flames, and Justin at the threshold of her room, ready to leap into the pyre.

Oh my God, oh my God, oh my God . . .

Everyone, crowding into her room, beating at the flames, all the footmen and servants, and Rajit and Jhasa with long poles, lifting away the flaming bedskirt and curtains, and Justin, covered in wool, diving onto the bed, and wrapping her in a woollen blanket, and lifting her out of harm's way . . .

Justin . . .

Servants everywhere with buckets and blankets and water and the stench of burned cotton and singed hair—her hair . . .

Oh my God, oh my God, oh my God . . .

She was like a statue; she couldn't move. She was so horrified by the scene and the sight and the fact that moments before she had been in the middle of it with fire leaping everywhere . . .

Oh my God, oh my God . . .

. . . oh my God—

She felt faint. She felt as if her heart had stopped. Someone waved smelling salts in front of her and she coughed.

Someone brought her water. Someone else, a robe. Leonie, she thought, who was properly staying out of the way.

And Justin, kneeling before her. Singed. The blanket, badly burned. And him. His shirt. His trousers.

"Oh my God," she whispered, her eyes skewing toward the bed which was now a sodden smoking ruin.

"Who?" Justin demanded.

"I don't know . . ." Her voice was smoke-clogged and barely above a breath. *A hissing noise in the sounds of the night . . .*

"Goddamn whoever it was to hell . . ." He didn't say the obvious: she could have died. She could have been disabled and disfigured forever. She could have been burned alive—

A funeral pyre . . .

Jesus—

"Serena . . ." she tugged on his shirt. "Where's Serena?"

The connecting door was closed.

He walked over to it, listened a moment, and he turned the knob.

The door was locked.

Oh my God, oh my God . . . no . . . no—no-o-o-o—

"Gita—go get Miss Serena."

She bowed and hurried out, and she was back almost instantly.

"Miss Serena's door is locked, sahib."

"How strange," he said tightly, and his voice was like ice. "Jhasa—I need help."

The two disappeared into the hallway. But she couldn't sit still and wait. Only that could propel her from her chair and compel her to walk—out the door and into the hallway.

They were battering their shoulders against the door.

"She's put something against the door," Justin said. "Leonie—get the keys from Tuttle."

Tuttle came himself, picking the key from the chataleine and handing it to Justin.

He turned the knob and the door gave way, and then he and Jhasa pushed with all their might until they had made a crack large enough for Justin to fit through.

He squeezed his way in. "It's the armoire. How in hell did she—it doesn't matter. The room is empty; none of her possessions are here. She's gone."

Everything in her life was evanescent. Everything.

She sat in the drawing room, bundled up in blankets and warmed with tea, and she couldn't think. She didn't think she could breathe. She thought maybe she wasn't even alive.

The betrayal was almost too much to bear.

"It *was* attempted murder," Justin said.

"Don't be ridiculous. It was an accident. Serena would never hurt me." But she didn't believe the words. She had to defend Serena, just as she always had.

"It was not an accident, and there may be someone in complicity with her—she could not have moved that armoire by herself."

"Maybe the ghost did it," she said bitterly. "Maybe Pamela, with superhuman, supernatural strength. Maybe they were in collusion . . ."

"Don't fall apart now," he warned.

"Oh no, I'm perfectly fine, Justin."

"I can see that. Do you want something stronger?"

"I've had enough for one night, thank you. But where could she have gone—alone and without money?"

"Far enough away that the constabulary would be wasting its money chasing her."

"Don't say that."

"Don't be a fool," he said roughly. "She'll never come back. She tried to kill you."

And if only you knew what else . . .

"I won't believe it."

"Believe it."

"There's no reason." But she had thought of a reason in the glimmering moment before she had awakened to horror.

"Jealousy," he suggested.

"Typical . . . ridiculous. Jealous of what? She was the one being pampered and given the season. Hugh insisted on it. Not for me. For her. She wanted it. She knew it."

"Then what changed?"

She thought for a moment. "Nothing." *Something, but Serena hadn't known that.*

Had she?

Her breath caught in her throat. *Surely not.*

"You thought of something."

She had to regain her composure. He was too attuned to her, could read the slightest nuance in her expression.

She shook her head. "No. I didn't see her at all after she left the drawing room, except I looked in on her when I got back to the room. But she was sleeping. Soundly."

"Maybe not."

"Dear God, would you stop?"

"No. You could have died."

"You would have saved me."

"Rajit saved you. He was sleeping outside your door and roused the house. But we can assume that Serena was gone by then."

"She didn't like the cards I dealt her," she murmured, attempting to make a feeble joke.

It didn't distract him. "So what changed, Diandra?"

"You tell me. You were there." *Place it on him. Let him speculate; she would defend.*

"She had never read the cards for anyone in the house before."

"Except me. It was an ongoing thing with her. She's very superstitious, wears charms, casts circles, chants spells. And Leonie did not like her cards, did she?"

"If she felt that strongly about it, she would have torched Serena's room, don't you think?"

"But she *has* been a little too involved with the spirits around here."

"So has Serena."

That was too true, and she didn't have an answer for it.

"There was *nothing* in Serena's room?" she asked after a while. But she knew the answer.

"No."

"She had her own cards, you know. Maybe she thought those other ones brought her bad luck."

"So she set fire to your room? There's no sense to that at all. And anyway, I think there's something else, something you know but won't tell."

"Truly I don't." Did that sound sincere enough? Or scared enough? "And anyway, how far could she have gone all alone and without money?"

"You don't know she doesn't have money. Have you checked your wallet yet?"

She hadn't thought of that either, and he offered to bring it to her. Her feeling of dread increased proportionately with his absence.

Dear God, why, why, why had Serena done this?

But she knew . . .

"It's a mess up there," he said, handing her the case that contained her papers and checks.

She rummaged through quickly, and it was obvious that someone else had been through it as well: all the papers were disarranged, and those pertaining to Serena were missing, as well as cash she had had to hand, and the letter of credit from her bank.

Which meant Serena could now draw on all her funds—whatever she wanted, whenever she wanted . . .

Jealousy? To go to those lengths to obtain a bank authorization and that much money? She would have given it to her, she would have.

"It's all gone, including the letter of credit."

"So—" He didn't seem at all surprised.

She threw the case on the floor. "I won't believe it."

"Of course, the other interesting thing will be—if Serena is gone, is our ghost gone too?"

She froze. "What do you mean?" She meant, *what do you know?*

"You know what I mean," he said evenly. "Was she responsible and did she have help?"

She drew in a deep breath. The ghost—the endless rapping tapping ghost that appeared so conveniently to make accusations of murder—or to attempt it.

And she refused to believe Serena was capable of it?

Ah, Serena . . .

She closed her eyes and she could almost see the flames and smell the smoke.

She could have been badly burned. She could have died.

Serena . . .

She must have come back for the extension rods and seen her manipulating them. And Serena couldn't take the chance she would tell.

Serena . . .

All back to Serena—

No ghosts, just Serena . . .

He watched her; watched the progression through her mind of all the ramifications of Serena's culpability. Watched her realize the larger implications of Serena's guilt. Watched her pain as she couldn't quite acknowledge the depth of Serena's treachery.

She hated that he could see it, and that he had any knowledge of what Serena had done. It changed things forever.

Everything.

She couldn't stay there. She couldn't even bear to face Leonie. Serena's betrayal was too great.

And now, she thought, all she wanted to do was go home.

Nightmares. She had them, even though she was safely ensconced in the family wing, next to Leonie and with Rajit guarding her door.

Fire flaring, crackling, burning, blistering heat, thick choking smoke, magic rods reaching for her to lift her into the fire: she woke up coughing, tears streaming down her cheeks, the sensation of the flames and smoke as real as if it were happening at the moment.

She couldn't sleep.

Serena was out there somewhere, absolved of complicity, spending her money, and laughing at her.

Serena had left her destitute. She had nothing. She hadn't even thought of the complications of that.

The knowledge cut her like a knife.

It meant she was stranded. That she would have to beg. And that she would be dependent on whatever Justin chose to give her.

Serena had hated her that much.

But Serena hadn't expected her to survive.

She felt a wave of pure ice wash over her body.

Serena wanted her dead.

She knew Serena's secret.

But she didn't conceive of why Serena had chosen to perpetrate the deceit.

She would never know.

She couldn't sleep. There was too much . . . too much—and it was all mixed up together . . . and it all had to do with Serena—and Guthrie . . .

. . . Guthrie—yes . . . something to do with Guthrie, and she didn't know what—

And Serena's tricks and betrayal did not explain everything else . . .

It was too hard to think, but she couldn't sleep. She punched the pillows down and burrowed under them.

. . . oh yes, everything else . . .

Including the deaths. Including her—almost . . .

She stood on the threshold, looking at her scorched bedroom. The reality of it was chilling; and the truth was, Serena had done it.

"Mem." Gita, softly, at her elbow. "Come."

She shook her head.

"Mem." Gita was insistent.

She let Gita lead her away. All of her possessions had been transferred to the other room already; she hadn't needed to come back to this wing, apart from her morbid curiosity.

It had proved nothing, except that Serena's intent had been particularly vicious and lethal. And she had known that already.

Leonie was waiting for her in the family dining room, and handed her a cup of tea. "We'll return to London tomorrow."

"I'll be glad of that."

"You must come to terms with the fact that she's gone."

"I have." She hadn't, but that was not for Leonie to know.

"You should eat something."

"Yes." Toast would do, and she munched on it determinedly. It tasted like dust. And her tea tasted like water. And nothing would ever taste good again.

How would she ever tell Hugh?

Oh God, Hugh—she hadn't given one single thought to Hugh in all the confusion . . .

But Hugh was so far away.

Serena was so far away . . .

Leonie's voice broke into her thoughts. And just in time. "Justin wants to see you in the library after your breakfast, Diandra."

That got her attention. Justin had been waiting all this time? "Of course." She drained her cup. "If you'll excuse me . . ."

She hesitated at the door of the library, and then pushed her way in.

"Justin?"

"Come in. Sit down. How do you feel this morning?"

"I'm still shaky, I still can't believe . . ."

He could, he thought. He could believe anything. She looked wan and pale, with dark circles under her eyes. She obviously hadn't slept, and he hadn't even been able to go to her and hold her.

But there were other things he could do.

"No," he said briskly. "It doesn't seem real. However, the question of your money can be dealt with; I've sent my man early this morning to attend to business. The accounts on which Serena could draw will be closed and transferred back to you in joint account with me—for the time being. You'll be provided with new checks and a new letter of credit. She will not be able to access any of your money as of ten o'clock this morning."

"Thank you for that."

"Easy to do, Diandra. She might be looking to convert to cash this morning at the earliest, depending on how far your money took her last night. So she'll be in for a nasty surprise."

Poor Serena . . . She was shocked at the thought. But then, Serena had chosen to cross swords with Justin, who had the means and wherewithal to thwart her.

So what if she ran out of money and died?

Insanity thinking that way. But she had always looked after Serena; she didn't suppose she would stop now.

"We'll return to London tomorrow. There isn't much else we can do here."

We can find a ghost . . .

She had to stop this; she still didn't believe, after everything, she still didn't believe it could be Serena.

It was a very quiet day, the kind of day she did not like. Leonie was adamant that she was going to stay still and read or write or do needlework or something. No one wanted to play cards or hear music.

She dozed off, she knew that. She could hear George and Leonie discussing Serena in low tones. And she could have predicted Leonie would have nothing good to say.

"I never liked her. I'm sorry Justin felt obligated—but then, what could he do? Such an insipid girl. Who knew she was full of such deadly instincts? It makes my flesh crawl that I even had anything to do with her . . ."

"Don't be unkind, Leonie. You fell right into all that mumbo-jumbo."

"Nonsense. Never. In any event, we'll be back in Town tomorrow and things will get back to normal. And I hope we may never see either of them again."

"Unkind, Leonie. Diandra upheld the family honor very well."

"She should go back where she came from and leave us all alone."

"And so she shall, in due time."

Kindly George, she thought, in her slumbrous netherworld. He knew just the right turn of phrase. She wished she had the years of training in tact.

Dinner was deadly. They could only talk about Serena's defection and horror of the night before.

And she definitely did not want to relive that.

But again, she couldn't sleep. Gita stayed with her, this time, and together they packed for the trip back to Town. And sometime, early in the morning, she fell back to sleep again.

Gita roused her at eight; she breakfasted with George, and they were on the road by nine-thirty.

No gray ghosts in the far fields. No wisps of fog disappearing around distant corners.

She had imagined it all.

Three hours later, their four carriages drew up in Cheswick Square. Millbank was waiting.

"My lady." He addressed Diandra. "You just missed Miss Serena."

It took a minute for his words to sink in.

What did you say?

"Miss Serena. She came yesterday in advance of the party, and left this morning. I was asked to tell you she left you a message in your room, my lady."

She started shaking. "Serena was here?"

"As I said, my lady."

"And left me—a message?"

"Yes, my lady."

"She didn't say where she was going?"

"Just out, my lady—to do some shopping, I believe."

And she knew in which store: the Bank of England. That galvanized her. She took the steps two at a time. The ghosts were gone, no ghosts in the hallway. Nothing. Just the doors behind which there were secrets.

She thrust open the door to her room and stopped short.

Propped up against her bed—the message: the two magician's extension rods.

Everything was arranged and cleared by late that afternoon. She had checks in hand, which were countersigned by Justin, she had her letter of credit, and she had money.

And she had the rods safely packed away in a suitcase where no one could find them.

She wasn't going to tell Justin. She wasn't going to tell anyone.

It was time for her to go.

The timing was perfect. Everything was already packed. Justin was at his offices. Leonie was out visiting. George was at his club.

And she knew with a certainty where Serena must have gone: where else, without money or resources, but back to Hugh.

Exactly where she needed to go. To mother India, to save her soul.

Chapter Seventeen

Collusion.

It was the only thing he could think as he surveyed her empty bedroom when she didn't come down for dinner. Leonie had said she was resting, that she had been restless and querulous the entire day, that she'd gone upstairs at four to relax and change for dinner. Leonie had–said.

And so sometime between four and six she had spirited her retinue and her wardrobe out the back door, and no one had seen her? He couldn't credit it, but there it was: she was gone as well, as neatly incised from his life as if she had never been there.

"Just as well," Leonie said when he told her. "Now we can get on with things."

"What things?" he asked suspiciously.

". . . Things," she said, evading his eyes, his question, her feelings. They were alone at Cheswick Square for the first time in her memory. The only ghosts between them were his memories and perceptions. He had never looked on her as anything but a member of the family. His aunt. His *younger* aunt.

But surely now—he hadn't asked her to leave, not yet.

And Diandra and her mettlesome sister were gone, thankfully of their own volition, and there was just herself and Justin and the intimacy of being in the same house, in the same place.

Surely now he would see . . .

But no—he didn't see *her;* he saw nothing but that Diandra, the provincial tart, had left his home and his care. What was it about her? She never could figure it out. He wasn't besotted. They had acted as if they hated each other—but *she* knew better.

Still and all, he had known it wasn't proper for him to make overtures in public. And he hadn't. At least he had had that much good taste.

The rest—well, it had been an uphill battle, and still he wasn't seeing what was before his eyes.

She was ecstatic the sisters were gone. But she didn't want to make too big a thing of it; he would defend them as soon as he would defame them, and she couldn't risk that either.

She was walking a tightrope, a line so taut and fraught with danger that she hardly dared open her mouth.

"At least," she ventured, "at least you made sure that murderous Serena couldn't get hold of her money."

"And now Serena is without, and Diandra has the wherewithal to do and go wherever she wants. This is incomprehensible."

"What hasn't been in the last three months?"

"And *you*—with all that business about Pamela . . ."

"My dear Justin," she said, affronted. "You've *never* had a question or a qualm about how your mother died? You don't think it's conceivable that her spirit is restless and wants justice?"

"Jesus. No, I don't. No, no, and no."

"You don't want to know. You're still angry at how they left you. After all this time. When *does* a man grow up, for God's sake? When does he stop assigning blame and start living his life?"

"Thank you, Leonie. I'm sure I merited that rebuke. We will not, of course, mention your living in Pamela's shadow, and refusing to marry, and saving yourself for God knows whom when George has been in love with you these five years."

He shouldn't have said that. She went very still and he knew that he did not want to hear what she was going to say.

But there was no escaping it.

And for her, it was the one and only chance—she had to take the risk, the humiliating risk.

"For you," she whispered. And then she drowned in the deep silent moment that resonated with everything else unsaid, while she watched his eyes turn sad and sympathetic. Pitying her for her futile misplaced love.

It was unbearable. It was the wrong time. Just wrong altogether. She wanted to sink through the floor. She wanted to die.

"Dear Leonie," he murmured. "I wish it could be more."

A tiny curl of hope. "Why can't it be?"

But she knew already: his mind and heart were far away from her. That too was reflected in his eyes. And his posture. And his impatience.

"You have always been my aunt."

Chilling words, final words.

She had to strike back. "*She* is your stepmother."

It was a hit. "Indeed she is. And I am responsible for her, and I am going to find her."

"And then what? Or don't you see how futile *that* is?"

"I don't know, Leonie. I just don't know."

"You can do nothing for her that your father hadn't already done."

"You are treading on very thin ground, Leonie. Don't let your disappointment skew your words."

"Oh indeed, I have watched her these three months, Justin. She's a pretty piece, and obviously well versed in certain *arts*, shall we say? But in your world, after the scandal of her sister . . . what could she be to you but your Indian mistress?"

"And that is just enough to send me out the door to find her," he said brutally. "And I might never come back."

It was a full frontal attack, but she was prepared for it. In her anger and her pain, she was ready to use every weapon at hand. "Childish, Justin. But what can one expect? You've never grown up. And she is just the toy of the moment. But obviously you must find that out for yourself. It is always the good women who suffer—and wait." And she turned on her heel and left him.

He was just a little shell-shocked as he watched her go.

Leonie, wanting him . . . never in his life would he have considered it. Poor Leonie, putting her desire on the line for him to crush with the merest word out of his mouth.

And so he had, and he couldn't even remember the whole conversation and she had only left him five minutes before. He couldn't think of anything but Diandra.

Nothing made sense. And Diandra's defection was so complete and inexplicable, he wondered whether it had been her decision to go. What if Serena and some accomplice had returned and spirited her away?

But then, Serena didn't know if she were alive or dead. Serena had brazenly stayed the night at Cheswick Square, but by now, she must be miles away. It could not have been Serena.

So Diandra's decision to leave had been compelled by some other factor.

She would not have wanted to go after Serena after what Serena had done.

Or would she?

And where could Serena go if her source of revenue were abruptly cut off? Serena was wily, Serena could fend for herself, if no other way than by telling fortunes with her cards. But that could not have been the existence she envisioned for herself when she had set Diandra's room on fire.

She had wanted the money. And now that there was none, she would either have to live by her wits—or go home.

And he couldn't have predicted which she would choose. But Diandra was another matter altogether. Diandra's job was done. And she couldn't, wouldn't believe that Serena would ever try to harm her.

Diandra was still in danger.

And he had to find her.

Three weeks at the minimum to travel to Bombay. She had forgotten the long, waterlogged trip through the Mediterranean and up the Red Sea through the canal, and now it would all be in reverse; the ship was leaving from Liverpool as soon as there was a complement of passengers. They were nearly to capacity now.

There was no reason to suppose that Serena would be on this ship. Taking the boat-train to France and going overland by train to Italy and across by boat to Cairo was arguably a faster way to travel, but it required too much reacclimatization and too many changes of venue. And it just wasn't as comfortable as settling in to one ship with storage for everything, and activities to while away the long hours out at sea.

But it could have been Serena's choice on the run. And it would have meant she could get moving sooner and have gotten farther away in less time.

She was sure Serena would not turn up on the docks of Liverpool, waiting in line for a cabin.

Two days at the most, she was told, as she purchased tickets for herself and her servants. One night at the hotel, and hopefully boarding on the second day, the usual double storage rooms available, one for items that would not be used at all, and the other to which she would have free access at certain hours of the trip.

She spent the time getting together a provision basket for herself and her servants, and rearranging her trunks for the most convenience. Small tasks that required a great deal of thought as to what edibles she would need for the trip and which clothes she would want immediately, which she could dispose of along the way, and which would go into storage.

She took short naps, with Gita watching over her, and she ate, sparingly, but she ate. The night was the hardest; the nightmare of *that* night was there full force, and she woke up screaming.

She bought biscuits and boullion and tea, a spirit lamp for cooking in her cabin, some tinned goods, some dried fruit, sugar, utensils, a candlestick, and a fair amount of bottled water. She bought towels and soap and spices that were known to be effective against seasickness and useful in cooking besides.

She was strangely ready to be going home. And India was home. Her brief sojourn in London had proved that to her, if nothing else. And that she could move successfully in the highest circles.

All she wanted now was to return to Hugh's plantation

and manage his household, just as she had done before. Serena would be there, and they would tussle good-naturedly over her deep dislike of living in India and it would be—eventually—as if this interlude in England had never happened.

She felt stronger, being away from London, and that much closer to Bombay. The sea air made her stronger. And lure of home.

And Serena would be home; and she could ask her all the questions she wanted and there would be explanations and hugs, and everything would be as it was before.

She couldn't wait to get home.

They were a week out and on the Mediterranean when she caught a glimpse of him. She had spent most of that time reading every book in the ship's library and conversing idly with the wives of civil servants who were on their way out for a tour of duty. The stories were all the same, she had heard them all before, and she answered questions mindlessly because it required no effort to do so.

And then—just as she had thought she was healing from the scourge of her time in London, there he was—and gone.

Ghosts. They were haunting her even here, and it wasn't Pamela or the gray cloaked wraith, then of course it would be him.

She had hardly given a thought to him as she stealthily removed herself from Cheswick Square. That way lay danger. And emotions she would sooner not evoke because it was just easier that way.

She had imagined him too. It was safer to believe that.

She had taken her pleasure like a man—and paid for it too.

. . . This evening never happened . . .

Hours at the rail, watching the dancing waves as the ship plowed through. Musicales at night, little parties, endless cards; what would they have done without cards?

But no Serena to tell a fortune, and certainly *she* couldn't.

And did she not see him moving elegantly through the crowd one evening when they had dressed for the Captain's Dinner? She would know those shoulders anywhere, but when she finally pushed her way through the crowd, he was nowhere to be seen.

Imagined him. Couldn't let it get to her. There was too much else on her plate. And the nights were not easy, the horror had not faded.

She saw him one morning as she came up on deck early to catch a breeze and take a walk. Surely that was he a hundred yards ahead of her . . . ?

She began to run, and she caught the wind.

He wouldn't do this to her—not after everything that had happened.

Two weeks passed. On a journey like this, one got to know more people more intimately than she had expected.

And while she felt asexual, the gentlemen swarmed around her like bees. The interest was palpable; any number of them would have bedded her and given her anything she desired to do so.

The voyage was obviously way too long.

The weather was getting hotter and hotter. They were wearing their lightest clothes, and sleeping out on the decks some nights, the men separated from the women by a curtain. They slept in their clothes, and discarded them over the side when, after several days, they changed, instead of trying to do laundry in that heat.

Had she awakened one night to find a stranger hovering over her, so familiar and so near?

She had imagined it, she was certain, and yet the touch of his hand was engraved in her memory, and the way he smoothed her hair back from her forehead and her neck, and loosened the buttons at her neck.

She wore white. She didn't care; no one on board knew

her for a widow. She gave them all her maiden name, Hugh's recognizable name, and there was no question, no censure.

They sat in the shade of the after decks and drank lemonade and water and ate biscuits and jam, and talked and talked and no one threw quoits or played shuffleboard. It was too hot even for that.

Had she seen him?

She thought, as she made her way down to her cabin to change for dinner, she thought she saw someone speaking with Jhasa.

"No, mem—" he denied it. "No. It was merely the watchman." As if that explained anything.

Three weeks out and just through the beautiful blue of the Red Sea, and the game of identifying biblical landmarks. It was questionable how much anyone could see to shore, but everyone knew his Bible.

It passed the time.

She was sleeping better at night, in the cooler night air, out on the deck and under the stars. And sometimes she thought that somebody touched her.

They were beginning to be a raggedy lot. The exigencies of the trip were finally getting to them. The days were hot, the nights were long. Their cabins were hot boxes, and the only escape was the deck and the company sometimes of those they really wished to avoid.

The fourth week out and they were steaming into the Indian Ocean, and soon within sight of Bombay.

Ghosts. There were ghosts everywhere; she had only to reach out and touch—Guthrie in Bombay, in the full panopoly of his office, with her by his side, at the quay to meet whatever dignitary was scheduled to arrive.

He would disembark, just as she was doing at this moment, and he would be met by the sights and sounds that were India, a vast canvas of color and noise and scent, and motion, motion, motion.

She stood at the top of the ramp and closed her eyes and inhaled. Sandalwood first, and spice, smoke; and then the sound of carts and carriages rumbling over stone. Music, faintly in the distance, the distinctive cawing of birds, and a babel of mellifluous voices, music to her ears.

She opened her eyes and moved down the ramp, jostled by others who who didn't feel quite as romantic about it as she and couldn't wait.

She had all the time in the world; the distance between the ship and the shore was as clear as a dream. She hadn't imagined a thing.

Justin was waiting for her at the bottom of the ramp.

And then, just as suddenly, he was gone.

She went by train from Bombay to Nagpur, a two-day trip on hard leather benches, with periodic stops to remove animals from the tracks or to obtain food. She and the servants slept on the benches that folded out into pallets, and she bought fresh water and fruit rather than eat the railroad food.

He watched them from afar, dining on whatever he could purchase out the window at each stop. He and the servants took turns on watch, even if she didn't know it; he had arranged it with Jhasa weeks before.

To him, the danger was real. They didn't know if Serena was travelling in this very train or had somehow managed to go on ahead. But wherever she was, she was a threat to Diandra.

And Diandra looked too fragile and not at all up to confrontations. The journey had been exhausting and tedious both to him, so it must have been torture for her.

He had planned not to let her see him, even though

once or twice it had been unavoidable. But his best weapon was surprise, and the clearest course was just to follow her out and wait to see how the whole would play out.

He itched to touch her, to hold her; he had given into it once or twice when she had slept on deck, and he was sure she had been aware of him.

And he had made the mistake of coming to watch her disembark. She had seen him then, clearly, and the expression on her face, when he melted into the shadows, was one he didn't want ever to see again.

He lay low on the hard leather bench and watched the scenery roll by.

The fascination of India—he hadn't let himself feel it, he held himself removed from it, and he was shocked to find it was seeping into his bones.

India enfolded him, from the moment he stepped onto the dock and into her arms. She beckoned him, promising him untold adventure and fulfillment of his dreams. She was as exotic as a mistress, and as familiar as a rhyme.

And he didn't want to resist her.

The miles clicked by; dusk fell, night. He slept fitfully, awakened, drank the lemonade he had bought earlier, ate some curry, and took up watch again from his position in his railroad car.

Quiet. Murmuring souls in the dead of night who couldn't sleep. The wail of the train whistle. The sound of lowing cattle somewhere in the distance. Keening voices urging them on.

Daylight then, and approaching Nagpur. More houses, gardens, people. Heat. Dust. The scent of burning cow dung mixed with garlic, cumin and tumeric. Sun, blazing hot relentless sun, as they emerged from the train and bought water and food from the vendors, and arranged for transportation on the next leg of the journey.

She would go by carriage from there to Bhaumaghar,

Jhasa had told him, and he would be wise to ride. He could keep pace with them that way and still stay out of sight. It was only another half day's journey; they would arrive at the house by sundown.

And it was nothing like he expected. It was situated on a rise overlooking the town, and it was approached by a long winding uphill drive, a commodious, whitewashed, two-storied building, surrounded by shuttered porches and generous gardens and lawns.

The grounds workers had already signalled their approach, and Hugh Morant was outside waiting by the time the carriage came in sight of the house; when it drew to a stop, a dozen chattering servants converged to see who the visitor was and what they might do for his comfort.

And then Diandra stepped out of the carriage and fell into Hugh's arms. It was impossible to tell what he was thinking: he hugged her, set her aside to look at her, murmured a few words to her, and then they disappeared into the house.

And there was no way to tell whether Serena was in there too.

"What an unexpected pleasure," Hugh murmured. "You must be exhausted. You're too pale, Diandra. What on earth are you doing back here? And where is Serena? You were supposed to stay in London for another three months at least. Truth to tell, I was expecting you'd stay on forever. I was so sure you'd fall in love with it. Tell me, was the Earl too beastly? Would you like some tea? Ah, I see Gita has anticipated. With sandwiches. Just right. Nothing too heavy after that enervating journey. You needn't talk yet. There's lots of time."

She smiled wanly and took the cup that Gita offered.

Singing warmth touched the palms of her hand. And this house. She loved this house.

She took a sip of tea, relaxed back against the cushions of the sofa and looked around the familiar comfortably cluttered room before she asked, her voice tentative, "Serena's not here?"

Hugh shook his head. "I see there's a mystery afoot. You didn't travel together?"

"No. She went off without me. I can't begin to explain."

"Is she safe?"

"I have reason to believe she is, but I don't know."

"Too puzzling, dear girl. Drink your tea and tell me."

She looked into his dear face, and she didn't know how she could. All the business about the spirits and then Serena's attack on her . . . he'd never believe it.

And now that she was a thousand miles from London, she didn't know if she did either.

"I'm sure she's right behind me, and she'll explain everything."

"I'll send a boy down to the road to look for her." He clapped his hands, and he gave instructions to the servant who appeared. "Now—you look all done in."

"Yes, but I'm home now." She jumped up and began pacing the room. It was funny how familiar and strange it seemed to her. As if her being away had given her new eyes with which to see.

And yet nothing was different. There was still the same grouping of chairs around the sofa and fireplace, the same worn oriental carpet on the floor, fresh flowers, as always, and an overflowing bookcase in the corner. Piles of books and newspapers on the floor by the chair where Hugh did his reading. And on his desk by the window, reams of paperwork for him to go through.

Yes, everything the same. The wall hangings, slightly faded now, and the groups of pictures on the tables, walls and shelves, wherever there was a space. Everything familiar. But still strange.

She picked up a framed picture, one she had seen a hundred times before: Guthrie and Hugh. Guthrie long before she knew him, youth in his face—Justin in his features—when Pamela was still alive.

She set the picture down slowly and picked up another. Hugh in this one, among mates at the club, men and women both. Another picture at a picnic. And another beside a kill on a victorious hunt.

Something about that . . . yes, Guthrie in this one too, the young Guthrie, not the one I knew . . . his tiger, his victory.

"My dear, you've seen those pictures all your life."

"I know. It just all looks—a little strange."

"Not to fear: India will reclaim you. You need some sleep. But you do have me worried about Serena."

"She will be all right, wherever she is." She tried to temper her voice, but it sounded harsh even to her.

"Why don't you sit down and tell me?" Hugh said.

"I can't. I don't know how. Everything was fine. I thought everything was fine, and then strange things began happening: we started seeing apparitions and summoning spirits. Leonie Hull was Serena's sponsor; Justin insisted, even though she dearly did not want to, and it got even more complicated because she really began to believe that her sister Pamela was the spirit. But it turned out that Serena was responsible for a least one of the manifestations, and when I discovered it . . ." No, she couldn't tell him about the fire. "When I discovered the apparatus she had used to do it, she . . . she left."

"My dear girl: that's the most inconceivable story I ever heard. Serena doing tricks—well, maybe. You know Serena. But the rest—and Guthrie's first wife involved— you know, I'm glad you had the sense to get out of there. Did you . . . did you confront Serena?"

"No. I think she saw me and she thought the better tack was just to leave so she wouldn't have to explain herself."

"I see."

"So she's probably on her way here. She took money, and I'm glad of that; I would have given her more. I wish she could have explained. I wish we had come back together."

"Of course you do. But that will all take care of itself. And everything will look better by morning."

"I hope you're not too shocked to see me back so soon."

"This is your home, Diandra. And anyway, where else do you have to go?"

And there it was again, one of those pinprick reminders of her status in the household. She didn't know why it grated on her so; Hugh probably didn't even realize how he had phrased it, or how it sounded to her.

"I should go to bed."

"The servants have readied your room, my dear." He helped her up from her chair, and walked with her to the staircase, his arm around her waist. "You get some sleep. We can talk more in the morning," and, as she mounted the first step, he added gently, "I'm so glad you're here."

"So am I." She walked slowly up the stairs, more tired than she ever could have believed possible. Gita awaited her to help her to her room, her lovely light and airy and shuttered room.

When she walked in the door, the first thing she saw was the long-missing divining board and planchette right in the middle of her bed with the velvet pouches folded neatly beside.

There were so many spare bedrooms in the house, it was no trouble for Jhasa to find him one where no one would know he was there.

He had already gotten the lay of the house, and where Diandra's and Serena's bedrooms were located, and he had been given food and water, and now he was settling in for a long night of surveillance.

She wouldn't thank him for it. She wanted to forgive and forget, but he was certain Serena only wanted to finish what she had begun in Cheswick Square.

He sat on the floor by the door, which was open just a crack so he could see down the long hallway toward Diandra's room.

Four weeks ago he had been *in* Diandra's bedroom. How mightily things had changed.

And what had changed to precipitate Serena's attack? He hadn't stopped asking that question, even though she had denied anything had changed.

And now he was in India, the place he hated, his rival, his antagonist, his foe; India—the entity that had taken his parents from him. And in the home of Hugh Morant, his father's close friend, who had promoted his marriage Diandra . . .

Ah, the gods were laughing.

What had changed?

What, of all the inexplicable things that had happened? When, in all the business of the spiritualists, the ghosts, the rappings, the messages, the deaths, had something changed enough to drive Serena to attempt murder?

Not her negative fortune. Or the floating table—her hands had been fixed on it almost as if they were stuck there. And it went down and she went with it.

After that, then. Confusion—lights out, the servants running to search the house, Serena on the floor near the couch . . .

What—what changed then?

Lights on, Tuttle with the brandy. Serena hoisting herself on the couch. His own demand that everyone be escorted to their rooms.

*Diandra remaining, after everyone had gone, on the floor,
picking up the cards . . .*

What else had Diandra picked up off the floor?

He felt a chill. He had been busy chopping up a table.
He tried to envision the moment he returned to the room.
Her face had been strained, her arm under the sofa.

Retrieving something?

Or *hiding* it?

And someone had seen.

Serena . . .

But what? What was worth killing Diandra for?

And did she still have the thing in her possession?

And was Serena planning to come and get it?

Not if I find it first.

It wasn't even a conscious plan. He would search her
room in the morning, and he would tear the place apart,
but he would find it—whatever it was—before Serena
stepped one foot back in Bhaumaghar.

Chapter Eighteen

And now she felt haunted; she didn't sleep all night. She just sat and stared at the board which she left where it lay on her bed.

The board: Agatha's board. They hadn't seen it in weeks. There was just no earthly way for it to have gotten here, and yet here it was.

And she didn't know quite what to do about it. Her first instinct was to hide it. But she was already concealing one too many secrets.

She was home now; she was safe. She oughtn't to be feeling threatened any more.

She should have been down having breakfast with Hugh.

The board held her back, delayed her, wielded a frightening power far beyond its physical presence. She wanted to touch it, and she wanted to destroy it. She felt as if it knew things it would tell her, if only she would ask.

She couldn't even conceive of a place to hide it.

Another nightmare.

When she finally got downstairs to Hugh, she felt as if her every secret was written on her forehead.

He was waiting for her on the screened verandah. It was one of her favorite places; they used it as a second dining room when the heat got too debilitating. And it was the perfect place to have breakfast every morning.

"You don't look rested at all," Hugh said when she joined him.

"I'm fine." She poured her tea, took some toast, and waved away his offer to serve her some eggs.

"That's not nearly enough . . ."

"That's all I want right now." She bit into the toast. It was dry, crumbly, and she almost choked.

What was wrong with her?

"So . . ." Hugh murmured. "I have a little time this morning, Diandra. Do you think you could make clear to me just what happened in London?"

She did; she told him everything, everything but the fire and the board, and it all sounded fantastic even to her.

"Absolutely bizarre," Hugh said when she finished. "Unbelievable."

"Exactly, but don't you see? If Serena could create that kind of illusion, then it's possible that all the manifestations were faked." And those were the words she didn't want to think let alone say.

"Well, of course—anything is possible. But why?"

"I don't know. That's the thing that makes no sense."

"Serena could not have been responsible for everything. The table levitation was a trick, most likely, in line with everything else that was happening. So there was no need for her to run away, was there?"

No, Hugh, except she tried to kill me.

"Maybe she thought I would tell Justin about her part and having found the apparatus."

"Would you have?"

"I hadn't intended to, no. But she didn't stay around long enough to know that."

"And we don't know where she is."

"No."

"Well—" Hugh set aside his napkin. "I've never heard such a curious story in my life, Diandra. I don't know what to make of it. I'm glad you're back home, however. And now, I do need to spend some time at the office. I hope for all our sakes that Serena is here by the time I get back."

She poured a second cup of tea as she watched him go. And she wondered who she was protecting by her lies of omission—Serena or him.

And then she was curiously at loose ends.

She was not going back to her room. She had buried the board under her mattress and she was not going to look to see if it was still there.

She couldn't even remember what she used to do in the house before she'd gone to England.

She wandered back into the parlor.

Strange how things still looked so different and so the same. And the room was tidy and everything was dusted. Hugh obviously had everything in hand.

She would have to look at the accounts and see to laying in more stores. She could order some lighter dresses in half mourning—surely it was time. And there were surely events and invitations to be organized now that she was home.

There was a stack of unopened mail on one of the parlor tables, and she picked it up and carried it into the dining room, set it down, and went back into the parlor to pick up one of the framed photographs that was on the table.

Guthrie again, the younger Guthrie, fresh-faced, eager, the man who had been Pamela's husband. And where was Pamela?

She picked up another photograph. The one she had looked at last night of a group of men and women on the verandah of the club.

Guthrie. Hugh. People she didn't recognize. She wondered if one of them was Pamela.

How long had Hugh known Guthrie? He must have known Pamela too. Curious that hadn't occurred to her before. And that Pamela must have been in Bhaumaghar with Guthrie. How could she not have known that?

Which of the women in the photograph was Pamela?

Why was she so fascinated by photographs that had been in her house for as long as she could remember?

Because . . . because—it was all interconnected somehow, and she had the feeling if she could just figure it out, everything would make sense.

She went back to the mail, methodically opening each envelope and sorting it according to importance.

. . . everything came back to Guthrie . . .

Yes. She kept thinking that. And there was something about the photographs, but she didn't know what.

It was an awful lot of mail . . .

She pushed it aside impatiently and picked up another photograph. The hunt. Hugh in the background. Guthrie beside the kill, surrounded by the guides. Ah—and there, behind Hugh—*behind him?*—a woman, her face partially obscured by shadow.

Pamela.

If it was Pamela . . . then she too had come to Bhaumaghar and Hugh had known her.

Why had she thought that Guthrie had come only after Pamela's death?

She picked up the picture at the club. So many unfamiliar faces. She couldn't tell if one of them were the woman in the hunt picture. But she could have been. She probably was.

But so what? Why was she feeling so disquieted about this?

It was the appearance of the board, so eerie, so unexpected, so mysterious.

Or—there could be as simple an explanation as Gita having found it someplace and put it among her things when she was packing.

And then just set it on her bed where it would scare her half to death?

. . . Agatha's divining board had just followed her to Bhaumaghar as if it had a life of its own . . .

Maybe it did—

Maybe she ought to ascertain the thing was still where she had left it—

She was up the stairs before the thought was fully formed. But she stopped short as she passed Hugh's room; the door was open and one of the servants was inside . . . unpacking a suitcase.

"Bhati—what's this?"

"Mem?" He bowed. "Sahib Hugh has only just returned—not a hour before mem arrived yesterday."

"What?!"

Immediately his expression changed and he turned away from her and back to his work.

"Bhati—?"

"I know nothing more, mem."

"No—you're saying Sahib Hugh has been away?"

"I know nothing more, mem."

"For how long, Bhati?"

"I cannot calculate—a month . . . maybe—"

She felt a chill. "That long . . ." But perhaps he had had business in Calcutta; any number of problems could have arisen after she and Serena left for England. That was probably what had happened. He'd gone to Calcutta, and there was no reason for him to have mentioned it last night when she arrived.

Explanations for everything, if only one looked.
Even a divining board . . .
Which was sitting right in the middle of her bed once again when she entered her room.

She had put it under the mattress—she knew she had.

"Gita!" Her voice was so loud and angry even in her own ears.

Gita came running, and stopped abruptly when she saw the board. "Mem?" And her tone—cautious, wary.

"Did you take the board out from under the mattress?"

"Oh no, mem." Gita began to back away. "Oh no. I know nothing of the board." She was out in the hallway by then. "I know nothing of how it came to be there."

Gita was scared of the board.

She was scared of the board. She closed the door behind Gita and contemplated the board.

It *was* the same board, and it had disappeared that night from her room, with the table. Justin hadn't been able to remove it, and yet here it was, on her bed, the same board.

She put an experimental finger on the edge of the planchette and felt the vibration all the way down to her toes.

She couldn't remove her finger.

It was like something was holding it fast—a pressure, unseen, barely felt, but so strong she could do nothing but keep her finger on the planchette.

And then it began to move and spell out a message.

Loved you.

Her heart started pounding painfully.

Guthrie?

And just as she thought that, the pressure was gone.

Oh my God . . . oh my God . . . oh my God—

There was no end to this; her ghosts and demons had followed

her right to Bhaumaghar. She felt their presence right in her room.
They were watching her, waiting for her . . .

She didn't know what to do about the board.

It will do something about itself.

To be thinking that way—she was going crazy; it was the only
explanation.

She needed to get back to mundane matters. Kitchen
matters. Housekeeping matters.

She edged out of the room and closed the door behind
her.

Back down the hallway toward Hugh's room, the door
shut now.

She paused and then turned the knob and entered.
Bhati was gone, everything was neatly in place.

Away for a month . . .

She opened his armoire on the pretext of looking for
anything that needed pressing.

Everything lined up by color, by article. Jackets, trousers,
suits, ties, hats, formal wear. His suitcase stowed neatly
beneath.

She pulled it out, she didn't know why, and she knelt
down and opened it. *Nothing inside. But what had she*
expected? He would take a minimal amount of clothing and one
body servant for a month's journey—

Who had gone with him, then?

She shoved the suitcase back into the armoire and went
downstairs to find Bhati.

"Who went with Sahib Hugh on this journey?"

"I know nothing more."

"Who attended to him?"

"I cannot say." His expression was calm, but his eyes—
his eyes reflected fear. Why?

"Tell me just that. Who went with him?"

"I was not here."

An outright lie. "Who was here then?"

"I cannot say."

And it was the same with all the servants. No one would tell her anything. She was outraged, and beginning to feel very uneasy.

Hugh would tell her. There were simple explanations.

She tended to the mail. She checked the day's menu and the stores. Anything to take her mind off the mysteries. And Serena.

And the board with its eerie message.

Loved you.

Her hands were like ice in spite of the heat. At tiffin, she returned to the verandah, and picked at her food. Surely Serena would turn up soon. Hugh would come home and answer her questions. And that would be the end of it.

She heard the humming of the house servants as they went about their chores. The cawking of the birds. The musical drone of distant conversation. Reassuring sounds that made her feel sheltered and safe.

Now why would she think that in her brother's house?

She cupped her tea to warm her hands. Only a matter of time now and all the little mysteries would be cleared up.

Loved you.

Except that one.

But—*Hugh had returned not an hour before she did, and never said a word? Had been great good friends with Guthrie long before Pamela's suicide; had even known Pamela, it would seem, from the evidence of the photographs.*

But—so what?

She didn't know, but her feeling of apprehension was escalating by the minute.

Who had identified Pamela when the ghostly manifestations had begun?

She couldn't even remember. Was the first time during

the visit of the Hoxton-Shopes, when Justin had deliberately brought her to the *voudrais?*

She wasn't even sure, it was such a jumble in her mind.

No, wait—they had been there, and then they had heard that awful rapping sound ... yes ... and had gone upstairs—and the table—had that been the first time that the table had levitated?

No ... no—that was the night before ...

... and Serena's hands had been on it both times ...

They had heard the rapping the second night, in the *voudrais.* And the table had gone flying ...

And now the conclusion was inescapable that Serena had made it levitate, both times ...

And—and ...

She didn't want to remember this—she didn't—but it had been Serena as well who had taken charge that night; and she was the one who had challenged the entity and ultimately identified it as Pamela.

All interconnected. All.

She sat still as stone in her wicker chair, her hands around the lukewarm cup of tea, and she saw her life crumbling before her eyes.

Everything came back to Guthrie.

She didn't know how to make sense out of it. But one thing was very clear: Serena had made those tables levitate and Serena had perpetrated the illusion that the so-called spirit was Pamela.

What else could have been a deliberate deception?

Any of it. All of it.

No wonder Serena had wanted her dead.

Oh now—wait, wait ... no—the thing was just not that critical. Whatever it was, it couldn't have warranted killing someone.

And yet—and yet . . . four souls had died . . .

The thought was so stunning she almost dropped her cup.

All those deaths had something to do with—ghosts?

That didn't exist . . . ?

And a murderer whom no one could catch.

She could not warm up. She felt cold as the grave. She hated what she was thinking; it would have been easier to believe in ghosts than to comprehend this.

She went into the parlor, gathered up all the photographs, brought them out to the verandah, and arranged them on the table.

What did they tell her?

Hugh loved taking photographs. He was fond of his friends and happy to be able to offer hospitality and a season of great hunting. He was convivial and well-liked.

And he had known Pamela.

Why did that disturb her so?

She went to Hugh's desk and took his magnifying glass to look at the woman in the hunt photograph more closely.

She was standing behind him, so she was slightly out of focus. She was dressed in the fashion of five or six years before and she was holding a broad-brimmed hat, and part of one side of her face was obscured by the shadow of Hugh's head.

Smudgy eyes in a heart-shaped face, and thick heavy hair coiled behind her neck.

Justin's mother.

And now, she could identify her in the club photograph as one of the women seated on the bottom step of the verandah. And again, in a group of picnickers along the bank of a river.

In every photograph, in fact. Subtly sometimes, but she was always there, in the background, like a hovering angel.

She didn't know why she felt such shock that Hugh had

known Lady Pamela so very well. And had kept her with him all these years.

She and Serena had probably been at boarding school then. She would have known otherwise. And she hadn't met Guthrie until well after Pamela's much publicized suicide.

They never found the body . . .

Guthrie had had her declared legally dead and asked the social-climbing Diandra Morant to be his wife, and in so doing, unleashed the power and the passion within her.

So why had Pamela come to life again suddenly? Who was Pamela supposed to be haunting?

But the entity had never done anything but make mysterious accusations of murder . . .

Her head was spinning. It still didn't make sense. Pamela had been dead so long by then. And Guthrie too.

Why ghosts?

Why did Hugh still have her pictures all around the house?

Why would Serena set fire to her room?

Why hadn't Hugh told her he had been away?

She felt like her brain would burst. She needed to lie down. She felt like she was moving through molasses as she brought the photographs back to the parlor and arranged them just as she had found them on the tables; and then she headed upstairs.

She had the awful sense that she was both alone in the house and that someone was watching.

The door to Hugh's room was closed. And her own. The next room down was Serena's—and that door was open.

She felt a familiar chill. It hadn't been open this morning.

Where was Gita?

Where was anyone?

She thrust open the door to her room: the board was

still in the middle of the bed. She slammed the door shut
and walked slowly down the hall toward Serena's room.

Serena's room was empty. The bed made. The shuttters
open. The scent of jasmine emanating from fresh flowers
on the bureau. Faithfully dusted. The mosquito netting
drawn back from her bed, making a gauzy foreground for
the armoire. No sign of occupancy, so Serena hadn't yet
returned.

She was worried sick about Serena.

*Don't forget she took all your money. She is not stranded. She
will make her way home; she's old enough to figure out how.*

*But—she hadn't wanted to leave London. She'd wanted to stay
there forever; she'd felt deprived of its amusements and social life.*

For all she knew, Serena was there now.

*But Serena could never survive there on her own, and surely
she wouldn't have the nerve to reapply to Justin for protection.*

That would utterly humiliate her.

*He'd probably foist her off on Leonie again—gullible, pitiable
Leonie.*

*Well, she had a clear field with Justin now. He didn't want to
marry anyone, so it could just as well be Leonie as anyone else.*

And poor poor George, relegated to the sidelines once again.

. . . Justin, grieving like a child . . .

She made a movement of denial. There was no reason
to think about him ever again.

There was nothing odd in Serena's room, except the
fact the door had been open.

And just as she concluded that, the door suddenly
slammed shut.

And hanging on a hook on the back of it was a long
gray hooded cloak.

Chapter Nineteen

She had never felt such terror in her life.

The cloak, the ominous hooded cloak of the vanishing gray ghost—as corporeal as her own body.

She stood rooted, unable to move even a finger, her heart pounding, sinking, dying.

Who—what?

"Put on the cloak, Diandra."

Oh God—Serena!

She whirled—no Serena.

"Put on the cloak."

Her voice seemed to echo everywhere.

"Where are you?"

"Put on the cloak, and everything will be revealed."

She couldn't move, not even if it meant discovering the meaning of heaven itself. But this was a nightmare in hell.

"Damn it, Serena."

The door to the porch flew open, and Serena suddenly appeared on the threshold, and she was fresh and vital and bright-eyed with malice.

And in her hand was a shotgun. And she was pointing it straight at Diandra's heart. "The cloak, Diandra."

She moved toward it so slowly, it felt as if someone else were in her body, and she took it from the hook and swirled it around her shoulders.

It was too long, and too thick for the heat. And she hated the feel of it around her; her body felt clammy and cold suddenly, cold as death.

"It's Pamela's cloak, you know."

"I don't know. I didn't know. I don't understand anything. Serena!"

"Oh, please, Diandra. Hugh kept it for years after she died. He had a long passionate affair with her. You didn't know that either, did you?"

And Serena did? But the evidence was there in all those photographs he had kept all these years.

"All right," she said carefully. "Hugh had an affair with Pamela."

"He wanted to marry her. She didn't want to divorce Guthrie. She just wanted to run away with Hugh. But you see, she didn't understand—Hugh wanted the money."

. . . the money . . .

"And she wouldn't; she wanted it for herself, and as long as they were just having an affair, everything was right and tight with Guthrie, and she had everything she wanted.

"Think about this now, Diandra. If she had divorced Guthrie, there would have been some kind of settlement, a large settlement to smooth the scandal and ease her out of Guthrie's life. He probably would have left her here, and she could have married Hugh and they would have had pots of money to live like kings."

. . . pots of money—someone else had said that: if she had stayed in India, she could have lived like a queen . . .

"But then—follow me now, Sister dear, Hugh got a better idea. We were away at school, you might recall, and on the verge of returning. And Pamela was being singularly uncooperative. So it was time to put a new plan into effect. And the first component was, Pamela had to die."

That bald statement jolted her.

Pamela had to die. Pamela had committed suicide. No one knew why. Except Hugh . . .

"Hugh is a very patient man, Diandra. He hates it here. Abhors it. But if he could have gotten the money—well, there was another plan: he was going to make Guthrie fall in love with you. He didn't know I wanted him myself. Wouldn't that have been something? The Earl of Skene and his baby bride. I always hated Hugh for that: he told me straight out I was too young and he wouldn't even consider it.

"You were the chosen, and he made sure that Guthrie came to Bhaumaghar as often as possible and then threw you in his path."

Had she been so gullible, so naïve? She hadn't known for one minute what Hugh's intentions were; he had been so hospitable, so sincere in his concern for Guthrie and his loss and his grief.

And all the while plotting and planning and using anything to hand.

She felt sick. Sick, sick, sick. Maybe it was the cloak; she felt an overpowering sour scent emanating from its folds. Or maybe that was her churning stomach.

"I don't want to hear any more."

Serena snorted. "If you hadn't found the rods . . . but that's just like Pamela refusing the divorce: the thing hangs in the air and you never can be sure it isn't going to be used against you."

"I wouldn't have. I was shocked, but I wouldn't have."

Serena shrugged. "But who could know that, or what you would deduce from it. Yes, I can see you came exactly to the conclusion I thought you would. That everything else was a hoax."

"People *died.*"

"Negligible. And besides, I couldn't let Justin get interested in anyone else. He was going to be *mine* after they
hauled you off to prison for Guthrie's murder. Perfect
happy ending: Hugh would get his money, and I would
get what I had always wanted: the Earl of Skene."

"*You* killed those two women?"

"Oh no no no—you still don't understand, Diandra. It
was me and Hugh. The whole thing, the two of us together.
The gray ghost, the spirits, the rapping, the glowing figure
at the *séance*—scared me to death even though I knew he
was going to do it. But Madam didn't, and she was going
to find out it was a hoax, so of course she had to be silenced.
He came about a week behind us; we'd planned the whole
thing out together. And he knew all about the houses:
Pamela had told him everything, and he had her keys too."

"Oh, dear God—and what, all in aid of what?"

Serena let loose an exaggerated sigh. "The *money,* Diandra. *Your* money. All that money that Guthrie settled on
you that you wouldn't give Hugh any of. The money he
would have controlled if you had been convicted of
murder."

She was so utterly dumbstruck by the intricacy of Hugh's
machinations that she had no idea what Serena was talking
about. "What do you mean, murder? Murdered who?"

"Guthrie, of course. He didn't die a natural death at
all, Diandra. Hugh killed him because he was out to get
you."

Byzantine.
Deranged.
*They were both crazy. Her sister, her brother, out to get her
money through a convoluted plot to have her convicted of murder-
ing Guthrie.*

What lengths they had gone to.

And now she knew everything, so they would kill her too.

"Ghosts—" she said desperately. "Why the ghosts?"

"It was dramatic, wasn't it, the spirit of Pamela accusing *someone* of murder. Who else could it be? And Justin already so suspicious of you. We didn't even know that. We just wanted to provoke his curiosity enough so that he would reopen the case. And then have the *ghost* provide the clue that would prove Guthrie was murdered—by *you*. Who could pin down a ghost, after all?

"Hugh is a very patient man, you see. He didn't care how long it took to get the money. And meantime, I was right in the house, and I had the best chance of slowly and subtly fixing Justin's interest."

"That's what you meant," Diandra whispered.

"What else? It really was quite clever. But I wasn't quite as clever as you, Diandra. I wanted to kill you just for taking him away from me."

"He was never yours."

"We could debate that, but we won't. I need to tidy things up here so that I can get back to London. I'll have him yet, Diandra, and you'll be dead, and that's the way it will be."

Cold-blooded. Fury raging in her. She'd never seen it, never felt it. Always thought Serena loved her.

But now—the reason for all those inexplicable changes in her were clear: they had planned that far in advance. Laid the groundwork in case the first plan didn't work. Or maybe Serena had been casting spells and chanting on her own at first.

She would never know. And she felt as if she had been living another life, parallel to the one in which Hugh and Serena existed.

How was it possible to be so oblivious to such hate?

She had been in love.

They had always been too poor. Never quite good enough. Never quite anything. Equal only in a country where a common man could be an aristocrat. It didn't take a fortune, and Hugh had accomplished that much at least. But it hadn't been enough.

Maybe nothing would ever be enough.

Not even her silence.

Or her death.

"What are you going to do?" she said finally.

"What do you think? You know too much now, and nobody will question the gunshot. We'll say you went back to London, and later, that you decided to stay there, permanently. I think it will wash." She lifted the shotgun. "And I know you made provisions for my dowry. I hope you were generous. I guess I should be grateful I didn't have to . . ."

The sound of a gun blast stopped her cold; she stiffened, and she fell to the floor, murmuring, ". . . beg."

There was blood everywhere, gushing from a wound in her side.

"Oh my God—oh my God . . ." Diandra was on her knees instantly, pulling off the cloak to cover Serena and reaching under her skirt to tear off a piece of her petticoat to wrap around her hemorrhaging midriff.

Where were the servants?

"Gita! Bhati! Jhasa!"

Bhati was the first in the room. "Ooohhhhh," he moaned. "Mem is wounded. I know nothing about . . . about—"

"You are *useless*. Jhasa—to the village for the doctor. Gita—help me get her onto the bed. And then get me bandages. And pads. And hot water. Quick! Hurry!"

There was no gentle way to do it. They made a makeshift litter out of the cloak and jolted her up to the bed. She was moaning and losing consciousness, and Diandra was scared she was going to die.

Rajit entered with a tray full of towels, pads and bandages. A moment later, Bhati brought a bucket of hot water.

Diandra sank down on the bed and removed the tourniqet. Useless. The blood just wouldn't stop. She rinsed the towels and began wiping it away, as Serena moaned in pain.

"Find the bullet." *Dear God, let there be an exit wound . . .* but she didn't think she was experienced enough to tell that. All she could do was clean it and bandage it tightly and make Serena as comfortable as possible until the doctor could get there.

Who had shot Serena?

"Stay with her."

"I will, mem."

She had blood all over her dress, and the sight of it made her sick. It could have been her. She could have been dead by now. Serena had been going to kill her.

So someone had tried to kill Serena instead.

Who? A ghost? Her guardian angel?

Was there no place on earth that wasn't haunted somehow?

She burst into her room, shrugging out of her dress as she made for the closet. She wasn't even going to wash the blood off her hands. And any dress would do.

The thing was going to end *now*.

She was going to find a killer.

He was waiting for her in the parlor with a gun in his hand.

Dear Hugh.

"Such excitement," he murmured. "Do sit down, Diandra."

"Did you shoot her?"

"I? Shoot my compatriot, my partner in crime? Oh no, there is some honor among thieves, my dear. I could not have done any of it without her. I love her for her feral instincts and her utter loathing of you."

He looked up as Jhasa appeared on the threshold.

"The doctor sahib is here."

"Take him up." He was so cool, so imperturbable.

"I should go with him."

"Oh no, Diandra. This time you can't escape your fate."

"I see; you'll leave me here in a bloody bath. You'll have witnesses—the doctor is right here, and he won't be able to save me."

"Something like that. I wish you had given me the money."

"How could I have done that? You never asked."

"But you see—*you* should have. You should have seen that it was through my auspices that you married well, and ultimately inherited a fortune. Surely I deserved some gratitude for lifting you above your station. You really should have asked, Diandra."

She was chilled to the bone, and she would never get warm again. Hugh was insane. And Serena was dying upstairs. "What should I have said?"

"Tch—you could have asked if I was in want of anything."

"Were you?

"Oh—about fifty thousand pounds."

Shell-shocked again. He had nerve, she had to say that for him. "Fine. Are you in want of fifty thousand pounds, Hugh? I could write the check right now."

"Ah! So kind. Too late. Too much has happened."

"What if Serena dies?"

"Oh. Well. Then it all comes to me, doesn't it?" He waved the gun in her face. "I hope poor Serena survives."

"Sahib." Jhasa at the foot of the steps. "Doctor sahib requests that you come."

"Of course." He gestured with the gun. "You first, Diandra. Don't try anything. I'm feeling skittish today."

She felt the hard nose of the thing in the small of her

back as they walked up the stairs. The doctor met them at the door. "She's lost too much blood. The bullet is embedded in her spine. She would be paralyzed in any event. There isn't much I can do."

Hugh pushed her into the room.

Serena's face was pale, beautiful. Her eyes were closed, her breathing labored. But she must have sensed them there. Her lids flickered open and she saw them, and smiled, and murmured, "Everyone is here, Guthrie. Now I can go . . ." And she took one more breath, and she was gone.

"*Serena!*"

"You can't—" the doctor, pulling at her one way and Hugh the other while tears streamed down her face and she tried to get to Serena, to infuse her with her life and her strength.

"She won't—" Hugh, his hands rough, merciless.

"Did you hear what she said? She spoke to Guthrie— Hugh, she *spoke* to Guthrie . . ."

"Diandra—this is not a parlor trick; get away from her."

"No, no—she can't go, not like this . . . *Serena*—!"

She was so cold, so lifeless. So beautiful. If she just hadn't listened to Hugh—

She fell to her knees, her anguish unbearable. She didn't care about Hugh or the past or the money or anything. Serena . . . Serena . . . never as calm as her name—

She heard Hugh in the background speaking in a low voice to the doctor and then the servants, instructing them to prepare Serena's body.

Serena's body . . .

"No-o-o-o-o-o-o . . . !"

Hugh's hands were lifting her roughly from the floor and shoving her out of the room. "No one comes in the room."

"As you wish, Sahib." Bhati, ever faithful.

Hugh punched the gun against her side. "Downstairs, Diandra, so we can continue our conversation."

"Stay where you are." Did she imagine it, or was it there? She couldn't see a thing through her tear-drenched eyes.

"Guthrie—" she whispered.

"Stay out of my way!" Hugh's voice behind her. "Get out of my way."

But he came toward them, the avenging knight, and so relentlessly and inexorably Hugh had nowhere left for flight; he backed up and up and up as the vengeful vision came closer and closer and closer still—

Guthrie! She saw him standing there as clear as a bell, watching, waiting for the final disposition . . .

There was no way out anywhere—Hugh's boot slipped on the top step, he lost his balance, and he fell on his head, and then he rolled over and over and down, until he landed with a gut-wrenching thump at the bottom of the stairs.

And then there was a dead hollow silence. Long. Deep. Punctuated by her anguished sobs.

And then, slowly, her vision cleared. And Guthrie was gone.

And Justin was there.

Some things couldn't be explained. She didn't want them explained. Like how Justin had turned up there. And whether she really saw the avenging face of Guthrie meting out justice to the man who had betrayed him.

None of that.

It was hard enough coping with her losses.

And the fact she must vacate the house to the newly appointed interim governor. And face Justin after everything Hugh and Serena had done.

All of that.

Hugh had murdered six souls in the name of his greed. But Justin had fired the shot that brought Serena down.

And how could she come to terms with that?

She was numb from the shock. And she had to arrange for their burials, and clear out the house, and arrange for somewhere to live while she spent her grief and tried to make sense of the whole.

Justin handled it all. He found her a house, he got the furniture moved, though in the crunch and crush, things got lost and mislaid; and the servants who would go with her. He took care of the burials, the expenses, and her life, and all she had to do was mourn and cry.

There wasn't much to say. He had heard it all while he kept watch over her against the moment Serena would strike again.

He stayed on at the hotel, never intruding, always there. Finding the India that had lured his father to his destiny and his death.

She gave him the photographs—the ones with Guthrie and Pamela, and he took them.

And she insisted that Guthrie was there that day.

"I won't argue with you about it."

They were in the parlor of her little house just off the main street of the village, and Gita was laying out plates and utensils for dinner.

"Every time I think—"

"Don't."

"How can't I? How do I live with what they did?"

"You just do."

"I never saw—"

They'd been over that too. Neither had he. He had thought Serena insipid and uninteresting, but never did he perceive the depths of her hate and rage.

That comforted her—somewhat.

She wanted him to go back to London, back to his life.

He didn't know what he wanted.

He wanted *her*.

But she wasn't nearly ready for him.

On a late summer's morning, three months after he had gone back to London, she awakened to find the misbegotten divining board on the bed beside her.

The thing was a cruel joke. A horrible reminder. She should have burned it herself. But it was the one thing in all the catastrophe that no one could explain. How it always turned up, how it worked, how it *knew* . . .

Loved you.

That potent message was always with her.

She reached out her finger and touched the planchette. Immediately she felt a pressure holding it there.

And then slowly it began to move and spell out a message.

Love him.

She felt the chill right through her body.

But the thing wasn't done. It started to move again, and she caught her breath at the word it spelled out next.

Go.

And then the pressure was gone. She could move her finger. She touched the board, tracing the letters.

Go.

She pushed at the planchette and it floated across the board and then lifted up, flew through the air and out the open window.

She jumped out of the bed and ran to the window.

This was a dream, wasn't it?

The thing wasn't there. Anywhere.

And when she looked back at the bed, she saw that the board had vanished too.

* * *

She arrived in London on a late September day, knowing full well that everyone was in the country and Town would be empty of company.

She wanted it that way. She wanted to come to London on her own terms, and find her own accommodations and live her own life.

Sons of deceased husbands need not apply.

She settled in at Brown's, with Gita and Jhasa in adjoining rooms, and she found that she eased into Town life just fine; there was so much to do even with the gentry off shooting pheasants. There was theater and the museums, and the libraries; and long walks, and country jaunts. And the titillation of the *Tatler* every day.

She was healing, slowly slowly slowly. She felt calm and secure.

Curiously, it was Leonie who discovered she was there.

"My dear. It's been an age. How *are* you?"

So cordial. But people were listening, and appearances must be kept up at all costs, especially in Burnham's Tea Shop.

"Come, let's have a cup. Right now. Sit down and tell me everything."

"I expect you know everything," Diandra said.

"I didn't know you were out of mourning."

"Two years is enough, don't you think?"

"Justin is away, did you know?"

Her heart stopped. "No."

"Went to the colonies—to some godforsaken place called Wyoming. Riding horses and chasing cows. But he's coming back for the wedding."

"The—wedding . . . ?" She felt faint. *The* wedding. But she had the presence of mind to say, "Whose wedding?"

"Mine. To George. Dear George. I would be honored

if you would come. If you are to be in Town in three weeks."

She could barely breathe. "I will. And I would be delighted."

"That's settled then. Where are you staying?"

"Brown's, for now. I'm looking for a house."

"Did Justin know?"

She shook her head.

"I see. I'd send him a message, but by the time it got there, he would be back here. And I'm so busy with the wedding."

"Of course you are." She remembered weddings. All the fittings, details, anxiety and joy. She had loved her wedding to Guthrie.

"But—we should have dinner, you and I and George."

"My pleasure."

"Good. I know where to find you. I'll be in touch soon."

She left then in a flurry of skirts and packages and Diandra eased back in her chair and stared out the window.

Three weeks. Three weeks and he'd be there.

On a late September morning, on the Punta Pass Trail in New Mexico, beside a dying fire, Justin awakened suddenly when he rolled over onto an object in his sleeping bag.

He was so tired; no one had ever told him that riding all day every day would just about kill him. This wasn't a fox hunt. This was pure unadulterated bone-jolting hard work. And he was loving every minute of it.

But damn, he was still aching from the day on the trail. Damned soreness never went away. And he slept like a house every night, with no time for memories to intrude.

They were taking the herd down to Abilene, and they had another hundred miles to go. Another week maybe, down through New Mexico and over toward Texas.

Sights and sounds he had never dreamt of; experiences not to be replicated. A man needed that kind of freedom of the soul.

He reached under his body impatiently to retrieve the object.

And he knew just what it was.

Nor was he about to question the vagaries of fate: he opened the velvet pouch and pulled out the divining board and planchette.

There was just enough early dawn light to see by. He pushed himself up on his elbow and lay the board on the ground beside him, and put the planchette on the board.

Now what?

He touched the planchette with one finger and instantly he felt a holding pressure.

The planchette began to move.

Always love you.

He felt the chill all the way to his hair.

The planchette moved again.

Love her.

His hand started shaking.

Go.

And then his hand was free suddenly. He pushed the planchette experimentally with his finger, and it floated across the board and lifted into the air and fell into the fire.

He scrambled to try to save it, but the fire consumed it in an instant. And when he turned back to look at his sleeping bag, he saw that the divining board was gone.

The Hull family always held its weddings at St. Peter's Church.

The crowd was so big you could get lost in it, and Diandra

was grateful for that. She slipped in to the back of the church and took a seat on the bride's family side.

The whole thing was a crush, and the church was crowded to the walls. This was the wedding of the season: Lady Leonie succumbing at last.

It took a good half hour before the crowd was settled. And then the music, and the long line of attendants.

And Justin.

She watched him enter, saw his eyes veer to the exact spot where she sat, watched him down the long red carpeted aisle to the altar, watched him, watched him, watched him until she could see him no more.

And then the service, and the vows, and Leonie's low choking voice promising to love, honor and cherish. And George, his voice so strong, so certain, bedrock.

The rush back down the aisle. The posing for photographs. The mass of carriages blocking the avenue as everyone raced to join the happy couple for the wedding supper at Claridge's.

She was among the last to depart, purely and simply to avoid seeing Justin.

She wasn't ready. She wasn't.

She was.

And just when she was aching to see him, he was nowhere there. Not at the church, not in the crowd on the avenue, not at the reception when she finally arrived there.

It was a test of her endurance. Her strength. Her will. Her desire.

She felt it creeping up on her, as fresh and green as spring grass, and as hot as the sun.

She felt the interest of men and the envy of women. She felt her starving body unfurling and demanding surcease.

She could have anyone. She wanted him.

One glimpse . . .

Love him.

The most powerful message of her life.

Go.

A command for a lifetime.

She was ready.

How long had she been ready? The minute she saw Leonie draped in bridal cream.

. . . do what you will . . .

Yes. That too.

Perhaps only that.

. . . you take your pleasure like a man . . .

But even a man mourned sometimes. Even he. Why had he immured himself in the frontier of Wyoming?

Even he.

But now—he was ready too. The memory of *them* was in his eyes as deeply as it was in her soul.

This was what she wanted; this was what she had been waiting for. She had only needed to see that he wanted it too, and that the past, finally, was no impediment.

Love him.

She would go to him now, naked and free.

She stepped into her carriage, feeling proud and bold and ready for anything.

And as if she conjured it, he was waiting for her, and she grasped his hand in wonderment as he pulled her up, in and against him.

"Justin . . ."

"I'm taking you away."

"Are you?" she whispered.

"I found my India—come and share it with me."

She understood exactly, what he was saying: he would go and never come back—never need to come back. But unlike his father, he would leave nothing behind.

Except her.

His India. The place of adventure and fortune. Success and prosperity. And postponed marriage—

Serena's predictions shockingly coming true . . .

"Come with me, Diandra. I need you."

Love him.

She would.

"I want you."

Love her.

He did.

"Come with me now."

Go.

A lifetime of his potent loving in place of no memories but the ones they would make.

Yes.

Yes.

Yes.

They lay naked, side by side, in the narrow bed of the ship's cabin. It had been slow, slow delicious lovemaking. It had been hard and fast and explosive. And now it was the languorous aftermath where his hard body partially covered hers, and she was wrapped in his legs, his heat and his desire.

So perfect. So right.

The motion of the ship lulled them; the call to adventure was dead ahead. She could do anything. But the best thing she could do was love him.

She couldn't get enough of him. He was so hard and hot against her already, nudging her, making demands of her.

She grasped him tightly in her hand, and he immediately thrust against her fingers.

"The only thing I want," she whispered, "is to wear bridal cream."

"Let me dress you then."

"Hurry."

But it was her hand and her desire, and she was in no hurry whatsoever.

All she wanted to do was adore him, his power, his length, his potency. All of that in her hands as she felt him, caressed him and pumped him and brought him just to the explosive moment of ejaculation.

And then she held him, just at the tip, just waiting, waiting, waiting until they both couldn't stand it—

Love him . . .

Forever—

And then she pulled her hand up abruptly and then slowly and firmly down, and she felt him erupt—hot and thick and wet all over her belly and thighs, luscious perfect bridal cream to bind them together forever.

And sometime during the night, he felt an unfamiliar object against his foot; he kicked at it impatiently and it fell off the bed and clattered to the floor.

He turned and looked sleepily over his shoulder, and he knew what it was, and he was sure he was dreaming.

Maybe . . .

On the floor, in the dim light of cabin, was the divining board and planchette, and the velvet pouches folded beside.